Disappearing
Ink

Disappearing Ink

Ink

The Other Side of the Door

SUNNY ALEXANDER

Book design by Maureen Cutajar
www.gopublished.com

Print ISBN: 978-0-9982029-0-7
E-book ISBN: 978-0-9982029-1-4
LCCN: 2017903248

To Dotty
Olav ha-sholom
May she rest in peace.

I will go and if I perish, I perish.
The Book of Esther, 4:16

CHAPTER 1

Los Angeles, California
1973

"Ha!" said Marley triumphantly, swinging her mother's rain-splattered four-door 1967 Buick Special Series sedan into the handicapped parking space at Brooks Medical Center.

Best spot in the parking lot, and I got it!

"On a scale of one to ten, not much of a victory," her inner voice commented. "Look around you, the lot's almost empty."

Her mother's disembodied voice chimed in: "Marley Chambers, no cheating allowed. You know the handicapped parking sticker is for Papa. Nothing handicapped about you."

"Oh, really? Come on, Mommy. I think you need to redefine that term. Plus, it's not as if I'm taking the last parking spot."

She heard Mommy's familiar "Tsk, tsk," the phrase that said more than any of the historical documents she had read in her years of higher education.

"Okay, okay," she mumbled as she threw the car into reverse and pulled into the space next to the handicapped spot.

The rain was really coming down now. *It was a dark and stormy night*, she thought, picturing Snoopy, Charlie Brown's whimsical

1

beagle with the rich imagination, perched atop his doghouse and pecking away on his typewriter at the mystery novel he would never finish. What was the rest of that purple prose cliché? Oh, yeah: "The rain fell in torrents."

It fit the weather she was now facing.

Brushing the medley of donut crumbs from her coat, she checked inside her purse for her inhaler, transferred it to her coat pocket, and proceeded to open the car door.

A sudden gust of wind caused the rain to pelt against her face. She buckled her all-weather film noir-style trench coat, adjusted her twill fedora low over her brow, and made a beeline toward the covered walkway.

The rain and wind were unusually strong, but in spite of the dual attack, Marley felt strangely invigorated by the force of nature.

She walked at a hurried pace but stopped suddenly to pick up a waterlogged leaf.

"I am not dead yet...not yet," it seemed to say to her.

She gasped, suddenly reminded of why she was at Brooks Medical Center. *Don't be dead, Papa. Don't be dead.*

She felt her chest tighten and picked up the pace until she reached the passageway to the hospital.

She stopped at the two doors leading to the lobby. The automatic door was meant for those who needed assistance, and the revolving door...she froze. *I hate revolving doors. What if I get stuck?*

She glanced at the automatic door control with its image of a stick figure sitting in a wheelchair. Mommy's *tsk, tsk* reverberated as she debated her choices. One door promised safety, the other evoked a lifelong fear of being trapped. She grasped her inhaler, placed both hands on the revolving door, and entered the lobby.

Visiting hours were long over, and the room was empty except for a few stragglers sitting on the faux-leather couches and chairs.

A group of five people huddled together, exchanging stories, smiling and laughing. A skewed tower of cheerfully wrapped packages lay on the side table. Festive balloons, welcoming a new life, were tied to the chairs' armrests.

A middle-aged couple, looking worn and exhausted, waited forlornly in the corner. The woman sat with her head in her hands; the man gazed into nowhere.

She had sat with Papa on the same couch after Mommy had her stroke. Was it only a year ago?

∞

"They called in Dr. Mathis, he's the best there is, and Uncle Curtis is with her. He'll watch over Mommy."

She had tried to take courage in Papa's reassuring words. Then she saw the agony in Papa's eyes before he began to rock back and forth, back and forth, muttering, muttering; a litany of sorrow spoken in an indistinguishable language.

The minutes ticked away, becoming hours.

Curtis Balfour opened the swinging doors leading from the Emergency Room. His shoulders slumped while unabashed tears streamed down his face. This wasn't the Uncle Curtis she knew, who played Santa Claus every Christmas, or even the Dr. Curtis whose comical bird whistles made her forget, in the throes of a violent asthma attack, that she felt as if she were drowning.

Even Uncle Curtis cries, she thought.

Curtis said hoarsely, "Andrew...Marley...Abbey's gone. We did everything to save her. I'm so very sorry."

Marley stood next to Papa. Her throat was dry; she struggled to swallow. She felt her chest tighten, accompanied by the sound of an all too familiar wheezing. She kept hearing the words, "Abbey's gone. Abbey's gone." *Mommy is gone? Gone where?* Her inner-child questioned.

She looked at Papa. Crevices of pain twisted his face; his eyes focused on an empty corner of the room.

Uncle Curtis held her tenderly. "Marley, you'll have to be strong for your dad."

She hung her head. *How can I, when I don't know how to be strong for myself?*

Papa said, "I want to see Abbey."

They walked solemnly through the double doors toward the ER. Staff lined the long hallway. Silent words of grief filled their path: trembling lips, hands held out to comfort, tears rolling down stricken faces.

They entered the high acuity room. Teresa Reyes was standing guard, her hands resting softly on Mommy's forehead. She reached out to Papa. "Andrew..."

Papa moved into her arms. "I know, Teresa. You and Abbey worked together for...what was it, twenty years?"

"Almost twenty-two," she said mournfully.

Andrew put his hand on her shoulder. "Abbey spoke so highly of you. Thank you for being here and for being her friend."

"I was finishing my shift in the Hospice Unit when I got word. Everyone loved and admired Abbey."

"I'll leave and give you your privacy, but I'll be right outside if you need me."

Papa nodded.

Teresa held Marley. "You know how to reach me," she whispered.

"Thanks, Teresa, for being here with Mommy, and—and for everything."

Marley watched as Papa leaned over to kiss his Abbey's forehead, murmuring words meant only for her.

Was this her mother lying motionless on a hard table? She looked like Mommy, only sleeping. *Is she still warm or has the chill of death taken over? I'm scared to touch her if she's cold.*

Marley wanted to shake her, to say as she did when she was a little girl, "Wake up, Mommy, wake up. It's Sunday and time to read the comics."

Now a second deathwatch was taking place. A few months after Abbey's death, Papa had a mild heart attack, with reassurances from the doctors that he would make a full recovery. A few months later, a second heart attack followed, and Marley knew her Papa couldn't go on without his Abbey. The promised recovery never came, and all that remained was a whisper of a man.

Marley made her way to the reception desk. Vivian was working the night shift, her head buried in a book, completely oblivious to her surroundings. Marley knew she would be reading *Our Bodies, Ourselves,* the frank guide to women's health and sexuality that had enjoyed tremendous popularity—and raised some eyebrows—since it was published in 1971.

An infectious smile crossed Marley's face.

"Still trying to figure it out, Viv?" she teased.

Vivian looked up. Her blue eyes widened, and a broad smile lit up her face. "Hey, kid, I was hoping you'd show up tonight." She stood, stifled a yawn, and moved away from the desk. "Lack of sleep." She ran her fingers through her pixie haircut.

"Your mom would kill you if she saw all your ringlets cut off," said Marley.

"If it's good enough for Mia Farrow, it's good enough for me."

Marley cringed at the memory of *Rosemary's Baby,* whose scariest parts she'd watched through the fingers of the hand she'd kept in front of her face.

Vivian winked. "Besides, what she doesn't know won't hurt her."

She smiled again, showing the slight gap between her front teeth.

"You may have cut your golden locks, but your goofy smile hasn't changed."

Vivian looked down self-consciously. "You know how I hate that gap."

"I've always loved it."

"Well, I envied your braces."

"And *I* envied the way you could jump off the swings and land on your feet."

"Ah, childhood; those were the days, weren't they?"

"The best," Marley agreed.

"I've been trying to reach you," said Vivian. "I left messages at your apartment and at your folks' home. I know you must be on overload, but I thought you might want to join our women's group for a short diversion from everything."

Marley shook her head. "Overload is putting it mildly. You know how they say things come in threes? My dad's dying, the proposal for my dissertation got turned down, and I think John and I are about to have the 'let's just be friends' talk."

"I do get it. Is there anything I can do? Anything at all, Mar."

"Not really, but if I think of something..."

"I'll hold you to that. I've been peeking in on your dad on my breaks. Teresa said he's stable, at least for now. You might get some relief if you get out. You know all the women in the group. Let's see," she said counting on her fingers, "there's Betty Louise, Agnes, Esmeralda, and—"

"Betty Louise?" Marley interrupted. "I thought she was going to be a nun."

"Not any longer," Vivian replied playfully.

"Hey, Mar, don't be shy; it might help to change the energy."

"You're doing your seductive thing."

"You mean, talking like Lauren Bacall?

"We're doing the self-exam mirror thing," Vivian said, doing her best Bacall imitation, a most convincing throaty purr.

"Oh, Viv, I can never be like you. How do you manage it all? Law school, working here, demonstrating...even doing the mirror thing?"

Vivian had invested in a self-exam kit that included a flashlight, a mirror, and a speculum. Enamored by her heretofore hidden parts, she instantly became an advocate of self-examination and the book, *Our Bodies, Ourselves*.

"I am woman, hear me roar! If we weren't demonstrating, do you think the government would have paid attention to us? Would Roe v. Wade have made it to the Supreme Court? And what about Vietnam? We got the ceasefire by demonstrating, now we'll be out of that stupid war, and soon.

"I know how hard it's been for you, but you're isolating from your friends, and I'm worried. It's after nine. Have you even been home today?"

"No, I had to meet with Dr. Holbrook. He didn't like what I've done on my proposal. Admittedly, it was almost nothing. He thought the title was 'smashing,' but then said I got lost in the complexity."

"Throw the title by me again." Vivian closed her eyes, the better to appreciate her friend's academic savvy.

"Folk wisdom, idioms, and proverbs: Their historical meaning and impact upon society."

Vivian opened her eyes. "Wow! It's impressive. What happened?"

"He thought I was in over my head. He said if I want to be writing my thesis for the next ten years, go right ahead. Then he whispered, as if telling me some great secret, 'Proposals and dissertations are really an exercise in futility.'"

"Where does that leave you?"

"I got a three-month extension," she said miserably.

"What a bummer! Geez, Mar, give your brain a rest. Getting out, being with friends, might do the trick."

"I'm not up to being with...well, anyone. Look at me: a water-logged, pudgy, twenty-seven-year-old, about to get kicked out of a Ph.D. program. Mommy's gone, and Papa's hanging by a thread. Plus, I can't wait to get home to John and our conversation."

"Hey! Stop putting yourself down. What do these pompous, elitist committee people know about real life? And as far as being pudgy, take a look at Marilyn Monroe's pics. You have a woman's body, not a skinny kid's like mine. And John?" She guffawed. "You know how I feel about that narcissistic, egotistical asshole."

"Couldn't you be more direct?"

"I'm trying. Accept who you are, Mar. And that's what our women's meetings are all about. That's all I'm saying. *The times they are a-changin'.*"

Marley sighed. "You know how I *love* Dylan."

"That makes both of us. I know, as a woman, I've got to work twice as hard for half the pay. It won't always be that way, but I'm willing to fight for our rights to the end.

"Whew, there I go again, being preachy like my Grandpa Liam. Boy, could he deliver a sermon."

Vivian lowered her voice. "I believe in the changes we're fighting for, and I believe in you. Stop selling yourself short."

Marley felt a lump in her throat and heard the crack in her voice. "I don't have your strength, Viv. I never did."

"Not true. It's there, and I've seen it. As my grandpa used to say, 'When you least expect it you'll find your strength.' And as far as John goes, well, fuck him."

"I tried that." Marley tried to keep a solemn face, but couldn't control the smile that was followed by a hearty laugh. "It didn't quite work."

"It's good to hear that laugh again."

"Feels good, too. Hey, what is it, Viv? You have that expression; you know the one—like when you're really struggling with something? Anything you want to tell me?"

"We've always done everything together, and I miss you...I miss us. Things aren't exactly great between my mom and me. She'd bust a gut if she knew about my extra-curricular activities. I know you talk to her sometimes. Promise you won't say anything, will you?"

Marley held up her right palm with mock solemnity. "I am the holder of all your secrets, from the day we first met. That makes about a million."

Not all. Oh, Mar, how I wish I could tell you this one. "Glad you see it that way. And I'll keep yours, too." Vivian added in a little girl whisper: "About your still sucking your thumb late at night, that is."

"Shh! Only when I have a nightmare," Marley joked back. She looked hard at her friend. "You're biting your lip, Viv. It's what you do so you won't cry."

"I'm trying to be Ms. Tough Chick, who can handle anything and everything. I don't always have it under control."

Vivian wiped her tears away with her hand. Marley reached into her purse and handed her a tissue.

"Thanks. I didn't want to admit it, but it was rough seeing your dad. Your Mommy and Papa were second parents to me. Mommy had a way about her that my mother didn't have."

Marley nodded. "I think about it all the time."

"I don't mean to hang anything more on you, but the way our two families were, celebrating all the holidays together. Shit, we lived right across the street from each other. We must have worn out the asphalt the way we were always going back and forth. Now my parents have moved to New York, your mom's passed. I get it, I mean about your dad." She glanced down the empty hallway, and then back at Marley. "I really miss the all of us," she concluded wistfully.

Marley planted a quick kiss on Vivian's forehead and whispered, "We had some great times growing up together. I don't know what I would have done without you. You're my closest and dearest friend. No matter what happens, that will never change."

Vivian sniffed and blew her nose. "It better not, or I'll tell my mama on you."

She motioned to the coffee pot behind her desk. "There's some left. And I saved a donut for you."

"Thanks." *Oh my God, if she knew I ate three on the way here. Oh, hell, why not top it off? And four is one of my lucky numbers.*

Marley dunked her donut in her coffee. "Still working weekends at the old hospital?"

"Yep, pulling double shifts for the next few weeks. I tell you, it's a real trip going through those old files. I have to shred the ones that are more than ten years old. Did you know old man Brooks built the hospital in honor of his kid, Teddy? The Teddy Brooks Memorial Hospital."

Marley rested her elbows on the counter. "I know that piece, but not the details. Tell me, and don't forget I'm a real history buff."

"Well, when Teddy Brooks was eighteen, he enlisted to fight in WWI, the war to end all wars. Got killed in Belleau Wood, France."

Marley recited, "Near the Marne River."

"You do know your history."

"Try eight years of higher education."

"The end is near." Vivian patted her hand.

Marley shook her head. "Maybe of the world, but with my Ph.D., it's wishful thinking at this point—two half-assed proposals and two strikes. If I wash out on number three, I have to take remedial classes.

Either way, I'm done." She forced a smile. "Please go on with your story. No need for me to get more depressed."

"Got it. Old man Brooks built the Teddy Brooks Memorial Hospital, and what do they do now? They rename the hospital and scratch out Teddy as if he never existed. Old man Brooks must be tossing in his grave."

Vivian sat on top of the reception desk, swinging her legs.

"Hey, you should come down there sometime. It'll be like old times—you, the shredder, and me. And I'll even include the leaky pipes and rats at no extra charge. I'll give you the grand tour of the inner sanctum," she added seductively, purring like Bacall.

Marley shuddered. "You know how I feel about rodents."

"Nah, I'll protect you. Don't forget, I'm Jack who climbs the beanstalk to rescue the princess."

"You'll have to give me more to tempt me."

"You wouldn't believe the secrets in those old files—lots of stuff about the old movie stars. I had to sign a nondisclosure agreement. There's one big star—I won't tell you who—but in her file, appendectomy was a code word for abortion. I could make a fortune selling this stuff to *The National Enquirer*."

"You're forgetting the nondisclosure agreement," Marley reminded her.

"Oh, yeah, gotta keep that in mind, my being an almost attorney and all." Vivian frowned. "Hey, that's where Mommy and Papa used to take you, isn't it? I mean, to Brooks, when you had an asthma attack."

"More times than I care to remember. Not only did my parents work there, but with my asthma, I think I won the prize for the most trips to Brooks."

"Yeah, I remember our moms talking about it. I used to eavesdrop all the time. It was all pretty boring stuff, mostly about recipes and decorating and sewing. Yuk!"

Vivian became thoughtful. "Except once, when they were talking about your asthma."

"Tell me."

"My Grandpa Liam was having one of his healing revivals, and my mom began to push your mom into taking you. It was getting pretty intense."

"How did it end?"

"Your mom kept calm and said they would have to agree to disagree. Then they got back to talking about dress patterns for us."

"They were quite a pair—different in many ways, but they stayed friends through thick and thin."

"Like us, huh? Mar, promise me you'll call if you need me—day or night."

"I will, Viv. You are my forever bestest and, right now, only friend. It's been a really rough ride."

Marley looked at the wall clock. "I better get going. Thanks for the invite and the provisions." Marley raised her coffee and donut in a combined gesture of thanks and parting. "It'll keep me going."

"My pleasure. I meant what I said—day or night."

They hugged before Marley turned and walked toward the elevator.

The conversation with Vivian had stirred up the memory of the first time she had her nightmare: such a haunting dream for a little girl of four.

She was in a dark tunnel of a room surrounded by screaming and crying shadow-beings, their hands raised as if that motion would give them more space, more air to breathe. She was squeezed from every side until she woke coughing and gasping for air.

Mommy came running, scooped her up, and rushed toward the bathroom. She shouted out to Papa: "It's croup. Steam, she needs steam. Andrew!" Her voice was stern. "Turn the shower on hot. Full force."

Papa froze.

"Andrew, you know what needs to be done—you, above all. Now!" Mommy shouted. Then her tone softened. "She'll be all right," Mommy murmured in a soothing voice.

She slept the rest of that night tucked safely between Papa and Mommy.

She forgot about the nightmare until it returned with a fury, this time accompanied by an asthma attack.

Did she remember the old hospital? Inside and out.

Wheezing, coughing, her chest oh so tight. Mommy held her in the backseat of the car, while Papa drove the winding road to Brooks, the scary old hospital overlooking Los Angeles. A replica of a French medieval castle, it was a bleak stone edifice surmounted by turrets and soaring towers.

She remembered Papa carrying her, Mommy rushing ahead, crying, "This way, Andrew. It's a shortcut to the ER."

Marley glimpsed the bas-relief of babies reclining in a garden as they ran past the night clerk. *Can't breathe...can't breathe.*

Long hallways twisting and turning, past the double doors with the sign INCURABLES WARD. Is that where they would take her if they couldn't cure her? She knew now it was the beginning of hospice care: hospice, a much kinder and gentler name for death's approach.

Her conversation with Vivian was unsettling and had triggered a return of those early memories. She reached into her coat pocket, felt the presence of her inhaler, and sighed. It was, as it had been for many years, her bridge between life and death.

She pushed the elevator button: sixth floor. Hospice Unit.

For once, she was glad that the elevator moved slowly. She could finish the donut, and if she wiped all the crumbs away, no one would be the wiser. Leave no evidence. Exactly like the old Brooks Hospital, with proof of illegal abortions and God only knows what else, now shredded into oblivion.

The elevator inched up. Everything in the hospital seemed to move at half speed, except when death was knocking at the door. Then, the tempo increased, and a common goal was put into place: keep death away. She was by her father's side, following his second heart attack, when he coded. In a matter of seconds, the ICU was filled with staff and additional equipment. She was pushed outside the room to watch by pressing her face against the glass partition. This wasn't a TV show like *Medical Center* or *M*A*S*H*. This was real; this was her Papa. She saw the franticness change to a calmer, steadier pace. A sign of hope, she thought. She was certain she saw a nod of reassurance from the doctor. Timidly, she reentered the room. The doctor walked over and with a solemn look told her Papa would not recover. His nod had been a figment of her imagination, a child's wish for her Papa not to die.

Stunned, she had stared at the shadow of the man lying silently in a hospital bed. Her Papa who had sat her on his lap and read to her every night. Who never passed by his Abbey without stopping to touch her lightly on the shoulder and whisper words that made Mommy smile, and at times blush. She wondered now if he could be dying from a broken heart.

She knew what Papa would say: "No one dies from a broken heart, Marley. That's just a romantic phrase created by some dreamy-eyed poet. While it sounds sentimental, and even quite lovely, research and science are the paths to truth, not speculation, and not religion. Hard facts, that's what counts."

But what if there aren't any hard facts, Papa?

The elevator bounced twice, then stopped on the third floor, fetching Marley back from her reverie. The door opened to a hospital aide standing next to a gurney. Marley moved aside. She averted her eyes, but not before seeing a woman, seemingly in deep repose.

How embarrassing to be on display for the world to see. I'd want them to cover my face.

She swept away the stray hair that had fallen over her eyes. She reached into her coat pocket, searching for the single rubber band among the paperclips and leftover candy wrappers. She would make a ponytail as soon as she escaped from the elevator.

She could hear Mommy's gentle admonishment: "Marley, rubber bands will damage your hair."

Her mother would have brushed the wisps with a soft touch that said I love you. A small smile would have crossed her face as she reached for a ponytail holder. "Shall we try hot pink? That will go nicely with your swirled tie-dye shirt."

Marley would have nodded her head.

"That's my beautiful girl."

Mommy always thought she was beautiful in spite of her pudginess and the out-of-control locks that plagued her.

The elevator stopped, and the doors opened. Marley followed the gurney through the double doors labeled HOSPICE. She still thought of it as the INCURABLES WARD, even though Teresa, the night nurse, had clarified the purpose of the east wing.

"The dying deserve the most tender care when they come to the end of their lives. It's about faith in the process of living and dying." Teresa paused. "I believe that our lives are a succession of entrances and exits. Death is merely one of them."

Faith, a foreign concept to Marley. She had taken religious study classes at Boston University but believed in no particular religion or in the existence of a god. She hesitated at the entrance to the Hospice Unit, with its invisible sign above the doors: One Way Only.

She paused before entering room 660. She noted there was no room numbered 666. *How droll*, she thought. She wondered if others had realized the absence of the number of the beast. For a moment, she imagined patients being rolled into room 666, as if the number of the room itself had decided their fate. A subdued smile curled the corners of her lips.

She opened the door to the room knowing she would not be greeted by Papa, but by medical equipment playing its symphony of sounds, whirring, humming, and beeping in concert. In spite of the hospital's efforts to disguise the odors of approaching death, she knew that no matter how diligently she scrubbed her body, the smell of pending death would linger long after her visit and continue to flood her senses.

The room looked the same as it had earlier in the day: a heroic attempt that failed to turn a hospital room into a home-like setting, with the trappings of nondescript framed paintings and faded artificial flower arrangements only augmenting the room's unfriendliness, not softening it. On a moon-filled night, the light would have filtered through the loosely woven beige drapes, but tonight, the lamp on the side table provided the only illumination. She took off her raincoat and sat on the paisley club chair next to the bed. She sighed, remembering how their home was once filled with the cozy smells of stew bubbling on the stovetop, or Mommy's biscuits baking in the oven. Even the aroma of Papa's favorite pipe tobacco, Erinmore Flake, was missing. She bought it for him every year for his birthday. "Ah, this is the best," he would say, opening the tin with the tiny pineapple logo. He would sniff the tobacco and declare, "Big, and hearty! My daughter knows exactly what I like."

Then he would wrap his arms around her, and she would feel the tickle from his five-o'clock shadow. Papa never shaved on his birthday. "It's my day off, " he would say, rubbing his emerging whiskers.

But here, in the Incurables Ward, there were no days off from shaving. Freshly shaved skin looks more alive. She remembered reading that in Viktor Frankl's *Man's Search for Meaning*. It was advice given to him by a fellow prisoner about surviving in the notorious Auschwitz concentration camp. "Shave daily...even if you have to use a piece of glass to do it. You will look younger. If you want to stay alive, there is only one way: look fit for work."

Would shaving help keep Papa alive?

The bedding was turned down to Papa's chest, his hands resting palms up as if waiting to catch a falling star. She sat on the chair and pulled it closer to the bed, lightly placing her hand over his.

Once, light years ago, they went camping in the Mojave Desert. She must have been around ten. Lately, time seemed to get twisted, the past creeping more and more into the present; the future looming further and further away.

Papa had rented a pop-up tent trailer, complete with a kitchenette. They stopped at the Kelso Depot Visitor Center and had dinner at The Beanery, now in disrepair, but not then. Then, the Beanery provided a welcome rest spot for hungry and tired desert travelers. They sat at the wraparound counter with its swivel stools and after she had twirled around a few times Papa said, "You can order anything you want." Marley gave a final twirl and chose the hot dog special. To this day, it was the best hot dog she had ever eaten.

That night they slept out in the open and watched the show of shooting stars in wonderment.

Mommy had a beautiful singing voice. She had told Marley that she had sung in a choir as a young girl. Surrounded by rock formations and cacti, Mommy sang *Catch a Falling Star*, popularized by the smooth crooner Perry Como, for her audience of two. She had wanted to ask Papa if she could catch a falling star and put it in her pocket, but she knew that was silly, even though Papa had said that all questions were worthy of an answer.

The sky had been clear, and the air pristine, on that night years ago. Now, the rain cascaded down the room's single window and a nasal cannula delivered oxygen to Papa. His source of comfort came not from Mommy's melodious voice but from a morphine drip. The heart monitor's continuous beep told her he was alive, but did he remain her Papa?

He looked fragile, this man who knew how to speak multiple languages, could change his accent at will, and never failed to find the answers to her endless, childish questions.

They would sit, as they did most evenings after dinner, in the room Papa called his study. The room, no greater than twelve by twelve, was lined with floor to ceiling bookcases filled with books on every subject. Best of all, Marley loved the rolling library ladder that scooted across the dark wood floors.

Every evening Mommy would bring in two cups of tea. Marley's in a flowered cup from her tea set, Papa's in a hand-thrown mug with the image of the biblical tree of life. Marley liked to close her eyes and trace the tree with her fingers. "The process is called *sgraffito*," said Papa. "It means 'to scratch' in Italian. The artist applies coatings of differing colors onto an object and then scratches off parts to create the image. Much like life," he mused. "We must scratch off layer after layer to get to where the truth lies."

Mommy interrupted. "I can't leave the two of you alone for a minute," she lightly scolded. She bent over to kiss them both on the top of their heads, always lingering before she left for her shift at Brooks Emergency Room. "Don't forget: homework checked, teeth brushed, and in bed by 8:30 p.m."

"Me too?" Papa winked.

Her mother smiled and leaned over to give Papa a kiss. "No, you may stay up until nine."

It always made Marley feel extra safe when they smiled and kissed.

"Now down to business," said Papa. "You know Mommy means what she says. I think she is connected to radar and knows what we are up to even when she's at work. And I also know you have some homework tonight."

"It's done, Papa. It was only spelling and ten arithmetic problems."

"Good, but you know I have to test you on your spelling."

"Later, Papa? I have a question, but it might be kind of dumb."

"There is an adage so old that no one knows who said it first. 'The only foolish questions are the ones unasked.'"

"This is a big one," she whispered. Her eyes widened, and her lips trembled.

Papa patted the chair. "Come sit next to me and tell me what you're thinking about."

"Papa," she said seriously, "you have two boo-boos." She took his hands in hers. "The little boy in 'The Selfish Giant' had boo-boos on his hands too." She pointed toward the angled and misaligned fingers on his right hand. "One boo-boo."

She turned his left hand over, looking at his forearm and the rectangular patch of pale skin that never seemed to tan. "Two boo-boos. This is a *biiiiiig* boo-boo," she said with a child's melodramatic flair.

"This happened a long time ago when I was a boy. Not like the child in the story. An accident."

Papa became silent. Marley knew he was thinking. What did Papa call it? It was a big word. She struggled—contra, contem... "You contemplating?"

Papa smiled, not his usual wide grin that lit up his eyes and showed all his teeth, but a cautious smile, with eyes that seemed to have lost their luster.

"Many years ago, when I was a child, something heavy fell on my hands. When I was finally freed, I could see a deep wound on my left arm. And the fingers of my right hand were broken. It was very long ago."

"In the time of the Selfish Giant?" Marley was a well-read little girl, and adored the Oscar Wilde short story.

Papa smiled. "Not that long ago. The doctors did their best, but not nearly the way doctors can do things today to make us all better."

"Like Uncle Curtis does?"

"Yes, Uncle Curtis is an excellent doctor."

"He wouldn't be selfish like the Giant?"

"No, not at all. Your Uncle Curtis is probably the most generous person I know."

"I love Uncle Curtis, even when he sticks me. He tells me I'm very, very brave. And Papa"—she lowered her voice—"he always gives me an extra Tootsie Roll for being his best patient. Can I ask you another question?"

"Of course."

"Can I stand on the library ladder, and will you scoot me across the room?"

"It would be my pleasure." Papa's eyes sparkled as he lifted Marley onto the ladder, making choo-choo sounds as it moved from one end of the room to the other.

The book that had prompted that long-ago conversation, *The Happy Prince and Other Tales*, occupied the table next to the hospital bed. What had her high school physics teacher said about a book lying on a table? She remembered Mr. Wilson looking very professorial wearing his tweed jacket with leather elbow patches and carrying a chalkboard pointer that he used as a baton: a conductor attempting to lead an orchestra of disinterested teenagers. He tapped the top of Marley's desk. "Miss Chambers, what makes this book stay in place?"

Dead silence.

"Come on, Marley, take a risk."

Pause.

Marley blushed at the attention. She spoke hesitantly. "It's Newton's law of inertia. Two equal forces are acting on the book. The downward force caused by gravity, and the upward push of the table on the book."

"Is that your final answer?"

"Yes, sir."

"Good. I knew you had it in you."

Could the same law of physics be applied to her? Could this be the cause of her emotional inertia? Were there two forces working to keep her static?

Well, there you go, Marley, off on one of your tangents. No wonder you can't finish your proposal, let alone your dissertation.

Marley held *The Happy Prince and Other Tales* in her hands, tracing the leather-embossed tree of life cover with her fingertips. Why was that image so important to Papa? It was on his mug as well on the custom-made book cover for this, his favorite book.

She sank further into the chair, opening the book to "The Selfish Giant." Falling into a dream-like state, the child began to read to the father.

∞

"Every afternoon, as they were coming from school, the children used to go and play in the Giant's garden.

It was a lovely large garden, with soft green grass. Here and there over the grass stood beautiful flowers like stars, and there were twelve peach-trees that in the spring-time broke out into delicate blossoms of pink and pearl, and in the autumn bore rich fruit. The birds sat on the trees and sang so sweetly that the children used to stop their games in order to listen to them. 'How happy we are here!' they cried to each other."

Marley lifted her eyes away from the faded words printed on aging paper. She hoped for a sign that Papa had heard her: a flickering of his eyelids, a twitch of his lips. She silently pleaded for a way to transfer her energy to him. The bony knobs on his fingers seemed larger than ever. She stared at his left arm as if seeing the scar for the first time. It had always been there, ever since she was. Part of Papa, no different than the way he ate his soup with a slight slurp or the way he would do imitations, using different dialects for her amusement. When she was five, he bought her a children's book of geography. They went around the world, using their fingertips to follow the roads and seas from country to country. As they crossed the borders, Papa would shift his accent. He whispered, "I used to entertain my family this way. My sisters would have to guess what country we were in by my accent." Suddenly, he slammed the book shut. She wanted to say, "You have sisters?" but something in his eyes told her to hold that question deep inside. *I'll put it with the others that never get asked.*

Papa had said, "Let's find something else to do, Marley. Would you like to play a game of Candyland?"

"Yes, Papa. But the winner gets a piece of real candy. Deal?" She held out her hand.

"Deal," said Papa, shaking her hand.

Memories that had been hidden for years began to impinge upon the present. What did she know about Mommy and Papa? It was as if they had presented her with an outline of their lives with the barest structure and the fewest possible levels. Why hadn't she confronted her parents? Insisted on answers? Even had a tantrum? Marley Rose Chambers: always the good little girl. She had stored the unasked and unanswered questions deep inside where the half-human beasts with two heads and fangs lived. Never let them out, she had told herself. Never let them out.

Suddenly alert, Marley reached inside her 1960s olive green hobo bag, a dead ringer, style-wise, for the one Carly Simon carried on the cover of her *No Secrets* album from 1972. Mommy would have loved it; she would have considered the bag the thrift shop find of the year. Her hands dug deep inside, moving beneath her creased, chocolate-stained proposal until she grasped her camera.

She studied Papa's scar as she would a work of art. No jagged edges, only a pale layer of skin in the shape of a perfect rectangle. And the fingers on his right hand, so terribly deformed. Why weren't they set or even reset before the pain and swelling took over? Why had she accepted his explanations without hesitation?

No flinch, or any movement at all when the flash went off. *Are you still here, Papa?*

"Marley?"

Marley turned to see Teresa standing in the doorway.

"Whew, I'm glad it was you, Teresa. Anyone else would think I was weird for taking a photo of my dad on his deathbed."

"Weird? Well now, join the weird club." Teresa straightened her nurse's cap. "Did you know that relatives used to take photos of their dearly departed?"

"Seriously?"

"Mid-Victorian times. Meant as a memento. I have a few from my great-grandmother's collection. Long before these modern cameras. State of the art, huh, Marley?"

"A gift from my mother." Her lips trembled. "Kodak Instamatic with a Magicube flash," she recited. "My last gift from her. I'll keep it forever."

Teresa placed a tray on the bedside table. "I got you a turkey sandwich, tea, and rice pudding." She spoke quietly, as if a tone above a whisper would disturb the withered figure lying in the hospital bed.

Marley tried to smile. "Thanks, Teresa."

Her father stirred.

Marley put her hand over his. "Papa?"

His eyes opened. "Rachel?"

"It's Marley, Papa." She put her ear close to his mouth. He spoke indistinctly.

"Teresa, do you know what he's saying?"

Teresa nodded. "It's been happening off and on today."

"Is it Hebrew?"

"Yes. It's the Shema prayer."

"I'm confused. My Papa knew many languages, but I can't remember his ever mentioning Hebrew."

"Come here, Marley." Teresa held out her arms, and for a moment Marley melted into her comforting embrace. They would part soon—two women brought together through a sorrowful vigil.

"I've been working with the terminally ill for more than twenty-five years, and I've been with patients of every faith. One of the first hospice patients I had as a young nurse was a rabbi. Back then it was called The Incurables Ward."

Startled, Marley replied, "I remember seeing that sign over the entrance door to the ward."

"Nasty way to think of it, wasn't it? We've come a long way in understanding the boundaries between this world and the next. I learned so much from the rabbi. More than I learned in all the courses I have taken on caring for the dying. He was a scholar, a teacher, and a person of great wisdom. I noticed that he recited this prayer upon waking and before going to sleep at night. He told me that it is the most significant sign of faith and, if at all possible, is recited during the moments before death. Hundreds went to their death with this prayer on their lips during the Inquisition, and millions more recited it as they were marched into the gas chambers.

"I don't recall the full prayer, but I do remember the first part. *Hear, O Israel, the Lord our God, the Lord is one. Blessed is His name, whose glorious kingdom is forever and ever.*"

As if responding to Teresa's recitation, her father began to mutter the Shema.

"I don't understand. Papa isn't Jewish."

"Maybe it's something he heard when he was young, from a friend, or even a nanny. I remember your father telling me he was born in England."

"Yes, he came here right after WWII. Mommy and Papa met in London during the war. Mommy was a nurse in the Army and Papa worked as a lab technician. She said it was love at first sight. They had to get permission to marry, though. Mommy said it was a lot of red tape. You know Curtis Balfour?"

"Of course. Everyone who works in the hospital knows Dr. Balfour."

"He was Mommy's commanding officer, and he helped them to get permission to marry. Mommy said they had the ceremony in a bombed-out registrar's office. They laughed all the time about Papa being a war bride. Well, he was a war groom, but there weren't many of them. Then when Mommy became pregnant, Curtis arranged for transportation back to the States. Mommy and Papa said he moved heaven and earth to get them back in time for me to be born in Los Angeles. I was born in the old Brooks Hospital. We became part of the Brooks Hospital family. Mommy as a nurse, Papa as a lab technician and me, I guess best remembered as a patient."

Teresa smiled nostalgically. "That was years before I started working at Brooks. Whatever is happening to your father must be something that rests in the deepest recesses of his mind. While you may never know the answers, I do believe it's giving him comfort."

Teresa motioned to the tray of food. "Come, Marley. You haven't touched your dinner. You must be starving."

Oh my God, if you only knew. Marley took a tentative bite of the sandwich.

Her father continued to mumble the Shema.

What could be behind his praying? He was a man who had denied the existence of God with such intensity.

"It seems so strange," Marley mused, "both Mommy and Papa without any family. Mommy's parents were still alive for a few years after the war, but her brothers had both died fighting. And Papa said his parents died when he was young. He grew up in an orphanage."

"I worked closely with your mother, and she never was one to talk much about her past. You and your father were her world." Teresa smiled. "She entertained me with stories about all your antics."

Marley choked on a bite of sandwich and sputtered, "Nothing too embarrassing, I hope."

"No, no, I promise," said Teresa. "Marley, I know this might be hard to hear and difficult to understand, but some things never get explained. Mysteries...we are all left with a few. Perhaps over time they can be puzzled out—or not. Try to keep that in mind, will you?"

"I'll try. Really I will."

"I've got to check on other patients, but I'll watch over your father and pray for and *with* him."

Teresa walked toward the door, stopped, and turned around. "Be careful driving home; the streets are flooded, and some main thoroughfares are closed. Your father would want you to be safe. There's time, and I'll call you if anything changes."

Marley sat for a while longer before leaning over to kiss her father goodbye.

She whispered, "Papa, who is Rachel?"

∞

"KNX 1070 weather alert," said the announcer in a Ted Baxter-ish baritone voice, reeking with self-importance. "Near record rainfalls have flooded the intersection of Beverly Boulevard and Fairfax Avenue. Alternate streets are reporting heavy traffic. Allow extra time and, above all, folks, drive safely."

Traffic was at a standstill even at this late hour, and Marley felt as if time was slipping through her hands. Teresa had said there was time. Time? An hour, a day, a week?

She would have to face John and his "we need to talk" messages. She was an expert at putting things off, but John was onto her ways of avoiding anything unpleasant.

She tried to get herself in the right frame of mind. *If not tonight, when?* She could hear Viv's comment when she was too scared to try something new. *Take a leap, Mar. What do you have to lose?*

She dodged the puddles and swore when someone purposely hit one and splashed mud all over her car. "Fuck you!" she screamed. *Was that a big enough leap, Ms. Viv?* She fumbled around the passenger seat and found a loose Andes Mint. She couldn't finish her proposal, but she was an expert at unwrapping mints with one hand. What if she did finish, and what if she actually graduated? Then what? A Ph.D. in History usually led to teaching. Did she even want to teach? She got a vision of being in front of a class of fifty young, eager faces, all daring her to be interesting and challenging—or else. College level, of course. What could she possibly have to say that would inspire them?

She sped through a large puddle, spraying two cars with muddy water while also managing to splash a lone pedestrian trying to cross the street against traffic. "Bull's-eye!" she shouted, with a fleeting sense of righteousness followed by an overwhelming sense of shame.

She pulled into the apartment's underground parking, space 203, right next to 202 and John's car. John's car was spotless. She knew he must have wiped it down before heading to their apartment. Hers, on the other hand, would be caked with mud by morning.

She hastily chugged some water from her avocado green thermos, hoping to erase the aftertaste from the Andes' Mint. She laid her head on the stirring wheel. The horn went off, echoing throughout the garage.

She unpacked her car: briefcase, umbrella, lunch box, and a bag of groceries. The car smelled of bananas. She thought about cracking the window open, but worried about a rat sneaking in.

She glanced again at John's car. Pristine. Could things get any worse? Surrounded by death and now a failing relationship. Not a failing relationship, a failed relationship, with only the final nail to be placed in the coffin.

The elevator had a handwritten note taped to the door: OUT OF ORDER. It was the perfect summary of her life for all to see. She took off her shoes and, after adding them to the lopsided bundle she was carrying, began to climb the four flights of stairs to their apartment. Everything was slipping from her grip, she thought. Did she even have a grip? Four flights. Fuck!

Marley stopped at the second landing to catch her breath and readjust her packages. She sat on one of the metal steps, rested her head in her hand, and sighed.

How did she get here? Was this how life works? You make one decision years ago that sets you on a course, and that's it?

∞

Marley's high school friends had chuckled when she told them she was accepted and would attend Boston University (BU).

Viv had commented, "You'll freeze your butt off, Mar."

"I've been skiing. I have some idea of snow."

"Ha! That was up at Big Bear on manmade snow, and it was so warm we skied in T-shirts."

She supposed Vivian was right, after all. She might be a California girl, but these freezing metal steps were reminding her of good old BU, and a May blizzard that changed the course of her life. She should get up and keep moving, but what was waiting at the end of her climb? *Five more minutes,* she bargained with herself.

∞

She was nearing the end of her freshman year at Boston with an undeclared major.

She made her customary Sunday call home, knowing that Mommy would be the one to pick up the phone. They would chat about the week's goings-on and end the conversation with Mommy telling her a care package was on its way. She could hear Papa in the background chanting, "My turn, my turn!" Mommy would shush him, and Marley could tell they were both smiling.

With Papa, it was a more serious conversation. "I'm still undeclared," she bemoaned.

"Don't fret about it, Marley. You have until the end of your sophomore year to declare. That's the purpose of college, to explore and grow from your experiences. You'll know when it's right."

Even after having been encouraged to take her time, she felt unsettled. Students all around her had a five- and ten-year plan. She had none. It wasn't that things didn't fit; the problem was they all interested her, one way or another. If Marley were to lay the blame on anyone, she could fault Papa for exposing her to so many subjects and making each and every one fascinating.

The turning point came near the end of her freshman year at BU when the fifty-five degree May weather suddenly changed to near blizzard conditions. She had a two-hour break between classes and thought about returning to her dorm. One look outside at the swirling snow, and she decided to sit it out. If not comfortable, she could at least stay warm.

She shivered, in spite of wearing a wool sweater underneath her parka. The school's idea of a heated building was not hers. Her friends were right after all: She belonged in California.

She sat on a bench opposite a lecture hall, and opened the paper sack with a capital M followed by much smaller letters: a-r-l-e-y. Like a box of Crackerjacks, her school lunches, packed by Mommy, had always come with a hidden prize. Marley had continued that tradition, even though she packed her own lunch. Today, in addition to a ham sandwich and an apple, she had put four Hershey Kisses in a plastic bag with a big heart written on it.

She noticed students entering the lecture hall and wandered over to read the announcement taped onto the half-opened door.

GEORGE SANTAYANA:
PHILOSOPHER, ESSAYIST, POET, AND NOVELIST
LECTURE FROM 12:00 P.M. TO 1:30 P.M.
PRESENTED BY: DEPARTMENT OF HISTORY CHAIRMAN,
PROF. THOMAS WHITMAN

She peeked through the open door to see students scattered throughout the auditorium, eating their lunches and drinking from cups of what she surmised was either hot chocolate or coffee.

She found a seat in the back row. The warmth of the room and a full stomach caused her to nod off.

Dr. Whitman stood behind the podium. He looked up at a group of students standing by the door, chatting softly.

"In or out, it's up to you," he called out to them. "Hiding from the weather? No problem, any port in a storm, as the saying goes. However, I must warn you, the joke may be on you. Did it occur to any of you that perhaps the storm was sent so that you would be forced to gather here and perhaps learn something about a subject you have no interest in at all?"

The loitering students began to find seats.

"Latecomers have missed the first part, but can catch up in the handouts. We're about to get to the meat of the lecture."

He turned the transparency viewer on. The first slide showed a handwritten, twelve-word sentence: *Those who fail to learn from history are doomed to repeat it.*

"This quote has been attributed to George Santayana, but it's important enough to be repeated by others in one form or another."

Startled awake, Marley reached for a notepad and copied the quote.

Dr. Whitman continued, "You may well ask, how can a quote be so important as to be repeated time after time throughout history, and yet hatred, war, and bigotry continue? Are we simply doomed to repeat history? To make this more enjoyable, there are twelve words in that quote. Here's a challenge for those who want to seek an internal refuge as opposed to an external refuge, such as a lecture hall during a snowstorm.

"Write a sentence in twelve or fewer words about why history continues to get repeated."

Marley must have written hundreds of sentences over the next few weeks. The snow had melted, the sun came out, and she was due to take the train home for summer break.

She spent the next few days being lulled by the motion of the train until she wrote her final sentence of ten words: *Repeating the known is less painful than discovering the unknown.*

She sat her pad down and, with a huge sigh, felt her destiny was to major in history.

She heard the metal door from the parking garage to the apartments open and clang shut. *Jesus, that five-minute break I took might just end in my demise.* She shivered in fear as the thump, thump, thump of heavy steps advanced in her direction. She froze, and then felt relieved when "Un bel dì vedremo" ("one fine day we'll see"), the beautiful soprano aria from *Madama Butterfly,* suddenly echoed throughout the stairwell. Oh no, Alice Nottingham, the apartment building's resident snoop, and frustrated opera singer. How fitting, she thought: an aria about a woman scorned reaching out to another scorned woman, sitting bedraggled on cold metal steps in a rundown apartment building. Were the gods mocking her plight?

She stood, readjusted her packages, and, wanting to put some distance between her and Alice, began to climb the stairs at a rapid pace.

Panting, Marley managed to rap on the apartment door without dropping anything. She stood in her stocking feet; shifting her balance from one cold, wet foot to the other. *Well, Ms. Vivian, the here and now is right here, now!*

John opened the door and made a face at her disheveled appearance.

"Christ, Marley, what happened? I was freaking out. I left you a dozen messages. How's your dad? Here, give me all that shit."

She stepped back from his reach. "I can manage, John," she said tersely.

"Just trying to help." He shook his head. "Jeez, you look like a drowned cat."

"Thanks, for the compliment. You seem nice and cozy." *And trim.*

"Do you want some dinner?" he said, ignoring her remark.

She shook her head. "I got your 'we have to talk' messages. Look, I need to get out of these things...then we'll talk.... *And say goodbye. Civilly, always civilly.*

Moving into the bedroom, she surveyed the all-white room.

John loved white. They had gone furniture shopping before they moved in together. He salivated, and his eyes glistened when he saw the oversized baseball glove-shaped sofa made by Heller. The novelty item was popularly known as "Joe."

"I like modern," John had said, a mite pompously. "And white."

Why had she murmured, "I love white too," instead of telling him that white was a Marley disaster waiting to happen?

She peeled off her clothes, letting them drop onto the white carpeting in one soggy mess. She purposely avoided looking in the mirror but finally couldn't resist glancing out of the corner of her eye. She wasn't a size two or an eight. Or even a ten. Maybe a twelve, if she stood up straight and sucked in her belly.

She turned the shower on full force and hot! Not quite scalding but close enough. Maybe it would help if she cried. Weren't showers the perfect place for crying? The showerhead played its own symphony of tears; hers would not appear.

She ran a brush through her hair. It was the one thing about her that no one could tame: tight curls that would spring up again and again, no matter how much wave set lotion she plastered on, or how many empty frozen orange juice cans she used as rollers. She set the hairdryer aside and put on her flannel pajamas. Why bother? You're about to be dumped. May as well be comfortable.

∞

"You look comfortable, Marley. Coffee? Wine?"

She shook her head. *Something you would say to a sister.* They sat on the black and white tuxedo sofa facing the fireplace. Not close and not far apart. Not adversaries and not lovers, just two individuals who were never meant to be together.

"I'm sorry about your dad. So soon after your mom."

She nodded. "At least my mother went quickly." She tried to keep it light, but her voice quivered, and her lips trembled.

John cleared his throat, a habit of his before making an important announcement. "I got the fellowship at Sloan-Kettering."

"I knew you would. Congratulations, John. You accepted, of course."

"Yes. You know it's been in the works. I thought by now we'd have our plan in place. You'd graduate and get a teaching job, and I'd get the training I need in neurology. We'd buy a house, have two or three kids, maybe a dog, and live the good life. We've gone in such different directions."

"You followed the plan, and I haven't budged."

"That's the problem. I have to move on. I'd like us to be friends. Can we do that?"

"Sure, why not?"

"We can split up the furniture. Why don't you take this couch?" He looked longingly at the big white mitt. "I'd like to keep Joe. Do you mind?"

She thought, Why would I want that monstrosity? "Nix to the sofa and Joe is all yours." She finally confessed: "I've always had a problem with keeping white, well, white."

"I noticed," he replied with an edge.

Wait until you get a look at the bedroom carpeting. "All I need are my clothes. I'll pack my stuff in the morning."

John said, "I'm going to spend a couple of days at a friend's house. Will that be enough time for you?"

"More than I'll need. I can't leave my parents' house vacant, and Papa won't be coming home."

CHAPTER 2

Marley woke to see the sun streaming through the blinds. Groaning, she glanced at the clock: 11:16 a.m. She threw the comforter aside and surveyed the room. Hurricane Marley had hit! She wondered if she should take the king-sized down comforter—after all, they had picked it out together and split the cost. Why should John get everything? She had a rush of anger followed by a wave of sadness when she remembered her bed at home. A twin size meant for one.

The first time she and John had spent the night together, they had lain in the center of the bed, face-to-face, arms and legs wrapped around each other, talking and making plans for the future. *Wait! Let me rewind that memory. John talked and I agreed. So much for being a partner in a relationship.* Why was it easier for her to acquiesce to everyone else's needs?

Over time, they began to retreat to their respective corner of the bed, until the place in which they had lain was empty. Not unlike prizefighters. The bell rings, and they move to neutral corners.

She threw on her sweats and scooped up last night's pile of damp clothing and stuffed it into a plastic bag. She stripped the bed and retrieved fresh linens from the closet. She didn't want to leave any trace that she had once lived here, not even her scent.

It was 4:00 p.m. by the time she had made six trips to the garage, filling the car with all her belongings. She spot-cleaned the bedroom carpeting and ran the vacuum before leaving the key and a note on the kitchen table. What was that line in the Beatles' song, "She's Leaving Home"? She remembered: "Leaving the note that she hoped would say more." She had no interest in giving John that satisfaction. She'd resisted the urge to write, "Screw you, John. " Instead, her note simply said:

JOHN,

GOOD LUCK.

MARLEY

It was the last time she would drive from John's apartment to Mommy and Papa's house, and the first time she would be spending her days and nights alone.

She wondered why she and John had never used pet names. No darling, no sugar, no honey bunch; it was boring old Marley and John to the end.

The late afternoon sun glared into her eyes. The radio news was predicting temperatures for tomorrow in the mid-seventies. Was it only last night that the rain had gushed, and the streets had flooded? If anyone doubted it, they only had to look at her car. She rolled down her window and made a mental note to get it washed. She'd be generous with her tip—a dollar instead of the usual fifty cents.

Marley turned left onto Plum Lane and stopped in front of the Spanish-style house, built in the 1920s. It stood out from the other homes on the street. "Custom built," Mommy had told her, "and on a corner lot. That means lots of natural light filtering into the rooms. The previous owners wanted a larger home, and I thought this house would be perfect for us. It's got the details I love."

Roughly textured stucco helped to keep the house warm in the winter and cool in the summer. An archway led to a walled patio and the speakeasy entry door, used by Marley and Vivian for planning and carrying out their mysterious escapades.

Marley's lips trembled when she thought of how much Mommy loved her home. Flaws were seen as adding to the house, not taking away from it. When an earthquake left hairline cracks on the yellow and black tiled kitchen counter, Mommy said of the house, "It adds to its charm." Mommy was like that, always seeing the best in things, in people.

Marley went around the corner to the side street, got out of the car to lift the wooden garage door, pulled the car in, and closed the door before taking the covered walkway to the back entrance and the service porch.

Over the years the windows had expanded and contracted until small gaps allowed the wind to whistle through. Even so, the house smelled fusty, and she walked from room to room opening the windows and letting fresh-smelling, post-rain air into the house.

She stopped at the door to Papa's study, but her hand refused to obey her command to turn the doorknob. She trembled. *I can't go in. Not yet.*

She went into Mommy's sewing room to check the Ansafone message machine. Her heart began to pound when she saw the *calls received* light flashing. The message from Teresa was brief but warmhearted. "Hi, Marley. Wanted to give you an update. Your father is stable. Why don't you take the rest of today and tomorrow off? If there's any change, I'll call."

She sighed with relief. She would use the time to put things away and try to settle in.

She wondered what it would be like when the sun went down and darkness and fear invaded her heart.

Maybe she should have taken the comforter after all.

∞

Teresa had been right. Papa's death would not come as it had for Mommy.

She drove to Brooks twice a day, sometimes sitting silently by his bedside or reading a poem by Dylan Thomas or Maya Angelou. Poetry directed to the soul, Papa had said.

Papa seemed to be struggling between two worlds. Most of the time he lay motionless, and during those times she sat anxiously awaiting his next breath. Occasionally a sudden burst of laughter or an anguished cry would escape his cracked lips and startle her. She was curious, at first, and wished she could see the movies in his mind. After a while she began to count his breaths, wondering when his final breath would carry him away.

∞

She had missed one Sunday morning's vigil. Vivian had called, insisting that she leave the house and go to the movies.

"Hey, Mar. There's this dark comedy that's getting tons of great reviews. *Harold and Maude*. About a young man morbidly obsessed with death that teams up with an old woman with a zest for life, and they go on a shitload of adventures. Ruth Gordon's the old woman. You know, from *Rosemary's Baby*."

"Oh, no! Don't remind me."

"Trust me, it's going to become a cult film someday. My treat."

"Really? Your treat? I don't know. Teresa might call."

"Please," she whined. "I'm missing my best friend."

"Talk me into it."

"It's on me, for one thing."

"Snacks included?"

"You drive a hard bargain."

They sat in the theater as they had done as children, sharing a box of popcorn and a thirty-ounce root beer. They had decided years ago when they were pre-teens how to share and share alike: one handful of popcorn and one slurp of the drink. No gulping.

Afterward, they stopped for coffee.

Vivian said, "I hope *Harold and Maude* wasn't too hard for you to watch, being about death and all."

"No, actually it got me wondering about a life fully—or not fully—lived."

"Yeah, me too."

"I kept thinking about John and me. I lost myself in that relationship. But then, I'm not sure if I ever had myself."

"You have it with us."

"I have, haven't I? What about you, Viv? You always seemed to know what you want and were determined to get it."

Vivian laughed. "My mother called it stubbornness. I got more than one whack for it. She would say to my dad, 'She didn't get it from my side of the family.' I miss your mom. She once told me that we are all like flowers. Even if they look alike, they are different in some way. I've never known anyone to take such great pleasure from the smallest things."

"She was a lot like Maude in the movie. Full of a boundless love for life. Hey, thanks for forcing me out of my cocoon."

"That's my job," said Vivian.

∞

When Marley got into bed, she thought about the way Mommy had lived. Every moment seemed to be appreciated. Even the hard times, when an asthma attack struck and Marley couldn't get a deep breath, or when Marley crayoned over a newly painted wall. Mommy shook her head, patiently explaining that crayons were meant to go on paper, and then cheerfully repainted the wall. But Papa, who was patient and kind, had an aura of sadness surrounding him.

Sleep had eluded her until the early morning hours, and when the alarm sounded, she rolled over, turned it off, and fell into a deep, dreamless sleep.

It was past noon when she woke. She stretched, at first feeling peaceful, then remembered her Papa was lying in the Hospice Unit.

She fairly flew into Mommy's room and stared at the Ansafone message machine. With weakened knees and a sense of dread, she leaned over and moved the dial to *play messages*.

"Hi, it's Teresa. I think it's time, Marley. I'll try to stay with your father until you get here."

∞

Marley entered Papa's room and sat on the edge of the hospital bed. On the table was a note from Teresa.

I'll be back soon. I wrote down the Shema for you. I thought you might want to recite the prayer to your Papa. I think he'll be able to hear it or at least feel it. It seems to mean so much to him.

She held her father's hand and recited the prayer out loud.

"Hear, O Israel, the Lord our God, the Lord is One. Blessed is His name, whose glorious kingdom is forever and ever."

She continued to repeat the words, seeing an occasional flutter of Papa's eyelids, a trembling of his lips, a lone tear working its way down his cheek.

Teresa came in, checked the monitors, put her hand on Andrew's head, and listened to his breathing.

"There's been a gurgling sound, Teresa. Is he in pain? I don't want him to hurt," Marley pleaded.

"It's tied to his not being able to swallow. I don't believe he's in pain; he's transitioning, and it's hard work." Teresa stroked Andrew's face. "What he's experiencing is much like being born into this world—scary and full of uncertainty. He may be waiting for your permission to leave."

"Permission?"

"Yes, I do believe he is between two worlds, and he may need to hear you tell him it's okay to let go." Teresa glanced at the wall clock. "I need to check on another patient. Is there anyone you want me to call? Vivian, perhaps?"

Marley shook her head. "We'll be fine."

"I'll check back—soon."

Marley held Papa's hand, wrapping her fingers tightly around his. Her father's lower jaw struggled to move until a smattering of mumbled words were released, sometimes in Hebrew, sometimes in English. Israel... God...

She wasn't sure she believed in what Teresa was telling her. Two worlds? Papa would have scoffed at that. She remembered him saying,

"It's science that counts. That which can be proven." How could she know whom to believe? They both seemed equally sure.

She put her head close to his. "Oh, Papa, I wish you could hold me one more time, but it's okay for you to go. When you get there, give Mommy a kiss for me."

His eyes opened wide and he looked directly at Marley. As if being called away, his gaze shifted to the far corner of the room. He stared, and then spoke two words: "Miriam? Rachel?"

He struggled to draw in a breath, released it, and then—silence.

"I have planned everything—well, almost everything," Papa said shortly after Mommy's death. He handed Marley an envelope with the word "Afterwards" written on it.

"You must know what to do after I die. There are a few phone numbers to call and instructions to follow."

She shook her head and cried. "I can't open it...not ever!"

"I know this is difficult," said Papa. "For now, put it someplace safe."

She stood in the kitchen trying to remember where she had put the envelope. *Someplace safe,* Papa had said. Of course: the old cigar box.

She and Vivian had gone with Mommy to Mr. Kemper's Tobacco Emporium. Mommy had told them that this was a very grown-up store. "Look, but don't touch," she had said firmly.

Mr. Kemper said, "Now, young misses, if you walk around the store with your hands behind your backs and don't touch anything, I'll have a surprise for the both of you." Mr. Kemper was short in stature, not much taller than Vivian—who promised to be taller than Marley—with a little potbelly and a lilt to his voice.

Marley and Vivian dutifully clasped their hands behind their backs and paced around the store, looking wide-eyed at the treasure trove of pipes, cigars, cigarettes, and tobacco.

Vivian leaned over and whispered, "When I grow up, I'm going to smoke a pipe like your Papa."

Marley replied, "You can't. Pipes are only for men."

Vivian eyed her. "Then why are there tiny ones with jewels? And besides, I can do anything a man can do!"

"Oh, yeah? You can't pee standing up."

"Oh, yeah? I've been practicing!"

Marley's eyes suddenly widened. She whispered, "Viv, look at Mr. Kemper. I think he's a gnome in disguise."

Vivian shook her head. "No, he's not. I'm certain he's a leprechaun."

Mommy's voice sang out: "Time to go, girls."

Mr. Kemper walked over with two cigar boxes. "A wooden cigar box for each of you for being well behaved. My granddaughter loves to put her special trinkets in these boxes. Now, don't open them until you're in the car. There's a special surprise inside."

"Thank you, Mr. Kemper!" they said in unison.

"You're very welcome." Mr. Kemper leaned over and whispered something to each of the girls. They both paled.

Once in the car, they opened the boxes to find a pink bubble gum cigar. Later that evening, during one of their many sleepovers, Vivian asked, "What did Mr. Kemper whisper to you?"

"I'm scared to say it. Do you think a ghost will come if I say it?"

"What did he whisper to you?" Vivian insisted.

"He said, 'I'm neither a gnome nor a leprechaun.'"

"He said the same thing to me."

"Viv, I'm too scared to sleep alone."

Vivian bounced into Marley's twin bed. "I think I have it figured out. We were whispering so he couldn't hear us, right?"

"Right, but my Papa says my whisper is like a lion's roar."

"I've got it! Mr. Kemper is a spy in disguise, and his store is wired."

"Do you think the bubble gum is poisoned?"

"Well, I'm not chewing it."

"Me neither," said Marley, snuggling even closer to Vivian.

∞

She opened the box filled with childhood keepsakes. The envelope marked "Afterwards" was on top. She took it out and placed it next to her. She looked at the shells from a day at the beach, sand from the camping trip to the desert, and Valentine's Day cards. Strange, she thought, that she'd only kept the ones from Vivian. She counted them. Thirteen all together, from kindergarten through twelfth grade. Childish, puppy love sentiments and scrawled signatures decorated with hand-drawn hearts and arrows; best friend cards followed by funny ones bordering on teenage grossness. She wondered if Vivian had kept hers.

At the very bottom of the box rested the famous poisoned bubble gum cigar. For a moment she laughingly wondered about the cigar: Could it have been poisoned, after all? A part of her needed to believe that their adventures were real and the world was filled with spies and danger and poisoned cigars. She was tempted to take a bite of the stale candy and find out. She resisted. Marley smiled at those childhood memories with Vivian. *What would I do without Viv?* She could live without John, but even the thought of not having Vivian in her life made her heart break, her throat tighten, and tears well up in her eyes.

She opened the envelope marked "Afterwards" to find a single sheet of paper with the phone numbers of Papa's attorney and accountant, a notation that the house was paid-in-full and a list of bank accounts showing substantial balances. She stared at the numbers. *How did they do it?* she wondered. She knew they had worked hard and rarely took vacations. They both accepted overtime when they could. Her own work history had been spotty. Summer jobs at department stores. Once a job at a bakery, but that was not the best place for someone with a fledgling eating disorder.

Further down on the page was a referral to Downer's Mortuary, followed by Papa's strict wishes for Afterwards:

Cremation without any memorial service. Pick out an urn or dispose of the ashes as you see fit.

    With all my love,
    Your Papa

This was followed by a postscript.

A favorite quote of mine by Khalil Gibran—sadly, one that I was not always able to follow.

"Your living is determined not so much by what life brings to you as by the attitude you bring to life; not so much by what happens to you as by the way your mind looks at what happens."

What was Papa trying to tell her?

Vivian met her at Downer's Family Mortuary.

They waved at each other across the parking lot. Marley surveyed Vivian's outfit: black flared pants with matching vest and jacket, and a button-down shirt with a pointy collar. She looked at Vivian's chunky shoes with gargantuan platform heels—the latest style. She glanced at her own outfit, a simple black dress befitting a daughter in mourning.

She watched as Vivian hobbled over and joined her in a fond hug.

"Wow! You look beautiful," said Marley. "I didn't know you owned anything so stylish. But why the suit and briefcase, and what's with the limping?"

"Thanks. I had to borrow everything, and the shoes are too small—they're murdering my tootsies." Vivian groaned, then cleared her throat. "I'm here to represent your interests. In short, I don't want you to get ripped off. Today, I am your attorney."

Marley rolled her eyes. "Okay, Ms. Legal Eagle, let's go!" she said, taking the lead toward the mortuary.

Vivian stopped at the entrance to the building.

"Mar, check out the sign." DOWNER'S FAMILY MORTUARY flickered off and on in blazing pink lettering. "Jeez, Mar. Is that sign trying to tell us something? How'd you pick this place anyhow?"

"Papa picked it out. He said they had the best prices, and he didn't want me to overpay."

"If I smoked, I'd be lighting up right about now. Downer's? Really? Your dad must have had a hidden sense of humor."

"Let's get it over with," Marley said, walking toward the building.

They gave their names to the receptionist. She waved them over toward two chairs that squeaked when they sat down or moved. Pastoral paintings lined the walls. Why did business offices always seem to have artwork of shepherds herding livestock?

They glanced down the long hallway as a man approached, wiping his hands on a towel.

Vivian and Marley exchanged looks. "Are you thinking what I'm thinking?" Vivian whispered. "I bet he just got finished"—she shuddered—"embalming somebody."

The man wore funereally dark pants and a white shirt. He picked up a jacket hanging on a coat stand and then turned to Marley and Vivian.

"I'm Edward Downer," he said, looking at Marley. "And you are?"

"Marley Chambers."

"The next of kin, I take it?" he said as he extended his hand.

She nodded as she shook his drooping hand. *Just like holding a dead fish*, Marley thought.

"I'm very sorry for your loss," Mr. Downer said.

"Thank you."

He turned toward Vivian. "And this young lady is?"

"My—"

"Her attorney. Ms. Vivian Harris," she said with an emphasis on the Ms.

"An attorney? Most unusual," Mr. Downer said with a forced smile as he shook Vivian's hand.

Marley could tell Vivian was holding back her laughter. *Oh God, she's doing that weird thing she does with her mouth when she's trying not to get hysterical. Oh, poor Mr. Downer.* She tried to send a telepathic message to Viv: *Remind me to strangle you when we get out of here.*

"Please follow me to my office," Mr. Downer said.

In the spartan office, glass cases filled with sample urns lined the walls: a sewing machine, figures of animals, cars and trucks, and a variety of wine bottles.

"Please have a seat." He gestured toward two vinyl-stacking chairs.

Marley avoided looking at Vivian, but couldn't miss the theatrical groan as Vivian sat down.

Mr. Downer sat at the oak veneer desk and began to jot down notes on a legal pad.

"I understand that your father's wishes were for cremation without any ceremony."

"That's correct," said Marley. He gets right down to business, she thought.

Mr. Downer made a sweeping gesture toward the glass cases. "We are known for our extensive and unique selection of urns," he noted with genuine pride.

Marley looked the strange assortment over and replied graciously, "You've got some nice ones, all right."

Vivian recited a silent prayer; *Oh, Heavenly Father, please give me the strength not to get the giggles.*

Mr. Downer said, "It can be a difficult decision to find the perfect resting place for our dearly departed. The animal urns have a soft cover. It can be a comfort to be able to hug your loved one."

She could tell Vivian was about to burst. Her cheeks were puffing out, and her face had turned a bright red.

"Did your father have a favorite hobby?"

"Yes. He loved to read."

Mr. Downer went to one of the shelves. "The book urn may be perfect. It's handcrafted, and we can have the title of his favorite book engraved on the cover."

She could see Viv pressing her hands to her head. Getting herself under a measure of control, Vivian said, "Get him the motorcycle, Mar."

Marley flashed a look that said, *Viv, you're going to need Mr. Downer's services sooner than later.*

Mr. Downer replied, "Ah, that's one of our most popular urns. It's a Harley-Davidson Baja 100—commonly known as The Desert Rat. Very popular with the off-road crowd."

"What's that one?" Marley asked, pointing to a simple wooden box.

"I see you have excellent taste, Miss Chambers. It's our most classic urn—made out of acacia wood from the Holy Land."

What a perfect paradox. Papa would love it. "I'll take it."

"Very good. If you young ladies will give me a moment, I'll take care of the, uh, particulars."

Mr. Downer did some calculations on an adding machine, wrote an amount on a slip of paper, and slid it across the desk for their inspection. He smiled unctuously at Marley and said, "I hope the price meets your satisfaction?"

"Looks good to me," said Marley.

Mr. Downer looked at Viv, and his smile disappeared. "And your satisfaction as well ... counselor?"

Viv was squirming with suppressed laughter but managed to say, "An acceptable price."

"Very good," said Mr. Downer. "It will be ready for pickup in five days."

"Thank you," said both girls together.

Mr. Downer could not help overhearing the young women singing, "The worms crawl in, the worms crawl out" as they headed for the exit door. It was from the macabre children's classic "The Hearse Song," of course. In his line of work, he'd heard it a million times from other irreverent customers.

He sighed and looked at his manicured nails. The smug look on his face made it clear what he was thinking: *Those who laugh last, laugh best. Everyone comes through our doors one time or another.*

CHAPTER 3

Marley gazed out the kitchen window, her eyes fixed on the walkway of broken concrete weaving its way through the lawn. She felt a catch in her throat when she remembered the weekend when she and Papa built the path. It seemed strange the way memories kept popping up, seemingly random and disconnected.

Weekends were extra special because Mommy and Papa were both home. Mommy slept in on Saturdays and Papa fixed breakfast. Papa had a way of winking before he poured Sugar Smacks into Marley's Hickory, Dickory, Dock cereal bowl.

Papa filled his extra large bowl to the brim. At that moment, he was not a grown man; they were two kids loving the super-sweet cereal meant for children. Between mouthfuls, he would talk about their project for the day.

"We have a big undertaking today, Marley."

Her head bobbed up and down and her eyes grew wide at the sight of the bottom of the bowl with the drawing of a grandfather clock and a mouse. "Hickory, Dickory, Dock," she said out loud, reading the opening line from the familiar Mother Goose nursery rhyme.

The bowl had belonged to Mommy when she was a little girl. Mommy had told her how much it meant to her. "We had to save box tops from our Wheaties cereal," she had related, all smiles. "It took me forever; at least it felt that way. Finally, I had enough box tops, and my Mommy helped me to send away for the cereal bowl. I would sit on our front porch and wait for the mail. The postman would shake his head, and I would feel a wave of disappointment. Then one day the postman knocked on the door and handed me a package. I was so excited I jumped up and down. Inside the box was my very own Hickory, Dickory, Dock bowl."

Papa filled the bowl again. "Stoke your furnace, Marley," he urged, "because we'll burn at least a million calories."

"What are we doing today, Papa?" she asked, taking a big mouthful from her second bowl of cereal. Mommy would never give her an extra bowl of Sugar Smacks—she said the cereal would rot her teeth.

"We're going to make a pathway through the lawn to Mommy's flower garden."

"Why, Papa?"

"You know how much Mommy loves her flower garden?"

She bobbed her head up and down, all the while more than happy to "stoke her furnace" with the sweetest of treats.

"It will be easier for her to reach the flowers."

They had made the walkway with concrete remnants from a nearby house-remodeling job. "Why waste what is useable?" Papa had said.

When the sun got high, Mommy came out with tall glasses of ice water. Her hair hung loosely down her back, and her eyes looked sleepy, as if she had just woken up from a nap. "My two talented landscapers." she said drowsily.

Papa stood up and stretched, taking one of the glasses from Mommy and handing it to Marley.

"Marley's in charge of installing the sand bed."

She drank thirstily. "It's hard work, but fun too."

"Work can be that way," said Mommy. "But right now I'm calling for a Mommy lazy day. I'm thinking of doing a bit of sewing."

Marley's eyes lit up.

"How would you like matching dresses for you and Vivian?"

She jumped up and down. "Like twins, Mommy?"

"Exactly," she replied.

∞

Marley smiled at the memory. *Hickory, Dickory, Dock. Those were the first words I could read.*

She knew where Mommy kept the bowl. "Top shelf, all the way in the back," Mommy had told her.

Marley opened the cabinet, reached all the way in, and found the bowl, a little worse for wear, but the words could still be seen.

Marley poured a second cup of coffee. She wondered where those dresses were now. Had Mommy kept hers somewhere, or had it been sent to the Goodwill store?

She had loved the blue striped dress with tiny red flowers and a Peter Pan collar.

Mommy even made matching shorts. "You are going into second grade and will be playing on the big kids' playground. That means monkey bars and the high slide. You don't want your undies showing."

Marley and Vivian wore the matching dresses for their first day in second grade.

Somewhere, there was a photo of that first day of school. She felt a sudden compulsion to find it. There was something about that picture. She went into Mommy's sewing room and looked at the neatly arranged albums on the shelf under the window. She picked the one labeled 1951-1953 and flipped through the pages until she came to the one with Mommy's handwritten inscription: "Marley and Vivian, the first day of second grade."

She chuckled at their obvious physical differences. What was that children's rhyme?

"Jack Sprat could eat no fat. His wife could eat no lean. And so between them both, you see, they licked the platter clean."

Vivian would be Jack, of course. Lean as could be...then she would have to be Jack's wife. She smiled at the chubby little girl with a broad smile standing next to her best friend, who wore the grandest scowl plastered across her face.

After Mommy and Mrs. Harris had dropped them off at school, Vivian said, "I hate wearing dresses. Especially ones with this ridiculous collar."

"Don't you want to be my twin?"

"Mar, why can't we be twins wearing overalls?"

"Mommy says overalls and shorts are for summer vacation, and now that summer's over, we wear dresses and skirts. Except on weekends, of course."

Vivian grimaced the entire morning, causing their teacher, Mrs. Martin, to ask her if she had a tummy ache. When it was lunchtime, Vivian managed to spill chocolate milk all over her dress and never wore it again.

Now Marley saw an angry little girl in Vivian. A little girl who didn't want to wear dresses and to this day wore pants whenever she could, and carried a backpack instead of a purse. *How sad that Viv couldn't be who she was and is. But, who am I to talk?*

Marley put the album back on the shelf between the albums marked 1949-1950 and 1954-1955 and returned to the kitchen.

She stood at the sink, her hands swirling around in lukewarm water. As she stared out the window, she saw signs that spring was not far off. The Bermuda grass was turning from light brown to green. Clusters of daffodils were pushing their stems up through the soil, and would soon display their bright yellow faces, like trumpets heralding longer, warmer days. Signs of renewal were everywhere, except in her heart.

Mommy had once said, "Los Angeles is sometimes made fun of for not having seasons, but if you look with a California eye, you can see that winter is passing, and spring is on its way."

She lowered her voice, as if sharing her deepest secret. "I've never lifted the bulbs the way you are supposed to, with a spading fork, yet year after year, they struggle to find their way through the tangle of roots and the hard ground. It's like birth—the baby and mommy have to struggle, and struggle together."

"Was that how it was with me, Mommy? When I was born?"

Mommy was silent.

"Mommy?"

"Hmm? Yes, it was a struggle." She bent down to kiss Marley on top of her head. "You were my gift."

Marley looked around the kitchen. More dishes waiting to be washed, and a high-rise of takeout boxes pleading to be taken out to the trashcan—Chinese, Italian, and her favorite: Canter's Delicatessen. No one made a corned beef sandwich like Canter's, and their dill pickles—to die for!

Driving to Canter's was a Sunday ritual she had shared with Papa ever since she was six. Her birthday had fallen on a Sunday and Papa had said, "Six means you a very big girl now. How would you like to go to Canter's with Papa? And because you are so grown-up, Mommy and I thought you can sit in the front seat."

Marley grinned, showing the space from her recently lost front tooth. She had another loose tooth that wasn't quite ready to come out, but Marley wiggled it from time to time to encourage it.

Papa had kissed Mommy and whispered, but not so quietly that she couldn't hear: "Maybe you should take a nice soak in the tub while we're gone." Mommy put her arms around him and replied, "I love you, Andrew."

Papa put down a purple velvet cushion so that she could see out the window. He inhaled deeply and asked, "Can you smell it?"

She took a long sniff. She recognized the delicate floral scent Mommy often wore and nodded her head.

"That's Mommy's favorite perfume." He took great care in pronouncing its name: "L'Air du Temps. Mommy first got a whiff when she was in Paris during the war, and since that time, it has remained her favorite."

The lingering fragrance wrapped around her as she sat elevated on the purple cushion, and for the very first time took command of the front seat. Usually, she sat in the back and busied herself with her *Sleeping Beauty* book or played with her Shirley Temple doll.

This time she could pretend she was a real princess riding in a coach drawn by four white horses. She waved to her subjects: the three men and two women waiting at the bus stop, the kids playing on the slide as they passed the park, and clusters of "royal citizens" out for a Sunday stroll.

Papa grumbled at the Sunday traffic. "Canter's is close by, but we'll never get there with all these Sunday drivers clogging the road!" He gave the steering wheel a frustrated slap.

Marley didn't care how long it took. She loved the time spent with Papa, and she especially looked forward to plunging her hand into Canter's brine-filled barrel to find the biggest pickle.

They turned left from Olympic Boulevard onto Fairfax Avenue. She stopped waving. She was entering a foreign land where the men had beards and wore black slacks and long black coats. Their heads were covered with skullcaps or large hats. She liked the fur hats best. Papa had told her they were called *shtreimels*, and that the people they were seeing were Orthodox Jews. Papa knew almost everything, and what he didn't know he could discover in one of his books. She knew what Jews were. In fact, she knew all about different religions from a library book she had checked out with Mommy.

They passed families with infants in strollers and older children trailing behind. Their mommies wore long dresses that covered them from collarbone to ankle. The boys wore black slacks and white shirts, and the girls wore long-sleeved dresses that hung below the knee. Marley looked down at her bare legs and sleeveless top.

"It's going to be a hot one," Mommy had said. "Dress cool."

She wondered if those girls ever got to wear shorts.

The streets were busier than usual, and the line to Canter's snaked around the block. Marley never minded waiting in line, as there was so much to see and think about. She could look inside the Hadassah Thrift Shop with the sign painted on the window in big white letters: SUPPORT HOSPITALS AND YOUTH PROGRAMS IN ISRAEL. She knew where Israel was; Papa had taken out his big book of maps and pointed to the small country next to a sea.

As soon as they got to the door, she could hear Mr. Canter singing out, "Take a number!" as he hand-sliced lox from a side of smoked salmon. Bagels, lox, and cream cheese in a large brown bag and a big dill pickle picked by Marley from the "Pick Your Own" barrel had become their traditional Sunday brunch.

Bakery Lady gave her two butter cookies because it was her birthday. She whispered, "I know your mommy doesn't like you eating too many sweets. Brush the crumbs off before your mommy sees you."

When they came home, Mommy brushed away the remaining crumbs, smiled, and sniffed her hand. "Did you get a big pickle today?"

"The biggest, Mommy."

Papa smiled. "Would you like your birthday surprise before or after breakfast?"

Her eyes widened, and Mommy and Papa laughed.

"It's in your room!" Mommy sang out.

She could hear Mommy and Papa laughing as she ran to her room. *Wow!* A Princess bedroom set, exactly like the one in her *Sleeping Beauty* storybook. She bounced on the bed, then lay down and pretended to be asleep, with exaggerated snoring added for dramatic effect. Mommy and Papa laughed and whispered, "I guess she really likes it."

Mommy ran her hand over the desk. "You can do your homework or write stories. As an extra surprise, the bed has a trundle." Mommy slid the trundle bed out. "For when you have Vivian sleep over. And as a special treat, tomorrow is a school holiday, and guess who is sleeping over tonight?"

"Viv, Viv, Viv!" she chanted.

"Yes, yes, yes!" said Mommy.

Mommy took Papa's hand, "Come, Andrew, help me with breakfast. I can see Marley needs more time to explore."

Abbey opened Canter's brown bag, closing her eyes for a moment as the aroma of fresh bagels filled the air.

Sighing, she said, "I don't know if I'll ever get used to this."

Andrew put his arms around Abbey's waist, pulling her close until the space between them vanished. "You mean Canter's?"

"No, silly. Everything. You, us, our beautiful home—Marley. Sometimes it's hard for me to believe after everything we've gone through. I never thought I could be so happy."

"It was you, Abbey. You did it all."

"I have to admit there were times I had to push you." She smiled.

"You did—push and pull. I've never known a woman to be so forceful when necessary."

"It came from being a frontline nurse. Not a place for sissies. Andrew?"

"Hmm?"

"I don't say it often enough. Thank you for giving me Marley."

"It was my pleasure." he chuckled. "Marley's a delightful child, isn't she?"

"Everything I could have ever wanted. Yet, I do worry. Have we done right by her? Perhaps we've overprotected her. Marley seems unusually anxious and frightened."

"Don't forget, she has asthma. Not an easy thing for a little girl to deal with."

"But, her nightmares. Where do they come from? You don't think—"

"Shh," he said, putting a finger to her lips. "Children sometimes have fears, even in a perfect world. If you were having trouble breathing, you'd have nightmares too."

"What we've done, Andrew, do you think God can forgive us?"

"Abbey, look at me." His tone was gentle. "There is no God, and nothing to forgive. I thought we had agreed upon that."

"I know, I know. But sometimes, when I think of all the time I spent in church and how much comfort I received...."

"Mommy, Papa, look!" Marley stood at the doorway, grinning like a jack-o'-lantern. "Viv told me to wiggle my loose tooth, and it would come out, and I wiggled and wiggled and wiggled."

She smiled and handed Mommy her tooth.

"This is indeed a big event," said Papa. "And cause for a celebration."

"And for a visit from the tooth fairy," said Abbey in a conspiratorial whisper to her husband. "Now don't you frown, Andrew. If there's room for reading fairy tales, there's room for the tooth fairy."

"You won't get an argument from me, Abbey," Papa had whispered back.

Marley had overheard, but she didn't quite understand what all the whispering was about.

∞

That night, Mommy pulled out the trundle bed for Vivian, kissed them goodnight, and told them not to stay up all night giggling. Ceremoniously, Mommy placed Marley's lost tooth under the pillow.

Vivian said, "That was the best cake ever! I asked my mother for a fireman bunk bed for my birthday. With a pole, so I can slide down in the morning. You could have the bottom bunk, but I'll let you slide down the pole if you want."

"A red bunk bed? Like a fire engine?"

"Yes, and with a siren too. Except, my mother said no, because they're for boys. You know what else she said?"

"What?"

"She said I couldn't run around without a top on. She said that girls have to cover their chests up."

"Why?"

"Because she said pretty soon our chests will grow."

"Really?"

"Yep, like our moms'. And I told her I wouldn't let mine grow."

"What did she say?"

"She laughed and said that was the way God made us."

Abbey opened the door. "Okay, girls. Time to get some sleep. Papa has to get up early to go to work. Lots of work in the hospital lab on Mondays. Night, now."

"Night, Mommy," they said in unison.

After a while, Viv whispered, "It's lonely down here."

Marley patted her bed and said, "It's lovely up here."

"Do you think your Mommy would care?"

"No, Mommy loves you. She says you're like a second daughter."

The two girls giggled quietly and shared their deepest secrets until they fell asleep curled up in each other's arms.

The next morning, Marley reached underneath her pillow to discover that the tooth fairy had paid her a visit, and to her surprise and delight, she was a shiny new quarter richer.

∞

Marley lowered another stack of dirty dishes into the sink. *Maybe I should let them soak for a few.*

Washing the dishes on the weekends was her first real chore. She was seven, and Mommy had pulled a stool up to the sink. "Wash or dry?" she asked.

Marley picked washing because she loved to make swirls in the suds, and when she took the stopper out, she could hear the *whoosh* as the water escaped from the sink. *Was that what death was like? One moment you're breathing, then you're not—the stopper comes out and whoosh!*

Later, when she was ten, and the stool was no longer needed, she pouted, "Vivian's mom has a dishwasher."

"I don't need a dishwasher," Mommy had said firmly, "and neither do you. It takes away from our together time. Wash or dry, Marley, it's up to you."

"Wash," she had grumbled.

Her mommy was soooo beautiful, with long hair the color of summer wheat and plaited into a single braid that hung to her waist. And when she would get ready for her shift in Brooks Emergency Room, she would form the braid into a knotted updo and say, "*Voilà*," a word she had learned while in France. How she wished to have hair like Mommy's instead of her out-of-control mop that refused to follow any style.

Mommy always wore a starched apron over her clothes when she had KP duty, as she called it. Mommy was an Army nurse during WWII and said, "Once a soldier, always a soldier." Marley's favorite apron had little cherries all over it and a big pocket that ran across the front. From time to time, as she dried the dishes and put them away, Mommy would smooth the front of her apron. All the while she hummed merrily, which gave Marley to know Mommy was in a happy mood and it was the perfect time to ask for a story.

"Mommy, tell me the story about when you were little."

Mommy laughed. No one laughed like Mommy. At first, the sound was distant and faint, then it built to a crescendo that made it seem as if her laughter belonged to the ocean waves as they snuck up and kissed the toes of children playing on the shore.

"Again? You want to hear the story about when I was a little girl?"

Marley loved to play the story game.

"Once upon a time, I lived on a farm in..."

"Iowa."

"And on that farm there were..."

"Cows and chickens and horses and pigs and lots and lots of corn." Marley giggled at the game they were playing.

"And we even had..."

"A vegetable garden. And your job was to..."

"Get up very early in the morning. Seven days a week. And milk the cows. Then..."

"You would carry fresh milk to your mommy and..."

"Help fix breakfast. We would have a farmer's breakfast. Bacon, eggs, and pancakes..."

"As high as the ceiling."

"Almost. And my daddy would talk about the work for the day and my two brothers, Phillip and Daniel, who were older than I, would eat and nod, eat and nod."

"That's the best story, Mommy."

Her mother leaned over to kiss Marley on top of her head. "I love to tell it to you—and the fun way you help me tell it! Now, you wash the dishes with me, the way I washed the dishes with my mommy. I love you, Buttercup," she murmured.

Only Mommy called her Buttercup. She said Marley reminded her of the golden wildflowers that grew in the fields surrounding the family farm.

She thought she was neither golden nor wild. Maybe her dark hair could be considered wild, but she thought her insides were black, the color of terror. Terror without a known cause, she now thought. Except for the asthma attacks, and her recurring nightmare, she had had a near-perfect childhood.

She wished she was little again, and Mommy was standing next to her, and she could ask, "Why, Mommy? Why am I always on the edge of terror?"

Marley began to wipe the kitchen counter with a dishrag. She shivered from a sudden puff of chilly air. *Was it Mommy's spirit, or only the wind finding its way through ancient windows?*

She bit her lower lip—not a habit she cared for, but it helped to keep the tears away.

How much more could she take? She had exchanged a few calls with John; he offered his condolences against the background noise of a party. "I'm glad we can talk," he'd said, practically screaming. "Remember, I'm here if you need me."

She had gone to the movies with Vivian and a few of their friends a couple of times since Papa died, she guessed.

They saw *The Way We Were*. She wished she could be bolder, like Barbra Streisand's political activist character, Katie Morosky. She'd settle for being able to sing like Streisand, but when she tried, her voice sounded more like a frog croaking on a summer night.

And then there was *The Exorcist*. She clutched Vivian's hand throughout the disturbing film and made her spend the night. "I'm scared to be alone. You know how that house creaks."

Viv said, "We're too big to sleep in the twin. I'll be right here on the trundle. I ask only one thing: Don't step on me when you get out of bed."

"Get out of bed? Are you kidding me? If I have to pee, you're getting up first to turn on the lights and make sure there's no demons in the bathroom."

"I already checked," Viv reported groggily. "I flushed 'em all down the toilet. Have to sleep, Mar. Good night!"

A few minutes later, Marley's loud whisper broke the night silence. "Viv?"

"Hmm. Trying to sleep, Mar."

"Viv, I heard a sound. Check the closets, please!"

"Jesus, what are you, six years old?" Vivian grumbled. "I need to get my beauty sleep. And no cracks!"

"No cracks, I promise. But I heard a sound." There was no mistaking the tremble in her voice.

"You're really scared, aren't you?" Vivian sat on the edge of Marley's bed and held her hand.

"Mar, you are my best friend since we were in the playpen together. I'm getting worried. I read this article in—"

"*Ms.* magazine," Marley interrupted.

"Shush," Vivian said playfully. "They do have some terrific articles—and, Your Royal Stubbornness, you might actually enjoy them."

"Tenacious, not stubborn," Marley replied.

Vivian tittered as she shook her head. "You win. Actually, this was part of a lecture on grief I saw at the hospital. You know the monthly lectures they have for the staff? One of the handouts was saying that after a period of time, grief could become, uh, well..."

"Well, *what?*"

"A sign of depression. Maybe it's time for you to talk to someone. There was a list of referrals in the handouts. They're all licensed therapists and carefully screened. You can't go wrong."

"Go ahead, Viv. Say it: I'm crazy!"

"Crazy? Let me think about it—hmm, no more than usual." She jumped into the twin bed. "Move over," Vivian said, opening her arms. "I'm here to protect you from werewolves, demons, mummies, vampires, Frankenstein's Monster, Godzilla—"

"Okay, okay, smartass, I get it. Now, would you tell me a story, the way you did when we were kids?"

"Which one, Princess?"

"The story of 'The Brave Little Tailor.'"

"You got it. Once upon a time..."

Dust and disorder had taken over the house she now owned but continued to think of as Mommy's and Papa's. The mess wouldn't have bothered Papa—his office was filled with books and magazines and a few antiques he had purchased from time to time—but she could hear

Mommy's faint "tsk, tsk," a mark of her displeasure.

Her partially written proposal lay scattered on the desk in her bedroom. On top of the pile lay the official reminder of her failure: a letter from the University of California, Los Angeles (UCLA), extending her status by three months. At the bottom of the letter was the handwritten note from Dr. Holbrook:

"I am indeed sorry for your very recent, personal losses.

Here is my phone number, should you need to contact me regarding your dissertation proposal."

Tick-tock, tick-tock she thought as she eyed the crumpled pile of empty, single-sized bags of Cheetos stacked next to the sea foam green Hermes Rocket typewriter. The typewriter was a gift from Mommy and Papa after she had been accepted into the Ph.D. program at UCLA.

"This is the world's lightest portable," Papa beamed. "And made like a Swiss watch."

"Papa, Mommy, I love it!"

Mommy said, "You'll be the envy of all the other students."

Papa chimed in, "Nothing is too good for our doctor to be."

Now, the typewriter sat unused, its purpose changed from a colossus of creativity to a reminder of another failure. She felt like throwing a dirty shirt over the machine so she wouldn't have to look at it.

It was almost noon, and she was still in her pajamas. With a sudden sense of urgency, she rushed into the kitchen, slapped together a cheese sandwich, grabbed a diet soda along with a half-full bag of Fritos, and dashed toward what had always been called Mommy's sewing room. She flipped on the TV just as the wooden cuckoo bird peeked out from the Swiss wall clock to chime the hour, its goofy song mingling with the opening theme from *Days of Our Lives*. There were rumors that the show would be expanded to one hour; she had read that report in two different soap opera magazines while waiting in line at the supermarket. She hoped she could fit the extra time into her non-existent schedule.

She took a bite out of her sandwich and followed it with a single Frito and a swig of soda.

She became alert when Dr. Laura Spencer Horton appeared. If she couldn't sing like Barbra, why couldn't she be courageous like Dr. Laura? My God, what that poor woman had endured! Raped by her ex-lover, becomes pregnant from the rape, gives birth prematurely to a son—yet, she battled on. *Dr. Laura would never sink into a clinical depression.*

The light from the east window shined through the white cafe curtains with the hand-crocheted trim. How Mommy loved this room. "Look how the light filters through the curtains. Perfect for sewing or"—she winked—"catching up on the latest scandal on *Days of Our Lives.*"

Mommy would use the noontime break to eat lunch before returning to household chores. Marley wondered how she did it all—cooking and cleaning during the day, working at night as an ER nurse. When did Mommy sleep? Did she and Papa ever have time for sex? She shuddered at the fleeting thought of her parents with libidinous desires.

She looked around the room. How did everything get so...so sloppy?

Wait, Marley. Don't be hard on yourself. You did rinse and stack.

Yes, but I'm down to paper plates. Which reminds me, it's almost trash day. I've got to get control of this situation.

She took out a lined tablet and, during commercials, began to make a to-do list.

1. Call Dr. Holbrook and beg for a longer extension. *As advisors go he's not such a pill, but what if he asks me if I understood the letter from the committee? Maybe that should go further down the list.*

2. Make an appointment with a therapist.

She circled number two. *Could Viv be right? She knew her better than anyone. It couldn't hurt. God, this is Los Angeles. If you weren't a therapist, you were in therapy.* Most of her friends, and even John Lennon and James Earl Jones, were into primal therapy. Although, any therapist might call for the straitjacket if they knew she had been glued to the TV watching amnesiac Tom Horton, Jr. romancing his sister Marie. Of course, it was entirely plausible because Tom had had amnesia plus plastic surgery on his face, and no one could recognize him. Did she have to confess everything to a therapist?

3. Take out the trash and tidy up the house.

One of the pricklier issues between her and John was that she was an abysmal housekeeper. Mr. Neat Freak, meet Ms. Slob. It was an accidental meeting; she was rushing across campus, late as usual for her proposal class. Her briefcase came open, papers fell out, and a gust of wind scattered them across the quad. Seemingly from out of nowhere, John appeared. He wasn't riding a steed, or carrying a sword, but when he smiled the sun reflected off of his perfect white teeth, and she knew he was the one—the knight she had always longed for.

He gathered up her scattered papers, commenting, "I've seen you before, always rushing from place to place."

She knelt on the walkway to scoop up an errant piece of paper. "It's because I'm always late. I'm late now, and I've got to present my proposal to Dr. Holbrook, who I'm pretty sure hates me!" She began to stuff the papers back into her briefcase.

John smiled and held out his hand. "Come on, I'll walk with you."

Afterward, they met for coffee.

"How'd it go?" John asked.

"I got a reprieve," she smiled.

"You have a beautiful smile," he said.

The credit goes to Dr. Litton and his torturous braces. "Thank you."

John told her how much he wanted to be a neurosurgeon. "I can really help patients get relief from pain...it's a challenging field, and I thrive on challenges. What about you? Why history?"

"There's a saying that history is written by the victor. I want to discover the truth."

"And pass it on to students?"

"I'm not sure I want to teach. I think I'll fit best in research, and I've been thinking lately about writing textbooks."

"A bit on the shy side?"

She nodded.

"I like that."

Three months later, they moved in together.

Now she wondered, was there ever such a thing as truth... absolute truth?

She needed to take control of this funk. She would start by dealing with the mountain of trash and getting some super-sized garbage bags tomorrow. That was it: Tomorrow would be a new beginning. No more soda, no more chips. She took a long swig of soda and finished off the bag of Fritos.

Her list needed more detail. She ripped up the page and started a new one in outline form.

I. Set the alarm for six. Shower, eat breakfast.
   A. One soft-boiled egg and two slices of toast—dry. Coffee—black.
II. Toss out all the junk food and buy fruit, vegetables, and lean meat.
III. Exercise with Jack LaLanne.
IV. Eat lunch.
   A. Half-cup cottage cheese, half-cup fruit, and one slice of buttered toast. She crossed out the buttered.
V. Get my proposal notes in order.
VI. Call for an appointment with Dr. Holbrook. Beg for an additional extension.
VII. Call for a therapy appointment.
VIII. Eat dinner.
   A. Four ounces of lean chicken, salad, and lots of vegetables.

There, it's done! She sat back, pleased with the list. She sighed as the momentary supercharge of energy began to fade.

Could she accomplish all this in one day? And shouldn't she put *Days of Our Lives* on the list? All work and no play make Marley a dull girl.

Prioritize and plan for success, she thought, not failure. Maybe she needed to pare down the list...a tad.

She began afresh.

#1. Buy trash bags—lots
#2. Tidy up the house
#3. Make an appointment with Dr. Holbrook
#4. Make an appointment with a therapist

The order seemed right. She would finish the food in the house—*it's a sin to waste food, Mommy had always preached*—and cleaning was exercise, wasn't it?

Monday would be a good day to start.

CHAPTER 4

The alarm sounded at 6:00 a.m. Marley grumbled in her sleep. Rolling over, she pressed the snooze button three times, finally pulled the plug out of the socket, and fell into a nightmare-filled sleep.

She woke up gasping for air. She grabbed her inhaler and with a well-practiced routine gave the inhaler four shakes, removed the cap, breathed out, brought the device to her mouth and breathed in slowly. She counted from one to ten before breathing out. Sighing, she reached for a tissue and wiped the tears that had trickled down her cheeks.

The same nightmare since she was a little girl. *Would it ever go away?*

The handout with the list of therapists lay on the nightstand. She remembered Vivian's words of advice: "They're all licensed and carefully screened. You can't go wrong."

Filled now with a sense of desperation, she stared at the list. How to choose? She thought of hanging the list on the wall and throwing a dart. Did she have any darts? She stared at the names of four men and four women. First decision: male or female? *Female. Was that being biased or, even worse, sexist?* At least now, she was down to four choices. One name caught her attention: Esther Saperstein. She muttered, *Esther Saperstein, Esther Saperstein.* Esther, an old-fashioned sounding name with biblical origins, and not a currently popular one. She had taken a class on Feminism in the Bible. The biblical Esther was a beautiful Jewish queen that had risked her life to save the Jews from extermination. There was even a holiday in her honor: Purim.

Perhaps this Esther could help; they might be a fit.

Marley reached for the phone and then looked at her watch—7:30 a.m.—and realized it was too early to call. She thought, What am I doing, calling without rehearsing? That's like skiing down a slope wearing blinders. *Take control here, Marley. Be more like Queen Esther. What if Dr. Saperstein picked up the phone? Ah poo, doctors never answer their own phones.*

She rehearsed out loud. "Good morning, Dr. Saperstein. Marley Chambers calling. My life is one big mess, and I need to talk to someone... stat!" *Too revealing.*

She lowered her voice and spoke deliberately. "Hello, Dr. Saperstein, my name is Marley Chambers, and I found your name on the Brooks Medical Center Referral List. I'm interested in making an appointment. Please call at your earliest convenience. 213-555-7863. *Nondescript and contained; just might do.*

She picked up the phone and dialed. She could feel her heart beating. *Please, don't answer*, she pleaded. The phone rang, one, two, three times.

"Hello, Dr. Saperstein speaking."

Oh God, my worst nightmare.

"Dr. S-Saperstein, my name is Marley C-Chambers," she stammered. "You don't know me. Of course you don't, how could you? God, I'm rambling like an idiot. Doctor, I need to see a therapist." She began to cry. "Oh, I'm so sorry. My parents both died, and I've had this recurring nightmare since I was a little girl and had my first asthma attack and... and... I'm failing my proposal class, and my best friend thinks I might be depressed."

The phone began to slip from Marley's hand.

Dr. Saperstein's voice was calm and reassuring. "Marley, I want you to take a slow, deep breath. Can you do that for me?"

"In through my nose and out through my mouth?"

"Exactly!"

She inhaled and exhaled.

"Did that help?"

Marley nodded.

"Marley, are you there?"

"Oh, sorry. Yes, I'm feeling a bit calmer."

"Excellent! Now let's see if we can arrange something for today. I have a 1:30 opening. Can you make it?"

"Yes. Thank you, Dr. Saperstein."

Marley was surprised when Dr. Saperstein proceeded to tell her she had a home office. "My office is attached to my house, but with a separate entrance and exit. I'll give you the directions. Do you have pen and paper handy?"

Marley rifled through the mess on her desk. *Damn, that's where the phone bill went.*

"I'm ready," she said breathlessly.

Dr. Saperstein's directions were very specific.

"Take Sunset Boulevard heading west. Exit at Middleton Canyon, and turn right. The house is about two miles from the canyon's entrance. The number is 2567. You'll see a sign that says Patient Parking. After you park, open the wrought iron gate, and follow the brick path. You'll see a door to your left. Please enter, but no sooner than ten minutes before your appointment time. There is a call light to the right of the bathroom door. Please announce yourself by pushing the button."

"Thank you, Dr. Saperstein. I'll see you then at 1:30."

Marley hung up the phone. *What did I get myself into? The directions alone are enough to give any patient a nervous breakdown.*

She drove through the palm-lined streets of Beverly Hills and turned left onto Sunset Boulevard. As she passed the Northern boundary of UCLA's Westwood campus, a familiar feeling of panic washed over her. *How can I get this proposal finished? Maybe it's time to drop out. Dr.*

Holbrook would probably be relieved, but Mommy and Papa had been proud of me for getting an advanced degree; they would have been ashamed if I gave up now. I would be a disaster as a teacher anyhow. A scene from *To Sir, with Love* with foul-mouthed, rebellious students flashed in front of her eyes. *The kids would make mincemeat out of me.*

She overcorrected for a sharp curve in the road and swerved into the next lane. Thank the powers that be, no other cars, and no cops. Sweat began to form under her arms, dampening her black blouse. She turned right onto Middleton Canyon toward Dr. Saperstein's office. The view changed from gated celebrity mansions to rustic homes set on lots cut deep into stark canyon walls.

She kept her eyes on the road until she spotted a sign in calligraphic script with the house numbers and an arrow pointing to PATIENT PARKING.

Dr. Saperstein's home stood out from all the others and seemed out of place in a canyon filled with chaparral, oak trees, white alder, and black cottonwood trees. The driveway curved around a sprawling, green-shuttered Cape Cod with a steeply pitched roof and dormer windows. She looked at her watch: twelve minutes before her appointment time. She got out of the car and stared at her outfit: white jeans tucked into black high cut boots and a black blouse not tucked in.

Damn, why did she let Vivian talk her into buying this outfit?

"It's time, my best friend, for you to move into the seventies," Vivian had said firmly. "Women are becoming liberated in every facet of life, and we can wear anything we damn well please. Come on, step out of the box."

And the sweater...it was the sweater that delivered the deathblow in her attempt to be stylish. Why had she picked a cardigan ski sweater with snowflakes running across her chest? Mommy and Papa got it for her three Christmases ago. She thought it was ghastly then, and her opinion hadn't changed.

"In case you want to go skiing again with Vivian," Mommy had said.

Ski? Ha! She could barely walk without tripping over her feet. Her one attempt at skiing had been a total disaster. She kept screaming,

"Where are the brakes, where are the brakes!" and never did get off the bunny slope.

Marley felt her anxiety level rising as the minutes tick-tocked away.

She wondered about Dr. Saperstein. She had noticed a slight accent from the phone call, but couldn't place it. She clutched the directions in her hand and felt her palms begin to sweat.

What if she hadn't followed the instructions exactly right? What if Dr. Saperstein was an axe murderer? Had she told anyone where she was going? The directions were becoming a soggy mess. She put them in her purse and wiped her hands on her white pants. *Shit, I got ink on my hands and now it's on my pants.* She felt her face turning bright red as she pulled the ski sweater down as far as she could. *Oh God, all my stains will show.*

She pressed the call button and sat on the lone chair in the tiny vestibule. *Tick-tock. Tick-tock. She still had time to flee.*

The door opened. A petite woman with graying hair, in her late forties or early fifties, stood at the door with a welcoming smile. She wore a classic pair of beige silk pants with a matching long-sleeved shirt, neatly tucked in. *Oh, the thrill of being able to tuck your shirt in. Why couldn't I dress that way? I'm not cut out for Viv's liberated ideas of fashion.*

Dr. Saperstein held out her hand. "Hello, Marley. I'm Esther Saperstein. I hope my directions were clear."

Marley nodded. "Very." She wanted to add, "They gave me a ten-plus anxiety attack."

"Please come in," Dr. Saperstein said with a wave of her hand.

Marley glanced nervously at the office, noting how sparse it appeared. *Neat as a pin* was her first thought.

Two Scandinavian tan leather recliners faced each other. Next to them were matching side tables, each holding a tissue box and a marble coaster. There was a flagstone fireplace with several framed certificates neatly arranged on the half wall. Dimly lit floor lamps, a cream-colored couch, and a mahogany desk completed the furnishings. It was the view from the floor to ceiling window that held her attention. She was taken with the denuded canyon walls that seemed to match her feelings of despair.

Dr. Saperstein stood next to her. "We've had unseasonably warm weather and the canyon is bare, but rain is expected later this week and then we'll see the wildflowers and plants spring to life. You would think they can't survive in such an inhospitable environment, but they do, as do we. It is a miracle of rebirth."

Dr. Saperstein motioned Marley toward one of the recliners and sat opposite her.

"Is this your first time seeing a therapist?"

"Yes," Marley whispered. *And maybe my last.*

"It can be a challenge, coming to a stranger for counseling without knowing what to expect."

Marley took a tissue from the side table and dabbed her tears away.

"Perhaps I should begin by telling you about the way I work. As you can see, I'm not Freudian. No analytic couch." She pointed to the neutral couch with its handwoven pillows covered in green and pale coral. "Although at times some clients do prefer to recline; that is up to them."

Marley nodded. "I guess I kind of lost it over the phone," she said with a nervous laugh.

"You've nothing to be ashamed of," Dr. Saperstein replied. "I believe that all of us, at some time, feel alone and hopeless. It sounds as if you have been holding onto several heavy burdens—the loss of both of your parents, a repetitive nightmare, and the difficulty you are having in school. I hope you will allow me to carry some of that load for you."

"I wasn't sure if you would want to see me," she said apologetically.

"Why would I not?"

"I would think it would be boring to listen to a crybaby."

"Is that how you see yourself?"

"I guess I do. I have had so much more than others. I was given everything I wanted, and sometimes before I even thought of it."

"Everything?"

"Why, yes. Love and a lovely home, and my parents paid my college expenses. And even after their death they made sure to take care of me financially. I haven't had to struggle."

"You describe an idyllic childhood, and yet you are haunted by a recurring nightmare. Do you recall how old you were when you first had your nightmare?"

"It began the night I first had croup and couldn't breathe. Four, I was four."

"Would you tell it to me?"

"Yes, of course. It's always the same, and it's always with me."

"It may appear to be identical, but each time we repeat a dream there may be subtle differences, perhaps in the way you see it or something new that comes to light. This time I'd like you to focus on your feelings."

"Feelings? I know there's terror. But, okay." She could feel the color draining from her face. She looked at Esther Saperstein. She seemed kind and non-threatening, definitely not an axe murderer as she had earlier feared.

"Is it okay if I put my feet up on the ottoman?"

"Of course."

Marley took off her shoes, put her feet on the ottoman, and eased back into the chair.

"The dream always begins the same way," she said drowsily. "It's pitch black and I can't see anything. I have a feeling of floating, and at first it feels wonderful. It's as if I'm inside a cocoon and I'm being rocked. But suddenly the movement shifts, and I'm being pushed and shoved and pounded. I feel split in half. Part of me floats outside of that protective place where I'm surrounded by formless shadow-beings, making noises, screaming. The figures remind me of the shadow game kids like to play. You know, with your hands."

Dr. Saperstein nodded. "Shadowgraphs."

"Yes. Even though they look like shadows, I've always thought of them as human beings because they keep moaning and crying out. I can't tell if the sounds are a language. It's like if I heard a foreign language now, I might not understand the words, but I could tell they were words. This is different. I can't decipher what the sound represents."

Dr. Saperstein leaned forward in her chair. "Go on."

"There's not enough air, and everyone raises their hands above their heads, as high as they can, as if by doing so they'll have more room. I'm being squeezed in every direction. The part of me that's outside is being shoved against the part of me that's inside. I want to go back; I want all of me inside the cocoon."

Marley gasped for air. "Now the feeling of floating is back. This is different, it feels as if I'm underwater."

"What else are you feeling?"

"I feel … I feel pain. I feel pain in my heart from the moans and in my body from being squeezed."

Marley opened her eyes. "In the dream, no one comes, no one can save me!" she sobbed.

"What about when you woke up?"

"Mommy and Papa heard my screams and ran into the room. Mommy picked me up. Papa froze. Mommy shouted, 'You above all should know what to do.' Then Papa turned on the shower and Mommy kept holding me, kissing my head, making soothing sounds, and soon the bathroom was filled with steam and I could breathe. Papa took his arms and wrapped them around Mommy and me. And we're all damp from the steam and our tears.

"I can hear Papa whispering to Mommy, 'I'm sorry, Abbey.'"

Marley began to shake. "I'm freezing."

Dr. Saperstein stood and picked up the afghan folded over her desk chair. She covered Marley.

"Thank you," she said, opening her eyes and holding the afghan tightly. "This telling of the nightmare was different."

"Can you tell me how?"

"I never remembered being underwater. You asked about my feelings. Terror, like I said before. Sheer terror. Being suffocated and squeezed. And the figures, I was taking in all their pain. I could feel what they were feeling. The part of me outside brought the feelings to the part of me inside."

"Do you remember what you felt after Papa put his arms around you and Mommy?"

Marley closed her eyes. "Safe, but also confused. It's as if I want to tell Mommy and Papa that I'm okay, and I don't know why they are still crying. I don't understand why Papa froze and why Mommy said, 'You above all.' What could that mean? It seems odd.

"Oh, Dr. Saperstein," she sobbed, "are you positively sure you treat crybabies? Because I think that's what I am. And I know almost nothing about Mommy and Papa. Not really. No photos of their families at all. Why didn't I question things before?"

Dr. Saperstein said evenly, "There is a great deal for us to think about, Marley. The time has flown by, and I'm afraid our session has ended. I'm wondering how you would feel about coming back on Wednesday and then Friday."

"So often? I must really be sick."

"Not at all. I wouldn't suggest it unless I felt you were strong. I sense we are onto something, and I would hate to wait a week."

"Same time on those days, then?"

"Yes, same time."

∞

Esther Saperstein removed a hundred-page spiral notebook from her desk's file drawer and wrote MARLEY CHAMBERS on the cover. She opened it and for a brief moment stared at the blank page. She wondered how many sessions would pass before the pages were filled. She wrote down "pivotal dream" and circled the phrase several times. She began to write, wanting to capture as much as she could of the dream, as well as Marley's reactions during the session. She eased back in her chair, focusing first on the narrative and then on Marley's feelings.

She was faced with an onerous task, having to diagnose a patient. How do you begin to label a young woman who is dealing with multiple losses, recurring nightmares, and secrets that hang over her like specters from the past?

She read the description of the nightmare and, for a moment, felt drawn into Marley's dream. Suddenly, the air felt heavy—devoid of oxygen. She gasped and slammed the notebook shut. She knew that Marley's dream would enter her innermost self. It had happened before, but for now, she needed to put aside the haunting images.

She foraged deep into the back of the drawer and removed a journal containing her personal thoughts and reactions to her patients, never meant to be revealed, or read by another.

She wondered how many notebooks she had like this. Stored in a locked closet, they contained twenty-years of material focusing on a particular interest of hers: pre-birth memories expressed through dreams.

She wrote a brief entry. *A pre-birth memory in dream form?*

Moving from place to place, Esther began to put her office back in order—the slight displacement of the ottoman, the off-center tissue box. She looked at the clock. One hour before her next patient. Precious time to have a late lunch with Danni.

She entered the kitchen and smiled at the woman standing at the sink. Danni turned and held out her arms.

Esther rested her head on Danni's chest. "I don't say it often enough, but you make my very existence possible."

Danni cooed in a lovely, unmistakably French accent, "Essie, you know my arms are for you and you alone, *mon petit chou.*"

Esther murmured, "Your little cabbage? I hope I am more than that."

"You are the world to me." Danni traced the lines on Esther's brow. "You always furrow your brow after the troubled ones have entered your soul."

Esther smiled. "I can't hide it from you, can I, Danni?"

"Not when we first met, and not for all these years."

"I have to take her pain inside; it's the only way I can help her through this."

"Only someone who has suffered can fully understand another's suffering. That is your gift and your curse. But for now, lunch—salad from the garden and homemade lentil soup. And for dinner I'm thinking perhaps cheese, fruit, and yogurt, and I got a loaf of that French bread you love so much. We do have tonight, *oui*?"

"Yes, all night."

"Ah, then, you will discover how much more you are to me than simply being my little cabbage."

∞

Papa had told Marley, "The return journey appears to be quicker than the outward journey."

Not in this case, Marley thought. The ride home from Dr. Saperstein's seemed endless. Was it because she felt like a wrung-out dishrag? School buses clogged the streets, and she managed to hit every red light; no doubt the powers that be were against her.

Her thoughts returned to her session with Dr. Saperstein. Had she made a complete fool of herself? Blabbing away, telling her things she had never discussed with anyone, not even Viv. And why had she agreed to return in two days?

She honked at the driver in front of her. Damn idiot, hadn't he seen the light turn from red to green?

She pulled into the shopping center nearest her home and parked in the furthest corner of the lot. She leaned her head on the steering wheel and let the tears fall. Dr. Saperstein had asked for her feelings. Really? How about I feel like an eviscerated chicken?

This is all Viv's fault. Exactly like the time she told me to climb the tree with her and swing on a rope like Tarzan and Jane. Except this Jane fell and broke her arm.

Feelings? How about this one? "Dear Dr. Saperstein, I feel fucking pissed off."

She slammed the car door, strode to the family-owned hardware store, and threw two extra large boxes of trash bags into her cart. She waited in the endless checkout line, inching her way forward. No doubt the supervisor in charge of sales had purposely placed the display of candy bars next to her. Damn, and each one was her favorite. But which were her very most favorite? Oh, don't binge, she pleaded with herself. Four, she could limit it to four. Her lucky number, and heaven knows, she needed some luck right now. She paid for the bags and the four assorted candy bars. "For the kids," she remarked to the indifferent checker.

CHAPTER 5

Marley shivered in spite of having burrowed under two quilts and a blanket. She stirred; was it night or morning? Something was buzzing inside her head, a sugar hangover. She had the weirdest dream. At least it wasn't a nightmare. In the dream, she had called Viv and begged her to come over. "Help me, help me, Viv. I can't handle this mess alone."

Marley glanced at the clock: 10:00 a.m. She stuck her toes out from the covers. Another dilemma to face: the room was freezing, and her bladder was about to burst. She rushed into the bathroom, flipped on the switch to the overhead heater, and peed.

The memories from yesterday were beginning to surface. She was going to kill Viv for pushing her into therapy, and now she had committed to more than one day a week. *Who the fuck did Dr. Saperstein think she was, Woody Allen?* She hoped she never got addicted to psychoanalysis like that famously neurotic comedian. And she sure as hell didn't have his kind of money to blow on an expensive shrink.

She sniffed. Was that coffee she smelled? Damn. Was she hallucinating? Had she turned on the automatic coffee maker? Wait! Sounds were coming from the kitchen—a robbery in progress. She dashed back to bed and hid under the covers.

Her door creaked open. "Mar, are you hiding?"

"Viv, is that you?"

"No, it's Dr. Frankenstein's Monster."

Viv carried a tray with two mugs of coffee and toasted crumpets. "Come on, it's safe to come out," she said, putting the tray on the nightstand.

"Are you sure?" Marley said, peeking out from under the covers.

Vivian sat on the bed. "I'll bet you forgot," she laughed.

"Forgot what?"

"Our late night phone conversation."

"We had one?"

"Yeah, you called me at midnight."

"Oh, shit. I thought it was a dream."

"No dream, I can guarantee it. Close to a nightmare, though—woke my roommates, too. After last night's conversation, they really want to meet you."

"What did I say?"

"You begged me to help you clean. You said you loved, loved, loved the therapist, and you were now inspired."

"Inspired to do what?"

"From the look of the bags in the kitchen, I would say to throw out and organize. Come on, Mar. Coffee, then up and at 'em."

"Up and at 'em? I feel like I'm in a John Wayne movie." She sipped. "You do make the best coffee. Uh, Viv ... I had a mini-binge last night."

"I kinda figured that one out. You left some evidence in the kitchen." She stroked Marley's hair. "Did you purge?"

"No, I haven't done that for years. I'm feeling ashamed for having binged, though."

"Fuck shame. Where has that ever gotten us?" Vivian kicked off her shoes and moved onto the bed. "I've got all day to spend with you, you lucky thing."

"Thanks. I'm glad you came over." Marley snuggled closer to Vivian. "Yesterday, Dr. Saperstein asked me about my feelings. I've never really thought about them—well, other than scared and anxious. I didn't realize before that that those feelings are always there. She unlocked a door I didn't want to go through."

Marley munched on a crumpet. "These crumpets are superb."

"They are, aren't they, even if I do say so myself," Viv replied. "I made them the way Mommy did. You know, toasted on the dark side with a trace of blueberry goat cheese. Remember how she talked us into trying it?"

"Yeah, we were really gross, sticking our fingers in our throats and pretending to throw up."

"And now it's on my favorite food list." Viv picked up a napkin and wiped traces of her tears away, recalling her second mom. "Here," she said, handing Marley a clean napkin.

"But, I'm not crying."

"You've got blueberries on your lips." *And I would like to kiss them away.*

"Viv, are you ashamed of me? You know, I'm such a wimp."

"Ashamed of you? Do you remember when that Sammy kid in second grade called me a name?"

"It's engraved in my memory."

"You really pounded him. You think of yourself as a helpless princess, but at that moment you were the princess with a punch."

"I was, wasn't I?" Marley sighed. "I miss Mommy and Papa. I feel lost, really adrift. I wander around the house not knowing where to start or where to go. Their attorney called while I was out. It was at least his tenth call reminding me that the accountant can't move ahead with the estate until I get last year's bank statements—and if the accountant doesn't move, he doesn't move."

"All the more reason to tackle the cleaning. Are you going to finish this crumpet? I'm starving."

"Not after what I ate last night. Go ahead, take it." Viv did, and Marley continued. "I don't even know where they would have kept the bank statements. Probably in Mommy's room, although I haven't seen anything."

"Have you looked?" said Viv, chomping on the crumpet.

"Not really, and I can't even open the door to Papa's study or their bedroom, let alone go through their stuff. It feels as if I'm intruding."

"Let's take one thing at a time. We should start in the kitchen—it's getting pretty ripe in there. Then Mommy's sewing room. And for today, we'll call this our musical trash day. I've got the best music on my cassette player: The Jackson Five, Queen, Led Zeppelin, and a bunch of others. What's your pleasure, madam?" Viv said with a sitting bow.

"Any classical?"

"Why, I think I do. Hmm, classical, that would be from the forties and fifties?"

"You know what I mean."

"Do I ever. How does *Scheherazade* by good old Rimsky-Korsakov sound to ya?"

"I'd love that. Papa was fascinated by the way Scheherazade saved her life with a thousand and one stories."

"Okay then!" Vivian slapped her leg, stood up, and stretched. "We'll listen to that first, then move on to some dance music. And for every three bags we fill, we'll stop to dance."

"Even with my two left feet?"

"Especially with your two left feet." Viv held out her hand. "Okay, princess with a punch—time to rise and shine."

∞

They heard the cuckoo clock strike 11:00 p.m. Vivian yawned. "I've got to get going. I have classes in the morning and you, my dear, have therapy."

Marley pouted.

"Stop pouting, you. Come here." Viv motioned at the window. "Take a look at what we've accomplished."

They stared at the massive pile of trash bags waiting for pickup along the curb.

Viv put her arm around Marley's shoulder. "It looks especially impressive in the moonlight. We did a great job, huh, kid?"

"We sure did, even if we didn't find the bank statements. But the kitchen's clean and Mommy's sewing room is back in order."

"Come with me, I want you to see something." Vivian held out her hand for Marley's and guided her outside to the walled patio. "Look up, Mar. Look at the moon."

"It's huge. I don't think I've ever seen it as bright."

"It's at its closest point to the Earth: a supermoon. Remember how practical my mother was?"

Marley nodded.

"One time, she took me outside and pointed to the moon. At that moment, she didn't seem like my mom. You know, kind of like a young girl, all romantic and stuff. My mom said I should always remember this moment and keep my feet on the ground, but let my heart soar to the heavens."

"I'll remember those words. Thanks for today, Viv. When you talk to your mom, tell her I miss her."

"That's not all I'm going to tell her."

"What else?" Marley said playfully.

"That you're turning out to be one hell of a dancer. We're on for Thursday?"

"Yes. Papa's room. That's going to take some time. Hard time."

"I know. I'm leaving my cassette player and tapes. At least one dance a day, Mar. It's what this doctor prescribes. Promise?"

"Promise."

CHAPTER 6

Marley picked up the morning paper from the patio, brushed away some fallen leaves from her robe, and thought momentarily that the patio needed to be swept. She ambled into the kitchen and hovered over the table before toasting two leftover crumpets and pouring coffee into the pink floral stackable mug. She added two teaspoons of sugar and a small amount of half-and-half, exactly the way Mommy fixed hers. The crumpets popped up, just as she placed the mug on the table. A good omen, she thought. Everything is aligned this morning.

She read the *Times* headline and shook her head.

NIXON DENIES ROLE IN WATERGATE COVER-UP

She felt strangely relaxed. She wondered if it was from accomplishing so much yesterday or from being with Viv. Or...maybe it was the way the moon looked last night. *Feet on the ground, heart soaring to the heavens.*

She had slept soundly last night, no nightmare. Could it have been all the dancing she did with Viv? True to her word, every time they filled three bags of trash, Viv would press the cassette button and start dancing. "Come on, Mar," she urged, holding out her hand. "Get outta your chair, move those hips, and twist like there's no tomorrow!" They had even joined in a conga line of two. From room to room, the staccato beat had followed them: One, two, three, la conga! No wonder her legs and back were sore. She saw a hot bath looming in her near future.

She had made a promise to Viv to dance today, and dance she would. Marley opened Viv's faux-wood storage case and went through the neatly labeled cassettes.

No twisting today, she would dance to slow music. Afterward, she would soak in a leisurely bubble bath before her appointment with Dr. Saperstein. Marley thumbed through the tapes, past the ho-hum disco offerings and hesitated at Gentle Giant's self-titled first album. She liked progressive rock, but dance to it? No way. She stopped at a compilation cassette labeled "Romance" in Viv's tiny and illegible scrawl. She remembered the comment from Mr. Taylor, their grade school penmanship teacher: "Most unladylike, Vivian."

She looked at the index of titles. *Close to You*, The Carpenters. *Lean on Me*, Bill Withers. *The First Time Ever I Saw Your Face*, Roberta Flack. *Time in a Bottle*, Jim Croce.

It was obviously a homemade tape, which Viv must have taken some care to assemble. Viv certainly is eclectic, she thought. A bit odd, though. She's never shown much interest in romance—or dating, for that matter. Whenever she brought up the subject, Viv would make light of it. "No time for that. First law school, pass the bar, get a terrific job, and then we can talk about dating." Yet, Last night Viv stepped away from her 'close to the earth self' and spoke of a heart that could soar to the heavens.

Marley fast-forwarded the tape, hoping she would get to the song of her choice: "Close to You." She felt foolish but a promise was a promise, and when Karen Carpenter began to sing, she closed her eyes and swayed to the dreamy music, remembering how her parents had held each other and danced to the music of their time. What was that song they played over and over again? Not one that Viv would have taped. The music ended, and she walked over to Mommy and Papa's stack of 78 rpm records, moving them aside, one by one, until she found "Blue Moon," sung by Frank Sinatra.

The scene that she had seen so many times played again in her mind's eye.

Papa would blow any real or imagined dust from the record before placing it on the turntable. After the turntable began to move, he would lift the tonearm and, in what seemed like slow motion, place the needle on the record. Then, he would turn to Mommy and sweep her into his arms.

Mommy's head would rest on Papa's shoulder; from time to time, their eyes would meet and they would smile. Not wide grins, she thought, but shimmering and twinkling.

Marley listened to the lyrics as if she was hearing them for the first time.

Blue moon you saw me standing alone
Without a dream in my heart
Without a love of my own
Blue moon, you knew just what I was there for
You heard me saying a prayer for
Someone I really could care for
And then there suddenly appeared before me
The only one my arms will hold
I heard somebody whisper "Please adore me"
And when I looked, the moon had turned to gold!

Marley wondered if she would ever have a love of her own. She returned to Vivian's homemade cassette. Next up was one of her favorites, Roberta Flack's *The First Time Ever I Saw Your Face*.

She couldn't remember when she first saw Vivian's face. She was simply always in her life.

∞

"Joined at the hip," Mommy would lovingly say.

Wrapped up in a mystery worthy of Nancy Drew, Marley and Viv's shenanigans provided Mommy with no end of amusement. "What are the partners in crime up to?" Mommy inquired, hands on hips, catching the girls spying with binoculars out the window.

Marley said, "Mommy, we think Mr. Roland is a spy."

"Our neighbor, Mr. Roland?"

Both girls nodded. "We have proof," Vivian said.

"You do?"

Marley said, "We've been spying with the binoculars Viv got for Christmas."

"Yes, so I see. That's very rude of you girls, you know. Besides, I thought they were for bird-watching."

Vivian said, "That too. But Mommy, we saw some very suspicious activity. We saw Mr. Roland"—she looked at their notepad—"on Monday afternoon at 3:53 p.m. carrying out a rug—all rolled up. That can only mean one thing!"

Marley's head bobbed up and down in agreement.

Vivian continued. "We're certain it was a dead body. Mrs. Roland's, to be specific."

"Anything else?" asked Mommy, tapping one foot on the floor impatiently.

Marley chimed in. "The biggest evidence is the spy antenna on his roof. We're certain Mrs. Roland discovered he's a Russian spy, and he killed her. And now he's sending secret messages to Russia. Viv thinks we should call the FBI."

"That's strange, because I was at the cleaners when Mrs. Roland walked in to pick up her rug, which Mr. Roland had dropped off. As for the spy antenna, Mr. Roland is a ham radio operator. No more spying on the Rolands. Understand? Now, what about your homework?"

They both sighed and took out their math homework.

"I have some work to do in the kitchen. I'll be back in half an hour to check on you."

Abbey walked down the hallway toward the kitchen, holding her breath. She waited until she closed the door to the service porch before doubling over in laughter. *Wait until Andrew hears that we have spies in the neighborhood!*

∞

After Mommy had left the room, Vivian said, "I overheard my mom and dad talking about the Joneses."

"Ronny's parents?"

Vivian nodded and lowered her voice to a whisper. "They said Mr. Jones was in jail for a year for... for... embezzlement."

"Wow!" Marley looked puzzled. "Uh, what's embezzlement?"

"I'm pretty sure it's another word for spying. I think we're on to something. Tomorrow after school at the Joneses?"

Marley agreed. "We can hide behind the pomegranate bushes. Bring your binoculars and the notepad."

"And you can bring some snacks. We may be there a long time."

Marley smiled at the memory of that afternoon at the Joneses. They sat outside the unwitting family's house, making up stories about spies and eating the snacks until the sun dimmed and the streetlights went on, signaling the time to report home.

She would have been lonely without Viv to push her along, guiding her into new territory, sometimes getting them both into trouble. She thought about the way her heart smiled when Vivian walked into the room. *It smiled then, and it smiles now.* Her heart never smiled with John. For a moment, as she listened to the cassette playing, she imagined dancing with Viv, not as they had done yesterday but the way Mommy and Papa had danced. The music stopped; she jerked herself out of her dreamlike state and wondered what had happened.

Taken aback, Marley entered the bathroom, turned on the hot water spigot, and sprinkled lavender bath salts into gushing water. Steam began to fill the room, clinging to the mirrors. Impulsively, she wrote her name on the steam-filled mirror, something she had done when she was little, and Mommy helped her to bathe.

How Mommy loved the mirror hanging over the sink. She could hear her whispering, "Look at the etched floral design. Something you don't find in the newer homes built down the street. This house has character and history. Never forget about history, Marley. It may be filled with tears, but it is also filled with joy and love."

"How many tears are there in the world, Mommy?"

"Enough to fill the oceans and cover the mountains." Mommy held her close and whispered, "But there is more love in the world than tears, and it's love that filled the oceans with fish and made the mountains and meadows blossom with wildflowers."

Marley added a large question mark to the eerie mirror writing that tore at her heart.

Hadn't she told Vivian that Mommy and Papa's presence was everywhere? She flung open the medicine chest and began to throw everything that was a reminder of them into the trashcan: Papa's shaving cream, their toothbrushes, and Mommy's Ponds cream.

Marley lowered herself into the steaming water. She stayed until the water chilled and she began to shiver.

This time she dressed in jeans, a long-sleeved plaid shirt, and sneakers. Comfort before style, she thought.

Backing her car out of the driveway, she maneuvered around the pile of trash bags.

She didn't want to be late for her second appointment with Esther Saperstein, Ph.D.

∞

Marley smiled shyly when Dr. Saperstein opened the door to the waiting room.

This time she didn't ask permission before taking off her shoes and placing her feet on the ottoman. She blushed at seeing her big toe peeking out. "I didn't realize I had a hole in my sock."

Dr. Saperstein smiled benignly. *You want me to see the parts of you that are hidden.*

"I had a good day yesterday but a difficult morning," Marley said with a slight wiggle of her toe. "Yesterday, Viv and I cleaned the kitchen and Mommy's sewing room. Viv brought over her tapes, and she made me dance. And she had me promise to dance today." She smiled. "Viv is like that."

"Like what?"

"Always pushing me to stretch. When I left here on Monday, I was a tad upset." Marley cast her eyes downward. "Maybe more than a tad," she added shamefully. "I don't know why, because you were very kind. I think telling my nightmare stirred me up. And then I had a mini-binge and called Viv in the middle of the night. I didn't remember calling her, except the next morning she showed up, made breakfast, and helped me clean up the house. She even brought music and talked me into dancing."

Marley glanced around the room, as if the walls might have ears. "I've always thought of myself as clumsy," she whispered conspiratorially.

"This morning, I listened to Roberta Flack's 'The First Time Ever I Saw Your Face.' Do you know that song?"

"I do believe I've heard it."

"I began to think about Viv. And I couldn't remember when I first saw her because she's always been with me, or at least it seems that way. And I felt full. Heart full. I don't know how to explain what happened, except ... I never felt it with John. And I was startled."

"Startled?"

"Yes, like where did these feelings come from? And then I sort of had to shake myself awake as if I had been in some kind of weird trance. When I went to take a bath, I remembered that the bathroom was filled with Mommy and Papa's stuff. And I began to sob and threw all their things away. Out of sight, out of mind, you know? I didn't want any reminders."

"You said you sobbed."

"I felt angry, and scared. First my nightmares, then both of my parents die and then these feelings about Viv. It's as if something is off-kilter, but I don't know what. I wrote my name on the mirror after the bathroom got filled with steam. I used to do that as a kid. But then, I became furious and I wrote this giant question mark."

"What do you think that means?" Dr. Saperstein prompted.

"I feel lost and confused. Who am I? I think I've always felt that way, and I don't know why." Marley absently studied her naked toe. "Tomorrow we're going to start getting Papa's study in order. I haven't been able to open the door, and I'm a bit worried about going in."

"What worries you?"

Marley took a tissue and blotted her eyes. "This may sound silly, but it's as if I expect to see him standing in front of the bookcases, completely absorbed in the book he's holding, and even though I'm as quiet as a little mouse, he'll become aware of my presence. Then he puts down the book, looks at me, his eyes light up, and he holds out his arms."

She began to sob softly. "I didn't think I had any more tears left. I have all these memories of being in that room with Papa. He always told me that the answers to our questions lie in two places: within our hearts and inside books."

"Your father sounds like a wise and loving man."

"He is...was. I think Papa was more of a dreamer and Mommy more practical. Sort of like Viv and me. Viv can be focused and on task. And I...well, if my proposal is an indicator, very much of a dreamer."

After a long pause, Marley blurted out, "Dr. Saperstein, something happened in second grade, and it's been on my mind."

"I'd love to hear about it."

"Viv and I went through school together, kindergarten through twelfth grade. This happened in second grade, when we got to play in the big kids' yard. It was recess, and we were playing on the monkey bars. Viv would go across one, two, three, and I would get halfway and fall into the sand pit. Viv was telling me to try it again, 'Make yourself go one more bar. That what my mother tells me when I can't do something.'

"Well, I was just about to try again when this kid, Sammy, came over and stuck his tongue out and called Viv a bad name. And I saw Viv's face, and I thought she was going to cry. I did exactly what Papa had once told me. 'If someone ever calls another person a bad name, you have a responsibility to tell them to stop.' I told Sammy to stop, and he stuck his tongue out at me and said the name again. So, I stuck my tongue out at him. I was getting angrier and angrier.

"Then, I said he was inappropriate. That was the biggest word I could think of, and it came right out of my Papa's mouth. He said the word again, and I punched him right in the face. Blood spurted out from his nose. I thought I had killed him. The school nurse came running, the yard duty lady came running, and we all ended up in the principal's office.

"Sammy sat in the corner with an ice pack on his nose. Viv was crying. I was too angry to cry but down deep, I was certain I was going to jail. Before I knew it, Viv's mom was there, Mommy was there, and Sammy's parents were both there. Mrs. Phelps, the principal, looked very upset and kept sputtering about how the school doesn't allow bullying or fighting. I thought I was doomed—prison for life!

"My mother, who seemed the calmest of all, said, 'Mrs. Phelps, perhaps we can hear the children's versions of what happened.'

"Sammy sat there holding the ice pack to his nose, staring at me as if he was throwing daggers.

"Mommy leaned over and said, 'Marley, would you tell us what happened?'

"He called, her...." I sobbed and sobbed.

"He called her..."

"Mommy said, 'Whisper it in my ear.'

"And I did. And I could see Mommy was trying not to smile. She said, 'Mrs. Phelps, I think we can all take a deep breath.'

"Mommy turned to Sammy and said, 'Will you promise us that you will never tell Vivian she is as skinny as a beanpole?'

"Sammy nodded, and it looked as if his eyes were swelling up and turning black."

"I tugged at Mommy's sweater and whispered, 'That's not all, Mommy. He said she could never climb the beanstalk and rescue the princess from the ogre. Sammy said he's the only one who can save the princess.

"I finally found my voice and started speaking really loud. 'I stuck my tongue out at Sammy because if anyone is going to rescue me from an ogre, I want it to be Viv.'

"Viv's mother hugged her so tight I thought Viv was going to throw up. I knew she was still hurting, because she always saw herself as Jack climbing the beanstalk, or the prince rescuing the princess."

"Was that the first time you hit someone?"

"The first and the last."

"You felt protective of Vivian."

Marley nodded. "Yes, and I know her better than anyone else. I can tell when she hasn't had enough to eat. Viv has a killer metabolism, but sometimes she has a sugar drop and her hands begin to tremble. And when she feels little inside, her mouth quivers and her eyes tear up. Viv knows me, too. When I'm really scared, she makes me laugh. And when I'm stuck, she helps to unstick me. We're different, but it doesn't make a difference if you know what I mean."

"Yes, I believe I do." Dr. Saperstein added thoughtfully, "Vivian sounds like a wonderful person and a very special friend. When you told me the Sammy story, you were also telling me about you and Vivian shifting roles."

"Shifting roles?"

"Yes. From the one who needs to be taken care of to the one who defends."

Marley smiled. "Viv still calls me the princess with a punch."

"I like the sound of that. You can be a princess but also be powerful. You were ill as a child, and you needed to be taken care of—rescued in the truest sense of the word. Your asthma was a severe and frightening situation. How is your asthma now?"

"It's under control. I have my inhaler. Sometimes, I hold onto it like a security blanket. Oh, God, I am so ashamed."

"Tell me."

"Here I am, twenty-seven years old. But, you know, inside...I feel like that little girl who can't breathe and who always needs someone to take care of her."

"I do believe there is another side to Marley Chambers. In fact, you have shown that side to me."

"I have?"

"Most certainly. When you saw Vivian being hurt, you came to her rescue. That tells me that within you resides an alter ego that has more strength than you can imagine. As you share your stories, it will be my job to look for patterns. In some ways, psychotherapy is a bit like a Nancy Drew novel, with you as both the author and the heroine. It can be quite a thrilling odyssey, and one that I am eager to take alongside you."

"Thank you, Dr. Saperstein." Marley looked at the clock. "Friday then, same time?"

"Yes, Marley...same time."

∞

Esther Saperstein, Ph.D. followed her tried and tested routine. She surveyed the room and then returned everything to its rightful place. She sat at her desk, unlocked the file drawer, and took out the composition book labeled "Marley Chambers." Some patients had more than one book assigned to them, not because of the length of her notes, but as a testament to the number of years they had been in treatment.

She wrote the date, followed by a brief summary of the session.

Her fingers drifted to the drawer below. She could close her eyes and see its lone contents: a diary made by a child from lined paper threaded together with red yarn and a hand-drawn cardboard cover depicting the seaside at Gdańsk, Poland.

Esther unlocked the drawer and took out the diary. It had been years since she had felt the urge to return to the past. She was surprised to see how faded the yarn had become and that the pages had yellowed over time.

The cover showed a sandy beach and a blue-green ocean. The blue sky was filled with fluffy white clouds, and the wood boat that rested on the shoreline had been colored with yellow, green, and brown stripes.

Twice, she thought. Twice I have been to Gdańsk. The first time was the summer when I was seven and Father, Mother, and I took a brief vacation to the seaport city. The second time...she sat back in her chair, exhaled a cleansing sigh, and found herself drifting back to when she was seven.

∞

Her family stayed at a small hotel, the only one in Gdańsk that welcomed Jews *and* served kosher food. Those few days were perhaps the happiest memories she had of her childhood. She closed her eyes and saw the blue cotton bathing suit, complete with a matching hat, hand-sewed by her mother and decorated with soft ruffles and hand-rolled flowers. She never forgot the look in her parents' eyes as they gazed at their only child. If she had to use one word to describe them, it would be glowing. She struggled to find the Yiddish word her mother used: *kvelling* [bursting with pride].

Sometimes it's best to keep the past buried, she thought, but today she felt compelled to revisit the memories that began during a time of innocence when life was simple, and she only knew acts of kindness.

Esther opened the diary to the first page, filled with a childish scrawl.

Dear Diary and Close Friend,

Today I put my toes in the sea and Father held my hand. The water was freezing. Mama put a blanket on the sand, and we had lunch. The clouds were white, and when I lay on my back, I could see a pony and a dog.

Father had helped her with her spelling. He whispered to her, "You are already a scholar." Mama heard and said, "Samuel, stop putting such thoughts in our Esther's head. It's marriage and children for our daughter." Her mother's eyes lit up. "I can't wait to see my grandchildren."

Father had put his hands in the sand and let the grains fall through his fingers.

"Perhaps both, Freda. A scholar and a mother. *Aun vos nit?* [And why not?]"

She wondered, what would her parents think of her now? She was a scholar, but also a woman who loved another woman and who would bear no children.

She turned the diary's pages to an entry dated 1939 when, once again, she had taken the train from Warsaw to Gdańsk.

∞

Her father waved a large envelope filled with documents in the air and smiled. "I paid dearly for this: a visa from the American Consulate General and a passport to America. Esther, you won the gold prize."

"But, Father...I can't leave you and Mother."

"You must go. It's all planned. You will take the train to Gdańsk. Once there you will board the steamship for New York. Your occupation is listed as a governess; you are going to America to assist your Aunt Yetta. Everything you will need is in this envelope. Guard it well."

"But Father—"

"*Sha, sha.* You will go first, and we will follow as soon as we can. I want you to be safe, and it's no longer safe in Poland for Jews."

Her father handed her a note card. "Everything you need to know is here. Follow the steps, and you'll be free. And," he said with a flourish, "here is your train ticket. Your Aunt Yetta will meet you when your ship docks."

"Please, Mama, don't make me go," She ran to her mother and buried her head in her bosom.

Her mother kissed the top of her head. "Six months at the most and then we'll all be together again. Listen to me, Esther, you will be safe: You will be with *mishpocha* [family] and that will make us happy."

Her mother held her and used her Hebrew name. "No more tears, *Hadassah*. Remember, wherever you go we share the same stars, moon, and sun. We are always with you."

∞

Esther Saperstein turned the pages of the diary to the entry dated August 10, 1939.

Dear Diary:

Today is the strangest day I have ever known. My world has become one of utter confusion and chaos. I'm frightened, but Father tells me I must be brave. He came home yesterday, bruised and bleeding. Some thugs had attacked him. Mama was crying but Father tried to make light of it.

Oh, my best friend, my diary, I don't know when I'll be able to write again. Father says I must travel alone to America and stay with Aunt Yetta until they can get papers to leave Poland. I'm so terrified.

Farewell for now. I promise to keep you safe.

She closed her diary and placed it in the bottom of her satchel.

Father ordered a taxi. Her mother handed her a knit cap. "Promise me you will wear this and never take it off."

"What if it's hot, Mama?"

"You wear it and if anyone asks, you tell them you are a modest young woman and your Mama made it for you. Promise?"

"Yes, I promise."

At the train station, her father held her close, kissed her goodbye, and whispered, "There are three diamonds sewn into the hat. When you get to New York, you are to give the diamonds to Yetta for safe-keeping. Tell her the biggest one is for her to keep, from her brother, Shmuley."

"Shmuley?"

"Yes, a childhood name of affection. Tell her it's for all the times I teased her when we were children. Tell her that I love her and to take care of my Esther. Tell her the other two diamonds are for your education and to help others. Remember, to help others is to honor your mother and father."

"Yes, Father. But you'll see her soon. You promised: six months."

"We will do our best, but it's always good to have another plan in place. Listen to me carefully, Esther. We only have a few minutes. When you get on the ship, look for a family with children and offer to help. Stay close to them and you'll be safe."

Armed with a precious passport and carrying a worn satchel filled with two changes of clothing, a sturdy pair of shoes, and her diary, she boarded the train leaving the Warsaw Main Railway Station for Gdańsk.

∞

It was unusual but not without precedent for the past to invade Esther's thoughts while writing patient notes. Unbidden memories that she believed were laid to rest had returned with startling vividness. Perhaps they had been triggered by something Marley had said, or as she felt deep in her heart, something had been transferred from psyche to psyche.

∞

When she boarded the ship for America, she followed her father's orders. She said hello to the parents of two young girls and when they discovered she was traveling alone, they made her their third daughter. They saw that she ate and shooed away any young men who seemed enamored by a budding young woman of sixteen.

Aunt Yetta met her at the dock, scooped her up, and said, "I would have known you anywhere. You are the image of your mama."

Esther had been told by her school friends that the streets in America would be lined with gold, but as they got closer and closer to the east side it began to look more and more like the Warsaw she knew.

Esther salivated as the fragrances from the food carts swirled around in the warm summer air. If she closed her eyes, and took in the smells and sounds, she could believe she was in Warsaw, walking home from school to find her mother in the kitchen. Mother would turn around, and her face would light up. "Sit," she would say as she piled a plate with stuffed cabbage. "Scholars need to be well-fed."

Vendors crowded the New York streets, and the adult immigrants dressed as if they were still in Europe. It was the children that looked different. The boys wore colorful, tight-fitting caps and played a boisterous game in the streets in which one boy threw a small white ball toward another boy, who tried to hit it with a long wooden stick. If successful, the boy ran around something they called a diamond, trying to reach a place called home while the other boys scrambled to tag him "out." The girls wore pretty dresses and hopped around an arrangement of squares drawn with chalk on the sidewalk, occasionally stooping to pick up a coin. As with the boys' game, there were obvious rules that Esther didn't quite understand, but there was no denying both groups of children were having great fun, and she smiled at them in spite of herself.

Aunt Yetta explained, "The girls are playing hopscotch, and the boys are playing baseball. A dangerous game! They are all the time getting smacked in the head or breaking windows. A big waste of time, if you ask me. Wait until you meet your cousins. Three ruffians, if you ask me. They even changed their names. 'We're Americans now,' they tell me." She shrugged her shoulders. "Go figure. But you, my Esther...I can see the goodness in you, so much like my brother." She hugged Esther. "We'll enjoy each other's company. You'll like your Uncle Joseph. He's a quiet man and a hard worker, but what does he know about being a woman?" She laughed. *Gornisht* [nothing]! Now that there is another woman in the house, I will have someone on my side."

They trudged up three flights of stairs to the apartment.

"It's crowded," said Yetta, "but we'll make do. The three boys are in one bedroom. This couch will be your bed. I wish it could be better."

"It's perfect," lied Esther, eying the shabby tweed couch that looked about as comfortable as a mortuary slab. "There's something I'm to give you," she added, removing her hat. "Whew! I'm so glad to finally take that uncomfortable thing off. I'm to tell you that inside the hat are three diamonds. The largest one is for you, and the other two are for my education and to help others."

Yetta's eyes grew wide at the sight of the diamonds. "We'll hide these for now."

"Father wanted you to know your diamond is from Shmuley. And they should be here within six months." Esther thought she saw a change of expression. Intuitively she said, "Is everything all right, Aunt Yetta? You looked so sad just now."

"Yes, darling, it's just that it's been years since I thought of your father as Shmuley. It's the excitement of having you here, that's all. It's a bit overwhelming. If you ask me, six months isn't so long to wait, is it?"

That night as Yetta and Joseph lay in bed, she turned to her husband and told him about the diamonds and the note from Shmuley.

She put her head on his chest and began to cry quietly.

"We never used our pet names unless we were in trouble. They're in trouble, I know it. Could the rumors be true?" she whispered.

Joseph, a butcher by trade, knew how to process a beef carcass into cuts for the consumer, but he didn't know how to comfort his wife. He too, had heard rumors at work about work camps and ghettos.

"They are just rumors," he answered, before kissing her on the forehead and turning over to go to sleep.

At first, Esther wrote to her parents weekly. Aunt Yetta helped her mail the letters and each time, before giving them to the postman, she kissed the envelope. She wrote about school, learning English, and helping Aunt Yetta with her three cousins.

> Dear Mother and Father,
>
> Three boys are like ten girls, or so Aunt Yetta says. And Mother, they hate to bathe. We share a bathroom with several other families, and sometimes Aunt Yetta takes all three kicking and screaming to bathe them and scrub them with a stiff brush. Father, I hope to become a social worker when I graduate high school. I find that friends like to tell me their problems, and I like to listen!
>
> I hope to hear from you soon,
> Love,
> Esther

Everyday after school Esther walked past the *mikveh* [in the Jewish faith, a bath used for the purpose of ritual immersion and purification]. Aunt Yetta didn't believe in using the *mikveh*. "We are more modern," she opined, "but when you wed, you will choose to use or not use."

Esther had never thought about marriage. "Aunt Yetta, what if I choose not to marry?"

"*Zey shtil* [be quiet]," Aunt Yetta shushed her. "One day you will meet a young man, fall in love, and have many children."

Dare she say she didn't want children? She smiled as Yetta held her hand and thought of the unbounded energy and chaos that came with three boys under the age of fourteen.

Every Monday morning, Aunt Yetta gave Esther two shiny nickels for being such a big help to her. Her aunt's question never varied: "Now, what will you buy with these two nickels?" And Esther's answer was always the same: "I will stop at Mr. Dinnerstein's knish cart and buy two potato knishes."

Aunt Yetta laughed at their weekly ritual. "Put the money in your shoe and come right home after school, and after you buy—"

"Two knishes. One for you and one for me."

"Good! Then we will sit like two ladies in the movies and have tea. Which actress would you want to be like, Esther?"

"I'll be Paul Muni."

Yetta laughed. "Silly girl. You can't be a man. I said actress, not actor."

"But he's Jewish, Aunt Yetta. And I like his suits, and I like the roles he plays. Especially when he played Louis Pasteur."

"You can't be anything except what God made you. Let me think." Yetta tapped a knobby finger against her full lips. "Ah! You can be Hedy Lamarr."

"She's Jewish?"

"Yes, and as smart as any man. And I will be Claire Trevor." Aunt Yetta lowered her voice. "You know she's Jewish, yes?"

Esther would shake her head, dumbfounded by her aunt's knowledge of Hollywood, gleaned from the slick magazines she devoured.

While Mondays were filled with Hollywood gossip and trivia, on other school days Yetta would give Esther practical lessons about life, which went down easily with her aunt's delicious sweet tea.

Two by two, she would take the steps to the third-floor tenement apartment in New York's Lower East Side. Aunt Yetta would be in the kitchen, humming and stirring soup in a large pot.

"How do you feed a family of six?" Esther would ask.

"Very carefully," came Yetta's smiling reply. "We get what others don't want and make it into a feast! Three boys, Esther—what a handful! You know I love them, but do you think they want to know how to cook? Ha! They only know how to eat."

Esther went to the mailbox day after day, week after week, praying for a letter from her parents. One day she returned from school to find Aunt Yetta holding a letter in her hand. "From Poland. You open."

Esther said, "It's from Father's employee, Mr. Banaszak." With shaking hands, she opened the envelope to find a note:

Dear Esther,

I received these postcards a few weeks after your parents were transported to a labor camp. Your father had left your aunt's address with me with instructions to contact you should anything happen to them.

All the mail has stopped to America, but this was smuggled out and sent from Canada.

I know that your parents were thankful that you were safe in the arms of your aunt. I hope you have found happiness in your freedom.

Aleksey Banaszak

She looked at the two identical, preprinted postcards, one from her mother, and one from her father. The message on both cards was the same: "Things are going well, and we are enjoying ourselves." The cards were postmarked Oświęcim, Poland. She went to her geography book and looked at a map of Poland. Oświęcim was an industrial town. Her father was a well-known businessman; perhaps they would use his talents. And her mother, no one could make lace the way her mother could. She had tried to teach Esther, but after a while, her mother had thrown up her hands and laughed, declaring, "I think your talents lie in another direction."

She wondered if her parents had been afforded first class seats or perhaps even a private compartment. For a moment, she visualized them being served tea and pastries in the dining car, laughing and chatting as they loved to do. Mother would be wearing her long velvet dress and Father would be in his best navy-blue three-piece suit. From time to time he would look at the Gruen Curvex watch on his left wrist and sigh at the waste of time. Mother would shake her head and say, "You can't make the train go any faster, dear."

Mother always called Father "dear."

Her mother had bought that watch for his birthday. She remembered the astonished look on his face when he opened the package. "These are very costly," he gasped, admiring the stylish watch with luminous hands. He turned out the lights and said, "See how it glows."

"It's been carefully used," her mother replied, echoing the sales-clerk's words.

He put it on his wrist. "I'll never take it off," he said tearfully.

Months went by, and Esther waited for another postcard, or perhaps even a letter. Her Aunt Yetta and her Uncle Joseph whispered things not meant for her to hear. Some of the kids at school told her of stories coming from the few Jews who had managed to escape the onslaught of the Nazis. She refused to believe any of it and concentrated on her studies. She thought less and less about Father and Mother, though her vast love for them never dimmed.

It would be years before Esther discovered that the postcards were a Nazi propaganda measure used to deceive the recipients, and that Oświęcim was the site of the infamous Auschwitz Concentration Camp.

∞

Six months turned into six years, and Esther grew into a young woman. The dreamed of letter from her parents never arrived, but the flame of hope burned in her heart. She remembered the last words her father had spoken to her. *Help others, Esther.*

She began to apply to universities throughout the United States. She had her heart set on one known for their outstanding social welfare program: the University of California, Berkeley (UCB).

One momentous day, Esther reached inside the mailbox to find a letter addressed to her not from her parents, but from the University of California at Berkley.

She opened the envelope with trembling fingers. Dare she read it? She must! She unfolded the letter slowly and carefully, as if it might contain a bomb, and basked in the words it contained.

She bounded up the steps, two at a time, bursting into the apartment. She heard Aunt Yetta humming in the kitchen. She paused in the doorway.

"Aunt Yetta, I've been accepted to Berkley! I'll be leaving in the fall. When you get a letter from my mother and father, will you remember to send it to me?"

Aunt Yetta kept humming, resting her gnarled hands on the worn counter that always smelled faintly of bleach.

"Aunt Yetta?"

Esther put her hands on Yetta's shoulders. Had she not recognized how worn and bent over her aunt had become?

"You've waited years for a letter from your parents. It won't come Esther, not ever."

Yetta reached into her apron pocket and produced an ominous looking envelope. Yetta's voice trembled. "From the Holocaust Tracing Service."

Esther's hands shook as she read the letter.

The letters blurred after the first sentence:

It is with our deepest sorrow that we inform you of the death of your parents, Samuel and Deborah Saperstein.

Yetta said, "Most of our neighbors received these letters...even the rabbi. The rabbi has called for a memorial service tonight at eight."

Esther shook her head. "No, no! I won't go. This letter's a mistake."

"It's no mistake. You will go, and you will stand along with everyone else to pray for the souls of your parents."

"I can't. What if the letter is wrong? What if they're lost somewhere?"

"Come here, Esther." Yetta pinched her cheeks and called her "my *sheina meidala* [pretty girl]. So young and beautiful to have to face this."

Yetta wrapped her arms around Esther. "How I wish I were sending you off to your university with joy. Instead, I give you my tears and the tears of all who died and all who mourn."

It began as a silent supper that night. Harry, David, and Jack sat staring at their plates. Usually they would be laughing and arguing about the prowess of their favorite sports teams, pausing only long enough to cram gigantic forkfuls of food into their mouths. Tonight they sat quietly toying with their dinners, until Harry ventured a controversial notion.

"The fellas and I have been talking, you know after school or when we're playing baseball," he began. "There are ten of us, and as soon as we graduate, we're going to Palestine to help create a Jewish state."

"No!" his father shouted and banged the table. "Harry, I forbid it."

"You can't stop me!" boomed Harry. He stood up, knocking his chair over. "You can't stop me, and my name is Herschel, not Harry."

Yetta wiped the tears from her eyes with the corner of her apron. "They say it was in the millions," she whispered. "Millions of Jews, wiped off the face of the Earth!"

"Mama, I'll stay," said Jack. "And you don't have to call me Yonkel. I like being Jack."

"And you, my middle son? What should I call you?" Yetta asked.

"We usually don't talk about me," David muttered. Esther knew him to be the most quiet and introverted of the three brothers, and not one to crave being the center of attention.

Uncle Joseph, who usually sat silently through dinner said, "David, let us hear from you."

"I want to go to school the way Esther is doing."

"And what do you want to do?" asked Joseph.

The room became silent.

"I want to become an engineer. The war has torn everything and everybody apart. I want to build bridges that will bring people and nations together. Wait, I'll show you."

David went to his room and returned with a sketchbook.

Joseph looked at his drawings of bridges and housing surrounded by greenery.

David said, "Each room will have windows that open onto a view of trees or a park, or even a manmade lake."

Joseph passed the sketchbook to Yetta. She placed her work-ravaged hand over her heart and declared, "They take my breath away, David. But where did you get the money for the sketchbooks and colored pencils?"

David looked at Esther.

"You've been in on this, Esther?"

"Yes, Aunt Yetta. As you can see, David is very talented."

"Where will we get the money for school?" Yetta cried. "We barely have enough to exist." Her tearful voice trailed off. "Perhaps God will show us the way."

They heard the nearby church bells begin to ring.

Yetta whispered. "The church is also holding services for those who suffered. Mrs. Abramov told me it wasn't only the Jews—Gypsies, crippled children, gentiles who tried to help. Mrs. Abramov said, 'even the *feygeles* [homosexuals] were sent to these camps.'"

The bells rang once again. Uncle Joseph said quietly, "Come, all, it's time to go."

The family of six left their tenement apartment. Grief had put a crack in this tight-knit family, and as they walked the six blocks to the synagogue they were joined by neighbors, friends, and strangers who, through circumstances of birth, now shared the same tragedy.

The sidewalks became crowded with mourners, dressed in black, carrying the letters from the Holocaust Tracing Services in their hands, coat pockets, and handbags.

They crowded into the synagogue and joined hands as they stood in front of the wooden pews. Neighbors who hadn't spoken to each other for years set aside their petty arguments and reached out to one another, asking for forgiveness.

They sat when Rabbi Meir entered to stand on the *bimah* [the raised platform in the synagogue from which services are led]. Esther would never forget his face or the shape of the hand that held his letter. Rabbi Meir choked as he tried to speak of the horror that had descended upon them.

The fantasy of her parents arriving in luxury was replaced by the reality of an overcrowded cattle car and the ineffable horror of their death in an Auschwitz gas chamber.

Her youth died that night as she listened to the wailing from family and friends. Over and over again she heard the anguished cries of "the babies, the babies."

Aunt Yetta held her hand and said, "It's time to stand, Esther, while the rabbi leads us in prayer." Supported by Uncle Joseph and Aunt Yetta, she stood with weakened knees and recited the prayer twice, once for her mother and once for her father. She made a vow to be charitable for their sake. For in doing so, she would elevate their souls and fulfill her father's wish: "Remember, to help others is to honor your mother and father."

Esther stood on the train station platform with Aunt Yetta, who was fretting over her niece's travel arrangements as she cried noisily into a hanky. "You have everything? Tickets? Money? *Oy vey*, I don't like the idea of a girl traveling alone all the way to California."

Esther hugged her aunt. "I'll never forget the way you took me in and treated me like your own daughter."

"Oh, piffle! With those three ruffians, I was happy to have you."

Esther took an envelope out of her pocket and handed it to Yetta. "*Vas iz das?*"

"In English, Aunt Yetta."

"What is this?"

"It's half the money from the diamonds, for David's education. Tell David"—she choked back a sob—"tell him to get good grades. And to build those bridges and houses."

The conductor called out: "All aboard!"

"I have to go now, Aunt Yetta."

Yetta clung to Esther. "Be safe, and remember. *Remember everyone,* Esther."

"I will, Aunt Yetta. I will never forget."

Esther turned and crossed the platform that would lead her to a new and unusual life.

∞

Over the years, Esther had come to realize that understanding another's pain could only come after understanding and accepting one's own.

She pulled away from her reverie and focused on the task at hand.

She knew what was about to happen; it wasn't the first time. She had felt it seconds before the phone rang and heard Marley's voice for the first time.

One night, after falling into a deep sleep, she would enter into and share Marley's dreamscape. She shuddered for a moment, then finished writing Marley's notes, closed the notebook, and locked the file drawers.

CHAPTER 7

D r. Saperstein opened the door to her office. She hesitated for a moment before speaking.

"Come in," she said, motioning Marley toward the open sliding glass door overlooking the canyon. "It rained again last night, and if you look closely, you can see shades of green beginning to show on the canyon walls."

"Yes, I see," said Marley. "It's beautiful."

"The air is fresh. Shall I leave the door open?"

"I would like that." Marley took her place on the chair and immediately began to cry. "I can smell Mommy's herbs—she had an herb garden, you see. She told me that her mother used healing herbs all the time when she was a little girl."

Marley took a moment to compose herself. "I guess you think I'm a nut," she apologized, "for launching into this anecdote with no preamble, but Mommy's herbs have been on my mind lately.

"I think Mommy straddled two worlds. She was a nurse and believed in modern medicine, but she also believed in the healing power of herbs. Mommy told me that we were losing something by not paying attention to nature's creations. She would make chaparral tea for me if I had a chest cold. I miss her so much. The way she cared for me, but more than anything, her wisdom.

"I had a different dream last night. I had forgotten all about it until you mentioned how the hills and canyons were turning green."

"Tell me," Dr. Saperstein prompted.

"In the dream, I was young—maybe two, or not quite two. Mommy and I were in a car driving down a dirt road. There was dust flying all around, and Mommy had stopped to roll up all the windows. It was hot, very hot inside the car, and even though I had a bottle of cool water, I was fussy.

"We came to a farmhouse, like Dorothy's in *The Wizard of Oz*. Standing on the porch was a gray-haired lady wearing a worn-looking dress and a tall, thin man wearing overalls and a straw hat. They both looked dried out, like the dusty road we had traveled upon.

"The man and woman walked down the porch steps and waited for my mother to stop the car. This part seems extremely clear. I could see the windows on the front of the house facing the driveway. Hanging in the windows were three flags. They each had a silver background with a red band. Inside two of the flags were gold stars, and in the other was a blue star.

"I pointed to the flags and exclaimed, 'Stars, stars!'" And then Mommy started to cry so hard that the gray-haired lady had to take me from her and hold me. The old man had to keep Mommy from falling, and I heard him say, 'God's will, Abigail. God's will.'

"The woman held me to her chest, and I could barely breathe, but it wasn't horrible like in the nightmare. She smelled of love. There was softness to her, and I felt safe in her arms. She said something to Mommy: 'Gone, Abigail. Both gone.' She kissed me and said, "God has sent His blessings to us.'

"And that's when I woke up. Dr. Saperstein, do you think dreams can be memories? This one seems so real. As if I was watching a film."

Esther Saperstein thought for a moment. *This child/woman is groping for something that goes beyond ordinary comprehension.* All her training would tell her not to answer a direct question, but rather to deepen the therapy with a statement: "Tell me what you think." She chose her words thoughtfully. "I have come to believe that dreams can be created in many different ways. From within our hearts, for one. Or a very early memory—or even a wish."

"A wish? For what?"

"What comes to mind when you think about a wish?"

"Something I want. Like wishing on a star for true love, or that Dr. Holbrook would think my proposal was exceptional." Marley cast her eyes downward. "Or at least acceptable."

"Perhaps we can look at wishes in a different way. What if you are wishing to be understood or to understand?"

Dr. Saperstein's comment intrigued her; Marley sat in thought.

"When you spoke about Dr. Holbrook," the doctor prompted, "weren't you wishing to be understood?

"I hadn't thought of it that way, but I think you're right."

"Your dream last night—it seems quite clear and filled with detail," Dr. Saperstein remarked at length. "Tell me, what do you know about your mother?"

Marley shrugged. "Not much. I know she was raised on a farm in Iowa. She went to nursing school and then joined the Army. Her two brothers died during the war. She didn't give me a lot of details, but one was in the Navy and died at sea, and the other was a Marine and died in Guam."

"The two flags in the window with the gold stars. Do have any thoughts about them?"

"I remember seeing photos of them in a textbook on World War II."

"Then perhaps you know that the gold star represents a family member that died during service to their country."

"Yes, I do."

"What I notice in this new dream is the detail and clarity. In your nightmare, everything is diffuse and dark and filled with pain. In this dream, there is a balance. There is grief, but also love and support. The road is dusty, but you have a bottle of water. Your mother sobs and collapses, but the man supports her and tries to comfort her. You were fussy from the drive, but the woman holds you snugly and protects you. You describe her fragrance as love."

"I didn't think of it that way. Balance—I like the idea. It's something I think I lack. Gee, maybe there's some hope in my crazy, mixed-up world after all, huh, Doc?"

Dr. Saperstein smiled. "I will always encourage my patients to hold onto hope. I firmly believe that where there is life, there is hope."

Marley snapped her fingers. "I keep forgetting! I took a snapshot of Papa's arm before he died. A bit macabre, but I'd like to show it to you."

"I'd like to see it."

"I'll bring it in next time."

CHAPTER 8

Marley woke up, stretched, and yawned. She traced the outline of her body with her fingertips. Was she fat or not? Rubenesque, perhaps? She couldn't feel her ribs and guessed that must be a sign of being overweight. Her arms were muscular, as were her legs. How strange, she thought. Mommy was willowy and Papa downright skinny.

She wiggled her toes and let them peek out from under the covers. Her baby toes were turned outward and lay completely on their sides—an abnormality that had made her a minor schoolyard celebrity among youthful curiosity-seekers. She tried to remember the shape of Mommy's and Papa's feet, but her physical memory of them was getting fuzzy. Would her memories of them fade until they disappeared?

She remembered as a teenager staring at her reflection in the mirror, trying to see if she looked like Mommy or Papa. Her frizzy hair, her dark brown eyes, and her too-thick eyebrows stood out, but did not favor either of her parents. Although she was pleased with her nose, it wasn't anything like Papa's or Mommy's. Papa's had a slight hook in it, and Mommy's went up at the tip.

Viv's mom had once taken out a box of old family photos. "Vivian," she said, holding one up, "here's a photo of your great-aunt Vivian at your age. Look, you could be twins."

The two girls went through the photos, holding them up against Viv's face. Over and over again they saw traits of her relatives. Her eyes were like her Grandpa Liam's, her nose more like her father's, her skin tone alabaster like her grandmother's.

Of course, there were lots of photos of her growing up, alone or with Mommy and Papa. First as a baby, then when she went to school, and a few from infrequent vacations.

Her mother had made her a photo album that went from preschool through her graduation from Boston University. Why were there no historical family photos? The question had haunted her for years. She would have to put this subject on her "things to talk about with Dr. S." list.

Today was the day of reckoning: entering Papa's room. At least Viv would be with her.

If she got up now, she could dash to the store and get some real food for her and Viv.

Viv was on this healthy eating kick.

"Join me, Mar. I've been doing it for a week, and I feel like Wonder Woman," she had said, flexing her biceps. "It can be fun doing it with a buddy."

Maybe it could work. But, so far, a million diets haven't. Enough of this obsessing, Marley. She said out loud: "Time to rise and shine." It was a phrase her mother used every morning to rouse her for school. She glanced at the clock before getting into the shower. It was eight, and Viv would be over around 9:30. She would dash to the market; what a surprise for Viv to find real food in the house!

"Well, you look chipper," Viv said, dragging into the kitchen; she had never been a morning person. She stared at the food bags on the counter. "What's all this?"

"Food, my dear," Marley declared. "Real food—salad, veggies, fruit, and chicken. And steak, if you want to light up the grill."

"Steak sounds good. But right now, I need coffee. Got an IV ready?"

"I made a twelve-cupper," Marley said as she poured two cups of steaming coffee and sat down next to Vivian.

Vivian lifted her cup before drinking. "Here's to you, kid." Swig. *Ahh.* "The nectar of the goddesses. Wow, I have to say you look rested and energetic. Dr. S., Wonder Shrink, must be working miracles."

Marley said, "Let's just say it's like walking on the beach and the sand shifts right under your feet. But enough about me. You're looking a bit on the grumpy side."

"Now that's the understatement of the year. Did you ever get so angry you wanted to kill?"

"Yes," she said, thinking about John. "What about eggs and toast?"

"You cooking?"

"I do know how, you know. I've just been exercising my right not to. But for you, I'll make an exception."

"Great. I'll have two eggs, scrambled, well-done. Oh, and toast, medium, with butter and jam on the side."

The two women looked at each other and burst out laughing.

"You've gotten far too used to eating out. So, Viv, what makes you grumpy this morning?"

Vivian reached inside the pocket of her 501 Levi's and pulled out a letter. "From my mom."

"Is everything okay?"

"If you mean, are my folks okay, yes—they're full of piss and vinegar. And that's a phrase you can use for your thesis. If you mean is everything okay, not exactly. You cook, I'll read."

Dear Vivian,

I hope this letter finds you in good health. Your father and I are doing well. Moving to New York was the right choice for us; there is nothing like being reunited and surrounded by extended family.

Some very exciting news: a family reunion is planned for the summer. All your aunts, uncles, and cousins will be gathering in the Big Apple for a fun-filled week. There are probably sixty relatives coming from all over the world, plus their spouses and babies. Our family is truly blessed to be thriving and growing.

We are planning on attending your graduation in May. We are very proud of you, and I can hardly wait to hear about your job offers. Once they begin, I do hope you will consider New York as a possibility.

Daddy and I thought we would stay in town for a few weeks to say hello to our Los Angeles friends and return home sometime in June. We would like to make reservations for three for the trip back to New York.

What fun it will be to have you return with us and reconnect with your extended family.

Remember, family is everything.

Love,

Mom

P.S. Your cousin Michael knows a lovely young man, also an attorney, who is eager to meet you.

Marley's heart began to race. "You'd move to New York?" she said sadly.

"Hah! I'm trying to find an excuse not to go at all." Viv sniffed the air. "Mar, the toast is burning."

"Oh, shit!"

"Don't get your panties in a wad, it's just burned toast. Not the end of the world, like that fuckin' family reunion my mom's trying to shanghai me into going to." She patted the chair next to her. "Sit down and eat with me.".

"I will, in a minute," Marley said, popping fresh rye bread into the toaster and adjusting the heat setting. "Do you want gooseberry jam?"

"Got any peanut butter?"

"Sorry, I'm out. And don't get that I'm disappointed look."

"You mean this one?" Viv asked, pouting.

"That's it!"

"Damn, you make fine eggs, Mar. Wanna pass me that gooseberry jam? Thanks." Viv lavished the jam on her toast and reflected, "Look, you've romanticized my family. You've only seen the tra-la-la stuff. You don't see all the family shit—the gossip, the being in your face, the judgment for being different."

"I see a loving family. Your mom wants you to be close, and she wants grandchildren."

"I don't see you in a rush to have babies."

"That was step four in John's plan."

"Uh-huh. Hmm, this is great jam. More eggs, please. I'm starving."

"What are you going to do about your family reunion?" Marley said, piling the last of the eggs on Vivian's plate.

"Push it aside, at least for now. I want to focus on helping you get through your dad's study. We can listen to some jazz, and I got a new Joan Baez tape. So, when do we start?"

Papa's study was dark except for a single beam of sunlight entering through a slight gap in the drapes. The musty smell hit Marley before her eyes could adjust to the dim light.

Both women stood frozen.

Vivian thought: *Good Lord, this is a scene right out of* Great Expectations.

Marley thought: *Was the room always like this?*

"I should have forced myself to come in sooner," Marley croaked.

"No guilt trips allowed. I think we should start by opening the drapes. Okay?"

Marley nodded.

Vivian hesitated. "There's going to be a shitload of dust. Here!" She tossed Marley a red bandana. "Step back and cover your mouth and nose."

Vivian walked over to the linen drapes and pulled on the draw cord. She turned her head as dust got released, floated around, and then began to settle. Mid-morning sunlight filled the room.

Vivian whispered, "I haven't been in here for years." She began to wander around the room. "My God, your mother kept everything sparse and organized, but in here..."

Marley looked around the room as if seeing it for the first time through the eyes of an adult. *This was Papa's world.*

Books, magazines, and periodicals were scattered throughout the room in untidy stacks. Some books had been piled high enough to nearly hide the oversized leather chair from view.

Marley's gaze lingered on the chair and the pipe stand alongside it. She had sat there with Papa, night after night, long before she could comfortably reach the bookcase's third shelf.

She picked up one of the pipes. "I bought this for Papa the Christmas before last," she said, a nostalgic fire in her eyes. "I tried to get him one every Christmas from different parts of the world. Papa loved his pipes, and he loved his geography."

"That's a pretty one," Viv commented.

"It's from Denmark," Marley murmured. "It's made of brierroot with an ebonite stem. He said it was his favorite, but he said that about all the pipes I gave him."

Vivian said, "This room is like a museum, but one I've never seen before. Maybe more like a cathedral. Something about it makes me wants me to speak softly and say, 'We're on sacred ground.'"

She walked the perimeter of the room. "What are these pictures on the wall?"

"I know all about those," said Marley proudly. "Honoré Daumier was a French artist who drew political caricatures." She pointed. "This one satirizes the legal system—its pervasive corruption and greed."

"Thanks for mentioning the flaws in my chosen profession," said Viv with mock indignation.

"You're the one who will change all that."

"What if all those hours we spent as kids wanting to be like Nancy Drew was a rehearsal"—Vivian made a broad sweep with her hand—"for all of this?" She noticed one of Daumier's caricatures. "Hey, Mar, look at this cartoon of Don Quixote and Sancho Panza." She launched into a lighthearted imitation of Peter O'Toole in *Man of La Mancha*, which the girls had seen when it premiered in 1972. "To right the unrightable wrong!" she sang out, brandishing an imaginary sword.

"To dream the impossible dream," Marley replied in a ridiculously deep voice, getting into the spirit.

"I'll be Don Quixote," Vivian said.

With hands on her hips, Marley retorted, "Why am I always the second lead?"

"Okay, okay, we'll take turns. You know what? I believe our greatest mystery may be right here, in this room."

"You may be right," Marley agreed. "Maybe these pictures are clues to Papa's experiences when he was young."

Vivian was on a roll. "This lawyer one, for example, certainly could be talking about today's justice system for minorities and women. We're fighting now for laws that will protect women from spousal abuse. And from these drawings, it looks like the past and the present have met."

Vivian continued to walk the perimeter of the room, letting her fingers trace the contents of the bookcases.

"Damn, there's a book on every subject. No wonder you were such a whiz-kid in school."

"I spent evenings here after Papa came back from work. First, we would have dinner together; Mommy would always fix it before she went to work. Then after my homework, Papa and I would sit right in this chair. Plenty of room for two if I move some of these books."

She motioned to Vivian. "Let's test it out."

Vivian and Marley sat down.

"Mmm, comfy," said Vivian. "And plenty of room for two, for sure." *Dare I move closer?* "So, what you would guys talk about?"

"Oh, everything. Papa would read fairy tales, short stories, or poetry. For the most part, he liked prose and poetry that had a moral lesson to teach. He always said, 'Look beneath the surface to discover what the author had to say about the human condition.' He liked *Alice's Adventures in Wonderland* and anything by Oscar Wilde." She began to cry. "I read 'The Selfish Giant' to him as he was dying."

"You were a good daughter, Mar." Vivian put her arm around Marley. "Lean on me now."

"I always have. You're my best friend."

"We're quite a pair, huh?"

"I want to be braver, like you."

Vivian pointed to the desk. "Brave enough to tackle this? She ran her hands over the two-sided partners desk. Where'd your dad find it?"

"Oh, he liked to find old things. We would go antique shopping. It was his favorite hobby, and the one thing he would spend money on, besides Mommy and me."

"What's the story on the desk?"

"Papa bought it when I was in seventh grade. I thought it was the most boring day of my existence. We went to this estate sale in old Pasadena—one of those huge homes built in the very late 1800s. I wandered around, looking at the jewelry, and after a while, he called me over."

"He said, 'This is our new desk, Marley.'

"I thought, big deal. Well, you know what smart-asses we were in seventh grade. Papa was so excited, and I thought, how boring. I can remember his words: 'It's called a partners desk. They were originally designed for banking partners, you see, with drawers on both sides. My side is perfect for research or reading, and yours is perfect for homework.' Then he whispered to me, 'It's a real find. Solid walnut and the leather inserts and brass fittings look like new. You see the way the desk is curved? That style is rare. Plus, there's a hidden compartment.'"

"Are you shitting me?" Viv exclaimed. "A secret compartment and you never told me? Tell me you at least looked."

"Oh, I lost interest in the whole day. I was pining for Gene Oliver. I wonder what ever happened to Gene? Remember how he tallied all the horse races?"

"Mar, would you please focus? Nancy Drew would have thrown you out of her fan club if she had known you were pining over a boy and missing what could be the mystery of the century. I'll make a deal with you. We tackle the desk, I'll treat you to lunch, and then we look for the secret compartment."

"It's a deal! Since it's your treat, you get to pick the place."

"How about Dolores' Drive-in?"

"What happened to healthy eating?"

"That was last week. This week calls for comfort food."

"Suzy-Q curly fries, then?"

"And onion rings."

"You're on!"

∞

The cuckoo clock sounded 1:00 p.m.

"Is that your stomach?" Marley asked.

"The tank has been empty for an hour," Viv replied, "and I'm running on fumes. Find anything?"

"I've filled two bags of trash. Whew, one more file drawer to go." Marley collapsed in the chair and sighed. "It's stuck, and I'm getting grumpy."

"Let's head out for Dolores' and deal with it later."

∞

Dolores' Drive-In was located in Beverly Hills at the corner of Wilshire and La Cienega boulevards. With its vintage 1950s space-age design, the joint looked straight out of *The Jetsons*. Social status and money blurred as hot rods, junkers, and Jaguars circled the lot, vying for a parking spot. Vivian swooped her red 1969 VW Bug into the one available space. Two cars slammed on their brakes and honked their horns. The driver of the Mercedes convertible stood up and shook his fist while shouting expletives.

"That was fun," said Marley.

"It's survival of the fittest, Dolores' Drive-In style."

Marley patted her tummy. "Survival of the fattest, you mean, especially after we get through pigging out."

"Marley, you're not fat, you're—"

"If you say 'pleasingly plump,' I'll sock you!" Marley said good-naturedly.

"I was going to say 'charmingly chubby,' for your information," Viv shot back.

The car next to them was brimming with high school age girls, flirting and giggling with the male carhop as he took their order.

The carhop came over, tilted his brown and black carhop hat, and said, "Can I take your order?"

Vivian replied, "Two cheeseburgers, one chocolate and one strawberry shake, Suzy-Q fries, and onion rings. And we would like two trays, please."

"My pleasure to serve," he said with a wink. "Now that's what I call an order. The stiffs in the car over there"—he gave a jerk of his head—"only got diet sodas. You ladies know how to enjoy yourselves." He left them with a wink and a smile.

"Well, what about that!" said Marley. "He was flirting with us—me, especially, of course."

Vivian laughed. "Are you holding onto your seatbelt? Most of the carhops here are gay."

"How do you know? You mean all those crushes I had—"

"You and the rest of the girls. You know how gossip gets started—it may or may not be true. Anyway, I think he was hinting around that he thinks we're a couple."

"I must be living in a bubble. Why would he think that?"

Vivian shrugged. *Is this the opening I've been waiting for? The timing sucks. Geez, I am such a fucking coward.*

"Hard to know, Mar," Vivian said, tuning the radio to the country's first all-night radio station, KGFJ. The funky riff from Stevie Wonder's "Superstition" had both girls dancing in their seats.

"Roll down your window, Mar, our order is here," said Viv.

"I want your car," said Marley, resting her arm on the car door holding the carhop window tray. "I'm getting tired of driving my mother's wreck."

"A gift from my folks for abandoning me for New York."

"Do I detect a wee bit of hostility?"

"More relief than anything. Hey, are you going to finish that shake?"

"I've changed my mind," said Marley, handing Vivian her shake. "I don't want your car, I want your metabolism. Viv, when we get back to my place, will you help unstick that drawer?"

"Only if you let me finish your fries. Deal?"

"Deal."

∞

"Wow! You did get rid of a lot of papers," Vivian said, admiring the garbage bags stuffed to the brim.

"Mostly old magazines. Papa had them under the desk. Not much in the drawers, just a few old bills since Mommy died. She always took care of everything. Papa must have felt lost."

Marley pointed to the bottom file drawer. "This is the one that's stuck."

Vivian tugged until the drawer opened enough for her to reach inside. "Yeah, I can feel a bunch of papers crammed in there. This situation calls for an intervention. Back in a flash."

She returned with a long thin spatula and inserted it in the drawer. "Okay, when I say go, you pull as hard as you can. Get ready, get set—go!"

Marley ended up on her backside from the force of pulling on the drawer. "Damn, I hope I didn't break anything." She clambered to her feet. "Nope, everything seems to be in working order."

"Well, at least we got the drawer open," said Viv. "What's in there?"

Marley reached into the drawer. "Bank statements." She thumbed through them. "Just what the attorney ordered. Thanks, Viv."

"Don't thank me. Thank my trusty spatula."

"Phew! I must say, I'm wiped out," Marley plopped down on the desk chair. "I'll finish tomorrow."

"Nuh-uh, lazybones, let's press on."

Marley frowned. "You sure have a bee in your bonnet."

Vivian twirled Marley around in the chair. "It's just that I know you."

"Put on the brakes, you nut, I'm dizzy!"

Vivian stopped the chair. "Come on, you get them in order, and I'll put the drawer back. Then we'll stop. But first thing tomorrow, we look for the secret compartment." Vivian leaned down to put the drawer back. "Shit, I can't get it back in."

Marley yawned. "Wiggle it a bit."

"Wiggling isn't going to do it. It's bumping up against something." Vivian scooted underneath the desk and reached her hand into the drawer frame. "I found it, I found it! The holy grail! When we took out the drawer, a door popped open."

Marley said, "Move over, I'm coming in."

Marley scooted under the desk. "Hi, Viv. Cozy under the desk with you. Do you remember when your mother would put a sheet over the dining room table and we'd play house?"

"If it weren't so crowded I'd bop you one right now. This is the mysterious moment of discovery, not the time to play house. There's something inside the cabinet—feels like paper but it's stuck."

"It's got to be a hidden treasure map! One of Papa's other favorite books was *Treasure Island*."

Vivian pulled her hand out. "Mar, look me in the eye. What do you see?"

"You, rolling your eyes?"

"Right. Get me some tongs from the kitchen."

The salad tongs did the trick. Five minutes later, Marley held a manila envelope with her name written on the front. "It's Papa's handwriting. I'd recognize it anywhere. He was big on penmanship. 'The mark of an educated person,'" she said, sniffling. "Remember our handwriting practice paper?"

"Yeah. Given freely by Mr. Taylor in his weekly cursive class. We wrote while Mr. Taylor cracked and ate walnuts."

"I would sit right across from Papa with my head down so I could concentrate. I never wanted to disappoint him."

Vivian put her hand on Marley's shoulder. "I don't think you ever disappointed Papa or Mommy."

"I've always been a coward by not dealing with issues that came up. I couldn't be honest with John, and I haven't been able to deal with school."

Marley looked down at the floor and whispered, "Have I disappointed you?"

"How could you even think that? Not once. I can't stand to see you hurting this much."

Marley took a deep breath and let it out slowly. "Sit with me on the big chair while I open this?"

"Of course."

Marley's hands shook as she undid the envelope's clasp. "There are two envelopes inside, marked one and two." She picked up envelope number one and ran her fingernail under the seal. "It's a letter, a letter from Papa." She stared at the first page. "I'll read it to you," she said huskily.

Dearest Marley,

I open this letter with an apology and a prayer for your forgiveness. Yes, a prayer from your Papa, who taught you that there was no God. Not that God was dead, but that he never existed: a fantasy created by those who couldn't understand where the sun went when night fell, or the mysteries surrounding birth and death.

The writing of this letter was prompted by an incident that happened shortly after you had returned home from Boston for Thanksgiving. We shared the festivities with the Harrises, as we had for many years. You and Vivian were decorating the table and walls, and then as a final touch, you made us all wear Pilgrim hats.

I had to smile at the two of you, best friends behaving as if they were once again ten years old.

You were a serious child with a veil of sadness about you, and Vivian was always full of mischief. So many times her antics changed your somber expression into bursts of laughter.

A few days after you returned to Boston, your mother had a transient ischemic attack. It was a minor stroke that came and went almost unnoticed. We decided not to tell you, adding yet another layer to all the other secrets and lies that we created.

We had kept the truth away from you for so many years, so what was one more lie by omission?

If I have learned anything in my waning days, it is that the horror of secrets is far worse than any pain that may come from the truth.

Your mother changed after her stroke. Not anything that was readily observable, but something that rested deep within her soul.

She told me that at the time of her stroke, she had relived her past. She said, more than once, "Andrew, I was seeing everything from the moment we met to the present day. It was as if a veil had lifted and I could see our history together with new clarity. What a terrible thing we have done by keeping the truth from Marley. We must right our wrongs."

I put my arms around her, and she leaned against me, with a sigh. She had lost weight, and her clothes hung on her like rags. I hated to argue with her, for she seemed so fragile.

"Abbey, we raised Marley to be a good human being, and that's all that matters," I said gently.

She began to weep, and after she collected herself she looked me in the eye and said defiantly, "Andrew, I can't face my death with these secrets weighing on my heart and soul."

"You're not dying!" I shouted at her, and pounded my fist on the table. It was the first time I had ever lost my temper with her in our long life together. We dropped the subject by unspoken assent, but a small chasm had opened between us, and we were distant toward each other for some time.

Meanwhile, I saw your mother changing. Her eyes, that had always been bright, became dull. I wanted to blame it on the stroke, but I knew, deep in my heart, it was about her guilt and shame over what we had done.

One night, as we lay in bed, I held her in my arms, and her tears wet my chest. As we talked that night, I came to understand her needs, and while I feared opening Pandora's box, I suggested a compromise.

"What if Marley doesn't want to know about the past?"

Abbey had not considered this and became very still.

"Perhaps," I suggested, "we should leave it up to fate."

Your mother found that intriguing and after much discussion, we came to an agreement. We would write letters about our pasts, unveiling the host of secrets and lies layer by layer, until the naked truth lay in front of you.

We would put the first letter in the cabinet hidden within the partners desk. If you came upon it by chance, then it was meant to be.

Your mother finally agreed, and true to my word I began to write the letter you now hold in your hand.

I must say, as the months went on I wrote and rewrote it until I discovered the guilt and grief that lay beneath my unyielding facade.

Do you remember when I read "The Lady, or the Tiger?" to you? You were making the transition to middle school and were anxious about having to choose some of your classes.

"How will I know if I make the right choice, Papa?" you asked me.

I thought for a long time, and then went to the bookshelf, took down a collection of Frank R. Stockton's fables for children, and read "The Lady, or the Tiger?" to you. As you no doubt remember, the story concerns a man accused of a crime who is punished by having to choose between two doors, one with a beautiful lady-in-waiting behind it, and a hungry tiger behind the other. The story ends ambiguously; we don't learn the man's fate.

Afterward, I told you that we never know if we've made the right decision until all is said and done.

In case you have forgotten the story, I wrote a slightly different version for your entertainment and enlightenment. You will find it in the second envelope. Perhaps it will help you to decide which door you will open: the door of secrets, or the door of least resistance.

If Vivian is with you—and with a smile on my face, I suspect that this is true—tell her that Mommy and I loved her like a second daughter.

One last thing before I close this letter: I wish to reveal my birth name to you: Abraham Cohen. I was born in Vienna, Austria, in the district of Alsergrund. The year was 1912.

Your loving Papa

∞

Marley let the letter fall into her lap. She sat dazed, her body immobilized, her mind overwhelmed.

Vivian murmured, "Are you okay?"

Marley shook her head then looked up, her eyes widening. "Why, Viv? Why would Papa have to hide his identity? I want to open the second envelope, but I'm terrified. What else is waiting for me?"

Vivian's voice trembled. "Whatever it is, you won't have to face it alone. I'm here for the long haul—I promise you that."

Their eyes locked for a moment. "I'll hold you to it," said Marley.

Her hands shook as she opened the second envelope with three handwritten pages titled, "The Lady, or the Panther?"

Marley said tearfully, "He's changed the title—I wonder why? It seems strange."

Viv shrugged. "Poetic license, I guess. We are really into a mystery, Mar. Here, hold my hand."

"Your hand is warm and strong. I think I can do this if you're next to me."

"I'm not goin' nowhere, I promise."

Marley began to read. Her voice trembled, but soon she drifted off to a familiar place where books and stories were more real than life itself.

∞

THE LADY, OR THE PANTHER?

Once upon a time, there was a king by the name of Lither, who ruled over the kingdom of Litherland.

Lither was a cruel king who judged his subjects not by their deeds, but by their appearance or the way they worshiped.

Even though many of his subjects longed for peace and were kind, the king set the tone for hatred and bigotry. Loathing and fear began to replace the love that had once filled the hearts of his subjects.

With a twisted sense of pride, Lither devised a plan that would make his idea of justice unique—a model he was certain would be the envy of the civilized world. He would build an amphitheater, the grandest ever built, with raised seating and walls decorated with mosaic tiles depicting the power and glory of Lither and Litherland. Now the masses could gather to see how justice should be delivered: without thought or kindness, but left wholly to chance.

A subject accused of committing a crime against Litherland would be forced into the arena. Within the arena's walls were two creaky iron doors that led directly to hidden chambers. Hanging from each door was an iron ring that when pulled would open the door to reveal the fate of the accused.

Behind one door, waiting to tear the accused to pieces, was Lither's pet leopard. A leopard so fierce, that the very sound of his throaty roars made the crowd shudder.

Behind the second door was the carefully selected and, in Lither's eyes, the perfect mate for the accused. If that door was chosen, Lither would enter the arena and perform a gala marriage ceremony. As a gift, he would let the couple choose anything they wanted from the stockpile of jewels and gold that belonged to previous victims.

Can you imagine the horror of not knowing your fate? Would you pick the door to your left or the door to your right? Would you rather be married to someone you didn't love or be killed by a vicious leopard?

King Lither had one child: a daughter, Princess Daeva. The king saw in her a cruelty that was a reflection of him, and because of this, he loved her above all others.

It came about in this kingdom called Litherland that the princess fell in love and wanted to marry a young man from one of the hated groups. Hanzi had olive skin, hair the color of a raven, and eyes that were as deep and dark as a black lagoon.

In the king's eyes, he was the lowest of the low, and no matter how Daeva begged and screamed he refused to give her his blessings. Lither decided to solve this problem through the trial of the arena. "'Tis the perfect solution," he thought. For no matter which door Hanzi picked, he would be out of his daughter's life forever.

Princess Daeva had conflicts that clouded her mind. What if Hanzi picked the door with the leopard? She would suffer as she watched him being devoured by the leopard. But, what if he picked the door with the lady? She would have to watch as he took another to be his bride. Either way, she would lose Hanzi. Such an important decision should not be left to chance.

Daeva went to the Keeper of The Doors, and offered bribes and threats until he revealed the fate awaiting Hanzi behind each door. Armed with this secret and now feeling in control, she went to her beloved, who was languishing in the dungeon. With a voice dripping with honey, she told him to look at her before he picked the door. If she raised her right hand to her forehead, he should select the door on the right side. And if she raised her left hand, he should choose the left door.

That morning the sky was covered with ominous black clouds, and the rumble of thunder shook the arena. Hanzi stood alone in the center of the arena, confident that his fate was in the hands of the woman he loved and trusted. She would want to spare his life, even if it meant he would be married to another. Wouldn't she?

The crowd cheered, for never had they seen such a handsome and heroic figure. Hanzi glanced at the princess with pleading eyes, as if to say, "Which door?" She raised her right hand slightly to her head. Trusting her, Hanzi went directly to the door and pulled the iron ring.

Marley, this is where the story ends, and yours begins.

Which door will you choose: the door of safety, or the door of uncertainty? You can accept your life as you have known it or take the path that may be extraordinarily painful, but at the same time enlightening.

You must ask yourself if you want to remain with the memories that were designed for you, or do you wish to discover the truth?

I must warn you, if you decide to move ahead with this quest, you will have to face your fears, and at times, you may feel as if you are falling off a cliff.

Think carefully, Marley Chambers. Once you begin, there will be no turning back.

If you decide to take the next step, open the small envelope hidden in the book entitled *Dr. Hudson's Secret Journal*.

Love,

Papa

∞

The papers dropped from Marley's grasp, drifting downward and scattering onto the floor.

"How could they do this to me?" she snarled. "They drop a bomb, and I can't ask them anything or tell them I'm fucking pissed off." Marley reflected. "You know, Cohen is a Jewish surname. Papa's must have been Jewish."

"It's a lot to take in. What are you going to do?"

"Papa said I should think carefully."

Vivian became thoughtful. "I have one last final on Monday, then a quarter break. I don't work during school breaks so that makes me footloose and fancy-free. What say I move in and we tackle this together?"

"You would do that?"

"I wouldn't miss it for anything. Whatever you decide, I want to be next to you."

Marley nodded. "I want you here."

∞

Marley Chambers no longer existed. *My name isn't even Chambers. It's Cohen. I guess that makes me Jewish or half Jewish. Is that like a bagel sliced in half?*

She sat up most of the night, reading and rereading Papa's letter and story. She had cried so hard that the ink had smeared and the paper had crinkled.

In a few hours, she would make the trek to Dr. Saperstein's office. What did she expect her to do? Kiss her boo-boo the way Mommy did and make it all better? Who picks a therapist because of their name? What's in a name, anyway? Fuck you, Shakespeare. I'll bet you never had to deal with a mystery like this.

CHAPTER 9

Esther Saperstein glanced at the office clock: twenty minutes before Marley's appointed time. Unlike many therapists, she spaced her appointments half an hour apart. She never understood how some therapists could book their patients every forty-five minutes, with little or no break between sessions.

Danni had once compared therapy sessions to a hearty meal. "In France, we savor our food. Courses are served with time to enjoy, plus"—she emphasized the plus—"we want to clear our palate."

Esther had a certain level of anxiety before a patient's arrival. Her analyst had thought it was leftover from her childhood trauma. Perhaps so, at least in part. One never knew what to expect in Nazi-controlled Poland, and one also never knows what to expect during a therapy session.

Danni had a very different take. "It's not a bad thing. It's like stage fright. It goes away once the curtain opens."

She smiled as she saw Danni in vignettes throughout their lives together. *What would I do without her?*

Esther blinked. It was a well-practiced technique, one she used to bring her from the past to the present.

For now, she must focus on her patient, Marley Chambers: a young woman, whom in some ways she saw as a child.

The call light went on.

Dr. Saperstein's welcoming smile faded when she saw her patient.

Marley's face was puffy, her eyes almost swollen shut. She clutched a small sheath of papers in her hand.

"I have to vomit," she managed to say.

Esther motioned to the bathroom. She stood next to Marley as she retched. Esther reached for a small towel, wet it, and placed it on the back of her neck.

"A bit better?" she asked.

"Yes. I'm sorry."

"It's all right, Marley. I'll leave the office door open. Come in when you're ready."

Esther moved quickly to the kitchen and the bottle of chilled ginger ale.

She returned to her office as Marley was walking in.

"Sip this slowly," she said, handing her the glass.

"Thank you. I haven't been able to keep anything down since last night. And I don't know if I'll be able to get any words out. Will you read this?"

"Of course."

Esther Saperstein took the papers, sat back in her chair, and began to read. Some of the writing was blurred from Marley's tears; some because Esther Saperstein could not focus. She felt her throat tighten, and in spite of her years of experience in containing her emotions she felt her eyes filling with tears.

She put the papers down and looked at Marley.

"I'm so very sorry."

"What do I do, Dr. Saperstein?"

"For now, you take a deep breath. Your world, as you have known it, has been turned upside down. You may begin to suspect everything and everyone around you.

"Who can you trust, who can you believe? I do think that the answers will come from within, but only when you are ready. Perhaps we can begin by talking about your feelings."

"All of them?" she scoffed. "I'm sorry. Hmm, let me think—fear, disappointment, anger, and let's not leave out betrayal. How are those for a start?"

"At this moment, what are you feeling?"

"I'm pissed off..."

"At?"

"You. I can't believe I just said that. Oh, God. I feel so ashamed. But you're here and they're dead. And what good is it to be angry at the dead?"

"Marley, your anger will not kill me or even knock me over. In fact, I consider it an honor that you trust me with it."

Marley was silent for a long moment as she sipped her ginger ale. "I'm scared and confused. This is worse than any nightmare I've ever had." She continued, "I was raised with such security and caring—hovered over, not encouraged to take risks. And now I've been thrown to the wolves, or perhaps to the leopard. I'm also feeling impotent, as if I'm screwed regardless of the door I pick."

Marley continued, "Who the fuck does this to their child? My God! Oh wait, there's not supposed to be a God. God or no God, I feel like I'm in the middle of hell."

"The Holocaust was much like that."

"Why do you go there?" Marley said angrily. "Papa's letter only talked about his place of birth and his birthdate, but not his experiences."

"The patient asking the therapist for her associations. Brava. As a student of history, I'm sure you have taken at least one class on the Holocaust."

Marley nodded. "Actually, two."

"Then you've seen a few documentary films about the Holocaust."

Marley nodded. "Too many."

"You asked why I associated to the Holocaust. Your father's age and birthplace, for one. Born in 1912, he would have been in his twenties when Austria was annexed by Germany." Esther Saperstein wrote the name LITHER on a notepad. "Look closely at the name and tell me what you see."

Marley studied the word; her mouth twisted. "It's an anagram for Hitler! I'm more confused than ever. My father spoke with a British accent. Slight, but it was there."

Dr. Saperstein leaned forward in her chair. "Some survivors went to great lengths to hide their experiences. In doing so, they believed they could hide it from themselves. They only wanted to forget the horror and start over again."

"Papa had a scar on his left arm, and the fingers on his right hand were horribly twisted. Wait, I keep forgetting to show this to you. It's the photo of his arm that I spoke about."

She dug into her purse and pulled out the picture.

Esther Saperstein studied the photo. "I've seen this before on the forearms of Holocaust survivors. As I'm sure you well know, inmates had identification numbers tattooed on their arms. There were a few plastic surgeons who later removed the tattoos, leaving a telltale scar."

Marley began to sob. "He told me the scar and his broken fingers were from a childhood accident."

"But you don't believe that," Dr. Saperstein prompted.

"I just don't know! How can I ever trust again?"

"I wish I had a simple answer. I do know that, as human beings, we have a need to trust. That will be your quest, regardless of the door you choose."

"My father called himself a coward, and I have to know why. And so often, when I feel afraid for no good reason, I think of myself as a coward. And my mother, why did she have to lie to me? None of it makes sense. If I take the next step and open Papa's book, what will I find? Another confession? Another riddle?"

Esther's voice became softer. "I will be here for you, but I wonder how you see Vivian at this time?"

"I want Viv by my side. She's going to stay with me, starting this afternoon. I've always needed her; I'll always need her; Viv's my anchor."

Marley became thoughtful. "It occurs to me that I never thought that way about John. I think I agreed to marry John partly because I was flattered that he wanted me. But more than that, I could see Mommy and Papa's eyes light up at the thought of my being married and taken care of. I always wanted to make them happy. So much of what I struggle with, I think, is trying to please others. My parents, Dr. Holbrook."

"And with me?"

"Sometimes I do get very anxious about coming here. And now that I yelled at you, I suppose you won't want to see me again."

"Perhaps that fear of hurting your parents is why you couldn't express any anger toward them. It is perfectly normal for children to become angry with their parents. You might say it is nature's way for a child to separate and become their own person.

"There is so much for us to explore, but sadly it is time for us to stop. Marley, before you decide, ask yourself if you want to move into these unchartered waters for yourself, or for others."

She nodded. "I will and thank you for today, Dr. Saperstein. Would it be okay if I didn't come in on Wednesday? I don't know where this adventure will lead me... us. And with Viv staying home with me—could I come on Friday?"

"Of course. Friday it is."

Somehow, Marley felt calmer. The ride home was unremarkable.

∞

Marley found Vivian parked outside her house, the VW overflowing with all her possessions. "I just pulled up," she said, getting out of the car. "How was therapy?"

"I threw up."

"Wow! Well, better out than in, I guess." Vivian held out her arms.

Marley melted into the familiar comfort of her friend's embrace. "Thanks, Viv, for doing this. I don't think I could manage without you."

"This is as much for me as for you. I was on the phone with my parents. Whew! Two hours with them can seem like a month. I told them I wasn't going to New York after graduation. Boy oh boy, did my mom get huffy. Then she put my dad on; then he put my mom back on. She made no bones about telling me that I've absolutely ruined their precious family reunion." Viv sighed melodramatically. "So, if you can stand me, I'm here for the duration."

"What about your apartment?"

"Mar, have you ever lived with five other females and one bathroom?"

"I roomed with three other girls and two bathrooms at BU. That was bad enough.

"Hey, what's that in the front seat of your Bug?"

"It's pizza, salad, and the very famous Teddy."

Vivian took a rumpled, light brown teddy bear out of the front seat of her car.

She held him in front of her. "Remember the Three Musketeers?"

"Yes. You, Teddy, and me."

"Then it's all for one and one for all."

They sat outside on the brick patio enjoying the perfect weather and the intoxicating fragrance of gardenias.

Vivian said, "I'm glad we're eating outside. It's a beautiful day. Where else can you get an ocean breeze, 72 degrees, and no smog?"

Marley said, "Have to love West Los Angeles. Pass the pizza, please. Remember what your mom called a meal between lunch and dinner?"

"A dunch. Pass the salad, please. It's hard for me to stay mad at her for being who she is."

Marley said, "What exactly happened with your mom?"

"It was a mess from the first hello," Vivian said, piling the salad on her plate.

"Don't leave out one word." Marley took a second slice of pepperoni pizza. "To hell with my waistline!"

"You seem pretty chipper, considering everything that's going on."

"Dr. Saperstein helped put things into perspective. I'm scared about what I might discover, but I have you, and Dr. Saperstein, too. She intimated that Papa might have been a Holocaust survivor. I'm beginning to lean that way myself, but I need more proof. There's no escaping the fact that Mommy and Papa must have been holding onto demons. In my heart I believe they were trying to spare me. But maybe, they were also trying to put the past away so they wouldn't have to face their own pain."

"Wow, that's heavy, Marley," said Viv. "I hope you share that with Super Doc. Your Papa's letter got to me. It made me realize that life really is too fucking short not to be upfront and honest. That's what gave me the courage to speak with my mom. She lost it when I told her I wasn't returning with them for the family reunion." *Now, if I can only find the guts to tell you I'm in love with you.*

"Like I said before," said Marley, "don't leave out one word. Spill!"

Vivian put down her fork and leaned back in the chair. "I've been dreading the thought of spending the summer in New York, surrounded by relatives and their expectations. Here's the whole reunion scenario, if you can stomach it. As soon as the plane lands, my mom puts my dad and my luggage in a separate cab. Then Mom whisks me away to Macy's. We're not shopping for plain old dresses, but for *dresses*, if you know what I mean."

"Frilly?"

"Yes, plus with high heels. Do I strike you as a frilly chick? Look at me: flannel shirt, Levi's, and hiking boots. Oh, and did I show you my latest?" She held up a leather carabineer key holder. "Hooks right to my belt loops. No more lost keys for me."

Marley mused, "I do like your keychain. I'm always losing my keys. Maybe I should get one."

Vivian smiled inside. *Oh, Mar. You are such an innocent. Don't you know it's a lesbian thing?*

"Can you imagine her reaction when she sees my haircut?" She mimicked a high-pitched voice: "What have you done to your hair! Oh my, those beautiful ringlets, destroyed!"

Marley chuckled. "Your mom doesn't talk that way."

"Maybe not the voice, but the words are right on. And even if I suggested a sharp-looking pantsuit, she'd give me her patented devil-daughter look."

"I've seen it on more than one occasion," said Marley, nodding. "What happens after you shop?"

"The reunion week begins."

"A whole week?"

Viv nodded between bites. "There's the primo event—a formal reunion dinner at a swank hotel. The gents wear suits and ties, and the ladies get dolled up to the max in long dresses. They're starving themselves at this very moment. But I'm not!" Vivian took a mighty bite out of her slice of pizza.

"My mom and my aunts have already reserved a banquet room at The Ritz. Seventy-five to eighty of us, not including babies under the age of three. Then there's five days of smaller gatherings—a family picnic, and visiting different relatives' homes. After that, the fix-up dates begin. Mom's already getting them lined up, and at the end...I'd better be engaged."

"It sounds positively horrible."

"Yep, and all the time the pressure is on. Whew! Aunts, uncles, and cousins fawning over me." Viv made mock grand gestures while imitating singsong voices. "Oh, Vivian, you've made us so proud! Carrying on the family name, and the first female in our family to become an attorney."

"The family name?"

"Haven't I told you? I was named after Aunt Vivian. And with that comes this ghastly ring that is handed down from Vivian to Vivian."

"Becoming an attorney is an achievement, Viv. Why wouldn't they be proud?"

"I get that, and I am grateful. But it's all about what will make *them* happy. It's not about *my* happiness." She noticed Marley's sad expression. "What is it, Mar?"

"All these years I've idealized everyone. I thought we had perfect lives."

"We've had good lives, but not necessarily real lives. We're heading into some serious stuff, both of us. Have you decided if you're going to read the rest of the letters?"

"I want to go forward, and I'm scared. But I know I have you and Dr. Saperstein. Oh, and I almost forgot: Lither is an anagram."

Vivian sat bolt upright. "Some Nancy Drews we are! An anagram, and we missed it. An anagram for *what*?"

She handed Vivian a Post-it with one word written on it: LITHER. "Dr. Saperstein told me to study it and see if anything came to mind."

"Did you figure it out?"

"Yes, I did. And that's what gave me the courage to continue."

Vivian studied the word and looked up, her eyes as wide as saucers. "Sweet Jesus! Hitler. The Holocaust...it's all beginning to make sense. Oh, Mar, I wouldn't miss this journey with you for anything. I'll be here with you, every day, every step of the way."

"That's what makes this doable."

"I've been thinking, is it okay if I crash in your parents' bedroom? I've outgrown the trundle. Plus, there's going to be times when I'll have to study and get ready for my final quarter." *I don't know if I can stand being in the same room with you at night... so close to you, dreaming about what it would be like to touch you, to make love with you.*

"The room is yours, Viv. I think we should spend the rest of today getting you settled and then start on the quest in the morning."

Vivian said shyly, "I got a job nibble this week."

"You did!" Marley screeched. "I've been selfish, only thinking about me. Tell me, tell me, puh-*leeze*!"

"Smith, Klein, and Hopper. Corporate Law. They're one of the top firms in the country. I told my parents, and needless to say, they were over the moon with excitement. The telephone company probably exploded with all the bragging they did to the rest of the family. One more quarter of classes, then graduation—then bar exams and deciding what I want to do with the rest of my life."

"Be honest, Viv: What's your passion?"

Vivian sat back, her legs stretched out in front of her. *Besides you?*

"Don't laugh, okay?"

"Have I ever laughed at you?"

She winked. "There's always a first time. I want my own office. I want to take the cases no one else will take. Abused women, abandoned women who can't collect their overdue child support and end up on welfare."

"Then that's what you should do."

"It takes money. Money to open an office, money to live on."

"I love the idea. We renewed our sacred oath, and I take it seriously. All for one and one for all. That means you and me stick together, come what may. And what about poor Teddy?"

Vivian picked up the little bear. "Well, he is a little ragged." She turned him around, comically sniffed his bum, and pinched her nose between thumb and forefinger. "And his butt stinks, too." Both girls convulsed in laughter. "Oh, dear Teddy, are you feeling neglected?" Viv held Teddy to her ear. "He says he's sad, and that it's embarrassing going around without any clothes."

Marley made an exaggerated sad face. "Poor Teddy. So abandoned. A new outfit then?"

"A real musketeer uniform, complete with plumed hat and sword."

"We should go to the Rose Bowl Swap Meet and see what we could find," Marley suggested. "The rest of our world may be falling apart, but us sticking together hasn't."

"A toast then," said Vivian.

They raised their glasses and cried in unison: "To *Les Trois Mousquetaires.*"

CHAPTER 10

Vivian awoke sprawled across Papa and Mommy's queen-size bed. She was certain she had seen figures floating around the room seconds before she conked out. Vivian thought it could have been the one-too-many glasses of wine, but then again it could have been their spirits. She liked to believe they were still hanging around, watching over Marley and her. She whispered, "Mommy and Papa, I sure could use a little of your mojo. I've been told when you cross over you're given unique gifts. I sure could use one or two right now. See, I've been smitten with your daughter ever since I can remember and my heart's breaking, because I love her so damn much. I want to protect her, and have her in my life forever and ever. So if you can see your way clear..."

She heard a crashing sound. *A sign—it has to be a sign!* The crash was followed by a scream, followed by: "Oh, shit!"

Not a sign from the spirit world, it's Marley on a cooking roll. The princess may need to be rescued from herself.

Viv jumped out of bed. She felt lightheaded and heard her stomach grumble. Great, the old hangover and hunger duet.

She slipped on her bell-bottomed Levi's, dashed into the bathroom, splashed water on her face, and sniffed her armpits. She thought they passed muster, but dabbed on some water to make sure, and put on her Morrison Hotel T-shirt.

Let the mystery continue, she thought as she followed the scent of burnt bacon and eggs.

∞

"That was a great breakfast, Mar."

"The bacon wasn't overcooked?"

"Perfect, I like it really crisp. I mean, really, *really* crisp."

"Hardy har har. I never claimed to be any great shakes as a cook."

"Good, because you sure aren't. But I love ya anyway." Viv leaned back in her chair. "You know, Papa's room was always a bit intimidating to me."

Marley raised an eyebrow. "Because of all the books?"

"No. It was the darkness. The way the drapes were closed day and night. Never opened. As if he was in hiding. Remember all the dust when I opened them? Kinda creepy. And your mom, it doesn't make sense to me, her being a neat freak and all."

Marley was quiet.

"Are you upset with me for saying these things?"

"No, I'm processing."

"Oh, God...your therapy must be working."

Both women laughed.

Marley said, "I cried myself to sleep last night and had this super weird dream."

"Want to share?"

"Hmm, I dunno. I read someplace, that when you're in therapy, your therapist should be the first to hear your dreams. But anyway, when I woke up this morning, I felt different, as if I needed to find out about Mommy and Papa and what they went through. I think by doing that, I'll find myself."

"Wow! This therapist must be brilliant. Okay then, let's get to work."

∞

"The room does look different with the drapes open," Marley said walking over to the bookcase holding *Dr. Hudson's Secret Journal,* by Lloyd C. Douglas.

"Have you read this book?" asked Marley.

"No, never heard of it."

"It was one of Papa's favorites. It's about a physician, Dr. Wayne Hudson, who, through a series of fantastic events, learns about a secret power that comes from helping others."

Vivian scratched her head. "So how exactly does that work?"

Marley held tightly to the book. "Let's say someone comes into your life who could use a boost up. You decide to approach them with a proposition to assist them, but on one condition. They must take an oath to never divulge the name of the person who helped them. If they agree, your life will change for the better."

"Hmm...how?"

"It could be in different ways. It could be an improvement in a talent, or a financial windfall, or perhaps a deeper understanding of life. The catch is that anything you gain must be used to help others."

"I should read that book. Did your Papa practice it?"

"Well, he was always encouraging me to help others, so I'd say yes—in his humble way, of course, without wanting any glory for himself."

"Just like the book teaches," said Viv.

"Right," Marley agreed. "Shall we?"

"I'm ready if you are!" Viv replied.

Marley nodded and took a deep breath. "Here goes!"

She opened the book to find a small envelope marked *Marley.*

"Another envelope with something bumpy inside."

"Open it up! I can't stand the suspense."

"It's a key and a note."

∞

Dearest Marley,

By opening this envelope, you have made a decision to discover the truth, and for that fact alone, I am proud of you.

I remember your fascination with Nancy Drew mysteries. I feared you would always be absorbed in another's adventure and not undertake your own. I think Mommy was right, after all: We owe you the truth.

I blame myself for wanting to shield you, but perhaps underneath it all, I did not want to face my own pain.

In keeping with your love of mysteries, go to the third bookcase on the west wall. There you will find two latches that will allow you to swing the bookcase away from the wall. You will discover a door that leads to the cellar. The key that you hold in your hand will unlock the door to your history and the truth about our lives.

Once in the cellar, you will find a leather physician's bag. I was not always a lab technician; I was once a surgeon. Another surprise, no?

The bag holds your next letters, as well as my memories of a different time when I was young, and the world was open and without limits. A time when I thought I was larger than life and more important than God.

Love,

Papa

∞

"Shit, Mar! If I hadn't been scared of this room, I would have discovered that secret door years ago. Okay if I get the top latch and you get the bottom one?"

Marley nodded. "I'm ready. One, two, three—*pull*!"

The bookcase swung out into the room.

"Damn, a pocket door. These can be sticky." Marley handed Vivian the key. "Would you do it? I'm too nervous."

"No way, kid. This honor is for you and you only."

The key clicked into place; the door wobbled and then slid into the wall.

Marley said, "It's dark down there. I'll get a flashlight."

"Nah, candles are more fitting for the occasion."

"Viv, enough of the Nancy Drew drama. Look, there's a light switch right next to the door."

The switch turned on a single incandescent light bulb dangling over the stairway.

"Jesus H. Christ!" Viv exclaimed. "These rickety old stairs look straight out of *Psycho*. You think Norman Bates is waiting for us at the bottom?"

"You would have to bring *Psycho* up," said Marley. "Now I'm scared to go down."

"Here, take my hand," said Viv. *Wow, finally! Geez, her hand is so warm...and shaking and sweaty!*

They advanced slowly down the creaking stairs. When they got to the bottom, Vivian found another light switch and flipped it. A second naked light bulb sprang to feeble life—it, and a dust-coated window at ground level, were the only sources of light. It was a typical cellar with a concrete foundation; the walls were made of unfinished wood panels darkened by age and dampness. The dank cellar had the fusty odor of decay and disuse, a disagreeable tang that made the girls' eyes water. Viv noticed the dust motes swirling in the air and immediately thought of her friend's asthma.

"You okay, Mar? Not too much dust?"

Marley whipped a paper dust mask out of her pocket and slipped it on her face. "Nancy Drew always comes prepared."

Rays of sunlight hovered directly over an old leather bag with an envelope tied to the handles by faded twine.

Marley sat on a turned-over crate and opened the envelope. After lowering her dust mask, she read the letter aloud:

Dearest Marley,

You may be wondering about this satchel and why it has been so important to me.

Let me return to a pleasant time when my world was filled with innocence and hope.

There was a golden era in Austria when Jews were decreed to be equal by law—but, as I was to discover, not necessarily by heart. This freedom had begun long before I was born when Franz Joseph I, the Emperor of Austria, bestowed equal rights upon the Jews. We became lawyers, journalists, authors, doctors, and businessmen. There were even several Jews who were elected to parliament. We felt we had a promising future with a sense of safety. No longer would we have to roam the world at the whim of our host countries.

My father removed the garments of an Orthodox Jew. He shaved his beard, and we became secular Jews, although a few customs remained in our home. On Fridays, my mother would oversee the Sabbath dinner, and when I turned thirteen, I would follow tradition by becoming a bar mitzvah.

My father had opened a small chocolate factory some years before I was born. It grew and prospered until RAM Confectionaries were known throughout Europe.

And so, my childhood unfolded. I grew up in an affluent home with few worries except those typical of most young boys. Did my schoolmates like me? Would I make the swim team? Would I be tall like my father or short like my mother? All normal concerns that I weathered in due course.

When I turned thirteen I had my bar mitzvah. Now I would be a man! And I must confess, I began to think about girls and wondered if I would fall in love and be happy like my parents.

What a time in our home! My parents were bursting with pride and my sisters (yes, I did have sisters) were excited about the celebration. Miriam was two years older than I; at fifteen, she was utterly boy crazy and only thought about marriage and babies.

Rachel was a year younger than I and wanted in the worst way to have her own bar mitzvah and refused to understand why she could not. Today the girls are welcomed into adulthood through a bat mitzvah, but it was not so at that time.

We lived in the same neighborhood as Sigmund Freud, the renowned father of psychoanalysis. Believe it or not, Marley, he came to dinner the night after my bar mitzvah.

It was a Sunday and my mother had overseen the most splendid dinner. Chicken soup with matzo balls, brisket, and latkes—the fragrance of that meal lingers in my memory. Freud's daughter Anna was also there, as were many of my aunts, uncles, and cousins. My sister Rachel was running around wearing my prayer shawl, stopping in front of our guests, reciting blessings, and passages from the Torah. I always felt Rachel was the brilliant one in our family.

After dinner, we gathered in the music room where Mother had a string quartet of flutists playing "Flight of the Bumblebee" by Rimsky-Korsakov. You well know that he has been one of my favorite composers, and now you may understand why.

After the music, the men rose to go into my father's study for cigars and brandy, as was traditional. Freud and my father exchanged sly looks. Then Freud turned to me and said, "Yesterday, you became a man. Won't you be joining us?"

My mother looked at my father and Freud, shook her head, and clucked her tongue in disapproval, but she did not stop me from joining the others.

I thought all the studying and preparation for my bar mitzvah was worth this moment, my true entry into manhood. Once in the holiest of shrines, Freud reached into his coat and handed me a cigar. "Tell me about your plans for your future," he said, puffing away.

I smelled and rolled the cigar between my fingers as I had seen my father do thousand of times, looking for lumps that indicated a poorly constructed cigar. To my untrained touch, this cigar seemed perfect. Freud leaned over to light the cigar for me.

"I plan on entering medical school, Dr. Freud," I said, taking my first puff and then coughing.

My father said, "No, no! The family chocolate factory is for you."

"Father," I replied, as my voice went up and down an octave, "you should hand the business over to Rachel."

"A girl? I will not hear of it!"

Freud remarked, "May I respectfully disagree with you, Herr Cohen? My daughter Anna shall be the heir to my throne. None of my sons can match her extraordinary way of thinking."

My father dropped the subject and motioned me toward his leather chair. He handed me a snifter of brandy. I puffed and drank, all the time feeling grown up. After a while, I became nauseous. I ran out of the room to vomit, and I could hear the men chuckling at my initiation.

I never smoked another cigar in my life, but I did keep the one Freud gave me as a memento of that evening. I fancied it might have some monetary value someday, if I could provide proof of its provenance!

I enrolled in the Medical University of Vienna and graduated second in my class. I was satisfied since my closest and dearest friend, Oscar Mueller, was the top student.

This doctor's bag was a gift from my father upon my graduation from medical school. How proud I was: a Gladstone bag, made from the hide of an ox and only carried by the most prominent physicians.

It was 1938, and I was a surgical resident receiving accolades for my skills. It's difficult to put into words what seemed to be a gift from God. At that time, I still had an abundance of faith. Before I performed any surgery I would follow a particular routine.

I would be in the operating theater before the patient was anesthetized. I would take their hand and briefly close my eyes, asking for guidance from God.

There was something about the way my fingers moved as I performed surgery, with a concert pianist's consummate skill and instinct, as if an unknown force was directing them.

It shames me to admit I grew arrogant from this omnipotent, godlike power I felt I possessed, but soon, I would be tested in ways I never thought possible. It began with the rumblings coming out of Germany. Laws had been passed requiring Jews to register their assets. This was followed by being locked out of all professions and being forced to wear an identification badge with a yellow star.

But, surely that couldn't happen to us! Not in Austria! We were citizens and had the law on our side.

As we were to discover, freedom may be hard to win but tragically easy to lose.

It wasn't long before the Nazis entered Austria, and we were expelled from all that we knew and loved. Life as we had known it came to an abrupt and terrifying halt for most of us.

After the "Night of Broken Glass"—a pogrom carried out by Hitler's ruthless Brownshirts against Jews throughout Nazi Germany on November 9 and 10, 1938, in which synagogues and Jewish-owned businesses were savagely destroyed—that many Jews woke up and tried to emigrate. And yet, my father continued to feel safe and above it all. I must confess that I, too, could not believe the Nazis would not want to exploit my surgical talent.

I had returned home after a double shift at the hospital and was going into my room, when I heard my parents in a heated argument. My room was directly opposite my parents, and as their conversation became louder and louder, I remained by the door to listen.

My father was trying to calm my mother, who by this time was upset and frightened.

My father said, "Colonel Hoffmann has promised to keep all of us from harm, and Abraham can continue his duties at the hospital."

"At what cost?" my mother screamed. "At what cost?"

"Shush, shush!" my father said.

They lowered their voices to whispers. I crept closer to the room and continued to listen through the crack in the door.

"I signed over the chocolate factory to Colonel Hoffmann," I heard my father say. "He will keep his word."

"Keep his word? A Nazi?" My mother laughed hysterically. "And what else does this fine gentleman want?"

"I will run the factory and teach his employees how the candy is made."

"And?"

"Every day I will give him one of my secret recipes. And in exchange, we can continue to live in our home. We will have food. We won't be deported. Do you have any idea what that means?"

My mother became a bit calmer. "How many recipes do you have?"

"Enough for this year."

"And at the end of the year?"

"We will escape before the year is up. I have a plan."

And so we remained in our home.

All I could think about was what it would mean to me. I could finish my residency and continue to perform miracles. I looked at my hands: skilled instruments that could play the music of healing.

My father spent his nights in the basement. Not like this one, but a laboratory of chocolate. For, like Scheherazade and her thousand and one stories, he needed to give Colonel Hoffman a new recipe every night. That and that alone would keep us alive.

Time passed. Except for a few Jews under the watchful and greedy eye of Colonel Hoffman, Vienna was becoming devoid of Jews. I could see the roundups as a German officer escorted me from my home to the hospital and back. It was impossible not to hear screams and gunshots echoing throughout my Vienna.

Eventually, I became the only Jewish physician on the hospital staff. I was hated by some and ignored by most, but I was still called upon to perform surgery on the more complicated cases.

Late at night, I could hear the trains pulling out from the station. The sounds that had once soothed me to sleep now became the sounds of death. There were no secrets now, and little denial left. We knew the destination of the trains, either to a ghetto or a concentration camp. Even Freud and his family had left Vienna for England.

It was on one such night that Father called me into his study.

The local priest, Father Schaefer, was standing in front of the fireplace, a glass of brandy in one hand, the other reaching toward the fire for warmth.

He turned and held out his hand. "Herr Doctor."

"Father Schaefer." He took my hand, as if wanting to transfer his warmth and energy to me. I felt an immediate surge of peacefulness.

"Sit down, my boy." My father motioned me toward the chair nearest to the fireplace. "Your mother is keeping your supper warm."

I sat silently. Had they invited me into Father's inner sanctum to tell me that supper, however meager, would be kept warm?

"The noose is tightening," said Papa. "Today, while you were at the hospital, they came for the Jews in our building."

I felt panic-stricken. "The Kleins?" I had a mild, unrequited romantic interest in the Kleins' youngest daughter, Sarah.

My father nodded. "We are the only ones left in the building."

I stood up; my fingernails dug deep into the palms of my hands. The pain they induced was the only thing that kept me from screaming.

Father Schaefer spoke. "Colonel Hoffman has put you and your family under house arrest."

"But, my patients—"

"You are no longer welcome at the hospital." Father Schaefer became quiet. "You are needed, though."

I sat quietly, mesmerized by the thought that I was still needed, somewhere.

"We have been hiding Jews in the church basement. Some are in desperate need of medical attention. This, my son, will be your new practice."

And so, for the next few months in the late afternoon, when the streets were crowded with children returning from school and adults rushing home from work, I put on a coat without the yellow star and slipped out of our home through a basement window. I walked the three short blocks to the church and stayed there overnight. The church became my hospital. What miracles we performed with old sheets for bandages, and a small amount of medication smuggled in by a few brave parishioners.

Once morning came, and the curfew ended, I would walk home, trying as best I could to fit in. The streets by then would be filled with pedestrians either going to work or joining the long columns of people hoping to buy heavily rationed food at the grocers. I would nod at passersby and smile at children on their way to school. Then I would turn into the alleyway leading to our home and slip in through the basement window.

The cloak of privilege that had kept me from harm began to fall into tatters. Our food ration was cut again, and we knew our time was near. Father's plans to escape had fallen apart. Neighbors who were our friends were either too frightened for their lives or, at the end, aligned themselves with the Nazis.

My Papa was nearly crazy. He cared for all of us, but I knew he feared the most for my two sisters, Miriam and Rachel. The time to bribe corrupt officials for passports had run out, and every day the noose became tighter.

On one afternoon, as I approached the church, I saw trucks lined up and soldiers racing into the sanctuary. I hid where I could not be seen, but could still observe.

I heard the cries and screams as they threw Jews into waiting trucks. Father Schafer was dragged from the church. I watched as those parishioners who had come to attend mass were made to watch as he was shot.

I remained hidden until the trucks pulled away.

I returned home, watching my breath smoke in the frigid air, terrified that we would be next.

I was exhausted from the emotions that now flooded me. Why didn't I stop it from happening? Why did I take the cowardly way out by hiding? Once again my mask is falling away, and I am filled with shame. It is true that some of the happiest memories of the before time still exist, but others will continue to break my heart for the rest of my life.

Papa

∞

Marley put down the letter. "Viv, you're crying."

"Aren't you?" she sobbed.

"I'm trying not to." She rested her hand on the worn leather bag and began to wail, "My Papa! My poor Papa!"

Vivian pulled her handkerchief out of her pocket and dabbed Marley's tears. Then she held the hanky to her nose and commanded, "Blow!"

She blew loudly. "You're always here when I need you, aren't you?"

"I try to be." Vivian put her hand on Marley's shoulder and drew her closer until their lips touched fleetingly.

Vivian pulled away first. *What have I done?* "Christ, Mar, you look like shit!" she sputtered to break the tension.

Marley quipped: "Yeah? You should take a look at yourself." *What the fuck just happened?*

"I gotta get out of here," said Viv. "This dusty cellar can't be safe for you, and truth be told, I'm getting depressed sitting here with all this psychic pain floatin' around." There was a foreign tremble in Vivian's typically confident voice.

"Viv, would you carry the bag upstairs to Papa's study? It seems more fitting to continue in his room. I think his energy is there, not here."

"Great idea."

"Viv?"

"Yeah?"

"I'm going to make some lunch. And,...there's another letter in the bag."

∞

They sat outside at the redwood table. Marley had packed their lunch in paper bags.

"I'm so glad we won't be sitting in that basement," she declared. "It's hard for me to think about what Papa must have gone through. It's one thing to read about it in books; it's another when you know it happened to someone you love. Here we are, years later, in this beautiful setting, two best friends whose troubles don't amount to a hill of beans in the grand scheme of things. I just can't wrap my brain around the persecution the Jews endured. How can people turn on each other like that?"

Vivian toyed with the lunch bag. "It's why I do what I do. If we don't stand up, something heinous could happen here."

"I think I'm gaining some understanding. Not only for what you do but why my parents were so overprotective. Papa having endured so much, and Mommy, a nurse during the war. They wanted to spare me from the shittiness of life, but it's impossible. You can't make someone go through life with blinders on and expect them to be fit to tackle the world."

"Can I artfully change the subject?" asked Vivian.

"Please do."

"What's in here?" Vivian asked, waving the lunch bag in the air.

She opened the bag and placed two peanut butter and grape jelly sandwiches and a pair of overripe bananas on the table.

"Yummy for my tummy. It smells exactly like our school lunches. Look, you even wrote our names on the bag. Geez, Mar, you outdid yourself. Where'd you find the wax paper to wrap the sandwiches?"

"Mommy liked using it. She never got used to plastic wrap."

Vivian dug to the bottom of the bag. "Archway Windmill cookies for dessert. My fave! Where'd you find them?"

"There's this little store in Old Calabasas that used to be a stage-coach stop. They might be twenty-five years old, but who cares?"

Marley sat down. She tilted her head back, feeling the warmth of the sun as it beat down on her face, and seemed to go into a trance.

"Where'd you go?" asked Vivian. "Earth to Marley!"

Vivian's voice seemed to come to Marley from the bottom of a well. "Huh? I disappeared, didn't I?"

"You do have a way of doing that."

"I was thinking about how Papa used metaphors to teach me about life. Do you know the one about the contest between the sun and the wind?"

"Ah, yes. That's the one where the sun and the wind get into a big pissing contest."

Marley laughed. "You have a colorful way of putting things, you know that? In other words, they want to see who is the strongest. They see a traveler walking on the road, and they have a contest to see who can get him to remove his cloak first. So the wind gets furious and blows as hard as he can, and the man only pulls his cloak tighter. The wind finally gives up. The sun comes out and warms the man so that he no longer needs his cloak for protection, and he takes it off. The sun wins! I was thinking it's such a sweet way to teach children about kindness and values. I guess I'm in a weird place—the cellar, the dampness—all the secrets. What about you, Viv. Viv?"

Vivian was silent.

"Are you all right, Viv?"

She nodded, took a swig of water, and swallowed hard. "I couldn't talk. You know how peanut butter sticks to the roof of your mouth? I could hardly swallow. Now it's settled in my chest." *Secrets? She's talking about secrets? God, if she only knew what a fucking fraud I am.*

Vivian pounded her chest and drank more water. "All better. The cellar was getting to me too. It's good to be outside eating my very favorite food. Damn, this is best meal I've had in weeks."

"And what about the breakfast I fixed? Or are you making fun of my culinary skills?"

"Hey, just because we're old doesn't mean PB&J doesn't taste like manna from heaven. Thanks for restocking."

"You're welcome, but no jabs at my cooking or about how old we are."

"Deal." Vivian blinked at the sun and pulled at the front of her damp shirt. "The sun feels good. If I had a cloak, I'd be taking it off. Can you believe it? We're only a few years away from thirty. And that's a critical year."

Marley frowned. "What happened to the promise you made less than a minute ago?"

"Ah, screw that. You just don't want to admit Father Time is nudging both of us with his scythe. It seems like only yesterday we were twelve. Remember when we were practicing spin the bottle?"

Marley laughed. "How could I ever forget? We were rehearsing for Susan...what was her last name?"

"Slater," Viv supplied. "Susan Slater's thirteenth birthday party. There we are sitting on your bedroom floor with the door wide open and spinning that stupid Coke bottle. Your mom thought it was just more of our mischief, but I thought my mom was going to blow a fuse."

Marley said, "That night while we were doing the dishes, Mommy told me she understood we were practicing for spin the bottle. Then I got the whole birds and bees lecture."

"Oh, I got a lecture all right. It was more about girls don't kiss girls."

Marley said, "I think mothers worry about their daughters having homoerotic thoughts and turning out to be, well—you know."

She saw Viv squirm and thought she might have touched a nerve. Then she remembered their fleeting kiss a short while ago; she suspected it was on Viv's mind, as well. It was too much to absorb, with everything else going on. She felt an urgent need to change the subject.

"We sure were a couple of fearless partners in crime back then, weren't we, Viv?" she said with a nervous giggle.

Viv's heart sank. Marley had opened a door of opportunity and slammed it in her face. *Didn't you feel anything when our lips touched?* "Well," she said, trying to hide her disappointment, "these partners in crime have got to get back to the scene of the crime. Ready?"

"Ready, willing, and able."

∞

"It feels different in Papa's room," said Vivian.

"In what way?"

"Not troubling, like before. I read somewhere that when someone dies, and things have been left unfinished, their spirits can't rest until they right the wrong."

"Do you believe it?"

"Not sure. But the room feels warmer, more at peace. Do you think it could be true?"

"I hope so." Marley sighed. "The more I read, the more distressed I become. Papa must have been tortured by his secrets. If my reading these letters sets him free, then let's read on."

Marley opened the next envelope and began to read.

Dear Marley,

If you look inside the bag, you will find the remnants of the cigar given to me by Dr. Freud. Dig a little deeper, and you will find chocolate bars from my father's candy factory. He named it RAM Confectionaries, and while a picture of a ram became its emblem, it was named after his three children: Rachel, Abraham, and Miriam.

When I began to write this letter, I let my fingers wander through the bag. I even thought I detected the toothsome smells that always came from my father's factory. I wonder if, after all these years, the chocolate bars are still edible.

If I meander between the past and the present, please forgive me. After all, is that not how the mind works?

Now to return to that day when I saw the Nazis at the church. I made it home, trying to walk normally from the church to the basement window.

My parents were standing in the foyer and were surprised to see me returning so quickly. In between shallow breaths, primarily from fear, not exertion, I told them what I had seen. My mother began to cry softly, as I remember. "Father Shafer, such a good soul," she moaned. "A friend to all."

My father called Rachel and Miriam and instructed us to each pack a small suitcase with essentials. My sisters began to sob. I put my arms around them as we climbed the spiral staircase to our bedrooms. "I'll take care of you," I said. "Don't worry. You'll be safe with me." That gave them some comfort; they stopped crying, and we each went into our bedrooms to pack. I didn't dare show them my own fears—at first, fears of the unknown and now, fears of the known.

I hastily threw a few things into a suitcase. Primarily warm clothing, but also my toothbrush, toothpaste, razors, and a comb. I was vain about my appearance, and at the last moment splashed on my favorite aftershave lotion, Lentheric—advertised as being for men of action, which I suppose I had fancied myself to be—and carefully placed the bottle in my carryall.

I looked at my physician's case and, for a fleeting moment, was filled with a sense of purpose. I swore that this bag that you now see before you would become the depository of my life, as I had known it. I only had a short time to gather some things that would define who Abraham Cohen once was. Family photos, carelessly stuffed into a desk drawer, the copy of the Old Testament I received at my bar mitzvah, my medical diploma, and my stethoscope went into the bag. Items that would identify me as a skilled physician were left in the bag as well. It occurred to me that my years had been filled with pride. I fell to my knees, not to ask a God I had sometimes scoffed at for redemption, but to ask for strength to endure and help others.

I went downstairs with my suitcase and my physician's case and entered my father's study. It felt hollow except for the fond memories of that evening with Dr. Freud. I picked up the telephone and called Oscar Mueller, whom I thought of as a brother. I blurted out, "The Nazis are coming for us!"

Oscar had been involved in the underground, and he told me to run from the house and join him. I was tempted, but could not leave my family. I told him I hid my bag in the woodbin next to the fireplace. I then directed him to enter the apartment through the cellar window.

"Oscar, keep the bag for me. For afterward, should I return."

It was at that moment that I heard loud banging on the front door. I let the phone fall from my hands and, walking out of my father's study, went to meet my fate.

If you dig deep into the bag, you will find another envelope. For now I ask that you and Vivian, who I feel strongly is still with you, put everything aside and temporarily leave this house, with all of its pain and secrets, and steel yourselves for what is to come.

Love,

Papa

∞

Marley hung her head and spoke into her lap, where she had dropped the letter. "I don't know if I can leave. I feel like my guts have been torn out and placed on display. What do you think, Viv?"

"I think we should do as your Papa suggests. Let's get out of this house."

Marley turned to face Vivian. "Look at me, look at me good. Everything I was told about my father's life was a lie. A goddamn lie! Raised in England...a lie. Even his accent was another lie. I can hardly wait to read the lies my mother must have told me. Who am I, Viv?"

"You're Marley."

"What?"

"You asked me who you were." Viv gestured Marley to come closer. "Let me put my arms around you. That's right. Now put your head on my shoulder, the way you did when we were kids and you were having a bad day."

"Like this?" Marley asked.

"Perfect," Vivian murmured. *So very perfect.* "Now listen to me. You are not defined by your father's phony accent or the made-up stories they told you. I think they were trying to make your life easier. Okay, maybe that's not too wise, but they were trying to keep you safe. I can tell you're still Marley. Want to know how I know?"

"Yes."

"First of all, you smell like Marley."

In spite of her pain, Marley laughed loudly. "Thanks, best friend."

"Everyone has their own scent. I read a story where they took a group of newborns and mothers and switched the babies around. The babies cried until they got to their true mother. So, my friend, by your scent you shall be loved."

"How else do you know I'm still me?"

"Because, underneath that frightened Marley lies a princess with a punch, who can face anything, even Frankenstein's Monster and the Wolf Man!"

"I love you, Viv."

Vivian tried to smile. "I love you too." *In every way.*

"Where shall we go?"

"To where life began: the sea. We'll walk along the ocean shore and feel the sand between our toes. We can park at the Santa Monica pier and stroll down to Venice Beach. The beach has always been my salvation when things seem dark. Let it also be yours."

"Dark? Viv, I've never seen you like that. I've always thought I'm the sad one. I researched depression in the library, and found a diagnosis that fits me. Dysthymia—mild, chronic depression. I've got most of the symptoms, from fatigue and feelings of hopelessness to problems concentrating—I won't bore you with the whole laundry list. But you, Viv, you're the most, well, well-adjusted and happy person I've ever known. I've always relied on your...on your..."

"You mother used to call them shenanigans."

"Yeah, she actually liked it when we got into some mischief. She thought it was healthy. I wouldn't have, you know, on my own. You're perfect for me."

You don't know how long I've waited to hear you say that. "That's sweet of you, Mar. But maybe I'm not someone you really should have followed. I've made an awful lot of mistakes in my life."

"Huh? What the hell are you trying to say, Viv?"

Vivian shook her head. "It just, it's just... Your Papa's letters really got to me.

It's making me think about my parents. My dad was in the Navy during the war. He never talked about it, and I thought it must have been like that old musical we saw with your mom. You remember the one?"

"Yeah. *Anchors Aweigh* with Gene Kelly, Frank Sinatra, and Kathryn Grayson. Remember that great scene with Gene dancing with Jerry Mouse, from the *Tom and Jerry* cartoons?" She smiled. "Mommy went around singing some of the songs for weeks afterward."

"I remember," Vivian said. "Anyway, I was thinking how my parents scrimped and saved to pay for their house and had such wonderful plans for their retirement, and now I've disappointed them. I'm struggling with not wanting to hurt them, yet trying to be my own person. I don't even know if they'll come out for graduation. You're coming, right?"

"I wouldn't miss it for anything, you know that. Hey, Viv...no need to cry. I'll be here to support you."

Will you, Mar? Will you really be able to understand and accept me?

"When are you going to tell you parents?"

Startled, Vivian replied, "Huh? About what?"

"You know, about wanting your own office."

Vivian looked down at her shoes. "Maybe after we solve your mystery."

∞

Vivian pulled the Bug into the Santa Monica Pier parking lot. "Smell that sea air," she said grabbing onto Marley's hand and pulling her bodily past the carousel.

"I want to ride the carousel," Marley pouted. She could be such a little kid at times.

"Don't you dare have a tantrum, Mar. I've got this figured out. We're going on the bumper cars. And every time you hit someone, I want to hear a primal scream."

"Are you serious?" Marley whispered. "And how exactly do you know about primal screams?"

"Ha! Another lunchtime workshop at Brooks with Arthur Janov, the dude who invented primal therapy. See, the whole point is to reenact a past trauma and then express your anger and pain through screams. If we had a pillow, you could hit that too."

"Do you think it can work?"

"I don't see that it could hurt. I'm going to do it, just because my parents want me to be someone I'm not."

"Okay, you're on, but I want the red car," Marley said.

"I'll take yellow."

"Let's go—primal all the way!"

Marley had to admit it helped. She was wobbly and hoarse after the third round of bumping into Viv and perfect strangers while screaming as loud as she could. Both young women gleefully ignored the stares of surprise and annoyance their antics fetched.

Exhausted, Vivian and Marley held hands as they walked along the beach, stopping every now and then to let the water lap at their feet.

"I have to admit, that felt really good," Marley said, letting her toes wriggle into the wet sand.

"You were hell on wheels," replied Viv, "and my sore neck is proof. I oughta sue you for whiplash!"

They followed the boardwalk, stopping to mix with the crowd standing near the fence that surrounded Muscle Beach Gym.

"Arnold Schwarzenegger used to work out here," said Vivian.

Marley made a puzzled face. "Arnold Whosis?"

"The bodybuilder. He's been Mr. Olympia and Mr. Universe multiple times. They call him the Austrian Oak. You don't get out much, do you?"

"Well, I may not know who he is, but I do know I want that body." Mar pointed to a super-tan, incredibly attractive woman with rippling muscles lifting weights.

"You and me both," Viv murmured, wondering if Mar would pick up on the double entendre.

Sometimes, she wondered if Marley spent too much time inside her own head and therefore was blind to all the hints she dropped about her sexuality. Maybe there were clues about her parents' secret history all along, too, and she simply didn't want to see them. *I guess I'm one to talk,* Vivian thought. For all her bravado, why couldn't she confide in her best friend? She scuffed at the sand lying on the cement walkway. She looked at Mar, her gaze fixed on the same shapely female bodybuilder. A bevy of bronze goddesses had been working out, but this particular woman monopolized Marley's attention. Vivian couldn't help but wonder if Marley just admired the woman's physique, or if she was also attracted to her sexually.

How could she ever risk telling her that she was the love of her life? What if Mar freaked out and she lost her? And how could she tell her parents, who were so proud of her for being the first attorney in the family? "Hi, Mom, hi, Dad. Hi to all my relatives at the reunion. Guess what? I'm a card-carrying lesbian."

At this moment, Mar looked as if she was miles away; her face was relaxed, as if the only other person that existed was the female body-builder. After finishing her workout, she began to wipe the sweat away with a towel and the crowd began to move on down the boardwalk, their attention now focused on the shops and restaurants.

Marley turned to Vivian. "I wonder how long it would take for me to develop a hot bod like that?"

"Your bod's hot the way it is," said Viv. *Another hint, and I bet it sails straight over her head!*

Marley smiled. "We should eat healthier and join a gym. What about trying Cafe Gratitude for dinner?"

"Perfect."

"Damn, I don't know why I'm feeling happy and lighthearted. Maybe all that primal screaming really worked."

"Could be, and maybe it's because you're letting the ghosts out."

Marley gave Vivian a quick peck on the cheek. "I think you're onto something."

CHAPTER 11

Danni looked at the bedroom clock with its bright red pronounce-
ment: 3:00 a.m. My, but time is fickle, she thought. It moves at a
snail's pace when it's late at night, and you can't sleep, or at lightning speed
when you fear a separation or a loss. She sighed, letting her body relax and
half closed her eyes. She became aware of Esther's soft breathing, in and
out, in and out. A light snore followed by a fluttering of her lips. She smiled.
A quarter of a century of being together, and she never tired of that sound.

She propped her pillow against the headboard and let her mind
drift to the past when they were both young, idealistic students at the
University of California at Berkeley.

It was 1947, and Berkeley was teeming with veterans using their GI
benefits. Danni, a foreign exchange student, was desperate to get units
to maintain her full-time status. The registrar looked through the list of
open classes. "Aha! Hard to find anything this late, but here's one that
has room—A Brief History of Psychotherapy." She added almost
seductively, "That'll score you three units."

Great, thought Danni. A biology student in with a bunch of aspiring
therapists and do-gooders. How bad could it be? she rationalized. It is

called A *Brief* History. I'll sit in a lecture hall with at least one hundred other students, take a few notes, perhaps doodle or snooze during the lecture, get the grade and count it as a step toward my goal.

"I'll take it," she said.

The registrar took out a campus map and circled the location. "Oh my, this post-war Berkeley—bursting at the seams. It's in one of the temporary classrooms. Bungalow 12A. Follow the map." She smiled at Danni and hollered "Next!" at an astonishing volume.

Danni stood outside the classroom, her ears still ringing. Could this possibly hold a hundred students? Could it even hold fifty? She opened the door and paled at the sight of chairs placed in a circle. No more than twenty-five, she estimated. *What have I done?*

There was a man off to one corner talking to a small group of students. She looked at her class registration; it had to be Professor Alfred Kingsley. She surveyed his rumpled, faded brown suit, beige shirt, and lace-up Oxfords, cow patty-brown and in bad need of polishing. *Monochromatic, symbolic of things to come.*

She slumped into a chair.

Professor Kingsley joined the students in the circle. He crossed his legs, revealing the pill-covered white socks tucked into those sensible shoes. Danni wondered if he worked at creating the caricature of a college professor, or if it just came naturally.

"Welcome. I'm Dr. Kingsley. Before we begin, I'd like to know how many of you are aspiring therapists?"

Fifteen hands were raised.

"And how many are here to fulfill a social welfare requirement?"

Six hands went up.

"Others?"

Danni raised her hand.

"And your major is?"

"Biology."

"Budding physician?"

"No. Research."

"Let me guess, this was the only available class."

She smiled.

"Welcome to our world, Miss—?"

"Blanchard. Danielle Blanchard."

Dr. Kingsley nodded. "I was stationed in France during the war. *Bienvenue*, Mademoiselle Blanchard."

"*Merci.*"

"Now, did everyone get a syllabus?"

The students nodded and mumbled affirmatively.

"Miss Blanchard?"

She shook her head, and he handed her a single-page syllabus.

"You may be wondering about the arrangement of this class—it's size, the fact that we are sitting in a circle. I had to really jockey around to get this class accepted. Thus the title: The Brief History of Psychotherapy. You will get your lectures, let's say during the first ten minutes of class. Does that sound brief enough?"

The class laughed.

"The rest of the time we will spend not on my pedantic prattling, but on finding out what makes you tick. I firmly believe one cannot expect to help others without first conducting a thorough self-examination. I mentioned I was stationed in France during the war, and throughout that time of monumental tragedy, I kept a diary of my observations, thoughts, and feelings. I believed that if I were killed my family would know about my final days, and that might help them to have some closure. Entries were sporadic—after all, there was a war going on—but I believe it allowed me to survive, mentally and perhaps even physically. The purpose of this class is to write about how you have survived in this world, and how you—as psychologists, social workers, and yes, even biologists—will survive in your chosen field.

"These are all challenging careers. At times, you will be carrying your patient's pain. Or, in Miss Blanchard's case, frustrations at failed experiments or lack of funds for research. Now, has anyone kept a diary or a journal?"

A few hands, mostly female, were raised tentatively.

"Excellent. I will be reading your journals, and I know that can be off-putting. I will make comments, but I will not judge. I hope my insights will deepen your thoughts and help you to make the most of every moment.

"Now, would anyone care to define a kaleidoscope?"

Several hands went up.

He pointed to one of the women. "You are?"

"Esther Saperstein."

He nodded.

"A kaleidoscope is a tube containing mirrors and small pieces of colored glass. The glass is finite, but when the kaleidoscope is turned, an infinite number of patterns can be created."

"Excellent, Miss Saperstein. What if we were to think of our experiences, thoughts, feelings, and memories as pieces of glass within a mental kaleidoscope? Except, in our mental kaleidoscope, as we go through life we are able to add new pieces of glass. Following me so far?"

The class nodded and murmured in agreement.

"Good. Now, let's say in the case of a personal trauma, the kaleidoscope gets jammed. If we give it a good shake, the pieces of glass might become unstuck and begin to make new combinations. And that, in a nutshell, is your journal: a kaleidoscope. In other words, we're going to shake things up. Any questions?"

There were none—or at least none voiced. To a person, the class looked at once intrigued and somewhat trepidatious.

"What I want to see in your journals are entries wherein you reflect upon your two worlds. Two worlds, you say? Yes, your outer and inner worlds."

He pointed to Danni. "Miss Blanchard?"

"Y-yes?" she stammered.

"What comes to mind when you think about your outer and inner worlds?"

For a moment she remembered hearing German tanks and cars entering Paris. She awoke that fateful day to the announcement of a curfew beginning that evening at 6:00 p.m. Her brother Paul came into her room.

"Danielle, the Boche [a derisive term for Germans, particularly German soldiers, used by the Allies in WWII] have entered Paris.

Father went to get the Abramses." He sat down on the edge of her bed. "I'm sorry, little sister. You will have to be brave, as brave as I must be. As an accomplice in hiding the Abramses, you will be in extreme danger."

She clung to Paul's hand. "When will I see you again?"

"Once I leave to join La Résistance, I am dead to you and everyone else who knows me."

Professor Kingsley said, "Miss Blanchard? Two worlds..."

She spoke haltingly, in an unfamiliar language. "The world inside me is the one filled with fear. The outside world is that which I cannot control. The circumstances of birth, of war..."

Dr. Kingsley spoke softly. "I think you have a great deal to teach us, Miss Blanchard."

She looked down at her hands, a mite embarrassed. When she glanced up again, she noticed the young woman who had defined a kaleidoscope was staring at her. Their eyes met, and they both looked away quickly.

"Class, for the rest of this hour, you are going to be paired with another student and get to know each other. To make that process more interesting, I'm handing out these slips with numbers one through ten written in pairs. Locate your partner, head outside, and try to learn about each other. It's a beautiful day here at Berkeley. Find a nice spot. Begin by sharing something about yourself. You've got thirty minutes before class breaks."

There was a bit of a hubbub as the students found their matching numbers and, two by two, left the room. The two women who had made eye contact were the last to pair up. They walked toward each other, holding their slips aloft.

"Hello. My friends call me Danni."

"Pleased to meet you. I'm Esther Saperstein."

"And your friends call you?"

"Esther."

Danni frowned. "I think we can do better than that."

She crinkled her forehead, a gesture that Esther would learn to love. "I hereby dub you Essie."

Esther beamed. "I like it. Your English is quite good. Barely an accent. I had to struggle for years to erase mine."

"I had the benefit of knowing a teacher who was quite skilled in languages. I was eager to learn, and the war taught me how uncertain our time on earth is and not to waste a moment of it. Anyway, the prof wants us to get to know each other, and I'd like to get to know you. Say, I'm dying for a cup of coffee, and there's a stand at the quad. Shall we?"

"My treat," said Esther "and thanks for the nickname."

"*Surnom* in French. It was my pleasure."

The ice broken, the two young women discovered over coffee they had worlds in common. In half an hour's time, they felt as if they'd known each other all their lives. And later that day, when Danni shared a long-kept secret, and Essie responded with a depth of understanding, their bond was sealed.

When Danni described their meeting as accidental, Essie suggested another, far more poetic term: *Beschert.*

"What does that mean?" Danni asked quietly.

Essie took her hand. "It was meant to happen. Destiny."

Esther's whimpering brought Danni back to the present. She waited. She knew that, sometimes, Essie's dreams would fade, and she would fall back into a deep untroubled sleep.

This was different. Crying out in her sleep—tormented, anguished sounds.

Danni leaned over, and, placing her hand on Esther's shoulder, cooed, "Essie—Essie, my love."

Esther gasped and bolted upright. Groaning, she reached for Danni. "Did I wake you?"

"No, I've been up for hours. You were having a nightmare."

"I'm freezing."

"You're shaking, and your gown is wet through. I'll get you your flannels."

"Then I'll be too hot."

"Ah, the joy of menopause! Another gift from God."

Danni went into the bathroom and returned with a warm wash-cloth and towel.

"Thank you, my angel."

Danni smiled. "I'm returning the favor."

"You know what works for these dreadful hot flashes, don't you?"

"You've always given me too much credit. I know what used to work for me. Now, tell me about your nightmare, love."

"Oh, Danni, I wish I could say it was mine."

"Your new patient's?"

"Yes. You know how it happens: Their dreams become mine. After all these years, I still don't understand it."

"There are some things that we are not meant to know. Will you tell me your dream?"

Esther spoke softly. "In my dream, I'm inside my patients dream. I can see my patient and the shadow figures she described. Everything was blurry, but I could see what appeared to be a large rectangular room made of wood—old wood, rough, unfinished. I could hear moaning that became screams, and then returned to moans that became softer and softer until they disappeared. There are sounds from the outside. My patient acknowledges hearing sounds, but can't decipher what they mean. I can. I hear shouting in German and dogs barking."

She trembled, and Danni held her close.

"I don't want to revisit it. But the feelings, ach! I can't imagine how my patient has managed for all these years. I fear for her."

"Remember, Essie, the only way you can help her is to let it unravel at her own pace."

"You, my darling, are the voice of reason."

"It comes from being around you all these years."

"Danni?"

"Hmm?"

"Remember when we first met?"

"How could I ever forget the most important day of my life?"

"There's something I've never told you, Danni. When you walked into the room, you took my breath away. I never understood my disinterest in boys until that moment. There was something about your face—not just beauty, but also intelligence and, yes, sauciness—that reminded me of the lovely French woman in Renoir's 'Dance At Bougival'—except you didn't smile."

"Because I was furious! Imagine, a budding scientist thrown into a class with a bunch of touchy-feely types. To tell you the truth, I felt a little, well, superior."

Esther laughed. "Well, my love, you shouldn't have waited to register until all the other classes were full. Although I do think you got something from that class."

"You, I got you." Danni pulled her close. "And what a lucky twist of fate that turned out to be."

"Do you remember when we sat outside drinking our coffee?

"Every moment."

"You were everything I wasn't and wished I could be. Outgoing, tall, with long straight hair, self-assured, and your French accent. *Oo là là*!"

"My dear, we both had accents," Danni reminded her. "We started talking, and then, I don't know why, but I blurted out the secret I had not shared with anyone in America. We hid a Jewish family from the Gestapo. Then you cried. And I didn't know what to do."

"For a moment I thought. I prayed...I almost collapsed."

"I put my hand on your shoulder—"

"—And I begged you for the name of the family. I thought perhaps my parents had gotten out of Poland and found their way to France. Perhaps they were spared. Perhaps, perhaps, perhaps." Her throat began to tighten. "I can't speak. Danni, does it ever go away?"

"No, I don't think it goes away, it hides until something triggers it. I still remember the deeply rooted terror. If the Gestapo discovered we were hiding the Abramses, we would have all been shot, or worse. We hid them for years in the attic; they became part of our family. We had to share our rations, and we nearly starved to death. The soup was watered down, with only a few vegetables we had managed to hide from the Nazis."

Essie put her head down. "I didn't want anyone to know about my heritage and humble beginnings...to perhaps pity me or—"

"Hate you...judge you."

Essie nodded. "I got out, but many did not. Throughout history Jews have been persecuted, hated, stigmatized. You were the first and only person I had told my story to up to that point. When I got to Berkeley, I wanted to erase the past. But the past doesn't let you go. I remembered my father's words when he gave me the diamonds: 'Help others.'"

"And you have. You continue to honor the memory of your family and the six million who died. Perhaps that is the only way to make peace with the past."

Esther gave Danni a soft buss on the lips. "You always did know the right thing to say."

"That's because I've always been smarter than you, my dear," Danni teased. "Essie, there's a reason this young woman selected you from a list. I don't believe it was simply chance. You have something she needs, and perhaps she has something you need."

"What could that be?" Esther said, snuggling closer to Danni.

"Would you like me to be the therapist to the therapist?"

"Yes."

Danni sighed. "That day when I came into the class, I was furious because of the war, and then when Dr. Kingsley asked me about the inside and outside of me, I blurted it out. Then I became ashamed that I had. I was a child when Paris was occupied and couldn't fully understand what was happening. I only knew what my parents told me about needing to hide the Abrams family. I resented that my brother had to go away, perhaps never to return. We were hungry all the time and I didn't want to share my bread.

"All I could think of was America, America. Someday I'll live in America, the land of freedom, and plenty. You know how kids think— everything is black and white. Then, when I got the opportunity to study here, I left France, with all that I owned in a small suitcase. I was still angry for having had my childhood taken away. I wasn't thinking about leaving my family behind. The house was damaged, and the

Boche, wanting to show they held our lives in their hands, had burned down our barn. But my parents blessed me, and my brother said, 'Fly, little sister, I will be here.' That he was spared is a miracle in itself.

"That day when we first met and began to share our secrets, I began to see things through your eyes. And that's when my anger started to leave. I was ashamed for having been selfish. I began to feel your pain, and at that moment I stopped thinking as a child.

"So, my Essie, through your experiences I was healed, in a sense. My anger became gratitude and love for the family I left behind, and for the family we had helped.

I think Marcel Proust said it best: 'The real voyage of discovery consists not in seeking new landscapes, but in having new eyes.' Perhaps through your patient's voyage, you will finally find peace."

Essie reached for Danni's face. Danni responded to Essie's touch with a kiss that spoke of passion and longings.

"I want you to be free," murmured Danni. "Now, no more hot flashes and no more pajamas. Only the warmth of my body to comfort you."

Danni slipped off her gown and eased back into bed. She wrapped her arms around Esther. "Essie, my love," she murmured.

Esther turned and sighed. "I thought you'd never ask," she said seductively.

CHAPTER 12

"Mmm, I smell coffee," said Vivian, ambling into the kitchen. "I didn't make breakfast. I thought we could have toast and jam. I really want to get to Papa's letter."

"As long as we have coffee I'm okay. Aren't you eating?"

"Viv, it's the miracle I've been waiting for. I lost my appetite."

"Can't say I'm surprised, with everything that's been going down. Don't worry, I'll be quick," Vivian said, filling the four-slice toaster. She picked up the *Los Angeles Times* and scanned the headlines. "Damn this Energy Crisis! I can't help thinking it's something Tricky Dicky dreamed up to deflect scrutiny on Watergate. It looks like we're in for another round of gas rationing. Odd-even system, according to our license plates. Are you odd or even?"

Marley smiled. "Definitely odd."

Vivian stood as the toast popped up. "I'll take these along with me," she said, gingerly placing the hot bread on a paper plate.

"Let's go," Marley said with a sigh. "I can't wait to get this over with."

They entered Papa's study. A cloud of dust particles danced in the thin beam of sunlight that stole through the small slit in the drapes. Vivian sat mesmerized as Marley took item after item out of the Gladstone bag, arranging the contents on the desktop. Six labeled bottles in a neat row: alcohol, aspirin, morphine, and tincture of iodine, peppermint oil, and clove oil.

"Do you think they're still good?" Vivian said, studying the bottles.

"Don't get any of your screwy ideas. I'm sure not going to be the guinea pig," Marley remarked. "This reminds me of our chemistry set adventure. Remember that debacle?"

Vivian rolled her eyes. "A minor disaster," she corrected. "I never could figure out why Mommy was so upset."

"Remind me to kill you later. You ran home, screaming, 'I think I hear my mother calling.' And I was stuck cleaning the rotten egg volcano off the kitchen cabinets."

Vivian hung her head. "Jeez, Mar, have you been holding onto that for all these years? Admittedly, that wasn't my finest hour. But, I'm here now."

"I know you are. I guess I'm just disappointed. I don't know what I was expecting, but so far nothing too surprising."

"Keep digging."

Marley reached deep into the recesses of the bag, placing each item on the desk: a leather case holding an injection syringe, various sizes of bandages, a stethoscope, scalpels, thermometer, needles and sutures, and lastly, obstetrical forceps.

"God, those look positively barbaric," said Vivian with toast in her mouth. "Imaging yanking a baby out with those wicked-looking things. Marcus Welby would not approve."

Marley couldn't help but snicker. "There're a few more things in here. Look, a photo! It's marked 1925. I can't read the rest of the writing—it's in German. Wow, it must be Papa's bar mitzvah photo."

They stared at the teenage boy, wearing a yamaka and a prayer shawl, posing with two girls and an older man and woman.

"That's Papa, all right," said Marley. "I'd know the shape of his face and his nose anywhere. The older girl would be Miriam. And the younger one, Rachel."

"Look at her expression," said Vivian. "She's pissed off."

"Remember, Papa wrote that she wanted her own bar mitzvah."

"We could use somebody like her today—she'd probably make a

helluva woman's libber," Viv quipped. "Your grandma is beaming, and your grandpa looks like he's going to bust his buttons with pride."

Viv noticed her friend's glum expression. "Hey, you don't seem very excited for somebody that just found her first real family photo. What's the matter, kid?"

"They look like a sweet family," Marley replied, "but I guess I was hoping I would find someone that I looked like—you know, the way your mom was always comparing you to all your relatives. Maybe my hair is like Miriam's, but..." She shook her head and her voice trailed off.

Vivian reached for the photo. "Aw, c'mon, this makes Papa seem so much more real. And just look at what his mother is wearing—a fox fur stole, complete with the head. Gross!"

"There's more in the case," said Marley, reaching deep into the cavernous bag.

She held up her prize with a smile. "Chocolate bars, wrapped in foil. And the labels are written in German and English. They must have exported. Chocolate Cream, four cents; Munch for Lunch, five cents."

Viv said, "Shit, that was pretty cheap for a sugar high. Anything else?"

"A Bible." Marley placed it on the desk, and, swooped her hand around the corners of the case. "A pocket watch ... and Freud's cigar!" She placed the items on the desk.

Vivian said, "All that's left of an entire family. Kinda gives me goosebumps."

Marley nodded. "I'm glad that Papa wrote down some of his memories. Maybe, after all is said and done, it's all any of us have. Reminds me something Freud himself supposedly said: 'Sometimes, a cigar is just a cigar.' They lived, they died; why look for a deeper meaning? But I've got to! I've come this far. I need to read the next letter and get it over with. Would you mind?"

Viv nodded. "Hell no, let's keep on truckin'. I'm really proud of you, Mar. I can only imagine how hard this must be for you."

"I don't think there are words to describe it."

Marley opened the next envelope and began to read.

∞

Dearest Marley,

I remember how you struggled with your decision to leave the safety of our home and travel to Boston University. You had to declare your major, and how you grappled with that! First Anthropology, then Art History, and then Archaeology. And that was only the A's. I had to smile as you went through all the possibilities. You stopped at History, and I thought how curious that, out of all possible choices you should be drawn to the one thing you did not have: your very own history.

Perhaps somewhere deep inside, you knew something was amiss.

Your mother has been busy writing her memoirs. In some ways, this has brought us even closer. In reliving the sorrow we have wept in each other's arms, crying old tears for the scars that will never heal, and new ones for exposing the truth we know will break your heart.

I ended my last letter with the banging at the door. I will return to that time. I left my father's room with the physician's bag I'd hidden safely in the woodbin, picked up my suitcase, and went to meet my fate.

We gathered in the foyer. That scene is imprinted in my mind, and I suspect when I die, it will follow me to my grave.

My mother wore her winter coat trimmed in rabbit fur. I remember the way the fur collar fluffed around my mother's neck, tickling her nose at times. She would sneeze in a ladylike manner and say, "Forgive me."

My father wore his best light gray business suit with matching vest and double-breasted jacket. Father must have taken the time to shine his shoes because I could see the chandelier's reflection in them. His pocket watch dangled from his vest. He reached into his watch pocket and pulled it out by the gold chain.

"This, my son, is your inheritance," he said with great solemnity.

I was overwhelmed and returned to my father's room. I wrapped the watch in my handkerchief, and tucked it into the corner of the case. Perhaps you have discovered it by now.

I returned to the foyer. Miriam and Rebecca were huddled together.

I'd like to tell you a bit about my sisters. Miriam had fallen deeply in love with a conductor and composer, Isaac Bernstein. They married, and what a wedding that was! She made a beautiful bride. Although my family practiced Reform Judaism, she chose to have a more traditional ceremony. I must admit, it was gripping. Sadly, it would be a brief marriage. Isaac was sent to a labor camp, and we received a letter that he had died of pneumonia. Miriam returned home and we were once again a family of five.

As much as my parents wanted to see Rebecca married, she remained fiercely individualistic, an early feminist determined to be successful in her own headstrong way. I often wonder what Miriam and Rebecca's futures would have been if the Nazis had not come to power.

I can see Miriam and Isaac surrounded by children and grandchildren. And Rebecca would have been managing my father's chocolate factory!

As for me, I would have continued on as a surgeon. But then, I never would have met your mother or held you in my arms.

The pounding on the front door continued. My father squared his shoulders and opened the door.

Colonel Hoffman stood there quietly for a moment, his eyes cast down on the marble floor. He then did something unheard of. The colonel clicked his heels and slightly bowed to my mother. He extended his hand to my father, and the look on his face! Although we—Mother especially—had expressed reservations about his motives, the colonel seemed genuinely sorrowful at having to carry out his duty.

It taught me a lesson that good and evil can reside within the same individual. That thought remained in my mind throughout the years I spent as a prisoner, and followed me to this very day.

"I came to escort your family," Colonel Hoffman whispered. I swear I could see his eyes glistening with tears.

Our dignity was to be preserved for the last time. We entered the colonel's silver Mercedes sedan and arrived at the train station in style.

I will not burden you with the details of my journey from Vienna to Auschwitz. I know you and the world have seen the films, and I am not anxious to relive this horror. Suffice it to say that many who entered our cattle car did not survive; upon arrival at Auschwitz, their lifeless bodies were carelessly dumped into the backs of trucks. Those of us who were able to walk were pushed and herded like animals by vicious Nazis into a living hell.

It was late at night, but there were blinding lights and a haze of smoke hanging over the entrance gate. I could barely make out a sign that said, "Work will set you free."

We walked past a man sitting at a table, alternately pointing left or right to divide the new arrivals into two columns. I was sent to the left, my mother and father to the right. My sisters were grabbed by two guards and thrown into a car. Even now, I tremble in contemplation of their fate. I made a mad dash toward them and tried to pull open the car door and keep them with me. For this desperate action I received a rifle butt in the small of my back and fell to the ground. The Nazi bastard seemed to be debating whether or not to shoot me; luckily, he was called to a commotion toward the back of the line. That would be the last I would see of my family, but not the last time I would be rescued from certain death.

We were processed and tattooed like cattle. I'm sure you remember that time when you asked me about my boo-boos. An innocent question posed by a curious child. I told you that I had an accident as a child. What was I to do? Tell my daughter of the horrors I lived through? That the scar that you saw came from surgery to remove the Nazi identification numbers? Or, that my broken fingers resulted from an experience at Auschwitz?

Forgive me, I fear I am getting out of sequence.

That first night, we huddled together in our hut, wearing striped prison camp uniforms. Six or seven of us crammed onto wooden slabs meant for two, and throughout that night I kept hearing my mother singing a Hebrew lullaby called "Numi, Numi" [Sleep. Sleep]. It was one I heard her sing to Rachel when she was a baby and it seemed embedded in my mind.

In spite of being a surgeon, I was forced into hard labor, building roads. Eleven hours a day in the rain, hot sun, or snow. The body I had taken such pride in, being a natural athlete, had become a skeleton to which clung a thin, translucent layer of skin—a grotesque testament to man's inhumanity to man. And the talented hands that I had vaingloriously considered instruments of healing were now calloused and stiff.

I saw the worst in mankind, and I saw the best. One day, I was weak and slow to move a boulder, with a stout metal rod. As I lay on the ground, exhausted by my effort, a sadistic guard heaved the boulder and rolled it over onto my hand. My fingers were crushed. I cried out in pain and cursed the guard in German, using some of the coarser language I'd picked up in the camp. I would have been shot if it weren't for another guard who had once heard me humming "Numi, Numi." He had told me the lullaby reminded him of one his mother had sung to him. He intervened at the risk of being called a Jew lover and had some of the other prisoners carry me back to our hut.

I am haunted by these memories that have, once again, become all too real. I must stop for now. The past has become stronger than the present.

Papa

∞

Marley let the letter fall from her hand. "There's no doubt about it now. Dr. Saperstein was right: Papa was a Holocaust survivor."

"And now we know why his fingers were deformed," said Vivian.

"That Nazi fucker! I hope they hung him upside down until his eyeballs fell out of his head."

In spite of her agony Marley could not suppress a small smile. "You do have a way with words. Oh, Viv, I couldn't do his without you. I'm terrified to read the rest of the letters. And Mommy's letters...I don't know if I'm strong enough."

Viv said, "Do you remember when my mother would show us family photos, but skip over some of them?"

"Yes."

"That's because my Aunt Jenny was in them. She died in a mental hospital. We all have something in our family that's hard to wrap our heads around. You can take one letter at a time—you don't have to do them all at once."

"I want to get it over with."

Marley picked up the final envelope. Her lips quivered as she ran her fingers under the seal.

∞

Dearest Marley,

Are you continuing to read these letters? I am almost through with my story. I have used the term "coward" to describe myself. Your mother was always the braver one, the one with a plan, the one to take chances. I am haunted by guilt at not having saved my sisters, and tormented by nightmarish visions of their unknown fate. I promised to take care of them, and all it took was one blow to stop me. I've tried to console myself with the knowledge that, if I had succeeded in liberating them from the car, we all three would likely have been shot on the spot.

Where did my last letter end? Ah, yes, with the story of how my fingers were broken. Fate or God, if you wish to believe, must have been looking after me. That incident happened in the dead of winter and was followed by a terrible blizzard that covered Auschwitz and the surrounding countryside. Not even the guards would venture out unless forced to. Our rations were cut; indeed, some were never received, and yet we felt strangely happy. We had two whole days of rest. Some did not survive. We had become so immune to death that we removed their clothing and carried their naked bodies outside and left them in the snow.

Some of the other prisoners took large splinters from the wooden bunks and fashioned splints for my fingers. My hand was wrapped in scraps of cloth taken from a corpse's shirt. Every hour, another prisoner would bring fresh snow, and pack it around my hand until my fingers became numb.

During those two days, we huddled together, piecing together bits of gossip we might have heard.

"The Americans are coming," was an oft-repeated wish.

"No, it's the Soviets who will get here first," another optimist, with Communist leanings, might opine.

And in this way, we latched onto any small bit of hope that we could. You see, Marley, my love, hope can survive, even in a death camp.

The storm passed, the snow began to melt, and we began to hear the roar of American planes flying overhead. We would listen to the sounds of war, moving closer and closer. Hold on, hold on, we would tell each other, but some could not. A mass evacuation of prisoners began. "To walk to a safer shelter," we were told.

The guard who had saved my life, saved it once again. He pulled my number from the list of prisoners who were being marched out of camp. "*Nein, nein,*" he whispered, taking me by the shoulder. "They are to be executed." He motioned to a truck. "You will be taken to another camp where they need a doctor. You will be spared."

Typhus was running rampant throughout all the camps. I thought, what difference does it make: to die from a bullet or to die from typhus? Perhaps I can help a few patients before I die. I got onto the truck.

It was dark when I entered Dachau and the hut that was marked *Krankenhaus*; that translates to Infirmary.

There was little I could do to help, at least in a traditional way. "Medication" consisted of a small bottle of aspirin and a bucket of murky water; that was all. For a moment I put my head in my hands, and helplessness flooded over me. Not for myself, but for my patients. It came to me that the one thing I had left to offer was words of comfort. And once again, a spark of hope was kindled. I went from bunk to bunk and put my hands on my patients' heads. I leaned over and kissed their feverish foreheads and held their hands as they took their last breath.

"*Gey schluffen*," I said. Go to sleep: It was something my mother would say in a tender way when kissing me goodnight.

The Nazis left me alone, not out of pity or because they approved of my essaying the role of a priest, but because they had dire concerns on their minds. The sounds of war were coming nearer and nearer. Then, late in April, there was a deadly silence. Most of the guards fled or hid in the forest near the camp. The remaining prisoners wandered around, dazed. Free, but imprisoned within their souls.

I opened the door of the infirmary to let in some sunlight and air. A female prisoner came toward me. I tried to focus; I thought I was hallucinating. She wore the tattered clothing of a prisoner but was not as emaciated as the rest of us. I looked carefully at her as she approached. A prisoner ready to give birth? Was it possible amidst all this death? A more recent arrival, I first thought, but then I saw the identification number on her arm. The Nazis, in their frenzy to kill as many Jews before the war ended, had stopped tracking them with ID numbers and instead put them to death as quickly as possible. I helped her up the steps and, as if she was reading my mind, she spoke to me in Hungarian. "The baby must live!" she gasped in pain. "The others kept us alive. They fed me—they fed *us*—with stolen scraps."

I spoke to her in Hungarian, in which I was conversant, as I was in several languages. This natural talent I had became a benefit when I was imprisoned with a diverse population. "What is your name?" I asked.

"Malka," she replied.

"Queen," I said, putting meaning to her name.

"Malka Elek. Someone must know I have a name." She took my hand, grimaced, and screamed, "Help my baby!"

I closed the door. At that moment I was no longer a prisoner but a physician preparing to deliver a baby. I swept everything from the lone table in the room and helped Malka to lie down.

I had no equipment except for my hands, eyes, and ears. I could see Malka's pallor; I could hear her breathing change. With these hands, as she took her last breath, I brought a new life into the world: you.

And now you know the truth.

∞

The letter fell from Marley's hands. Vivian picked it up from the floor and, in a tone of disbelief, continued reading it.

I wrapped you in rags. I cried, I rocked you, and I sang "Numi, Numi."

It was at this point that the door to the hut swung open. The sunlight streamed in, catching me in my eyes, and for a moment, everything became blurred. At first, I thought I was seeing two angels. Yes, angels they were, but not the winged kind in flowing robes, but two Americans in uniform—a man and a woman, looking as shocked as I felt. I had never seen a woman wearing pants before!

The man walked over to me. "Major Curtis Balfour, at your service," he said. I stared at them. The woman approached me and knelt. "My name is Abigail." She opened the pack she was carrying. I had not seen such treasures for years: medicines, bandages, and food. She reached in and took out an Army-issue shirt. "Extra," she said with a slight smile. I looked into her dark blue eyes and felt as if I had fallen into a lagoon.

"May I?" she asked, reaching for you.

I hesitated, drawing you closer to me.

"I'll give her back to you, I promise."

I was frightened to let you go, but I trusted her from that moment on.

I handed you to her, and the next thing I remembered was waking up in a real bed, with sheets and blankets. I had been bathed and shaved. Was I dreaming? Had I died, and was there really a heaven?

I heard the cooing of a contented baby and, at first, was very confused. I looked around the room, trying to follow the sound and saw you lying in your first bed, a bureau drawer.

Later, I would discover we had been moved to the Nazi officers' quarters, where we would remain for two months.

This, then, is the story of your birth and how I met the woman who would become my wife and your mother.

This is only the first part of your story of how you came into this world. Mommy's letters will shed light on how we became a family and take you through the rest of this very strange journey.

In the basement, under a sheet, are a few belongings of your mother's. You will find a striped cardboard suitcase. This was Mommy's luggage that took her from her home in Iowa to the Army Nursing Corps.

Open the case, and Mommy will guide you on the next part of your journey.

I can only beg for your forgiveness. I know you will be filled with anger at your Papa and will have doubts that may never be resolved.

Love,

Papa

∞

"Mar, are you okay?"

Marley bit her lip and shook her head.

Viv said, "When do you see your therapist?"

"Friday," she croaked.

"I want you to call and see if she can get you in tomorrow."

"Can't ... can't ..." Marley stared blankly ahead, repeating the word like a nonsensical mantra.

"You look like you're going to pass out." Viv guided her to the oversized chair.

"Sit down—I'm calling, and I'm driving you."

That night, Vivian sat on a chair next to Marley's bed. She had been there since early afternoon—sometimes holding Marley as she sobbed, at times trying to feed her some broth.

"Mar, can you sit up? I brought you some soup. You have to eat something."

"I will, but only if you don't look at me."

"Why wouldn't I look at you?"

"Because...because you don't know who you're looking at."

"You are still my Mar. That's all that matters."

"Viv, it's not like the way it was with you, your mother always showing us family photos and telling us who you looked like." She sobbed. "I can't look like anyone because I don't belong to anyone."

"Listen to me, Mar. We will get through this. I called Dr. Saperstein. She wants to see you tomorrow morning at ten. I'll take you and wait for you."

"Will you Viv? Wait for me, because I don't know when I'll be back."

"I'll wait for you, for as long as it takes."

CHAPTER 13

"Wow, this is some setting," remarked Vivian as she pulled into Dr. Saperstein's patient parking space. She turned off the engine and sat back for a moment gazing at the stark canyon crevices that surrounded Dr. Saperstein's home office.

"Can I walk you to the office?"

Marley shook her head. "I'll be okay. You sure you don't mind—I mean, waiting here for me? I'm sure Dr. Saperstein wouldn't mind if you came inside where it's comfortable."

Vivian shook her head. "Pretty day, I might snoop around the canyon a bit. Besides, if I came inside, the doc might try to shrink my head too, kid. I'll be right here when you get back."

"Thank you, Viv. You are the one constant in my life." She leaned over and kissed Vivian on the cheek before opening the car door and walking toward the door marked OFFICE.

Vivian sat in the car with tears streaming down her cheeks. She wiped them with the back of her hand, hearing her mother's voice in the background. *A lady always carries a hanky.*

Was that going to be the extent of their relationship: a kiss on the cheek, and a hanky in my pocket? *Oh God, can't you see I want so much more?*

She focused on the canyon. *There's beauty even in these barren ravines. What forces of nature moved them, molded them, and carved them out over thousands or millions of years? Why does everything have to be so damn complicated?*

With a sigh, she opened the car door to stand by its side and fully take in the power of her surroundings. Not much to see from this vantage point. She looked at her watch. Three minutes had passed. *Shit, this is going to be one long hour.* Vivian yawned. *Time sure can move slowly.* She twiddled her thumbs, something her mother told her to do when she was bored.

"The hell with it," she mumbled.. "I'm heading out."

Walking to the edge of the property, she saw a path with a steep incline. She slung her backpack over her shoulders, made sure her keys were hanging from her pant loop, and followed the winding trail to a clearing.

Vivian stopped for a moment to catch her breath and observed a woman resting from her labors in the most beautiful vegetable and herb garden she had ever seen. So serene did she look, and so in harmony with the verdant place, that Vivian momentarily mistook her for an ultra-realistic garden statue. A pair of garden gloves, stiff with caked mud and long use, lay next to her, artistically mimicking the shape of her hands. An oversized panama hat shielded her face from the sun. Wisps of auburn hair fell from the hat onto her eyes. She brushed them away, looked up from where she squatted on her knees, and saw Vivian standing there.

Vivian said, "Hi, sorry to intrude on your little slice of paradise. My friend is seeing Dr. Saperstein, and I'm waiting for her. I took the path from the parking lot, and it led me here. I guess I couldn't resist."

The woman wiped her hands on her jeans and stood, wincing a little with the effort. "I should know better than to squat for so long at my age," she said, smiling and extending her hand. "Welcome. I'm Danni."

Vivian shook hands and introduced herself. "It's beautiful out here. Let me guess: You must be the gardener."

Danni chuckled. "Ah, what gave me away? And you must be a good friend to drive all the way out here and wait for your friend."

"She's having a rough time. I'm worried about her."

"Then you are a special friend, indeed."

"She's special."

Danni nodded, wiping her forehead with a calico kerchief. "The sun is brilliant today, and the crops abundant."

"Yeah. I don't think I've ever seen a garden this magical. I hope it's okay that I walked around. It got boring waiting in the car."

"I'm confident Dr. Saperstein wouldn't mind."

"I see this path becomes a fork. Is it okay if I keep exploring?"

"Why, yes." Her eyes, the color of a brilliant sapphire, bore into Vivian's. "You will have to decide which one you want to take. If you take this path"—she pointed to the right—"you'll find an easier route. It's been smoothed out, and there are few obstacles. But, it does dead-end in tangled chaparral. If you choose this one"—she pointed to the left—"it will take you to a waterfall."

"Wow, an honest to God waterfall?"

"Yes, I was amazed, myself, when I first saw it. You should know that there is more danger on that trail. It remains the way nature has intended it to be."

Vivian didn't hesitate. "I'll take the one to the waterfall. It's hard to think of one existing in this canyon."

"I thought you would pick that path; you seem like an adventurous young woman. It will be well worth it. I promise you that."

Danni fished among the garden tools leaning against a well-used wheelbarrow and handed Vivian a twisted walnut and mesquite walking stick. "You'll need this."

"Thank you. Will I see you when I return?"

"I'll be gone. You can leave the stick next to the wheelbarrow. I'll pick it up later."

With a wave and a thank you, Vivian began her trek to the waterfall.

∞

"Thank you for fitting me in, Dr. Saperstein."

Dr. Saperstein nodded.

"Vivian told me she filled you in. I'm very puffy; I've been crying since I read Papa's last letter." She began to sob. "I'm not theirs. And I was born in a prison camp. Place of birth: Dachau. I don't understand, because I saw my birth certificate when I went to get my driver's permit. Born in Los Angeles, California, to Abigail and Andrew Chambers.

"Dr. Saperstein, I think I may die from this. I don't know how things can become more fucked up than they are now."

Dr. Saperstein sat quietly.

"Viv stayed by my side; she sat in a chair next to my bed. She fed me broth. I felt like a baby being taken care of by its mommy."

"Vivian is a true friend," Dr. Saperstein remarked.

"The best."

"I had my nightmare again last night, but it was a little different. It started out the same, feeling squeezed, but then I began to hear different sounds. Loud sounds, but they didn't mean anything to me. It was as if I couldn't unscramble them. Then those strange sounds became louder and louder. Then, I heard a familiar sound, that I couldn't identify then, but I can now."

"What was that sound?"

"It was the sound of tears."

"It looks as if the dream is becoming more real than before."

"It is, but at the same time, I feel as if I'm falling apart. You know, like Humpty Dumpty. Please, Dr. Saperstein, help put me back together again."

Esther left her office the way it was. No organizing, no notes, no thinking, just feeling. She found Danni in the kitchen, humming and cleaning vegetables.

"Ah, I can see you were working in the garden."

"How could you tell?" Danni smiled.

"One, by the vegetables and herbs. Two, by the dirt under your fingers, and on your arms and clothes. You look like a naughty child let outside to play in the dirt. And three, your face is red from the sun. Did you forget your hat again? You know you shouldn't take too much sun."

"No, commandant, I wore my hat," Danni teased.

Esther held Danni's hands. "And your gloves?"

"Guilty as charged. What can I say, I like to feel the soil with my naked hands; it feels as if I am communing with Mother Nature." Danni noticed Esther's troubled look. "What is it, Essie?"

Esther shook her head and mouthed, "Nothing."

Danni pulled her close. "I know when you look that way and say, 'Nothing,' it's been a painful session. And I also know you can't talk about it."

"I'll be okay. I always am."

"I was planning on going to the university library tonight," said Danni. "Would you rather I stay home?"

"No need. I'm working for a couple of hours. The produce looks fantastic." Esther reached for a grape tomato. "Mmm, these are delicious. Danni, would you do something for me?"

"What's your pleasure, mademoiselle?" Danni said as she stroked Esther's hair.

"I need you to look something up at the library and copy a couple of articles for me."

She handed Danni a note card.

Danni stared at the card. "Are you serious?"

"Never been more serious in my life."

"Pre-birth memories? Essie, I thought you had given up on that notion."

"As a scientist, Danni, don't you believe in the adage, leave no stone unturned? It's not unusual for some unexplainable phenomenon to be proven by science, even hundreds of years after its original discovery."

"Or equally disproved. Essie, darling, I don't want to see you putting yourself through any more pain than necessary. I've seen you before, absorbing too much from your patients and paying the price for it."

"Please, Danni, it's important to me," Esther pleaded. "At least these three articles, and if there are any books on the subject, those too."

"I know when to let go of the rope." Danni wiped her hands on a dishtowel. "Now, would you like to help me get rid of this garden soil?"

"I do have three hours, but will that be enough, my love?"

"Barely," Danni replied. "Barely."

∞

Vivian was waiting by the car, gouging out the pebbles and mud from the treads of her hiking boots with a stick.

"What happened to you?" Marley asked.

"I explored a bit and slipped. No big deal."

"Don't tell me 'no big deal.' Your shirt is torn."

Vivian opened the car door for Marley.

"It's just a scrape, honest."

"What happened?"

"I can't talk about it now. Give me a few to wrap my brain around it. Later, okay?"

"Okay, but don't think you can wiggle out of this one."

Settling into the driver's side, Vivian asked, "How'd it go?"

"I feel better," Marley sighed. "Hey, where'd you get all the veggies?"

"I walked around a bit and met the gardener. Fascinating woman. There's a waterfall not too far from here. That's where I took my tumble. When I got back, there were bags of veggies and herbs. And get this, a recipe for using these veggies and a chart about the healing properties of herbs. Plus, a jar of balm. I think the gardener might be a witch; she must have known I would take a tumble."

"At least she's not a spy." There was a chipper note in Marley's voice.

"Well, you must be feeling better."

"A little. I hate it when you keep secrets from me."

"I'll be cooking tonight," Vivian said, ignoring her comment. She glanced at Marley. "Hey, that therapist performing voodoo on you?"

"Could be. I do seem to go into a trance. I'm going to see Dr. Saperstein tomorrow. Then I'll decide about reading my mother's letters or letting things go. So, tell me about the gardener."

"Her name is Danni. And she said something that got me thinking."

Marley looked at her quizzically. Do I get to know that part at least?"

"Oh, I'm pausing for dramatic effect. Let's say you have two paths to choose from. One is easy but leads to a dead end, and the other is filled with obstacles, but there's beauty at the end. Which one would you choose?"

"I'm hoping tomorrow will answer that for me."

CHAPTER 14

Marley was twenty minutes early for her appointment. She leaned her head against the car's headrest, hoping she would be invisible to passersby. Her head was swirling. It was no longer only about the bomb dropped by her parents; it was also about Viv. She was hiding something from her. She sensed it; she knew it. Was this her destiny, to have the people she loved hide the truth from her?

She closed her eyes and wondered which path she would have chosen. She dozed and woke to discover she was late for her appointment.

She dashed into the waiting room and pressed the call button.

The door opened. "Hi, Dr. Saperstein. I'm sorry I'm late. I fell asleep in the car."

Dr. Saperstein smiled benignly and ushered Marley into her office.

"I'm not sure of where to begin. I'm terribly worried about Viv. Something's not right. She seems withdrawn, and I think—no, I'm sure—she's keeping something from me. I've been selfish, only thinking about my problems."

Dr. Saperstein was a sphinx, silent and inscrutable. Marley went on.

"I had another dream—different, but also disturbing. I believe the dream got me to make a decision about reading Mommy's letters. Or should I call her Abigail?"

Dr. Saperstein remained quiet.

"I'm not sure what Viv could be hiding, but she seems pained and distant. I'm beginning to wonder if everyone sees me as being so fragile that they have to hide the truth."

Marley dabbed her eyes with a tissue. "Yesterday, when I got into the car with Viv, she told me she had walked around your property. That's no surprise, because I know how hard it is for her to sit still for an hour. She's an outdoorsy girl and loves to go exploring.

"Anyway, during that walk, she came to a fork in the trail. Your gardener was there, and she said something to Viv about choosing to take an easy path, or a more difficult one. Of course, Viv took the one that was challenging. And she fell. I could tell because her flannel shirt was torn. But, she sloughed it off. She said no journey is worth taking if it's without risk. I think she got that right out of the gardener's mouth."

Dr. Saperstein's only response was to uncross her legs.

"Last night I couldn't sleep, and I tossed and turned," Marley continued. "Finally, I fell into a deep sleep and had this dream. In the dream, I had gone with a group of people to an enormous lake. The kind you might see in Switzerland, like Lake Geneva. And everyone, except me, got into boats to get to the other side. It was raining hard, and the water was becoming rougher and rougher—heavy swells—and the boats were being tossed around. People were holding on to anything they could, but in spite of the choppy waters they cast off, but I remain standing on the shore. There was a small sailboat with room for one left at the dock. I'm not completely alone; someone is standing some distance away, close to a spruce windbreak. I knew it was a woman, but I couldn't tell whom.

"I'm terrified to get into the boat that can take me to the other side. And then, the fog begins to swirl up from the lake, surrounding me, and I've lost sight of the others. And that's the dream."

Dr. Saperstein said, "What about the other side?"

Marley turned a bright red. "Do I have to answer all your questions?"

"Of course not, but I should warn you, there is no such thing as an unanswered question, at least not in therapy."

"Touché. I wanted to be brave; I wanted to get into the boat and find my way to the other side. But the waves were high and pounded onto the shore. I was afraid to take a risk, to take the next big step."

Marley paused for a moment and said, "Dr. Saperstein, did you ever see the movie, *Portrait of Jennie*?"

"No, I don't believe I have."

"On Tuesdays, Mommy would pick Viv and me up from junior high and take us to The Art Theater—a retro cinema where they showed classic flicks. We'd get popcorn and Cokes and watch these old movies from the forties. Mommy said she missed a lot of them because of the war and the ones she did see, she wanted to see again. It felt very grown-up to us. Viv and I would share popcorn and a Coke, and sometimes we would hold hands when the characters would kiss.

"In this movie, Eben and Jennie—played by Joseph Cotten and Jennifer Jones—fall in love. But it's like a ghost love, because Jennie had died years before in a boating accident. At the end of the movie, Eben tries to cross the time barrier to save Jennie, but he can't change fate. I guess I'm thinking of that because Jennie was in a small sailboat and the sea is wild and crazy, and Eben can't hold onto her. She slips out of his grasp and drowns."

"And what about you?"

"Sometimes, I feel that I'm close to grasping something unknown. I'm so close, and yet it is out of my reach."

"You mentioned a woman in your dream."

"She's behind me but at a distance. She was supportive but not interfering. I was getting these vibes of encouragement. As if I could do it."

"Do you have any idea of who she was?"

Marley blushed. "I think it was you, Dr. Saperstein," she said shyly.

Dr. Saperstein nodded. "I think it's an important dream. What about your associations to *Portrait of Jennie*? Eben risks death to be with Jennie—any thoughts about that?"

"I don't think so."

"Your voice cracked."

"Wow, Dr. S., you don't miss a thing, do you? I think I was caught off balance by your question. I was thinking about the boat and the sea. And how Jennie and Eben were willing to risk everything to be together."

"What's on the other side, Marley?" Dr. Saperstein pushed.

Marley squirmed. "It's something that has to do with Viv and me."

"Did you feel I was putting you on the spot with my question?"

Marley's eyes widened. "Yes, I did. I know those feelings are there, but I'm not ready to face them, not yet. I am moving forward, Dr. Saperstein. I want to know all that there is know about who I am. I'm ready to read Mommy's letters. Perhaps there I will find some answers."

∞

Marley had never experienced a shift like that. It felt as if someone—or some deity—had reached inside and moved her heart. She wasn't sure how this was possible, but at the same time, she felt more open and available. She guessed that risks could come in many shapes and forms, including knowing Viv's secret or admitting her own longings.

She stopped at the market before going home. As she pushed the cart up one aisle and down another, she kept thinking about Viv and what she would enjoy.

She passed by the snack aisle; its siren song went unnoticed.

She pulled into the garage and entered the kitchen through the service porch. Vivian was sitting at the table, drinking coffee, and doing the *Los Angeles Times* crossword puzzle.

"Hi, Viv."

"Hey. Need some help?"

"No, I'm good. I stopped at the market to buy chicken and lean steaks. I thought we could whip up a stir-fry with all those veggies." She put the bags on the kitchen counter. "Your choice for dinner: chicken or steak."

"Whatever," Vivian said indifferently.

Marley moved a chair next to Vivian's. "Talk to me, please. I feel like I've lost you."

"Don't be so melodramatic, kid. I'm just trying to figure things out." Vivian cast her eyes downward. "Do you believe in miracles, Mar?"

"I don't know what I believe in anymore. Do you?"

Vivian shrugged. "I was raised to believe in miracles. You know, church every Sunday. And my Grandpa Liam in the pulpit, praising God one minute, and rattling off all the sins that'd send us straight to hell the next. Remember the Sunday school coloring books I had, with all those corny pictures of biblical miracles?"

"Do I ever! I was envious and couldn't understand why I couldn't go with you so we could color together." Marley smiled. "We were awfully innocent."

"I think we were both handed a crock. You know? Your folks telling you not to believe in anything, and mine tell me to follow a strict path to everlasting glory. Did you ever wonder how our moms stayed friends all those years?"

"Sure I did; they seemed so different, on the surface. I'm not sure we'll ever know. Do you think your mom might talk to you...us?"

"I wouldn't count on it. Something happened yesterday when I was walking down to the waterfall. I kept thinking about what the gardener told me about choosing two paths. I'm here to tell you the one I took was not easy."

"What was it like?"

"At first it wasn't too difficult. I was glad I had the stick Danni loaned me, though. It kinda broke my fall."

"You clammed up when I first asked you about it."

"Well, you know, my being the prince and all, I could hardly confess to being in pain. I stumbled on the path, hit some boulders with my arm, and thought I was about to die. But, when I finally stopped, I was lying on the softest ground. And the smell—damn, I'll never forget it. The way the earth must have been billions of years ago, when it first began to cool, and everything was fresh and clean. It had a primordial feel, as if life began there."

"Maybe you can take me there some day."

"I'd like to, but it was as if I got transported to another place and time. I almost doubt if I could find it again. The waterfall was completely out of place in that desolate setting, and yet it seemed to belong—you know, as a reminder that all life on earth began in water."

"Better not let your mom hear you say that," Marley joked.

"Damn straight. Anyway, I sat there for a while, and I felt a kind of peace falling over me. And I thought about what you're going through, and the way I'm feeling about my mom and dad."

A reflective silence fell over the two women, broken at last by Vivian's tentative voice.

"Mar, I have a secret, and I'm afraid if I tell you, you won't want to be my friend. And if I tell my parents, they'll only see me as a sinner."

"Please trust me, Viv. You've been taking care of me—now let me take care of you. Nothing you could tell me would change the way I feel about you."

"I'm not ready yet." Vivian smiled. "But, I feel better just being able to tell you that I'm struggling with something. Maybe after you've read Mommy's letters. You are going to read them, aren't you?

"Yes."

"Promise you won't push me?"

"I swear."

"Pinky swear?"

"Of course."

They hooked their fingers and repeated in unison:

Pinky, pinky bow-bell,
Whoever tells a lie
Will sink down to the bad place
And never rise up again.

"Okay, let's do it," said Marley. "The sooner we get to them, the better. Maybe we can move forward together."

∞

Twilight had fallen when they took the steps to the cellar. The naked bulbs over the staircase and in the basement proper were outmatched by the growing darkness. Like the true Nancy Drew devotees they were, Viv and Marley had each brought their trusty flashlights.

Marley took off the first sheet to find a tobacco-brown cardboard suitcase, with leather fittings and a brass latch.

Vivian said, "This is like staring at a time capsule. Look how scuffed it is. Ahh, if this suitcase could only talk."

"I'm hoping it will," said Marley, a small smile flitting across her face. "I want to bring it upstairs, to Mommy's room...the way we did with Papa's bag."

"I like that idea."

"The room meant so much to her. I have so many warm memories of being with her."

Vivian said, "Tell you what, you make some iced coffee, the way Mommy made it, and I'll dust off the case and bring it upstairs."

"No peeking?"

"I promise, no peeking."

∞

"I think this was a good idea," said Marley, holding a tray with two glasses of iced coffee.

"It seems fitting to be in her room instead of that depressing cellar. Mommy once told me that she never thought she would live in such a fancy house. She was grateful for everything she had."

Marley sat the tray down on the coffee table. "Mommy had her way of making iced coffee. Saving the leftover coffee in the fridge, adding half-and-half until it swirled to the top, then adding two heaping teaspoons of sugar and crushed ice."

She held up a handful of plastic novelty straws bent into fantastic shapes. "Look what I found in the cupboard! Remember when Mommy bought us these Krazy Straws in rainbow colors?"

"I haven't seen these for years," said Viv. "Your mommy was always doing things like that, and she never left me out."

"I know. I've been an ungrateful—"

"Asshole?"

"Thanks. I was thinking more of a brat."

Vivian smiled before taking a slurp of coffee that made its way through the twists and turns of the straw. "Damn, this is good. I may ask for a second, even if it means I'll be up all night peeing."

They lay the case on the coffee table flanked on either side with captain's chairs.

"Our moms loved finding old furniture. They found this on the curb and practically yanked it out of the garbage collector's hands," Marley said, rubbing her hand over the flawless finish.

"Yeah, that was one thing our moms shared," Vivian agreed. "Remember what they would say? "One woman's trash in another woman's treasure."

Marley said, "I thought it was a man's trash?"

"You forget I'm a feminist."

Marley rolled her eyes. "Anyway, they sure were serious about restoring stuff and making it look better than new. I remember them working away in the garage, stripping off the old finish, all the time talking about the latest recipes."

"Remember that time Mommy yelled at you?"

"How could I forget?" Marley mimicked her mother: "'Marley Rose, get your little keister out of here *right now*!' Wow, could she shout! I know now she was afraid of me being exposed to the fumes because of my asthma."

Vivian rubbed her hand over the solid maple and birch wood table, which had a storage area underneath two hinged lids. "I was always fascinated with this table," she said, opening one of the hinged lids. "Wow, lookie here, some of your school paintings from first and second grade. How did we miss this? I'm beginning to wonder about our sleuthing skills."

They sat down on the captain's chairs and began to go through childish drawings.

"Happy faces," said Vivian of the stick figure family with wide grins.

"Starry, starry night," said Marley of the three stick figures lying on their backs gazing at the star-filled sky. "This is the camping trip we took to the desert."

"What's this one?" Vivian asked. "It's foreboding, not cheerful like the others. It looks like monsters."

Marley paled. Her hand began to shake. "It's my nightmare—not the way I see it, but the way I feel it." She began to shake. "Viv, I can't let this inside me. Tear it up, please!"

"Can't." Vivian placed her hand on Marley's chin and lifted her face. "Don't you see, Mar? This is critical, and Dr. Saperstein needs to see it. Trust me on this one. I'll put it back, and when you're ready, take it to Dr. S. Okay?"

"Okay," she whispered. "Can we please get to Mommy's letters?"

"Of course," Vivian nodded, moving the straw to the bottom of the glass and sucking up the drops of sugar that had settled to the bottom.

"No more slurping."

"Fini!" Vivian declared. A most unladylike burp sneaked out of her throat. "Excuse me!"

"Gross!" said Marley.

She opened the suitcase. Everything inside the case was carefully wrapped in tissue paper with Post-it notes for easy identification. A pile of numbered letters lay on top.

"This is so Mommy," Marley sighed appreciatively. "Everything in apple pie order."

She picked up the first letter. "Here goes," she said, running her finger carefully under the envelope's seal.

∞

Dear Marley,

I have so much to say, and yet I am at a loss for words.

Where do I begin? How do I put a lifetime onto a few sheets of paper?

You must be feeling betrayed; I would be surprised if you didn't.

You have been given the facts by Papa: the place of your birth, and that Papa and I are not your biological parents.

My dearest Buttercup, that is only the beginning of our story. I say ours because if you are to ever understand and forgive, you must know how this all came to be. And to do so, I must take you back in time.

As I begin to write, I am flooded with thoughts, feelings, and images. So much so that pain and joy seem intertwined.

After I had my first stroke, something changed within me. It was as if another dimension had opened, and I began to have visions. At first, the doctors told me this was not uncommon. I think they forgot I was a nurse and had worked with many stroke patients. I knew these were different; instead of lessening, they grew in intensity. I let the doctors believe they had faded away. I didn't want any more tests or medication, and I sensed they had a purpose. I think of them now as a gift.

They began with small flashes of people I had known, things I had seen, very much like still photos. They changed to film clips, similar to a black and white silent film. Eventually, they came in color, complete with dialogue. Some of the images were touching reminders of a time long ago when the corn grew high on our family farm, and laughter and love rang out throughout our home. In the movies of my mind, I am seeing you for the very first time, minutes after you are born. To see new life surrounded by death filled my heart and soul with hope. Then there was that first moment when you were in my arms, and I felt a passion washing over me, to protect and love you with every fiber of my body and soul.

The film fast-forwards, and I see you trying to make your first smile. Your lower lip quivers, followed by the widest and happiest grin I had ever seen.

Soon you are taking your first steps, falling with such a look of surprise that your Papa and I had to laugh. You struggled, got up, fell again, but kept going.

Later, I was forced to relive that night when your nightmares started. At that time, something was telling me that your nightmares were beyond human comprehension, yet out of my own fears, I put those thoughts away.

More recently, as I was dozing off, I saw an older you, perhaps in your thirties, swathed in a veil of sadness. I came out of that trance with a gasp, and I knew I had been given this extra time on earth to right a wrong, and my final task in this world would be to bring the truth to you.

Do you remember when you wanted to peek at the end of a storybook? You told me it helped the butterflies in your tummy, but I explained that by doing so, you might miss the story's purpose.

I pray you are not alone while you are reading these letters. It helps to have someone to lean on during difficult times. Might you be with John, or perhaps Vivian?

I had your Papa, and although we did disagree on many things, we always seemed to find a way through—a compromise.

Are you willing to set aside all judgments until you have read, and, I pray, understand the whole story?

Love,

Mommy

∞

"I wish I could tell her I'm moving forward," Marley said. "It may seem at a snail's pace, but I am moving." She looked up at Vivian with pleading eyes.

"Maybe she knows."

"Do you think it's possible, Viv?"

"Yeah, I do. If you had asked me that question a couple of days ago, I would have made fun of it. But after going to the waterfall... For what it's worth, I feel like I'm watching you blossom."

"Thanks, Viv. I'd like to keep going. I needed time in between Papa's letters. But, I feel Mommy has some urgent things to tell me; things I really need to hear. And that vision of hers, seeing me sad at thirty. I want to shake this dark cloud away. I want to find where I belong."

Vivian quipped, "This is sort of like *Let's Make a Deal*. Let's see what Carol Merrill has behind door number two!"

"Jeez, Viv. You are such a goofball."

"It's so I won't cry. Don't you know that by now?"

"You can trust me with your feelings. Honest." Marley crossed her heart.

Vivian smiled wryly. *Can I, Mar?* She stood up, pointing her hand northwards. "Therefore, I command thee: Onward and upward! To Narnia and the North!"

C.S. Lewis would have loved you." Marley picked up the second letter and began to read.

∞

Dear Marley,

It is a rainy day, and I'm sitting in the living room watching the rain slide down the picture window. I'm not working as much as before. Papa and the doctors insisted on half-shifts. Perhaps they're right, I do tire easily, and it does give me more time to think.

Do you remember when you wanted me to tell you a story about when I was little and lived on a farm? The stories I told you were a version fit for a child who was already plagued by nightmarish sleep.

Yes, we sat at the table for breakfast, but not the breakfast I described to you. Those were memories from the before time, long before the War, and before the dust came and took over our land and lives.

Many of my most powerful memories are not of abundance, but of scarcity. The rain had stopped, and like a plague, the winds and dust swooped in. Dust so powdery that it stole its way into our house through every crevice. And bleakness settled over our lives.

When I went outside to do my chores, I had to cover my mouth and nose with a mask made from old sheets. In spite of that protection, the dust managed to find its way inside.

The outside of the house, that had always been kept freshly painted, looked badly weathered now. Bossie, our old milk cow, all but went dry. She barely produced enough milk for our own use, with nothing left over to sell.

At the time of the great dust storms, I was still a young girl, no different than the other girls in my class, wearing threadbare dresses either too large or too small and a single pair of shoes with holes in their soles. But, the holes in those soles did not make holes in our souls. On Sundays, we sang our hearts out at church, with eyes lifted towards heaven. How I looked forward to church services! I would sing along with the choir, and raising my voice upward to God brought my only solace.

The world seemed at a standstill. When would the weather change? Would it ever change? It wasn't easy to hold onto hope, but I did cling to a dream that rested deep in my heart.

One of the classes the girls took in school was called home nursing. It was assumed that we would marry and, in that role, care for a husband and children. There was a bed in the classroom, and we learned to make it with crisp hospital corners. We also learned how to take temperatures and dress minor wounds. I was intrigued by the thought of taking care of others, and I desperately wanted to be a nurse. I knew my brothers, Phillip and Daniel, would remain farmers; you could see their eyes light up when they talked about the crops they planned to grow when, one blessed day, the dust blew away for good, the rain returned, and the farm would flourish again.

I think my desire to be a nurse came from my grandma, who knew how to heal by concocting home remedies from nature's bounty. But, becoming a nurse would mean I would have to continue beyond the eighth grade, graduate from high school, and then attend three years of nursing school.

I became depressed. Where would I get the money for school? How could I leave my family with my chores?

I was horribly sad; my heart was broken, and any little thing would set me to tears.

My mother began to worry about my health. I stopped eating; I'd just twirl my food around and around on my plate.

My brother Daniel said, "Abigail must be pining." The boys loved to tease me, and they began to chant, "Abbey's got a boyfriend."

"Nonsense!" my mother shushed them. "Nothing that a dose of blackstrap molasses won't cure."

I was in the eighth grade, and come June I would graduate and begin working on the farm in earnest. My bedroom was in the attic. It wasn't a frilly girl's room with pretty wallpaper and cozy furniture. No, it was sparse as a cave, and hot in the summer and freezing in the winter. But it was my own private place where I could safely cry my heart out.

It was the night before graduation. I lay sobbing on my bed. My future looked bleak; I felt as if my world was about to end. I didn't hear the stairs creaking or the door opening. I could tell who it was even though I was facing the wall. You see, my father had the smell of a farmer—hay and oats and corn mingled with sweat. It may sound horrible to you, Marley, but to me, it defined him. A wholesome, earthy smell that lingers pleasantly in my nostrils even as I write.

He sat on the edge of the bed and, in that smooth baritone voice I remember so well, confided to me, "When I was your age, I wanted to be a musician."

I stopped crying. My father, who rarely spoke except to talk about the weather and crops, was sharing his boyhood longings with me.

"I had a dream, to follow the road wherever it might take me, and earn a few bucks playing the guitar in honky-tonks and saloons." He chuckled. "I knew it was just a dream. I never got past sixth grade—been a full-time farmer ever since."

I didn't move for fear he would stop speaking.

"Your mother and I have been downright concerned about you—the not eatin', all that cryin'. I told your ma, blackstrap molasses ain't goin' to fix this 'un. Went into town the other day and stopped by to see your teacher, Mrs. Powell. Fine lady. Said you're the best student she has, smarter than any of the boys. She thinks you could be a nurse like you want."

I turned over to face him. "But Daddy, the farm, the money."

He put his hand on my head; it was so big, it felt like I was wearing a hat. "You get the grades; that's all I ask. Mrs. Powell said if you get the grades, and she writes a letter, you could get a scholarship to nursing school. It means going off to the hospital in Des Moines, but you'll get room and board and an education. Three years. You'll need train money and uniform money. You let me worry about that.

"Come September you're going to start high school—the first in this family. Make us proud, daughter."

I leaned against him, and I thought I would hold onto him forever, and I have.

I threw myself into my schoolwork and completed high school at the age of 16. Mrs. Powell, may her soul rest in Heaven, fought to get me into nursing school at that tender age. She feared, and I believe she was right, that if I waited, I would follow the path of the rest of the girls—marry early, and become tied down to the farm.

I was turning seventeen when I entered Des Moines Hospital Nursing School, carrying all my possessions in the cardboard suitcase you see before you.

Revisiting these memories has taken a toll on me. It seems I need to sleep more often, and I do believe that I will be called back to the Lord sooner than later.

I think I'll stretch out on the couch and cover myself with the afghan my mother made while I was overseas. I can listen to the rain as I wrap myself not only with the afghan, but also with the memories of my life.

Love,
Mommy

∞

Vivian rubbed her hand over the surface of the cardboard suitcase. "I'm thinking of how your Mommy went off to nursing school with this very suitcase. She was a kid, barely seventeen. I think she must have been extraordinarily brave, and then to join the Army—your mom had guts. Did she ever talk about what she saw?"

"No. What gets me is how devout Mommy was when she was young, and then later she renounced God."

"Maybe she'll explain it."

"For God's sake, what else could they possibly throw at me?" Marley wondered as she picked up the next letter and began to read.

Dear Marley,

Where are you now? I mean in life?

I don't suppose I will ever know if you found these letters. My, but your father could be a stubborn man about leaving them hidden in that secret compartment of his. I have to laugh a bit, wondering if you'd find them, or would someone hundreds of years from now discover the secrets of a man and a woman whose bones, like the farmland of my youth, had long since turned to dust.

It was September 1938, and I would be taking the train to Des Moines to attend nursing school. It was still dark when I awoke. I lay in bed surrounded by familiar sounds and smells. I could hear my mother bustling in the kitchen, while the fragrance of chicken frying and peanut butter cookies baking in the oven drifted up to the attic. That day Mommy had made a double batch as a kind of going away present, and as soon as the rooster crowed, I heard my brothers tearing down the stairs, fighting and grabbing cookies off the hot sheet. I knew Mommy would be slapping their hands with a spatula but laughing all the while.

I wish you could have known my family. We didn't have a lot of material things, but our love warms my heart to this day.

We got through that morning and off we went to the train station. I was wearing the new dress Mommy had sewed for me. We must have had five fittings, because I kept losing weight from excitement. Finally, Mommy said, "If I have to take this in one more time, you're not going." Well, that was enough to get me eating again. We got to the station, and for once my rambunctious brothers were serious; they hugged me and wished me good luck. Mommy told me how proud she was, and her final words to me were: "Don't forget to eat."

Daddy held me close and said, "My dream goes with you."

I got on the train juggling my suitcase, plus the fried chicken and other goodies Mommy had packed into a picnic basket. I kept blowing kisses until everyone got smaller and smaller and finally disappeared from view.

I shared my feast with the other passengers, and by the time the train pulled into the Des Moines station, there was nothing left but a few crumbs and a lot of full tummies.

Nurse Potts met me at the train station. She looked me up and down and made me show her my hands, right then and there. She scowled, and I blushed because I knew my hands were still slightly greasy from the fried chicken.

She informed me in a clipped tone of voice: "Lesson one: a nurse always has short nails and clean hands."

I vowed never to have dirty hands again. It was a promise I tried to keep, but as I was to discover, later on, the war did not always allow it.

With my first lesson under my belt, we took the trolley to the hospital.

I was the youngest girl at school and earned the nickname of Baby. But, I kept up and then some. I was used to hard work and dirty work, and at the beginning that was all we did!

We had classes five mornings a week, followed by a quick lunch and a stint in the wards in late afternoon. I asked for extra shifts on the weekends; there was a nursing shortage, and they were glad to have me. I wanted to learn as much as possible, plus we got paid a stipend that I saved for the time when I would return home. Sunday, we spent washing our clothes, going to church, and once in a while we would sneak out for a movie. My favorite actor and actress were Fred Astaire and Ginger Rogers. If I wasn't going to be a nurse, I wished I could be a dancer!

It was 1941, and while my parents couldn't afford to come to my graduation, it was, up to that point, my greatest achievement.

Look inside my suitcase, and you will see a photo of our graduating class in our nursing uniforms. I kept the cap, out of style now, but how proud I was to have earned it.

I was thrilled to be returning home. This time when I got on the train, I was loaded down not with food, but with gifts. And along with the gifts, I had a secret to share, but not until after Christmas.

My career as a nurse would not begin in a civilian hospital but as an Army nurse. You see, I longed for more education, and the Army offered me the rank of Second Lieutenant, along with the opportunity to train as a nurse anesthesiologist. We all knew that war might be around the corner, and I thought it would be best to wait until after Christmas to tell my family I'd enlisted. I kept thinking this should be a holiday to remember. It was, but not in the way I had expected.

Everyone met me at the train station, and what a reunion that was! Mommy and Daddy looked a little bit older. Phillip and Daniel had filled out but were as silly as ever. They took turns twirling me around and whistling at the way I had changed. They told me I had filled out, too! I remember they called me a sweater girl, and that I could give Lana Turner a run for her money. They were just flattering me, as brothers will do, but I appreciated the compliment just the same.

Once again, I was a farm girl with chores to do. Milking cows is a bit like riding a bike: You never forget how. And that skill came in handy after you were born, but more about that a bit later.

After years of being plagued by drought, the rains had returned, and the farm was alive once again. I settled back into the routine and, although life as a farm girl agreed with me, I hankered to resume my nursing career. Amidst the chores and the anticipation of the holidays, there came a fateful day that caused the entire world to turn topsy-turvy. Sunday, December 7, 1941, to be exact, and you know what that day means.

We had returned from church, and I was helping mother with our early Sunday dinner. Ham had been slow-cooking in an earthenware crock since morning, and mother had made her famous potato salad and Parker House rolls, two recipes passed down by her mother. If you look through the suitcase, you'll find her cookbook. It's faded and raggedy, and her dishes wouldn't be considered healthy by today's standards, but it was good, wholesome food that would stick to your ribs, as Daddy liked to say. There wasn't much in the way of fresh vegetables, it being wintertime, but Mommy raided her vast store of canned fruits and vegetables in the cellar. And let me tell you, Marley, my brothers could sure eat! I have to laugh; I was no slouch in that department myself!

After we'd scraped out plates clean, we sat back and rubbed our stomachs—that was our countrified way of telling Mommy, "Quite a feast." By then, it was past two in the afternoon. Daddy turned on the radio to listen to the Washington Redskins and Philadelphia Eagles football game. Mommy and I were cleaning up when we heard Daddy and the boys shouting from the living room to come quickly, that something terrible had happened. We joined them around the radio and listened to the announcement: "We interrupt this program to bring you a special news bulletin. The Japanese have attacked Pearl Harbor, Hawaii, by air, President Roosevelt has just announced."

We all knew what that meant. I also knew from the look on my brothers' faces that, come hell or high water, they would be enlisting.

My mother grabbed her apron and put it to her face to hide her tears. Her tears changed to sobs when I announced that I had joined the Army. My father put his arms around my mother and me, but the boys joked around, saluting and saying, "Yes ma'am, General!"

I tried to call to see if my orders had been changed, but all the phone lines were tied up, and all I could do was wait. A week later, I received a telegram to report to Walter Reed for training as a nurse anesthesiologist.

We had an early Christmas, and I'm glad we did. It would be the last Christmas we would celebrate as a family.

Once again I packed my suitcase and left toward the unknown.

I had no idea of how my world was about to change. When I got to Walter Reed, I was immediately swept up into intense training as an anesthesiologist. Sometimes, at night, I would think about how my life had changed. I had no idea of what the future might hold, but I was determined to be the best that I could be.

There was a shortage of nurses, but when the call went out, they appeared in droves from all over the country. Some were innocent farm girls like myself that had just fallen off the turnip truck, as the saying goes, and some were gum-snapping city girls, streetwise and full of sass. Together, we learned how to use a gas mask, how to march, and how to salute. More than that, we learned how to work together and accept each other's differences, and in doing so we became sisters linked by a common goal.

It was at Walter Reed that I met Captain Curtis Balfour; you know him as Uncle Curtis. He didn't seem to have the same biases as so many of the other doctors who saw nurses as only being capable of performing the three Bs: bed pans, bathing, and bandaging.

Under Curtis's mentorship, we nurses grew and thrived. I had no idea that he would continue to play a pivotal role in my life after the war.

I have opened the chambers of memories, but now, I grow weary and must lay my pen down.

Love,

Mommy

∞

Marley said, "She was my mommy, wasn't she? But... but..."

"You're thinking about the nature versus nurture conundrum, aren't you?"

She nodded.

"No doubt, you got genetics from your biological mom," said Viv. "And don't forget, she kept you alive so you could be born. And think of what all the other prisoners did—giving up their food so you could thrive. But in my opinion, you won the grand prize with Mommy. Don't discount what she gave you—and what she's *still* trying to give you."

"You're right, Viv. I'm feeling ashamed right now."

"Look, you're confused, and who wouldn't be? I really want to hear more about your Mommy's story."

"I want to look for her cap and the cookbook."

"Maybe we can try a couple of recipes. Those peanut butter cookies sound yummy."

"Viv, how the hell do you do it? You're like an eating machine, but you never gain an ounce."

"Gee, Mar, you've got me blushing. But don't worry, my metabolism will betray me eventually. You haven't seen my mom recently. She's put on thirty pounds."

"Well, that's hopeful. How many years do I have to wait?"

"At the rate I've been shovelin' it in," Viv frowned, "I might balloon up by morning."

"I'd like to read one more letter, then break—dare I say it—for a quick bite."

Viv nodded, looked down, and said shyly, "I am a bit peckish."

Marley waded up a napkin and threw it, hitting Vivian right in her mouth.

"Next time throw a Snickers bar, wouldja?" Vivian said with a wink. "Now, get on with the next letter."

Marley obliged, and read aloud:

Dear Marley,

　　We nurses were eager to get overseas and put our newly acquired skills to use. But I discovered the military has a frustrating hurry up and wait policy, and we were not shipped out right away. We were kept busy taking care of military families, getting soldiers cleared to go overseas, and treating the more severely wounded casualties from Pearl Harbor. Most of the nurses and, yes, even the doctors, had trained in city hospitals, and were ill prepared to face the horrific war injuries that made one want to run screaming from the ward. This, then, became my baptism of fire. There were times when I doubted my ability, but the bravery of our wounded men and women set me straight. I wonder if they knew how much they gave us?

Here's something I bet you never knew about your Uncle Curtis. He came from a family with seven children, and he was the only boy. I do have to smile. What a benefit that was to the nurses.

One day, very early in our training, Curtis was lecturing the entire staff on what we might expect once in the field. He was using a slide projector when suddenly, the photos changed to pictures of his family. Our mouths dropped open.

He faced the group of doctors, all male, of course, who were huddled together. I'll never forget what he said. "If I ever hear one of you referring to one of the nurses as 'only a woman,' you'll catch hell from six angry women and their brother: me!"

Curtis showed us photos of each of his sisters. I don't recall all their names, but I do remember one was an engineer, several were wives and mothers, another one was an attorney who had argued in front of the Supreme Court, and the youngest sat in a wheelchair. I remember how Curtis's voice cracked with emotion when he spoke about Lilly. He told us that she was the bravest of all. "Think of her as the men and women you will treat, not cleaned up as you see at Reed, but fresh from the battlefield and in pain, frightened, and broken."

He pointed once again to Lilly. "Lilly wanted to be a dancer before she contracted polio. I remember her making pirouettes throughout the house. She was the happiest of us all. She had to put aside her dream and discover another one."

He changed the slide to an amazing painting of a flower. "Lilly did this. While she was in the hospital she became severely depressed. One of the nurses gave her a set of art pencils and a pad of paper. At first Lilly wouldn't touch them. Finally she picked them up, began to doodle, and realized she had real talent. Lilly went on to get a Masters Degree in Art and another in Education. She teaches handicapped children to be happy, useful, and self-fulfilled, despite their limitations.

"Even against overwhelming odds, the human spirit does not have to die. In the chaos and hell of war, when seconds count, a few words of comfort can make the difference between life and death. Let this practice become as automatic as inserting an IV or prepping a patient for surgery."

Curtis set the spirit for our group. We learned, we became a team, and I do believe he changed some of the other doctors' opinions. They treated us nurses with respect and spared us their risqué comments and wolf whistles.

Our training continued while we waited for an overseas assignment. As hard as we trained, however, nothing could prepare us for our experiences in France and Germany. More on that later.

I wrote and called home as often as I could. Oh, I forgot to tell you that Daniel had joined the Navy and Phillip joined the Marines early in 1942. I joked with Mommy and told her she should have had one more child who could have enlisted in the Air Force. Daddy expressed concern that his little girl would be placed in harm's way, but I know he was proud of me. Both he and Mommy had resigned themselves to the fact that, in the words of that old song, they couldn't keep their adventurous daughter down on the farm.

The push continued for more nurses to enlist. Did you know the government once entertained the idea of a draft for nurses? But it wasn't necessary, not at all. They came in droves, most of them barely out of school. Our task turned to training our replacements. It was important, yet we were itching to get to the war. "Is this what we signed up for?" we groused.

The newer nurses took over our assignments at Walter Reed,

and one day we were loaded onto a truck with all our belongings and taken to a base for two weeks of field training.

We were issued uniforms with pants, helmets, and packs. We marched along steep, rocky roads carrying full packs, scrambled over fallen trees, and even practiced climbing down rope netting.

We knew we would be shipping out, but all Curtis would tell us was that something was in the wind. At night as we lay in our bunks, we played guessing games about our destination until we fell asleep.

One afternoon, Curtis made the big announcement. We would be moving out the next day at 0700. Well, you can imagine the buzzing that went on. We were driven to the PX to get essentials. Would it be hot or cold? Rainy or dry? We all bought makeup. It wouldn't be long before I was wishing I had taken less lipstick and more chocolate bars. How innocent we were.

Well trained and eager to put our skills to work on the front, we stood at attention on a drizzly morning. We were a solemn group getting ready to face the moment of truth.

A bus pulled up and took us to Bolling Air Force Base where we marched rather smartly, I thought, onto a plane. Once seated, Curtis told us we would be landing in England to complete our training in a field hospital. We knew what that meant, and we all applauded. Not only because we would be going to where our hearts lay, but also because Curtis had been promoted to major, and would be heading up the field hospital. After our training in England, we were shipped to France.

We followed the battles, and sometimes we could hear gunfire right in our backyard. The days, weeks, and months seemed to blur together. First France, then Germany.

I never forgot what Curtis had told us about Lilly, and I never failed to utter a few words or a prayer as I readied someone for surgery or held their hand as they took their last breath. Sometimes, they died alone, but I always took a moment to offer a prayer.

How I came to hate war! My faith began to waver. How

could God allow this to happen? Treating horribly wounded soldiers was painful enough, but then there were the burned and mutilated children. Many died in my arms, crying for their parents. I've often wondered what became of those poor children whose lives I played a role in saving, those orphans of war who were its greatest casualty.

We also treated the enemy. That could be a challenge. Yet, I thought, how could I hate a young man just because he wore a German uniform? How could I tell if he was a bloodthirsty Nazi who believed Hitler's demented philosophy, or a draftee—just another cog in the Nazi machine, and likely anxious that the war should end, whatever the outcome. All I knew was that he was someone's child and in that respect my conscience is clear.

One of the prisoners of war taught me a few words in German: "Rest easy. We will care for you." They came in handy, more times than I can remember.

Now, Marley, I want to tell you about a significant chapter in my Army career that will be of special interest to you.

It began on April 28, 1945. Our field unit was now in Germany and very close to the front line. We had spent some frightening days and nights with shells falling much too close for comfort. But now, there was a lull. Looking back, it was the quiet before a different type of storm.

The fighting had scaled down; the Nazis were on the run. We were beyond being grimy and were taking turns trying to get clean under a makeshift shower. The shower itself was quite a clever project put together by some of our "boys." They rigged up 5-gallon cans of water and even put up enclosures made from old drapes discovered in an abandoned house. The nurses had heated water on a wood stove, and although it was tepid by the time we showered, it felt luxurious. Each can had to last for five of us, so our allotment of one gallon was frugally used, but felt quite luxurious. You can't believe how great a small of water could feel! I had finished showering and changing. My hair was not braided and hung down my back in wet strands.

Curtis stood at a tactful distance away, giving us the privacy we needed. He motioned to me. I must confess I was hoping it wasn't anything urgent. It had been weeks since any of us had had an uninterrupted night's sleep, and sleep was at the top of my list—right after a shower.

Curtis looked as if he had aged twenty years. His complexion had changed from ruddy to pasty, and I had to wonder, what now?

He looked down at the ground, scuffing at it with the toe of his boot. "Colonel Denning wants to meet with us. Umm... Abigail, your hair, would you mind? He's a bit of a stickler."

"Give me five."

You used to like the way I could braid my hair and whisk it into a French knot. I learned to do that in the Army.

Colonel Denning might have been a stickler, but on this night he looked like a man frustrated and sickened by the hell of war. He waved us over to two chairs.

"Please sit. Abigail, Curtis... He cleared his throat. "This conversation is off the record. I've been informed that the rumors we've been hearing are no longer rumors."

There's a saying that the Army travels on its stomach, but I would add, it also travels on rumors.

"Rumors, sir?" asked Curtis

"Tomorrow at dawn we will be entering Dachau Concentration Camp. Once you have secured the area, the Red Cross will follow to assist."

"It's true then, sir?" I asked.

He nodded. "What you will see will be embedded forever in your memories. Minesweepers will start clearing the roads at first light. Be ready to roll by 0900."

"Yes, sir," said Curtis. There was little else that could be said.

Curtis and I stood up, saluted, and left.

The sleep that I had prayed for eluded me. We had heard about work camps, disease, and mass movements from ghettos to concentration camps. We had even heard about gas chambers, but

I'm not sure any of us wanted to believe that humans could be that evil. I felt my faith crumbling.

We were up before dawn and the trucks were loaded with medical supplies, food, and water. The sound of land mines exploding surrounded us. We were a somber group. Curtis and I and the two interpreters were in the lead jeep; three trucks followed, two carrying supplies and the other the finest medical team available. For once, the GIs in the trucks didn't feel like trading wisecracks.

We left promptly at 0900.

When we entered Dachau, we were mobbed by what I thought, at first, were macabre skeletons. The unspeakable horrors we witnessed in those first hours do not bear repeating in this letter, even if I had the words to do them justice.

Curtis and I did a quick assessment. Where to begin? The emaciated prisoners crowded around the supply trucks, reaching and begging for food. We knew that food had to be carefully rationed out, but can you imagine how difficult it was, trying to tell people who have been starved that we must gradually get them accustomed to eating again? It might have been the biggest challenge of my nursing career.

Curtis and I agreed that we had to focus on staving off any more disease. His first order was to assign a burial detail.

Thank God for the Red Cross. They came through with more supplies, and volunteers. We couldn't have done it without them.

Curtis asked, with the help of an interpreter, if there was a medical clinic.

I heard a strange rasping sound, and turned to see the source. One of the prisoners was laughing, or attempting to. His head was a skull in which two tiny flames burned in the hollow eye sockets, and the mandible moved chillingly up and down exactly the same as a parody of a skeleton I'd once seen in a cartoon. He apparently found it amusing that we should be inquiring about an infirmary in this chamber of horrors. I found out later, to my astonishment, that he was only twenty-one years old. He pointed to a hut with a sign: Krankenstation. He managed to say, "Fleckfieber." I didn't need a translation. Typhus: It was one of the German words I knew. Dachau, like the other concentration camps, was overrun with the disease, and the infirmary was overloaded with patients in its death grip.

The infirmary door was ajar and when Curtis opened it, I saw the most unbelievable sight. Within this room of the dead and dying was a man in appearance much like the other prisoners, but holding a new life. That person would become your Papa. He was holding you, rocking back and forth and humming a lullaby. You were still covered in amniotic fluid and blood. I walked over, amazed that you appeared healthy in every way.

I had a clean shirt in my pack. I took it out and motioned to this man, whose name was unknown to me, to hand me the baby. At first, he held you closer as if he was afraid to let you go. I called upon the few words I knew in German and along with a lot of gesturing, managed to say, "I promise to give her back."

"English," he said. "I can speak English and I have a name; Abraham." He held out his arm and made a feeble but clearly contemptuous gesture at the tattoo there. "I am more than a number! I am a doctor!"

Curtis whispered to me, "There are officer quarters close by. We can go there."

I spoke to your Papa. "Abraham, can you walk?"

As hard as he tried, your Papa could not stand, let alone walk the short distance. He shook his head. "I can't leave my patients."

"Abraham, I'll be here," Curtis said. "I'll bring in nurses, and we'll do our best for your patients."

And with that Papa collapsed, sobbing.

I covered you with the shirt and held you so that you would not be noticed. There was so much chaos; we would be another anonymous group struggling through the fires of hell.

Curtis said, "Abigail, I'm assigning you to these two."

I started to argue with Curtis that I would be needed in the camp.

He leaned over and said, in a voice quiet but firm: "I need you to stay with them. The Red Cross is here in full force, and between them and our staff, I think we can spare you."

Those words were poetry to me, and I almost cried with gratitude, for by holding you in my arms, I had already fallen deeply in love.

Curtis left the infirmary and brought two soldiers and a stretcher, and we were escorted to a nice, well-appointed apartment, one formerly occupied by a camp officer. I could not help thinking of the swine enjoying this relative luxury while, mere yards away, innocent Jews by the thousands had been housed in squalid conditions and subjected to unspeakable barbarism. The teachings of my Christian upbringing had taken a beating, as I've said, and I hoped that the officer who had enjoyed these cozy surroundings would suffer for all eternity.

The two stretcher-bearers, Chuck and Norm, fussed over you. I put them to work helping with your father. I checked his vitals, which seemed good considering what he had gone through. I gave them orders about caring for your Papa and then turned to you. You had been quiet, but your eyes were wide open as if you understood everything. I knew it wouldn't be long before you started fussing to be fed.

I turned to Chuck and Norm. "I need a milking goat and baby bottles. Remember, this is top secret."

Chuck and Norm were relieved to be away from the camp, and in a short while they returned with a milking goat and two baby bottles. They told me they had found them in an abandoned farmhouse. The goat's udder was swollen and she was bleating to be milked. Chuck and Norm were amazed at my milking skills. As I wrote earlier, you never forget how!

The days turned into weeks. You blossomed, and Abraham began to regain his strength. It felt as if we had created a sanctuary filled with love and hope. Slowly, Abe told me his story, and

I listened, and listened. I fell more and more in love with you and Abe, each and every day.

On May 8, 1945, the war in Europe was over, and we celebrated, oh my, how we celebrated! Whoever had lived in this apartment must have been a connoisseur of fine wines. We had discovered not only an assortment of wines, but jars of caviar as well.

We opened a bottle of French wine and toasted to the end of the war and prayed for a peaceful world.

I knew we would be moving on, but to where? But my excitement was short-lived and quickly turned into heartbreak, for I couldn't stand the thought of losing you and Abe.

One afternoon, Curtis and I drove back to our unit. Before entering the camp, he pulled to the side of the road.

"Just wanted you to know," he said, "that Colonel Denning is making an announcement. Our unit's being sent home. First to England, then transported back to the States." Curtis lit a cigarette. "What are you going to do?"

"About what?" I could feel my heart beating in my throat and barely got the words out.

Curtis grinned. "I know head over heels in love when I see it."

I couldn't hold my tears back and began to cry.

Curtis put his hand on my shoulder. "You are in love with Abe, aren't you?" he asked softly.

I nodded.

"And the baby?"

"I don't think I can go on without them."

"That's what I figured. I took the liberty of speaking with Colonel Denning. He owes me some big favors, and I called them in. I'm going to tell you how we've arranged this."

I started to speak, but Curtis hushed me. "Listen to me, Abigail. We all stuck our necks way out to get this to work. And I need something to tell me this goddamn war wasn't for nothing."

He became blunt, almost as if he was giving me orders. "You need to ask Abe to marry you."

At this point, I stopped breathing. "Ask *him*?" I croaked.

"Yes, that's how it's going to work. Abe will be a war groom. It doesn't happen often, but we can make it happen. Denning will give you permission to get married. I'll write out the birth certificate listing you and Abe as the parents. We'll fudge on the place of birth and all the pertinent details. The child will be none the wiser. Trust me, it's for her own good."

"I don't know," I said. "It seems so deceitful, to deny her the true facts."

"Would you want her to know she was born in Dachau?" said Curtis.

I shook my head. "Maybe you're right."

Curtis sat back in the jeep. "Look, talk it out with Abe. And as far as the baby, why tell her anything? Does she need to be weighed down with that piece of her history?"

I couldn't argue with his logic. "Curtis, why would you do this? You'll be putting your career in jeopardy."

"Maybe I've seen enough of death. And the baby—do you want her to grow up in a displaced persons camp? Bring her and Abe to Los Angeles."

"Los Angeles?"

"Yeah, why not? I've got a long-standing offer at the Teddy Brooks Memorial Hospital in LA. With our experiences here, we can write our own ticket to any emergency department."

"I'm worried about Abe. He told me he'll never practice medicine again. I don't know what he's going to do with his life now."

"A small glitch. Bet you dollars to donuts, I'll be able to find a place for Abe at Brooks. Let me talk to him about that one."

It was then that Curtis laid out the details of the plan. I was to leave with my unit to England. You and Papa would follow. Once in England, Abe and I would marry, and we would sail back together to New York.

I didn't know if I would find the nerve to propose! So very strange in my day; it was the man who did the proposing. I set that aside for the moment, as I had a more pressing concern.

"Could you get a goat on board the ship back to the States?"

At first Curtis thought I was joking, but when he saw how serious I was, he took out a pad of paper and wrote a reminder: *Need goat on board.*

I smiled, and for the first time in years my heart felt light.

"I couldn't bear the thought of the baby not having her goat milk."

Curtis started the car and stared at me.

"The baby? Isn't it time you gave her a name?"

"Abe asked me to think of a name that begins with an M for his sister Miriam, and the baby's mother, Malka, and a middle name that starts with an R for his sister Rachel. I've always loved the name Marley, ever since I read it in a children's book. I've haven't been able to say it to myself, let alone out loud. I'm afraid if I say her name it will make her more real, and then I'll lose her."

"You won't lose her; I promise you that."

"Marley Rose," I said with sudden conviction. "That is her name."

Curtis grinned. "And a damn fine name it is."

The next night, I borrowed the jeep; yes, I do know how to drive one, a skill I'd picked up in basic training, and one I'd exercised when my nurse friends and I enjoyed a rare weekend pass.

Papa and I drove to a small tavern in a nearby town. It was here that something strange happened.

Somehow the tavern had remained unscathed. We were served a delicious seven-herb soup, with thick slices of pumpernickel bread. I had brought along a bottle of wine from the supply left by the Nazi officer.

Abe held out my chair. It had been a lifetime ago since that simple act of courtesy had been shown to me.

We held our wine glasses, and Abe said, "*L'chaim.*"

I shook my head in ignorance.

"It means to life. Thank you, Abbey, for giving me back my life."

"I've got orders," I blurted out. "I'm being sent home."

His lips trembled as he said the proper words. "I wish you a safe trip. Where is home, Abbey? You've never told me much about it."

"A farm in Iowa. But it's all changed now. I'll visit, but I'm thinking of settling in Los Angeles."

"Ahh, the movie capital." He tried to smile, but I could see his eyes tearing up. "When do you leave?"

"In two weeks. We'll be flown to England, and then go by ship to New York. I'll be separated from the service in New York."

"I—we—will miss you. We will have to go to a displaced persons camp until I can get papers and decide if I should return to Vienna." Amidst his sadness, a twinkle came into Abe's eye. "Have you decided on a name for the baby yet?"

"Marley Rose. That's her name."

"Marley Rose. It has a lovely sound to it. I'm pleased. Thank you."

We fell silent, as if a wedge of pain had come between us. I sipped my wine, trying to find the right words and the courage to say them.

Finally I stammered, "Abe, return to the states with me. You and Marley—come with me."

He sat there with the most stunned look on his face. I explained how Curtis had moved heaven and earth to make this extraordinary thing happen.

"Abe, I love you, but if you don't feel the same way, I understand. Even so, it would give you and Marley a fresh start."

"If I don't love you?" He took my hand. "When you entered the infirmary, I saw you surrounded by light. At first, I thought you were an angel." He looked down. "I still think of you as an angel. Of course I love you, but I don't know what kind of a husband or father I'll make.

"These last weeks, I've had time to think about starting over. My hands can no longer perform surgery, and will always be a reminder of the Nazis. I want to try and put that part of my life behind me."

He began to speak with the slightest British accent. "My name is no longer Abraham Cohen. Can you still love me as Andrew Chambers?"

"You've thought of a new name?"

"A new identity, Abbey. There is something I must bring up. These past weeks have given me time for deep reflection, and I find I can no longer believe in the existence of God. I don't want the baby—Marley Rose—to be raised with the notion that God exists. Can you live with that?"

I was stunned, as I had been struggling with this very thing. "Andrew is a good, strong, masculine name," I mused. "But Chambers?"

"A respectable British name." He smirked. "And a grim re- minder of the gas chambers. Abraham Cohen died in the Holocaust, and Andrew Chambers was born in England."

"Andrew, you're asking me to give up my faith, my beliefs. I do have to admit I've been struggling, but yet..."

Andrew became thoughtful. "I have no problem with Marley learning about all religions, as long as you understand that I will explain, appropriately, that the concept of God was created from fear of the unexplainable."

I looked down at the table. "I always thought it was love, not fear, that brought God to us."

"Look around you—would a God of love have allowed this? Abbey, I will understand if this feels too difficult for you."

At this moment, my mind was racing. I kept thinking, why wouldn't he feel this way, after the atrocities he'd witnessed and experienced firsthand. Surely with time, he might have a change of heart. But the harshness of his tone, and a certain coldness in his eyes, made me doubt it.

I stood up, and Andrew did the same. "I think it's time to go. Marley will need to be fed, and she's not that used to Norm and Chuck feeding her."

We left the tavern, and when we got outside, I looked up. The sky was overcast, but a few stars twinkled through the cloud cover. I saw it as an omen.

I said to him: "Difficult it will be, Andrew, but not impossible."

And on that day in June, and only a few miles from Dachau, your father kissed me for the first time and told me how much he loved me.

On our drive back to Dachau your father said, "I need to return to Vienna for just a day. There is something I left with a friend."

I didn't pry. When your father returned from Vienna, he told me about his friend Oscar and how he had risked his life to save Papa's physician's case.

Papa looked at me with the most soulful expression. "This is who I once was," he said, opening the case and peering inside. "Now, I wish to shut that door forever." And with that he closed the bag, and we began our life together as a family.

Love,
Mommy

∞

Marley set the letter down.

"I've been so angry with them, feeling betrayed and looking for every flaw I could find. But their letters..." Her voice trailed off. "I think Mommy wanted me to grasp a deeper world, even if it would be painful. Dr. Saperstein told me that understanding could lead toward forgiveness.

"There's one more letter. Shall I keep going or did you want to break for a few?"

"Let's not stop now," Viv said hoarsely.

Marley picked up the final letter.

∞

Dear Marley,

I struggled with that one demand made by your father. Did I do the right thing? Perhaps I took the easy way out so that I didn't have to face my own lingering doubts.

Where was God when we were trying save the dying?

Where was God when both of my brothers died?

Where was God when millions were sent to their deaths in concentration camps?

I know now that there are no answers. All I know is that during times of war, there are no victors and everyone is a victim, one way or another.

Lately, as I live out what I believe to be my final days here on earth, I have turned once again to God, who always remained somewhere in my heart, and have prayed for His forgiveness.

The other day, after I had finished watching my favorite soap opera, *Days of Our Lives*, I began to feel sleepy. I stretched out on the couch and fell into a deep slumber. I started to see more movies, but this time they were vibrant and filled with color. My brothers and parents sat on the porch of our farmhouse, waving to me. I heard the words: "The truth will set her free." I woke with a start, and it was as if my faith had been restored. I knew then that we had to tell you the truth.

I doubt that you have any memory of this, but when you were not quite two, I took you to visit my parents in Iowa. The farm had once again fallen into disrepair, but the Blue and Gold Star flags were still displayed in the window.

My mommy's face lit up when she held you in her arms. After all the loss of life, I think it gave her a sense of peace to see life beginning once again.

Do you remember running in the field of buttercups? You were always in my sight, but once you thought you were lost. Oh, my poor baby. Only a few feet from my arms and yet feeling so frightened.

My parents both died within a year after our visit.

They too were casualties of war. A house that was once filled with energy was now deathly quiet. All of their children were gone; two lost directly by the war, and the other lost to a different way of life.

My father died of a heart attack. He had gone to tend the crops as he had done since he was a child. My mother discovered him when she went to bring him his lunch. I returned to Iowa to help Mommy sell the farm and move into a small apartment in town, near the church and her friends. I called her every week and was planning to visit when I got a message from Pastor Miller that Mommy had died in her sleep.

I have few regrets, but I do regret that I couldn't bring my mother home to live with us. You see, your father and I had lived in a way that was so foreign to everything she knew and loved. How could I ever explain that I had given up so many of the values she held near and dear to her heart?

Do you remember when I had to leave for a few weeks? You were not quite four, and you still had your Papa.

I returned to Iowa for my mommy's funeral. When I came home I brought a few artifacts from my childhood. You will find those in the basement. I hope your father remembered to keep them covered with sheets. There is a rocking horse, used by all the kids in our family. His name is Pony and was carved by my father. Some of my mother's pots and pans are there; I could not part with them. Why those? I don't know, except as reminders of a simpler time, a time of peace and hope before the droughts came, followed by the ravages of war.

Mommy's cookbook is safely wrapped in tissue paper at the bottom the suitcase. Dig inside the suitcase, and you will also find the Gold and Blue Star flags. The flags are all that are left of my brothers. Death took them within a few weeks of each other, yet thousands of miles apart. They were so young, so very young.

I wish I could tell you more about your biological family. Andrew said that your mother had spoken to him in Hungarian.

She was dead when we opened the door to the infirmary, but I remembered the serial number on her arm. I recited them over and over again, committing them to memory. I also remembered the shape of her feet. Her pinky toe lay entirely on its side, like yours. So many times when I bathed you, I looked at your feet and spoke silently to your mother: "Malka, your baby is safe in my arms."

I have included her serial number at the end of this letter. You will have to decide if you wish to search for your relatives. You will know when the time is right.

I always felt that somehow you were haunted by your beginnings. I don't understand how or why, but your nightmares were so reflective of the concentration camp experience. How could that be? Apparitions from the past can be a horrible burden, and I hope and pray that these letters somehow set you free.

When you get to the very bottom of the suitcase, you find a letter for Vivian.

Thank you, Marley, for being my joy, my light, and my daughter.

Forever yours,

Mommy

∞

"Wow, Mar," Vivian said, wiping her tears away. "Everyone paid such a horrible price."

"I'm feeling like such a shit."

"Why?" Vivian scratched her head.

"You know, being so fucking angry at them. My Papa brought me into this world. Mommy gave me everything any daughter would want. I wish they were here. I'd like to thank them, and tell them I love them."

Vivian reached out and put her hand on Marley's arm. "Mommy wrote me a letter. I'm pretty overwhelmed." She paused. "And anxious as hell to see it!"

"I'll find it, just hold your horses," said Marley.

Marley emptied the suitcase, spreading the items on the coffee table one by one, as she had done with Papa's medical bag.

"Oh, look, Viv. Here's a photo of the house and the man and woman standing on the porch. I remember them. Mommy's parents.—my sort-of- grandparents. And the flags—look, you can see them hanging in the window. I remember seeing the stars, and the way Mommy's mother smelled like fresh baked bread and cinnamon rolls."

Marley came upon the final envelope and held it out ceremoniously. "Here's your letter, Viv."

"I can't believe Mommy wrote to me."

"Don't be silly! You know she and Papa loved you like a second daughter. They were all the time saying so."

"My hands are shaking, I hope I can open the envelope."

"Do you need help? Do you want privacy? I can always wait in another room."

"Why would I not want you next to me? I thought we were in this together."

Marley shrugged and her lips trembled. "I don't know," she whispered.

Vivian opened the letter and began to read out loud.

Dear Vivian,

I suppose I should call you Viv, since that was the nickname Marley gave you when you were both young. I think she had trouble pronouncing your name, and it stuck. But, it seems as if it only belongs to the two of you.

I'd like to tell you the story of how I met your mother, how we became friends, and how we managed to stay friends, although our views on life became very different.

Not too long after we moved into our home, the bean fields on the other side of the street were subdivided for homes. Smaller homes at first, for the thousands of returning veterans, then larger and larger homes on the sloping hills.

Your parents bought the house across the street from us. I walked over with a casserole in one hand, while pushing Marley's stroller with the other. I made my mother's macaroni and cheese. Believe it or not, the recipe called for 1/4 pound of butter, 1/2 pound of cheese and whole milk. Andrew jokingly called it my "heart attack mac!" I'd share the recipe with you girls, but you're probably both too health conscious to want to try it.

"Who's too health conscious?" Marley cut in, smacking her lips.

"I wouldn't mind diving into that myself," said Vivian. "Maybe later, but right now, I want to see what else Mommy has to say."

The top was still bubbling when your mother invited us in for lemonade. We talked for a while, and she told me she had been a Navy nurse. We found that we had much in common. Even our upbringings were not too different.

We spread a blanket on the lawn; there weren't any plants, but the grass was lush and green. That was when you woke up from your nap, Vivian. You and Marley looked at each other and smiled. You played on the blanket as if you had known each other forever.

It was a Saturday, and your dad and Andrew were carrying moving boxes into the garage. They also seemed to enjoy each other's company.

We settled in, and gradually Olivia and I began to depend upon each other. And although at times she bridled against what she called our very liberal political views and anti-religion philosophy, we decided to lay the discussion of politics and religion aside and let you children enjoy each other's company.

There was one event that caused a chasm in our friendship. And while we continued to share holidays, it was never quite the same. I do believe the change might have gone unnoticed by you and Marley.

∞

Vivian's voice trailed off; she finished reading the letter in silence. "Jesus Christ! I can't take it any longer," she shouted.

"Viv, talk to me," Marley pleaded.

"You want to know? You really want to know? Then read the rest of the letter yourself. Look, I've got to get out of here. Clear my head." The chair wobbled as she stood.

"Viv, what's wrong? Please talk to me."

"This is what's wrong." She moved over to Marley. "Look at me, Mar. Really look at me. Who do you see?"

"I see my best friend."

"Is that all you see?"

Marley cast her eyes downward and her voice became throaty. "No. I see someone I can't live without."

Vivian moved closer until there was no distance between them.

"Are you saying what I think you're saying? Remember our private game of spin the bottle?"

"Of course, we talked about it the other day."

"For me it was more than two girls practicing for boys. For me it was who I am, my identity, my loving you in every sense of the word. Do I repulse you now? Are you going to see me as some kind of a freak?"

Marley panicked inside. There was no way to answer Viv's desperate questions without getting into a subject she wasn't sure she'd ever be able to talk about. "Let me see the letter," she said, seizing on a diversion.

Vivian hung her head as Marley continued reading where they'd left off.

The day that you and Marley played spin the bottle, the strangest sense came over me. You see, the Army was much more than just being a nurse. The experience opened my eyes to a wide world far beyond the cornfields of Iowa. I became acquainted with women of many different temperaments and philosophies from every part of the country. I was shocked to discover that women could love other women. A couple of the students at nursing school had talked about it and made fun of it, but I had a hard time believing it could be true.

While we were still stationed in France, a few of us drove to a nightclub in Paris. Women were dancing together. I'd seen women dance with each other before and didn't think it was unusual, especially since most of the men were off to war, but this was different. These women were dancing together as a preference, not because there were no men around.

I have to admit that I was disturbed at first. But then, a couple of the nurses I knew and admired got up and began to dance, and I could see that they were in love. After all that we had seen, the brutality of war, who was I to judge? I was able to see and accept the beauty and naturalness of their attraction to each other.

For many years I set that memory aside. I subsequently had patients who were lesbian or homosexual, and I never had a thought other than how nice it was that they'd found love.

Your mother and I were having coffee while you and Marley were playing spin the bottle. We did have many things in common besides our military background; we both loved family, enjoyed sewing and cooking, and in some ways were like sisters. I called you girls to come in for lunch, but you didn't hear me, and that's when I walked to Marley's room. I peeked in the half-opened door and smiled. You both looked sweet, as if you belonged together in a way that surpassed friendship. Your mother had followed and became extremely upset. Later that night she called and told me she thought it was best for us not to see each other again. I asked her not to make such a rash decision, but to meet me for coffee the next day.

We talked from our hearts, and while we disagreed on what we'd witnessed, I felt her truth meant as much to her as mine did to me. I told her about some of the things I saw during the war and how that had shaped my values.

At the end of the two hours we spent together, we made a decision not to break up your friendship, but—and she was firm on this—if it happened again she and your father would transfer you to another school and you girls would not be permitted to see each other.

That night I spoke to Marley, and you might say we had the birds and the bees talk. Now, as I lie here in my bed, I think of the way you looked at each other. It reminded me of the two nurses whom I saw dancing together in Paris; if anyone looked upon them with open eyes, it could not be denied that they were in love. I wonder now if they stayed together after the war and are well and happy. I do hope so.

If I'm wrong in my observations, Vivian, know that I love you like another daughter. If what I suspect is true, you and Marley have my blessings.

Love,

Mommy

∞

A long, contemplative silence fell over the room, broken at last by Marley. "I remember that talk. Mommy was sweet, you know? She held my hand and told me about how you never know where love will find you. She asked me what it was like to kiss you."

"What did you say?"

Marley looked down. "I told her it was tingly. I hadn't thought about that talk until we were reminiscing. I remember Susan's party."

Vivian smiled. "Me too. I got Bobby."

"I got Morris."

"How was it?"

"Definitely not tingly."

"And kissing Bobby was about as satisfying as kissing a pine tree." They both laughed. "Mar, what about with John? You never talked much about it."

Marley looked down. "I kept waiting to feel the earth move—you know, the way it's supposed to be."

"And?"

She confessed. "Maybe a slight tremor now and then. Never an earthquake."

Vivian said, "Do you think we should see if we can find that Coke bottle?"

"Not necessary," said Marley, moving toward Vivian until their lips met. They lingered, lost in the moment...not wanting to part.

"You're crying, "Vivian murmured.

Marley rested her head against Vivian's chest. "Where do we go from here?"

"I could carry you up the stairs. You know, Rhett Butler style."

"That would be a feat. Especially since we don't have a second story."

"Well then, I guess we need to go to plan B."

"Which is?"

"We see where this path takes us."

"It might be a while. I'm pretty fucked up, in case you didn't notice."

"You seem perfect to me, and I don't mind waiting as long as I know there's a chance. Shit, Mar, I'll be here for all eternity, if that's what it takes."

CHAPTER 15

Marley sat in her usual place.

"How are you?" Dr. Saperstein asked.

"Stunned."

"By your mother's letters?"

"Partly. Something happened between Viv and me, and I'm more confused than ever. I wish Mommy were here. I never realized what a wise parent she was. Dr. Saperstein, I'm horribly embarrassed. I'm not sure I can get my words out."

"Would it help if you closed your eyes?"

"No, I don't think so. Umm, would it be okay if you closed yours?"

Dr. Saperstein closed her eyes.

"That's so much better. Now you can't see me. When Viv and I went through Mommy's suitcase we found a letter addressed to Viv. She said it would be okay if I shared it with you. Would you mind reading it?"

"I'd be honored, but I will have to open my eyes."

"It's okay now," Marley said with a shy smile.

Dr. Saperstein's eyes glistened as she read the letter. "Your mother was an unusually intuitive woman, and quite ahead of her time in her views on, shall we say, sensitive subjects."

"I don't think I ever fully appreciated her. What she went through as a child and then what she saw during the war. And yet, she was not destroyed by her experiences. I do wish they would have trusted me with the truth, though."

She sighed. "After I read the letter, I remembered how good it felt when Viv and I kissed. I always imagined it would be that way when I fell in love. But it didn't happen with John, and I thought there was something wrong with me. Then, when Viv finally told me her secret—that she's a lesbian—things just fell into place. I guess part of me always knew, or at least suspected. And, if I'm being honest with myself, I guess I've questioned my heterosexuality sometimes—at least I've wondered if I'd be comfortable playing for the other team. And that dream of wanting to get to the other side. Wow! All I know is, it seemed natural for Viv and me to kiss. And then it hit me. What does that make me?"

"Human."

"Huh?"

"Human. It makes you human, Marley. Let me set aside all my training and talk to you from my heart. Falling in love isn't black or white, although most may need to see it that way. Tell me what you felt when you and Vivian kissed."

"Besides the tingling?"

"Yes."

"I felt as if I had come home after a very long trip through a dark tunnel. I felt safe, as if we could tackle the world together." She looked down. "And, I wanted to keep kissing her. I wanted to know what it would be like to lay next to her, to touch and be touched. I'm frightened, Dr. Saperstein. I don't know where to put this. I think I'm afraid of another label."

"Label?"

"Lesbian. It's hard for me to say the word."

"What do you think your mother would have told you?"

"She said it in her letters. Despite all of her personal losses and the atrocities she saw, she still believed in love."

"This is all new for you, but perhaps you can keep that in mind and talk to Vivian. The most important part in any healthy relationship, regardless of gender, is to be able to communicate honestly and openly."

Marley looked at the clock. "Something I struggle with. Until next time then?"

"Yes, next time."

∞

Esther looked out the foyer window, watching Marley walking to her car. *Such a heavy weight on one who can be so childlike.* She moved away from the window and walked toward the kitchen.

Danni was leaning over the sink, washing fresh vegetables from the garden, and humming along with Edith Piaf's version of "La Vie en Rose."

Esther said, "Remember when we first danced to this?"

Danni turned around. "You reminded me of Edith. I asked you over for dinner."

"I couldn't wait."

"You brought flowers."

"You introduced me to a whole new way of eating."

"Oh, my Essie, that wasn't all I introduced you to."

"I was a quick learner, *oui*?"

"*Oui!*"

Essie said, "Remember our marriage ceremony?"

"Did you think I would forget it?"

"We had just moved into this house."

"No, it wasn't finished," insisted Danni.

"The roof was on."

"We sat on the back patio," said Danni. "With champagne and pate. Remember the stars?"

"The sky was overflowing, and the moon! Such a moon."

"It was just the two of us."

"Three, Danni—we had Merlin then."

"Wasn't he the best cat?"

"A magical cat," said Essie. "Capable of casting love spells."

"We put a bow tie on Merlin and pledged our love."

"It was the best ceremony ever."

"We made love under the stars."

"Merlin was discreet and left."

Danni said, "Do you remember our first kiss?"

"I surprised myself by being the bold one," said Esther.

"I had been waiting patiently."

"It took a while for me to understand. I was such an innocent child."

"What is it, Essie? Is it your patient?"

"Yes."

"Come, let me hold you."

They moved with familiar ease into each other's arms.

"Will she have the strength? I'm worried about what she may have to face. Remember when you thought you would lose your teaching position? And when I was in the hospital and you had to pretend you were my sister?"

Danni chuckled. "I could never forget. The nurse looked at us suspiciously, and I was convinced she was going to pin scarlet letters on us. But it's been worth it, yes?"

Esther kissed Danni's rosy cheek. "Yes, of course."

"If her love is for that young woman I met in the garden," said Danni, "they will find their way, as we found ours. After all, she has you to help."

"I pray it will be enough."

Marley felt an immediate void when she opened the front door and saw an envelope propped up on the entryway table.

Her hands shook as she took out the note.

Mar,

You now know who I am and how I feel about you. I have no further secrets to reveal. From that angle I feel greatly relieved, but at the same time I'm terrified to take you into my world.

I want to give you some room; some time to think. Especially with the other burden you are carrying. I'm going back to the apartment.

I'm really sorry I laid this on you.

Viv

Marley felt her face flush. *My blood must be boiling.* She threw her hobo bag onto the kitchen table and dialed Vivian's number.

It was picked up on the first ring.

"Nancy here."

"Is Vivian there?"

She could hear Nancy singing out, "Oh, Vivian, a phone call for you. I think it's one of your many lovers." Then Nancy made what sounded like kissing noises. Peals of laughter erupted in the background.

How immature! Marley thought. *And damn, what a squeaky voice. Like fingernails on a blackboard.*

Then she heard Viv shouting, "Quiet, you morons! Could you all please leave for five minutes and give a woman her space. *Thank you.* Hello?"

"Goddamn it, Viv. What the fuck happened to your, 'I'll be here for all eternity'?

"I didn't want to push you." She confessed. "I got scared."

"Don't you ever do that again."

"I'm sorry."

"Meet me at the park."

"The park?"

"Yes, be there at five."

∞

Beverlywood Park was tucked away at the end of a housing tract built in the 1950s. Ranch houses with gable roofs, board and batten siding, and attached garages filled the tree-lined streets. During the mornings, preschoolers would play in the sandboxes or on the swings. The older children who came to the park after school would climb the metal ladder to ride the "slide of doom" or organize an impromptu baseball game. The waning light signified it was time to return home, and the park now was empty except for an elderly man and woman sitting on one of the park benches. They were huddled together, lingering as they watched the sun begin to set. The woman wore a red wool coat with a tie belt, and the man a black car coat with oversized pockets.

Probably gifts from their kids, thought Marley. *I will never be able to buy Mommy and Papa another gift, not for their birthdays, or Christmas, or their anniversary. Why couldn't they have lived to grow old together?*

Marley observed the couple discreetly. From time to time they would hold hands and the man would rub the woman's hand to keep it warm. He took a pair of gloves from his cavernous pocket. They each put on one glove, grasping the bare hand of the other with their gloved hand.

She walked past the couple. They smiled; she smiled back and nodded.

Marley stopped at the tire swings. She remembered how she and Vivian had graduated from the toddler safety swings to the tire swings and, finally, to flat-seat swings. Marley would pump her legs as fast as she could and then wait for the swing to gradually stop. Vivian would pump and pump as high as she could go, and then jump off as if she was indestructible, always landing on her feet.

She looked at her watch, impatiently waiting for 5:00 p.m. She walked back to the car and got the picnic basket filled with everything that Viv liked. Spreading the feast on a picnic table, she returned to the swing.

She saw the VW pulling up.

Oh, God. What should I do? Should I stay where I am? Walk towards Viv? Instead, she sat on the seat swing and began to pump her legs, going higher and higher.

Vivian sat on the swing next to her, matching Marley's rhythm.

Marley pumped higher, moving beyond any previous height she'd reached as a little girl. Once again, Vivian matched her with ease.

Suddenly Marley let go, jumping off the swing and landing on her back on the bed of sand.

Vivian jumped off, too, landing on her feet exactly as she had done as a child.

She ran to Marley, crying, "Jesus Christ, Mar! Are you breathing? Are you dead?"

"Knocked the wind out of me," she gasped.

"You had me scared to death."

"I didn't quite make it."

"You were superb."

"I'm okay now—got my breath back." Marley reached her hand up and let Viv pull her to her feet. "Was I brave enough?"

"The bravest." Vivian touched her forehead to Marley's. "I love you, Mar."

"I love you, Viv, in every way," Marley sighed. "I think somewhere inside of me I always knew you were the knight I was waiting for."

Their lips brushed.

"Viv, would you spend the night in the trundle bed, for old time's sake?"

"Of course I will."

"See that couple on the bench? I think they were watching us."

Vivian looked at the couple. "That could be us in forty years."

"We should come back here every year. Today can be our anniversary."

"It's a date," said Viv. "Hey, look at them—they're smiling and waving to us."

"Let's wave back!" And they did.

In between whispering sweet nothings to one another, they feasted on the picnic supper. They giggled as they fed each other from the assortment of olives, cheese, and graham cracker peanut butter and jelly sandwiches.

"Let's go," Marley said dreamily.

They packed up the remains, and drove home, Vivian's car following Marley's at a safe distance. They got into their beds, Vivian in the trundle and Marley in the twin.

Vivian whispered, "It's lonely down here."

Marley tapped her mattress. "It's lovely up here."

∞

Vivian awoke and reached for Marley. "Mar," she said groggily.

Marley was standing by the side of the bed, putting on her sweats. "Shh. Go back to sleep."

Vivian glanced at the clock: 3:30 a.m. She stretched and groaned. "What are you doing?"

"I had this dream, and then an idea. Several ideas, actually."

Vivian reached out and tugged on Marley's waistband. "This is not the time for ideas. Come back to bed," she whined.

Marley knelt and kissed Vivian with a newly discovered hunger. She whispered, "You are the love of my life, the one I want to spend eternity with. It's just that Obsessive Compulsive Disorder I have been praying for kicked into overdrive." She threw on a raggedy sweatshirt over her naked torso and added, "Have to go now. I'm on a mission." She paused. "Viv, you won't leave will you?"

"Ha! Just try and get rid of me. But, I do think we might want to invest in a slightly larger bed." Vivian said with a smile before she rolled over and fell into a deep sleep.

She awoke to the *tap-tap-tap...ding...zzzzzip* music of Marley giving her neglected Hermes Rocket typewriter a brutal workout.

Viv glanced at the clock. *What could she possibly be typing at 8:05 a.m.?* She bolted upright. Did last night really happen or was it a dream? She lay back. From the contented way she felt, it was no dream. She threw on her clothes and followed the sound.

Marley sat at the partners desk surrounded by crumpled papers, two full trash bags, and a stack of fresh paper.

"Mar?"

She looked up.

Viv grinned.

"What's so funny?"

"Did you have to change the ribbon?"

"Yeah, how did you know?"

"You'd make a horrible spy. You've got more ink on your face than on the paper. What's up?" she cooed, stroking Marley's hair.

"I can't think when you do that."

"Do you want me to stop?"

"Just a pause."

Marley turned to type two more lines. "All done," she said. The platen made a loud *zing* as she yanked the page out of the typewriter and showed it to Vivian. "It's my cover letter."

Dear Dr. Holbrook:

I have completed and am enclosing the outline of my proposal.

Please review and call to set up an appointment.

Sincerely,

Marley Chambers

"Sounds good to me," said Viv. She pointed to a thin stack of papers on the desk. "That your proposal?"

"Yeah. I have to drop these off at his office today."

"Today? Mar, Holbrook isn't going to be anywhere near the campus on a Saturday."

"I called him."

"When?"

"Around four this morning. He had given me his personal number. He answered, and I told him it was urgent."

"That must have been one hell of a dream. I bet he wanted to kill you."

"It was and he did. There's more, but I'd like to take a shower and have breakfast before we head out to the campus. Uh ...Viv?"

"Yeah?"

"We have some time. And..."

"And?"

"I've been thinking. The *Times* headline this morning was 'Water Shortage Matches Gasoline Shortage'."

"Uh-huh."

"Are we really doing our part? Do you think we might try saving on shower water?"

"I think that can be arranged."

CHAPTER 16

"Hi, Dr. Saperstein."

"Hello, Marley."

"It's been a most unusual couple of days. Viv came with me again. I have an appointment this afternoon with Dr. Holbrook, and then we thought we'd have an early dinner at Rive Gauge Cafe. I've never been there before."

"It's quite a lovely setting."

"I'm wondering, do you think you can you fall in love with someone after years of knowing them? Do you believe that someone can fall in love with their best friend?"

"I think you have a story to tell me."

"I'm not sure where to begin. Perhaps I should start with the dream I had last night. It was different than the one that has haunted me.

"I'm in a room, and I can see a word floating around. It's in front of me at times but it keeps moving. I not familiar with the word, but I can see it distinctly. *Brausebad.*"

Dr. Saperstein flinched.

Marley said, "I don't know what that word means. I thought I would look it up in the university library."

"You may not find it. After the war the word became unacceptable and was stricken from new dictionaries. It translates to shower. A common term the Nazis deceptively used to refer to the gas chambers."

"Oh, that breaks my heart," Marley said mournfully.

She dabbed her eyes with a tissue.

"In the dream, naked people were being herded in to a room. They each carried a scrap of soap and a ragged piece of towel.

"Men and women held babies in their arms, and children hung onto their mommies' hands. After a while the door is shut with a bang, and I heard a hissing sound. There are cries and screams, and I'm being pushed and pulled in all directions. I don't collapse, but as *they* collapse, I can see their spirits rising. Instead of being dark, as they are in the other dream, they are clothed in white robes. They circle me and whisper in my ear. Then they rise to the ceiling of the room, where there are four openings. One by one, their spirits move through the openings and are set free."

"You mention four holes in the ceiling," Dr. Saperstein interjected. "Do you have any association to that number?"

"It's always been an important number to me. I had my first nightmare when I was four. I sometimes feel compulsive about that number, almost as if it's a ritual I must perform."

Dr. Saperstein chose her words carefully. "There were four openings in the gas chamber ceilings. That's where the canisters of poison would be placed."

Marley shuddered and said, "I don't know how I can have dreams about something, someplace I've never seen. The detail is beyond anything I ever saw in books or documentaries about the Holocaust."

"Marley, there are some questions that cannot be answered—at least not with the knowledge we have today."

"When I woke up, I felt strangely energized. I knew what I had to write about. I feel different. Not afraid."

"I'm curious," said Dr. Saperstein, "what did the people in the room whisper?"

"'Tell our story.' Over and over again: 'Tell our story.' And I think that was the real purpose of Mommy and Papa's letters. Not just to give me my history, but to let their experiences be known.

"I wrote the proposal outline late at night. It flowed, and I knew that was what I was meant to do."

Dr. Saperstein nodded. "Tell me about loving your best friend. I'm assuming that's Vivian."

"She is my heart. I think I've always known it. Viv thinks I should write my dissertation as a novel."

"That's a splendid idea."

"I want the world to know about those who hid their experiences after the Holocaust. I even have the title: *Disappearing Ink: The Other Side of the Door*."

∞

Vivian walked to the garden. The gardener was there, kneeling, her hands deep in the loamy soil. She looked up and smiled. "Hello."

"I wanted to stop by and thank you for the vegetables."

"Goodness, there are more than enough to share, and you're more than welcome."

"I wasn't sure you would be here."

"I'm here most days."

"You must have a green thumb."

"You are too kind. I think while I garden, and thank the plants for what they give me. Did you enjoy your walk to the falls?"

"I fell. And thank you for the balm. It worked like a charm. But, how did you know?"

"We all fall, one time or another. I thought you might need it."

"I was wondering if it would be okay to take my friend to the waterfall. She's with the doctor right now."

"I think it would be fine. I brought two walking sticks."

"Two?"

"Yes," she smiled. "I had a feeling you might return. Make sure you hold your friend's hand on your way down."

"Oh, I will. I will."

∞

Vivian leaned against the VW, watching as Marley walked toward her. She had a lifetime of thoughts she wanted to share with Marley: her dreams, her life, and most of all, her heart. She hoped she could be as brave as Marley when she spoke to her parents.

They lingered at the car for a while, holding each other, whispering secrets never uttered out loud before.

Marley said, "I figured out how you can have your own office."

"How?"

"Papa's study. It'll be perfect."

"Really? asked Vivian. "There won't be any income for a while."

"I guess you'll have to find another way to pay."

Vivian grinned. "With pleasure.

"I've decided to tell my parents when they come out for my graduation. I'm scared."

"I'll be there with you."

"Really? It might get pretty ugly."

"I can do ugly, as long as we're together."

"I want to take you to the falls," said Viv. "The gardener gave me two sticks. But, she told me to hold your hand."

"Promise me you'll never let go."

"I swear. Pinky promise."

Hand in hand, they walked toward the rocky path.

Danni tapped on Essie's half-opened office door before walking in. Essie was standing at the window facing the parking area.

"I wanted to check on the plans for our bridge game," said Danni.

"Two tables. There'll be eight of us. Six of the girls are coming. It should be an exciting night. You know those girls."

"Quite a group." Danni couldn't suppress a giggle.

"Come." Esther motioned for Danni to stand next to her.

They watched as Vivian took Marley's hand and guided her toward the path that led to the waterfall.

"You knew they would come together, didn't you?"

"I was hoping."

"Ah, you're a psychic-scientist." Esther smiled, and then became serious. "Do you think their life will be easier than ours?"

"Who's to say or know? Any regrets?"

"Not one. I hope they don't have to hide as we did. Perhaps one day, the world will know that love trumps all."

CHAPTER 17

Los Angeles, 1977

Marley and Vivian found shelter from the rain under the awning of the Empire Bookstore. The rain dripped off the awning, bouncing on the sidewalk before running into the gutter. They held hands as they gazed at the window display.

"Wow! Look at that poster," said Vivian.

EMPIRE BOOKSTORE IS PROUD TO PRESENT:
MARLEY ROSE CHAMBERS, PH.D.
READING FROM HER NATIONAL BOOK AWARD NOVEL
DISAPPEARING INK: THE OTHER SIDE OF THE DOOR

"The book display looks great, doesn't it?" asked Marley.

"I wasn't looking at the book covers, baby girl. I was staring at the photo of the woman next to them." She pointed at the picture of Marley, looking sophisticated and glamorous in a professional studio portrait commissioned for the book promotion.

They turned and traded smiles, then leaned closer to murmur an oft-repeated endearment: "I love you."

Marley held Vivian at arm's length, and straightened her black velvet jacket.

"Your sure I look okay?" asked Vivian. "I wasn't sure about the flared pants. But, I'm actually getting used to being a kept woman."

"It's stylish, you're stunning, and you definitely are a keeper," Marley said.

Vivian placed her hand on Marley's fat little tummy. "How's Sweet Pea doing?"

"Move your hand a little to the right and you'll find out."

"Wow! I think I felt a foot. We should get inside where it's warm. Are you sure you'll be okay?"

"I'll be fine, I'm an old pro at this by now. If New York didn't do me in, Los Angeles certainly won't. And I've got Amanda with me. Thank the lord for publicist's assistants."

"I'll be back in an hour."

Marley smiled and said, "Liar, liar, pants on fire."

Vivian crossed her heart. "Cross my heart and hope to die, if I've told a big fat lie."

"Bite your tongue."

"Ouch! It's a good thing we aren't superstitious. The longer I linger, the longer my meeting will take. I think I've got the plaintiff and his shady mouthpiece shaking in their booties. A teacher who owns her own home, is in a stable relationship, and her ex-husband wants to take her kids away because she's a lesbian. Let 'em try!"

"Do good, baby."

"I will."

"It went well, don't you think?" asked Amanda. "Only two baiters this time wanting to prove the Holocaust never happened."

"Yeah," Marley replied. "And Eve actually ate that damn apple."

"I thought the rest of the audience was going to murder them. You handled it well."

"Thanks. When does your plane leave, Amanda?"

"Tomorrow, noon."

"I'll bet you'll be happy to get home."

"Yes, Scott's about ready to send the kids to boot camp."

"Let's call it a night, then."

Amanda nodded. "You must be exhausted."

Marley rubbed her belly. "Sweet Pea has been kicking up a storm. I'm so ready to end this tour and sleep in my own bed. Vivian should be here any minute. She keeps buying more baby things, and it's driving her crazy not knowing the gender. Six more weeks to my due date; I'm looking forward to some downtime sleeping, eating, and sorting baby clothes. Don't tell her, but at the next ultrasound, I'm caving in on knowing the gender."

"God help the department stores after that," Amanda laughed. "Uh-oh. A couple of latecomers just walked in. Do you want me to excuse you?"

"Oh, look at them. They're soaked. Can you get some hot tea, and perhaps the elderly woman can sit in one of the overstuffed chairs."

"Will do. I'll explain that your time is limited. Well, look who walked in right behind them! Big surprise, your hero is carrying two shopping bags from La Infant's."

"She's impossible," Marley whispered dreamily.

"I'll fetch the tea, and then I'll give Viv a hand with her bags," said Amanda.

"I appreciate it," said Marley. She sat at the book-signing table. It had been a grueling, three-month bicoastal tour, hitting all the big cities, but she wouldn't have missed it for the world.

If only Mommy and Papa could be here. I would tell them that the world has read their letters and we've changed a lot of lives. Oh, how I wish you could meet your grandbaby.

Marley watched Amanda and Vivian going through the overstuffed shopping bags of baby items, both of them squealing with excitement. She smiled at the woman she called wife.

The young woman who'd just come in left her elderly companion to enjoy her tea and walked over to the table, holding a copy of Marley's book in one hand and a briefcase in the other.

"Excuse me for being late," she said.

Marley smiled. "No problem."

"I see someone is busy buying baby clothes. What a special time. I have three."

"Sounds like a handful," said Marley.

"It is, but I manage. I wanted to thank you for the tea, and for seeing us. I know it's late, and I'm sure you're dead tired. Our flight was delayed, and the trip was hard on my mother. We hoped to make it for your reading, but the traffic from LAX and the rain..." She smiled apologetically.

"Where did you come from?"

"Israel." The woman held out her hand. "My name is Hannah Shapiro."

"So far to come to be disappointed. The store doors are locked, and I've got time.

Please have a seat, Hannah."

"Thank you."

Hannah sat with a sigh. "I bought your book as soon as it came out. The subject matter fascinated me. My mother and I have been active in supporting survivor groups and in preserving their stories in the form of oral history. It's almost impossible to get the history of those who have decided to hide their experience."

"Perhaps my book will begin to change that."

"It must have been a big undertaking."

"It was."

"I was stunned when I first read your dedication page."

"I've had readers comment on it, but no one ever used the word stunned."

Marley opened the book to the dedication page and read:

To my mother, Malka Elek,
who through the worst of times gave me life.
To my Mommy and Papa, who showed me how to live it.

"What about it stunned you? It seems fairly benign."

"My mother's name is Sarah... Sarah Elek. My aunt's name was Malka Elek. I believe we are related."

Marley grabbed the arm of her chair.

"If I am correct," Hannah continued, "your birth father was Zalman Elek. He was a great poet, before...before the Nazis invaded Poland. My father was Zalman's brother, and by far the more anxious of the two. As soon as he heard rumblings, we left for Israel. Palestine at the time."

Hannah could see Marley was still trying to wrap her head around this bombshell. After a long moment she smiled warmly and asked, "Have you done any family research?"

Marley shook her head. "Not yet. Writing the book took everything I had to give. I came close to giving up several times. There were times when I was pulled in that direction, but as my very wise therapist kept reminding me, balance and prioritize."

"It makes perfectly good sense, especially when you are bringing a new life into the world. I've been involved in family research for some time. We lost so many." Hannah gave a self-conscious laugh. "I hope you don't think I'm some kind of crazy person, showing up like this."

"Crazy or not, I am so very grateful."

"I brought documents and photos to share with you."

Marley's eyes filled with tears. "I don't know what to say."

Hannah reached inside her briefcase. "Here's a photo of your mother. You look like her, especially around the eyes."

Vivian walked over. "What is it, Mar? You look like you're going to pass out."

Hannah said, "I'm sorry if I upset you. Perhaps I should have written, but I knew that letters sent to book publishers are often misdirected or lost. I can give you the phone number of where we are staying, and my phone number in Israel, if you should want to reach us." She reached inside her pocket, took out a card, and stood to leave.

"Please, Hannah, don't go." Marley gazed at the photo of her birth mother. "Our hair, our eyes; it's as if I'm looking into a mirror."

Hannah smiled. "We have much to tell you about your family. Mama is the holder of the family history." She nodded in the direction of the elderly woman. She was sipping her tea and enjoying a conversation with Amanda.

"Where are you staying, Hannah?" Marley asked

"With cousins—yours and mine—in Culver City."

"That's almost in our backyard. Please, will you come to our home tomorrow?"

Marley turned to Vivian. "Are you free tomorrow, darling?"

"Of course. Of course."

"Forgive me, this is my wife, Vivian."

Vivian extended her hand. "Wife in every way except legally. But, we're working on that."

Hannah reached out and hugged her. "*Mazel tov* on your work. I read all about you in Marley's book," she said. "I admire you greatly. *Both* of you."

Marley said, "I have a doctor's appointment in the morning. Could we make it around two?"

Hannah smiled. "That would be perfect."

Marley wrote down their address and phone number.

"There are survivors from Auschwitz who spoke of hiding a pregnant woman," said Hannah. "And there are rumors about a child born in Dachau at the end of the war. Perhaps I can tell you more tomorrow."

"I can't wait," said Marley, taking Hannah's hand. "We have so much to talk about. Hannah, I must say hello to your mother before you leave. What should I call her?"

"She would love to hear the word aunt." Hannah chuckled. "Don't be surprised if my mother touches your belly, blesses the baby, and cries."

"I won't. I would kneel at her feet, but I'm afraid I won't be able to get up."

The rain had stopped. Marley and Vivian carried the shopping bags as they walked toward the car.

"I have family," Marley said softly. "More family," she corrected herself.

"I'm so happy for you. For the three of us, I should say."

"How was your meeting?" asked Marley.

"Took fifteen minutes. We won hands down."

"I'm so proud of you. Look, the stars are coming out. It's a beautiful night."

"It's a perfect night," Vivian said. "I had time to go home and put Pony in Sweet Pea's room. Also, Mommy's suitcase is now filled with stuffed animals."

"What about Teddy?"

"He's top dog, or I should say top bear. He's waiting in the crib."

"You make me very happy. Thank you. Viv, we have an early appointment with the doctor tomorrow. Would you like to know if it's a boy or a girl?"

Vivian blew a kiss. "Really? I'd love that. It's getting really hard to buy neutral clothes. Especially in larger sizes."

"That's because you've already bought everything there is."

"I thought you were determined to be surprised."

"I think I was being stubborn," Marley confessed.

"Who, you?"

"Only on rare occasions."

Vivian said, "Hey, I've been thinking about names. How does Zachary strike ya?"

Marley said, "I'm processing." She furrowed her brow. "For some reason, it has a familiar ring. Zachary, beginning with a Z, after his grandfather, Zalman. I like it and it follows a Jewish tradition. But, what if it's a girl?"

"Zelda," Vivian said slyly. "But don't worry, a little birdie told me it's a boy."

"And what birdie is that?"

"Babe, do you have any idea of how much you talk in your sleep? It's become my nightly entertainment. You've been sleep-talking boys' names since the night you got pregnant. It started right after we did the whole getting pregnant ceremony."

"Thanks to your cousin Eddie and the baster. Not to mention—"

Vivian said. "Shh, the baby might be listening. Using Eddie as a donor was a brilliant idea, and he was more than happy to comply. He could finally get recognized for what he has been doing since he turned twelve. Plus, having someone in my family as the donor won my mother over. She said, and I quote, 'At least it'll be all in the family.' Her favorite show, by the way. I guess old dogs really can learn new tricks. When I spoke to my dad, he told me she's gone bonkers, with baby shopping. They'll need to hire a truck when they visit."

Marley burst out laughing. "And we'll need to add a second story to our home."

Vivian looked at Marley and stuck out her tongue. "Okay, say it."

"Like mother, like daughter."

"Guess you're right, Mar—the apple doesn't fall far from the tree."

"Tell me, what sold you on Zachary?"

"Because for the past few months, you've been mumbling 'Zachary' in your sleep. It followed us everywhere on your tour. I finally looked it up."

"What's the meaning?" asked Marley.

"Remembered by God."

Appendix

The Selfish Giant
by Oscar Wilde.
The Happy Prince and Other Tales (1888)

Every afternoon, as they were coming from school, the children used to go and play in the Giant's garden.

It was a large lovely garden, with soft green grass. Here and there over the grass stood beautiful flowers like stars, and there were twelve peach-trees that in the spring-time broke out into delicate blossoms of pink and pearl, and in the autumn bore rich fruit. The birds sat on the trees and sang so sweetly that the children used to stop their games in order to listen to them. 'How happy we are here!' they cried to each other.

One day the Giant came back. He had been to visit his friend the Cornish ogre, and had stayed with him for seven years. After the seven years were over he had said all that he had to say, for his conversation was limited, and he determined to return to his own castle. When he arrived he saw the children playing in the garden.

'What are you doing here?' he cried in a very gruff voice, and the children ran away.

'My own garden is my own garden,' said the Giant; 'any one can understand that, and I will allow nobody to play in it but myself.' So he built a high wall all round it, and put up a notice-board.

TRESPASSERS
WILL BE
PROSECUTED

He was a very selfish Giant.

The poor children had now nowhere to play. They tried to play on the road, but the road was very dusty and full of hard stones, and they did not like it. They used to wander round the high wall when their lessons were over, and talk about the beautiful garden inside.

'How happy we were there,' they said to each other.

< 2 >

Then the Spring came, and all over the country there were little blossoms and little birds. Only in the garden of the Selfish Giant it was still Winter. The birds did not care to sing in it as there were no children, and the trees forgot to blossom. Once a beautiful flower put its head out from the grass, but when it saw the notice-board it was so sorry for the children that it slipped back into the ground again, and went off to sleep. The only people who were pleased were the Snow and the Frost. 'Spring has forgotten this garden,' they cried, 'so we will live here all the year round.' The Snow covered up the grass with her great white cloak, and the Frost painted all the trees silver. Then they invited the North Wind to stay with them, and he came. He was wrapped in furs, and he roared all day about the garden, and blew the chimney-pots down. 'This is a delightful spot,' he said, 'we must ask the Hail on a visit.' So the Hail came. Every day for three hours he rattled on the roof of the castle till he broke most of the slates, and then he ran round and round the garden as fast as he could go. He was dressed in grey, and his breath was like ice.

'I cannot understand why the Spring is so late in coming,' said the

Selfish Giant, as he sat at the window and looked out at his cold white garden; 'I hope there will be a change in the weather.'

But the Spring never came, nor the Summer. The Autumn gave golden fruit to every garden, but to the Giant's garden she gave none. 'He is too selfish,' she said. So it was always Winter there, and the North Wind, and the Hail, and the Frost, and the Snow danced about through the trees.

One morning the Giant was lying awake in bed when he heard some lovely music. It sounded so sweet to his ears that he thought it must be the King's musicians passing by. It was really only a little linnet singing outside his window, but it was so long since he had heard a bird sing in his garden that it seemed to him to be the most beautiful music in the world. Then the Hail stopped dancing over his head, and the North Wind ceased roaring, and a delicious perfume came to him through the open casement. 'I believe the Spring has come at last,' said the Giant; and he jumped out of bed and looked out.

< 3 >

What did he see?

He saw a most wonderful sight. Through a little hole in the wall the children had crept in, and they were sitting in the branches of the trees. In every tree that he could see there was a little child. And the trees were so glad to have the children back again that they had covered themselves with blossoms, and were waving their arms gently above the children's heads. The birds were flying about and twittering with delight, and the flowers were looking up through the green grass and laughing. It was a lovely scene, only in one corner it was still Winter. It was the farthest corner of the garden, and in it was standing a little boy. He was so small that he could not reach up to the branches of the tree, and he was wandering all round it, crying bitterly. The poor tree was still quite covered with frost and snow, and the North Wind was blowing and roaring above it. 'Climb up! little boy,' said the Tree, and it bent its branches down as low as it could; but the little boy was too tiny.

And the Giant's heart melted as he looked out. 'How selfish I have been!' he said; 'now I know why the Spring would not come here. I will put that poor little boy on the top of the tree, and then I will knock down the wall, and my garden shall be the children's playground for ever and ever.' He was really very sorry for what he had done.

So he crept downstairs and opened the front door quite softly, and went out into the garden. But when the children saw him they were so frightened that they all ran away, and the garden became Winter again. Only the little boy did not run, for his eyes were so full of tears that he died not see the Giant coming. And the Giant stole up behind him and took him gently in his hand, and put him up into the tree. And the tree broke at once into blossom, and the birds came and sang on it, and the little boy stretched out his two arms and flung them round the Giant's neck, and kissed him. And the other children, when they saw that the Giant was not wicked any longer, came running back, and with them came the Spring. 'It is your garden now, little children,' said the Giant, and he took a great axe and knocked down the wall. And when the people were gong to market at twelve o'clock they found the Giant playing with the children in the most beautiful garden they had ever seen.

< 4 >

All day long they played, and in the evening they came to the Giant to bid him good-bye.

'But where is your little companion?' he said: 'the boy I put into the tree.' The Giant loved him the best because he had kissed him.

'We don't know,' answered the children; 'he has gone away.'

'You must tell him to be sure and come here to-morrow,' said the Giant. But the children said that they did not know where he lived, and had never seen him before; and the Giant felt very sad.

Every afternoon, when school was over, the children came and played with the Giant. But the little boy whom the Giant loved was never seen again. The Giant was very kind to all the children, yet he longed for his first little friend, and often spoke of him. 'How I would like to see him!' he used to say.

Years went over, and the Giant grew very old and feeble. He could not play about any more, so he sat in a huge armchair, and watched the children at their games, and admired his garden. 'I have many beautiful flowers,' he said; 'but the children are the most beautiful flowers of all.'

One winter morning he looked out of his window as he was dressing. He did not hate the Winter now, for he knew that it was merely the Spring asleep, and that the flowers were resting.

Suddenly he rubbed his eyes in wonder, and looked and looked. It certainly was a marvellous sight. In the farthest corner of the garden was a tree quite covered with lovely white blossoms. Its branches were all golden, and silver fruit hung down from them, and underneath it stood the little boy he had loved.

Downstairs ran the Giant in great joy, and out into the garden. He hastened across the grass, and came near to the child. And when he came quite close his face grew red with anger, and he said, 'Who hath dared to wound thee?' For on the palms of the child's hands were the prints of two nails, and the prints of two nails were on the little feet.

< 5 >

'Who hath dared to wound thee?' cried the Giant; 'tell me, that I may take my big sword and slay him.'

'Nay!' answered the child; 'but these are the wounds of Love.'

'Who art thou?' said the Giant, and a strange awe fell on him, and he knelt before the little child.

And the child smiled on the Giant, and said to him, 'You let me play once in your garden, to-day you shall come with me to my garden, which is Paradise.'

And when the children ran in that afternoon, they found the Giant lying dead under the tree, all covered with white blossoms.

THE BRAVE LITTLE TAILOR
The Grimms Brothers
1812

One summer's morning a little tailor was sitting on his table by the window, he was in good spirits, and sewed with all his might. Then came a peasant woman down the street crying, "Good jams, cheap. Good jams, cheap."

This rang pleasantly in the tailor's ears, he stretched his delicate head out of the window, and called, "Come up here, dear woman, here you will get rid of your goods."

The woman came up the three steps to the tailor with her heavy basket, and he made her unpack all the pots for him. He inspected each one, lifted it up, put his nose to it, and at length said, "The jam seems to me to be good, so weigh me out four ounces, dear woman, and if it is a quarter of a pound that is of no consequence."

The woman who had hoped to find a good sale, gave him what he desired, but went away quite angry and grumbling.

"Now, this jam shall be blessed by God," cried the little tailor, "and give me health and strength." So he brought the bread out of the cupboard, cut himself a piece right across the loaf and spread the jam over it. "This won't taste bitter," said he, "but I will just finish the jacket before I take a bite."

He laid the bread near him, sewed on, and in his joy, made bigger and bigger stitches. In the meantime the smell of the sweet jam rose to where the flies were sitting in great numbers, and they were attracted and descended on it in hosts.

"Ha! Who invited you?" said the little tailor, and drove the unbidden guests away. The flies, however, who understood no German, would not be turned away, but came back again in ever-increasing companies. The little tailor at last lost all patience, and drew a piece of cloth from the hole under his work-table, and saying, "Wait, and I will give it to you," struck it mercilessly on them. When he drew it away and counted, there lay before him no fewer than seven, dead and with legs stretched out.

"Are you a fellow of that sort?" said he, and could not help admiring his own bravery. "The whole town shall know of this." And the little tailor hastened to cut himself a girdle, stitched it, and embroidered on it in large letters,

"Seven at one stroke!"

"What, the town!" he continued, "the whole world shall hear of it." And his heart wagged with joy like a lamb's tail. The tailor put on the girdle, and resolved to go forth into the world, because he thought his workshop was too small for his valor. Before he went away, he sought about in the house to see if there was anything which he could take with him, however, he found nothing but an old cheese, and that he put in his pocket. In front of the door he observed a bird which had caught itself in the thicket. It had to go into his pocket with the cheese.

Now he took to the road boldly, and as he was light and nimble, he felt no fatigue. The road led him up a mountain, and when he had reached the highest point of it, there sat a powerful giant looking peacefully about him.

The little tailor went bravely up, spoke to him, and said, "Good day, comrade, so you are sitting there overlooking the wide-spread world. I am just on my way thither, and want to try my luck. Have you any inclination to go with me?"

The giant looked contemptuously at the tailor, and said, "You rag-amuffin! You miserable creature!"

"Oh, indeed," answered the little tailor, and unbuttoned his coat, and showed the giant the girdle, "there may you read what kind of a man I am."

The giant read, "Seven at one stroke," thought that they had been men whom the tailor had killed, and began to feel a little respect for the tiny fellow. Nevertheless, he wished to try him first, and took a stone in his hand and squeezed it together so that water dropped out of it.

"Do that likewise," said the giant, "if you have strength."

"Is that all?" said the tailor, "that is child's play with us," and put his hand into his pocket, brought out the soft cheese, and pressed it until the liquid ran out of it. "Faith," said he, "that was a little better, wasn't it?"

The giant did not know what to say, and could not believe it of the little man. Then the giant picked up a stone and threw it so high that the eye could scarcely follow it.

"Now, little mite of a man, do that likewise."

"Well thrown," said the tailor, "but after all the stone came down to earth again, I will throw you one which shall never come back at all." And he put his hand into his pocket, took out the bird, and threw it into the air. The bird, delighted with its liberty, rose, flew away and did not come back. "How does that shot please you, comrade?" asked the tailor.

"You can certainly throw," said the giant, "but now we will see if you are able to carry anything properly." He took the little tailor to a mighty oak tree which lay there felled on the ground, and said, "if you are strong enough, help me to carry the tree out of the forest."

"Readily," answered the little man, "take the trunk on your shoulders, and I will raise up the branches and twigs, after all, they are the heaviest."

The giant took the trunk on his shoulder, but the tailor seated himself on a branch, and the giant who could not look round, had to carry away the whole tree, and the little tailor into the bargain, he behind, was quite merry and happy, and whistled the song, "Three tailors rode forth from the gate," as if carrying the tree were child's play. The giant, after he had dragged the heavy burden part of the way, could go no further, and cried, "Hark you, I shall have to let the tree fall." The tailor sprang nimbly down, seized the tree with both arms as if he had been carrying it, and said to the giant, "You are such a great fellow, and yet can not even carry the tree."

They went on together, and as they passed a cherry-tree, the giant laid hold of the top of the tree where the ripest fruit was hanging, bent it down, gave it into the tailor's hand, and bade him eat. But the little tailor was much too weak to hold the tree, and when the giant let it go, it sprang back again, and the tailor was tossed into the air with it. When he had fallen down again without injury, the giant said, "What is this? Have you not strength enough to hold the weak twig?"

"There is no lack of strength," answered the little tailor. "Do you think that could be anything to a man who has struck down seven at one blow? I leapt over the tree because the huntsmen are shooting down there in the thicket. Jump as I did, if you can do it."

The giant made the attempt, but could not get over the tree, and remained hanging in the branches, so that in this also the tailor kept the upper hand.

The giant said, "If you are such a valiant fellow, come with me into our cavern and spend the night with us."

The little tailor was willing, and followed him. When they went into the cave, other giants were sitting there by the fire, and each of them had a roasted sheep in his hand and was eating it. The little tailor looked round and thought, "It is much more spacious here than in my workshop."

The giant showed him a bed, and said he was to lie down in it and sleep. The bed, however, was too big for the little tailor, he did not lie down in it, but crept into a corner. When it was midnight, and the giant thought that the little tailor was lying in a sound sleep, he got up, took a great iron bar, cut through the bed with one blow, and thought he had finished off the grasshopper for good. With the earliest dawn the giants went into the forest, and had quite forgotten the little tailor, when all at once he walked up to them quite merrily and boldly. The giants were terrified, they were afraid that he would strike them all dead, and ran away in a great hurry.

The little tailor went onwards, always following his own pointed nose. After he had walked for a long time, he came to the courtyard of a royal palace, and as he felt weary, he lay down on the grass and fell asleep. Whilst he lay there, the people came and inspected him on all sides, and read on his girdle, "Seven at one stroke."

"Ah," said they, "what does the great warrior here in the midst of peace? He must be a mighty lord."

They went and announced him to the king, and gave it as their opinion that if war should break out, this would be a weighty and useful man who ought on no account to be allowed to depart. The counsel pleased the king, and he sent one of his courtiers to the little tailor to offer him military service when he awoke. The ambassador remained standing by the sleeper, waited until he stretched his limbs and opened his eyes, and then conveyed to him this proposal.

"For this reason have I come here," the tailor replied, "I am ready to enter the king's service." He was therefore honorably received and a special dwelling was assigned him.

The soldiers, however, were set against the little tailor, and wished him a thousand miles away. "What is to be the end of this?" they said among themselves. "If we quarrel with him, and he strikes about him, seven of us will fall at every blow, not one of us can stand against him." They came therefore to a decision, betook themselves in a body to the king, and begged for their dismissal. "We are not prepared," said they, "to stay with a man who kills seven at one stroke."

The king was sorry that for the sake of one he should lose all his faithful servants, wished that he had never set eyes on the tailor, and would willingly have been rid of him again. But he did not venture to give him his dismissal, for he dreaded lest he should strike him and all his people dead, and place himself on the royal throne. He thought about it for a long time, and at last found good counsel. He sent to the little tailor and caused him to be informed that as he was such a great warrior, he had one request to make of him. In a forest of his country lived two giants who caused great mischief with their robbing, murdering, ravaging, and burning, and no one could approach them without putting himself in danger of death. If the tailor conquered and killed these two giants, he would give him his only daughter to wife, and half of his kingdom as a dowry, likewise one hundred horsemen should go with him to assist him.

"That would indeed be a fine thing for a man like me," thought the little tailor. "One is not offered a beautiful princess and half a kingdom every day of one's life."

"Oh, yes," he replied, "I will soon subdue the giants, and do not require the help of the hundred horsemen to do it; he who can hit seven with one blow has no need to be afraid of two."

The little tailor went forth, and the hundred horsemen followed him. When he came to the outskirts of the forest, he said to his followers, "Just stay waiting here, I alone will soon finish off the giants."

Then he bounded into the forest and looked about right and left. After a while he perceived both giants. They lay sleeping under a tree, and snored so that the branches waved up and down. The little tailor, not idle, gathered two pocketsful of stones, and with these climbed up the tree. When he was half-way up, he slipped down by a branch, until he sat just above the sleepers, and then let one stone after another fall on the breast of one of the giants.

For a long time the giant felt nothing, but at last he awoke, pushed his comrade, and said, "Why are you knocking me?"

"You must be dreaming," said the other, "I am not knocking you."

They laid themselves down to sleep again, and then the tailor threw a stone down on the second.

"What is the meaning of this?" cried the other. "Why are you pelting me?"

"I am not pelting you," answered the first, growling.

They disputed about it for a time, but as they were weary they let the matter rest, and their eyes closed once more. The little tailor began his game again, picked out the biggest stone, and threw it with all his might on the breast of the first giant.

"That is too bad!" cried he, and sprang up like a madman, and pushed his companion against the tree until it shook. The other paid him back in the same coin, and they got into such a rage that they tore up trees and belabored each other so long, that at last they both fell down dead on the ground at the same time. Then the little tailor leapt down.

"It is a lucky thing," said he, "that they did not tear up the tree on which I was sitting, or I should have had to spring on to another like a squirrel, but we tailors are nimble." He drew out his sword and gave each of them a couple of thrusts in the breast, and then went out to the horsemen and said, "The work is done, I have finished both of them off, but it was hard work. They tore up trees in their sore need, and defended themselves with them, but all that is to no purpose when a man like myself comes, who can kill seven at one blow."

"But you are not wounded?" asked the horsemen.

"You need not concern yourself about that," answered the tailor, "they have not bent one hair of mine."

The horsemen would not believe him, and rode into the forest, there they found the giants swimming in their blood, and all round about lay the torn-up trees. The little tailor demanded of the king the promised reward. He, however, repented of his promise, and again bethought himself how he could get rid of the hero.

"Before you receive my daughter, and the half of my kingdom," said he to him, "you must perform one more heroic deed. In the forest roams a unicorn which does great harm, and you must catch it first."

"I fear one unicorn still less than two giants. Seven at one blow, is my kind of affair."

He took a rope and an axe with him, went forth into the forest, and again bade those who were sent with him to wait outside. He had not long to seek. The unicorn soon came towards him, and rushed directly on the tailor, as if it would gore him with its horn without more ado. "Softly, softly, it can't be done as quickly as that," said he, and stood still and waited until the animal was quite close, and then sprang nimbly behind the tree. The unicorn ran against the tree with all its strength, and struck its horn so fast in the trunk that it had not strength enough to draw it out again, and thus it was caught. "Now, I have got the bird," said the tailor, and came out from behind the tree and put the rope round its neck, and then with his axe he hewed the horn out of the tree, and when all was ready he led the beast away and took it to the king.

The king still would not give him the promised reward, and made a third demand. Before the wedding the tailor was to catch him a wild boar that made great havoc in the forest, and the huntsmen should give him their help.

"Willingly," said the tailor, "that is child's play."

He did not take the huntsmen with him into the forest, and they were well pleased that he did not, for the wild boar had several times received them in such a manner that they had no inclination to lie in wait for him.

When the boar perceived the tailor, it ran on him with foaming mouth and whetted tusks, and was about to throw him to the ground, but the hero fled and sprang into a chapel which was near, and up to the window at once, and in one bound out again. The boar ran in after him, but the tailor ran round outside and shut the door behind it, and then the raging beast, which was much too heavy and awkward to leap out of the window, was caught. The little tailor called the huntsmen thither that they might see the prisoner with their own eyes. The hero, however went to the king, who was now, whether he liked it or not, obliged to keep his promise, and gave him his daughter and the half of his kingdom. Had he known that it was no warlike hero, but a little tailor who was standing before him it would have gone to his heart still more than it did. The wedding was held with great magnificence and small joy, and out of a tailor a king was made.

After some time the young queen heard her husband say in his dreams at night, "Boy, make me the doublet, and patch the pantaloons, or else I will rap the yard-measure over your ears."

Then she discovered in what state of life the young lord had been born, and next morning complained of her wrongs to her father, and begged him to help her to get rid of her husband, who was nothing else but a tailor.

The king comforted her and said, "Leave your bedroom door open this night, and my servants shall stand outside, and when he has fallen asleep shall go in, bind him, and take him on board a ship which shall carry him into the wide world."

The woman was satisfied with this, but the king's armor-bearer, who had heard all, was friendly with the young lord, and informed him of the whole plot.

"I'll put a screw into that business," said the little tailor. At night he went to bed with his wife at the usual time, and when she thought that he had fallen asleep, she got up, opened the door, and then lay down again. The little tailor, who was only pretending to be asleep, began to cry out in a clear voice, "Boy, make me the doublet and patch me the pantaloons, or I will rap the yard-measure over your ears. I smote seven at one blow. I killed two giants, I brought away one unicorn and caught a wild boar, and am I to fear those who are standing outside the room."

When these men heard the tailor speaking thus, they were overcome by a great dread, and ran as if the wild huntsman were behind them, and none of them would venture anything further against him. So the little tailor was and remained a king to the end of his life.

LOCHINVAR
Sir Walter Scott
(1808)

O young Lochinvar is come out of the west,
Through all the wide Border his steed was the best;
And save his good broadsword he weapons had none,
He rode all unarm'd, and he rode all alone.
So faithful in love, and so dauntless in war,
There never was knight like the young Lochinvar.

He staid not for brake, and he stopp'd not for stone,
He swam the Eske river where ford there was none;
But ere he alighted at Netherby gate,
The bride had consented, the gallant came late:
For a laggard in love, and a dastard in war,
Was to wed the fair Ellen of brave Lochinvar.

So boldly he enter'd the Netherby Hall,
Among bride's-men, and kinsmen, and brothers and all:
Then spoke the bride's father, his hand on his sword,
(For the poor craven bridegroom said never a word,)
"O come ye in peace here, or come ye in war,
Or to dance at our bridal, young Lord Lochinvar?"

"I long woo'd your daughter, my suit you denied;—
Love swells like the Solway, but ebbs like its tide—
And now I am come, with this lost love of mine,
To lead but one measure, drink one cup of wine.
There are maidens in Scotland more lovely by far,
That would gladly be bride to the young Lochinvar."

The bride kiss'd the goblet: the knight took it up,
He quaff'd off the wine, and he threw down the cup.
She look'd down to blush, and she look'd up to sigh,
With a smile on her lips and a tear in her eye.
He took her soft hand, ere her mother could bar,—
"Now tread we a measure!" said young Lochinvar.

So stately his form, and so lovely her face,
That never a hall such a galliard did grace;
While her mother did fret, and her father did fume,
And the bridegroom stood dangling his bonnet and plume;
And the bride-maidens whisper'd, "'twere better by far
To have match'd our fair cousin with young Lochinvar."

One touch to her hand, and one word in her ear,
When they reach'd the hall-door, and the charger stood near;
So light to the croupe the fair lady he swung,
So light to the saddle before her he sprung!
"She is won! we are gone, over bank, bush, and scaur;
They'll have fleet steeds that follow," quoth young Lochinvar.

There was mounting 'mong Graemes of the Netherby clan;
Forsters, Fenwicks, and Musgraves, they rode and they ran:
There was racing and chasing on Cannobie Lee,
But the lost bride of Netherby ne'er did they see.
So daring in love, and so dauntless in war,
Have ye e'er heard of gallant like young Lochinvar?

THE LADY, OR THE TIGER?
Frank R. Stockton
(1882)

In the very olden time there lived a semi-barbaric king, whose ideas, though somewhat polished and sharpened by the progressiveness of distant Latin neighbors, were still large, florid, and untrammeled, as became the half of him, which was barbaric. He was a man of exuberant fancy, and, withal, of an authority so irresistible that, at his will, he turned his varied fancies into facts. He was greatly given to self-communing, and, when he and himself agreed upon anything, the thing was done. When every member of his domestic and political systems moved smoothly in its appointed course, his nature was bland and genial; but, whenever there was a little hitch, and some of his orbs got out of their orbits, he was blander and more genial still, for nothing pleased him so much as to make the crooked straight and crush down uneven places.

Among the borrowed notions by which his barbarism had become semified was that of the public arena, in which, by exhibitions of manly and beastly valor, the minds of his subjects were refined and cultured.

But even here the exuberant and barbaric fancy asserted itself. The arena of the king was built, not to give the people an opportunity of hearing the rhapsodies of dying gladiators, nor to enable them to view the inevitable conclusion of a conflict between religious opinions and hungry jaws, but for purposes far better adapted to widen and develop the mental energies of the people. This vast amphitheater, with its encircling galleries, its mysterious vaults, and its unseen passages, was an agent of poetic justice, in which crime was punished, or virtue rewarded, by the decrees of an impartial and incorruptible chance.

When a subject was accused of a crime of sufficient importance to interest the king, public notice was given that on an appointed day the fate of the accused person would be decided in the king's arena, a structure which well deserved its name, for, although its form and plan were borrowed from afar, its purpose emanated solely from the brain of this man, who, every barleycorn a king, knew no tradition to which he owed more allegiance than pleased his fancy, and who ingrafted on every adopted form of human thought and action the rich growth of his barbaric idealism.

When all the people had assembled in the galleries, and the king, surrounded by his court, sat high upon his throne of royal state on one side of the arena, he gave a signal, a door beneath him opened, and the accused subject stepped out into the amphitheater. Directly opposite him, on the other side of the enclosed space, were two doors, exactly alike and side-by-side. It was the duty and the privilege of the person on trial to walk directly to these doors and open one of them. He could open either door he pleased; he was subject to no guidance or influence but that of the aforementioned impartial and incorruptible chance. If he opened the one, there came out of it a hungry tiger, the fiercest, and most cruel that could be procured, which immediately sprang upon him and tore him to pieces as a punishment for his guilt. The moment that the case of the criminal was thus decided, doleful iron bells were clanged, great wails went up from the hired mourners posted on the outer rim of the arena, and the vast audience, with bowed heads and downcast hearts, wended slowly their homeward way, mourning greatly that one so young and fair, or so old and respected, should have merited so dire a fate.

But, if the accused person opened the other door, there came forth from it a lady, the most suitable to his years and station that his majesty could select among his fair subjects, and to this lady he was immediately married, as a reward of his innocence. It mattered not that he might already possess a wife and family, or that his affections might be engaged upon an object of his own selection; the king allowed no such subordinate arrangements to interfere with his great scheme of retribution and reward.

The exercises, as in the other instance, took place immediately, and in the arena. Another door opened beneath the king, and a priest, followed by a band of choristers, and dancing maidens blowing joyous airs on golden horns and treading an epithalamic measure, advanced to where the pair stood, side by side, and the wedding was promptly and cheerily solemnized. Then the gay brass bells rang forth their merry peals, the people shouted glad hurrahs, and the innocent man, preceded by children strewing flowers on his path, led his bride to his home.

This was the king's semi-barbaric method of administering justice. Its perfect fairness is obvious. The criminal could not know out of which door would come the lady; he opened either he pleased, without having the slightest idea whether, in the next instant, he was to be devoured or married. On some occasions the tiger came out of one door, and on some out of the other. The decisions of this tribunal were not only fair, they were positively determinate: the accused person was instantly punished if he found himself guilty, and, if innocent, he was rewarded on the spot, whether he liked it or not. There was no escape from the judgments of the king's arena.

The institution was a very popular one. When the people gathered together on one of the great trial days, they never knew whether they were to witness a bloody slaughter or a hilarious wedding. This element of uncertainty lent an interest to the occasion, which it could not otherwise have attained.

Thus, the masses were entertained and pleased, and the thinking part of the community could bring no charge of unfairness against this plan, for did not the accused person have the whole matter in his own hands?

This semi-barbaric king had a daughter as blooming as his most florid fancies, and with a soul as fervent and imperious as his own. As is usual in such cases, she was the apple of his eye, and was loved by him above all humanity. Among his courtiers was a young man of that fineness of blood and lowness of station common to the conventional heroes of romance who love royal maidens. This royal maiden was well satisfied with her lover, for he was handsome and brave to a degree unsurpassed in all this kingdom, and she loved him with an ardor that had enough of barbarism in it to make it exceedingly warm and strong. This love affair moved on happily for many months, until one day the king happened to discover its existence. He did not hesitate nor waver in regard to his duty in the trial in the king's arena. This, of course, was an especially important occasion, and his majesty, as well as all the people, was greatly interested in the workings and development of this trial. Never before had such a case occurred; never before had a subject dared to love the daughter of the king. In after years such things became commonplace enough, but then they were in no slight degree novel and startling.

The tiger-cages of the kingdom were searched for the most savage and relentless beasts, from which the fiercest monster might be selected for the arena; and the ranks of maiden youth and beauty throughout the land were carefully surveyed by competent judges in order that the young man might have a fitting bride in case fate did not determine for him a different destiny. Of course, everybody knew that the deed with which the accused was charged had been done. He had loved the princess, and neither he, she, nor any one else, thought of denying the fact; but the king would not think of allowing any fact of this kind to interfere with the workings of the tribunal, in which he took such great delight and satisfaction. No matter how the affair turned out, the youth would be disposed of, and the king would take an aesthetic pleasure in watching the course of events, which would determine whether or not the young man had done wrong in allowing himself to love the princess.

The appointed day arrived. From far and near the people gathered, and thronged the great galleries of the arena, and crowds, unable to gain admittance, massed themselves against its outside walls. Theming and his court were in their places, opposite the twin doors, those fateful portals, so terrible in their similarity.

All was ready. The signal was given. A door beneath the royal party opened, and the lover of the princess walked into the arena. Tall, beautiful, fair, his appearance was greeted with a low hum of admiration and anxiety. Half the audience had not known so grand a youth had lived among them. No wonder the princess loved him! What a terrible thing for him to be there!

As the youth advanced into the arena he turned, as the custom was, to bow to the king, but he did not think at all of that royal personage.

His eyes were fixed upon the princess, who sat to the right of her father. Had it not been for the moiety of barbarism in her nature it is probable that lady would not have been there, but her intense and fervid soul would not allow her to be absent on an occasion in which she was so terribly interested. From the moment that the decree had gone forth that her lover should decide his fate in the king's arena, she had thought of nothing, night or day, but this great event and the various subjects connected with it. Possessed of more power, influence, and force of character than any one who had ever before been interested in such a case, she had done what no other person had done,--she had possessed herself of the secret of the doors. She knew in which of the two rooms, that lay behind those doors, stood the cage of the tiger, with its open front, and in which waited the lady.

Through these thick doors, heavily curtained with skins on the inside, it was impossible that any noise or suggestion should come from within to the person who should approach to raise the latch of one of them. But gold, and the power of a woman's will, had brought the secret to the princess.

And not only did she know in which room stood the lady ready to emerge, all blushing and radiant, loveliest of the damsels of the court who had been selected as the reward of the accused youth, should he be proved innocent of the crime of aspiring to one so far above him; and the princess hated her. Often had she seen, or imagined that she had seen, this fair creature throwing glances of admiration upon the person of her lover, and sometimes she thought these glances were perceived, and even returned. Now and then she had seen them talking together; it was but for a moment or two, but much can be said in brief space; it may have been on most unimportant topics, but how could she know that? The girl was lovely, but she had dared to raise her eyes to the loved one of the princess; and, with all the intensity of the savage blood transmitted to her through long lines of wholly barbaric ancestors, she hated the woman who blushed and trembled behind that silent door.

When her lover turned and looked at her, and his eye met hers as she sat there, paler and whiter than any one in the vast ocean of anxious faces about her, he saw, by that power of quick perception which is given to those whose souls are one, that she knew behind which door crouched the tiger, and behind which stood the lady. He had expected her to know it. He understood her nature, and his soul was assured that she would never rest until she had made plain to herself this thing, hidden to all other lookers-on, even to the king. The only hope for the youth in which there was any element of certainty was based upon the success of the princess in discovering this mystery; and the moment he looked upon her, he saw she had succeeded, as in his soul he knew she would succeed.

Then it was that his quick and anxious glance asked the question: "Which?" It was as plain to her as if he shouted it from where he stood. There was not an instant to be lost. The question was asked in a flash; it must be answered in another.

Her right arm lay on the cushioned parapet before her. She raised her hand, and made a slight, quick movement toward the right. No one but her lover saw her. Every eye but his was fixed on the man in the arena.

He turned, and with a firm and rapid step he walked across the empty space. Every heart stopped beating, every breath was held, every eye was fixed immovably upon that man. Without the slightest hesitation, he went to the door on the right, and opened it.

Now, the point of the story is this: Did the tiger come out of that door, or did the lady?

The more we reflect upon this question, the harder it is to answer. It involves a study of the human heart, which leads us through devious mazes of passion, out of which it is difficult to find our way.

Think of it, fair reader, not as if the decision of the question depended upon yourself, but upon that hot-blooded, semi-barbaric princess, her soul at a white heat beneath the combined fires of despair and jealousy. She had lost him, but who should have him?

How often, in her waking hours and in her dreams, had she started in wild horror, and covered her face with her hands as she thought of her lover opening the door on the other side of which waited the cruel fangs of the tiger!

But how much oftener had she seen him at the other door! How in her grievous reveries had she gnashed her teeth, and torn her hair, when she saw his start of rapturous delight as he opened the door of the lady! How her soul had burned in agony when she had seen him rush to meet that woman, with her flushing cheek and sparkling eye of triumph; when she had seen him lead her forth, his whole frame kindled with the joy of recovered life; when she had heard the glad shouts from the multitude, and the wild ringing of the happy bells; when she had seen the priest, with his joyous followers, advance to the couple, and make them man and wife before her very eyes; and when she had seen them walk away together upon their path of flowers, followed by the tremendous shouts of the hilarious multitude, in which her one despairing shriek was lost and drowned!

Would it not be better for him to die at once, and go to wait for her in the blessed regions of semi-barbaric futurity?

And yet, that awful tiger, those shrieks, that blood!

Her decision had been indicated in an instant, but it had been made after days and nights of anguished deliberation. She had known she would be asked, she had decided what she would answer, and, without the slightest hesitation, she had moved her hand to the right.

The question of her decision is one not to be lightly considered, and it is not for me to presume to set myself up as the one person able to answer it. And so I leave it with all of you: Which came out of the opened door,--the lady, or the tiger?

NUMI NUMI [SLEEP SLEEP]

Sleep, sleep, my little girl.
Sleep, sleep.
Sleep, sleep, my little one,
Sleep, sleep.

Daddy's gone to work -
He went, Daddy went.
He'll return when the moon comes out -
He'll bring you a present!

Sleep, sleep...

Daddy went to the vineyards -
He went, Daddy went.
He'll return when the stars come out -
He'll bring you grapes!

Sleep, sleep...

Daddy went to the orchard -
He went, Daddy went.
He'll return in the evening with the wind -
He'll bring an apple!

Sleep, sleep...

Daddy went to the field -
He went, Daddy went.
He'll come back in the evening with the shadows -
He'll bring you ears of grain!

BLUE MOON
Music by Richard Rodgers.
Lyrics by Lorenz Hart
1934

Blue moon you saw me standing alone
Without a dream in my heart
Without a love of my own
Blue moon, you knew just what I was there for
You heard me saying a prayer for
Someone I really could care for

And then there suddenly appeared before me
The only one my arms will hold
I heard somebody whisper "Please adore me"
And when I looked, the moon had turned to gold!

Blue moon!
Now I'm no longer alone
Without a dream in my heart
Without a love of my own

And then there suddenly appeared before me
The only one my arms will ever hold
I heard somebody whisper "please adore me"
And when I looked, the moon had turned to gold!

Blue moon!
Now I'm no longer alone
Without a dream in my heart
Without a love of my own

Blue moon!
Now I'm no longer alone
Without a dream in my heart
Without a love of my own

ACKNOWLEDGEMENTS

A book—either fiction or non-fiction—cannot come to life without those who support the author.

My most profound love to my family for their unfaltering support as I continue to do the dance called My Life.

I feel fortunate to have Kevin Cook and Pamela Cangioli (Proofed to Perfection) as my editors. Thank you Pamela and Kevin for your guidance and encouragement to reach higher and deeper levels of writing. (www.proofedtoperfection.com)

Jeannine Henning took my fantasy of the perfect book cover and created a work of art. I am so very pleased! JHenning. (jen@jeaninehenning.com)

As always, Maureen Cutajar provided a professional and insightful finishing touch through her formatting and talented interior design. (www.gopublished.com)

To my cast of characters, thank you for entering my life and trusting me with your story. I have laughed with you and cried with you. There were times when I felt my heart shatter, but most of all, I have learned to never give up on love or the goodness of humankind.

About the Author

Sunny Alexander lives in Southern California, near the beaches and the Santa Monica Mountain hiking trails.

Though she once struggled at school, she returned to college at the age of forty, became a Licensed Marriage and Family Therapist, and established a private practice in 1988. Compelled by her fascination with dreams, she continued her education and received her doctorate in psychoanalysis. The use of therapeutic storytelling is an important part of her private practice.

As a gay woman and author, she is moved to portray the suffering of those who feel they must hide their identities.

In her time off, Sunny enjoys walking and flying kites along the California beaches near her home and spending time with her family.